"One thing's fo... P9-DML-564

"We are not compatible, not one bit.

Brody didn't argue, although he'd been having a good time despite Melissa's absurd prejudices about firemen. He would have enjoyed showing her just how wrong she was. But then he'd lost control—he, Captain Brody, whose cool under pressure was legendary on the force. This proved he had no business dating.

Out of sheer, dogged politeness, he followed Melissa to her door. She stuck out her hand to shake his.

"Thank you for the nice evening. And just so you know—" but she didn't get a chance to finish. Before he knew what he was doing, Brody yanked her into his arms and covered her mouth with his.

What was he doing? He was insane. This girl despised him, she thought they weren't compatible; but none of that mattered. He had to touch her, had to feel her soft lips against his. She'd probably . . . but no. Her mouth opened on a sigh.

Her bare arms came around him, silky and maddening. Losing himself in the sweetness of her mouth, he let his tongue explore, feeling hers dance and twirl with his, as if they were still on the ballroom floor.

This was a bad idea, a very bad idea.

Romances by Jennifer Bernard

THE FIREMAN WHO LOVED ME

Forthcoming
HOT FOR FIREMAN

the FIREMAN WHO LOVED ME

A BACHELOR FIREMEN NOVEL

Jennifer Bernard

AVON

An Imprint of HarperCollinsPublishers

This book is a work of fiction. References to real people, events, establishments, organizations, or locales are intended only to provide a sense of authenticity, and are used fictitiously. All other characters, and all incidents and dialogue, are drawn from the author's imagination and are not to be construed as real.

AVON BOOKS
An Imprint of HarperCollins*Publishers*
10 East 53rd Street
New York, New York 10022-5299

Copyright © 2012 by Jennifer Bernard
ISBN 978-0-06-208896-3
www.avonromance.com

First Avon Books mass market printing: May 2012

Avon Trademark Reg. U.S. Pat. Off. and in Other Countries, Marca Registrada, Hecho en U.S.A.
HarperCollins® is a registered trademark of HarperCollins Publishers.

Printed in the U.S.A.

10 9 8 7 6 5 4 3 2 1

Acknowledgments

Many thanks to everyone who helped bring this book to life. Special thanks go to Rick Godinez, Fire Captain II of the Los Angeles Fire Department, for sharing his firefighting expertise. Any mistakes are mine, not his. Thanks also to Marlene Casillas for her assistance with news production details. Thanks to Alexandra Machinist for loving this book from the beginning, and to the wonderful Tessa Woodward for making it what it is today. I adore you both. Deep gratitude to the Alaska Romance Writers chapter, to my family for all their support, and, most of all, to Scott.

the
FIREMAN WHO
LOVED ME

Chapter One

Hot Men for a Great Cause.

The words on the poster were black, the background an orange fireball, and, front and center, a hunky fireman gripped his hose.

In the crowded lobby of the San Gabriel Hilton, Melissa McGuire stopped dead at the sight of the poster propped on the large easel. This couldn't possibly be right. She and her grandmother must have gotten their wires crossed. On Nelly's birthday, they usually gorged on hot butterscotch sundaes or the all-you-can-eat lunch buffet at the Bombay Deluxe. Had she misread "Hilton"? What else started with an H? Hooters? That seemed even more unlikely. But with Nelly, you never did know.

As she dug in her jeans pocket for the envelope on which Nelly had scrawled the directions, someone jostled her from behind.

"Hey!" she protested.

Oblivious, a pack of girls streamed past her, a blur of cropped tops and streaked hair. Now that she thought about it, the crowd was made up entirely of young women in their twenties and thirties. They were virtually stampeding in the direction of the ballroom. The last time Melissa had been here, she'd been covering the mayor's victory party for Channel Six. This had to be a mistake.

The envelope, when she finally found it, said otherwise. *San Gabriel Hilton, five p.m. I'll save us a seat at the front of the ballroom. Your loving grandmother, Nelly.* "Loving" was underlined twice. That meant trouble.

Melissa stumbled as a sharp elbow to her back nearly knocked her over. "Do you mind?"

"Oops, sorry," said a girl in a glitter-sprinkled party dress. "But all the good seats are going to be taken if we don't hurry."

Melissa took a step back. "What kind of event is this, anyway?" Whatever it was, it wasn't worth getting kneecapped over.

"Just get yourself a table up close and you won't be sorry." The girl disappeared into the crowd bottlenecked at the ballroom's double doors. A hum of chatter filled the lobby, rising and falling like swallows on an air current.

What had she stumbled into? Rather, what had her "loving" (translation, bossy and interfering) grandmother led her into? There was more text on that poster, if she could just get close enough to read it.

Two bruised ribs and a stubbed toe later, she stood in front of the easel. The silhouetted fireman in the poster looked so . . . manly. So heroic. A dynamo captured in mid-rescue. An ode to testosterone. It took her a moment to tear her eyes away and read the rest of the text. When she did, it took another moment for it to sink in.

The San Gabriel County Firefighter and Law Enforcement Officers Fourth Annual Bachelor Auction.

Nelly McGuire sat triumphantly at a linen-draped table right next to the ballroom stage. Her quilted purse was planted on the chair next to her. Inside it nestled tonight's program, which listed the bachelors who would be strutting their stuff that evening. She'd already underlined several names. The purse also contained a thick roll of hundred-dollar bills. It was a substantial chunk of her savings, but money well spent if it got Melissa a man before she, Nelly McGuire, kicked the bucket. Which would be sooner than—

"Excuse me, missy," she snapped as a shapely arm clad in white spandex reached for the chair with her purse on it. "That seat's taken."

"Excuuuuse me! Aren't you in the wrong place, Granny? Bingo's down the street." A smirk dented the girl's glossy, pouting mouth. Nelly had to admit she was gorgeous. All the more reason to cut her down to size.

"I'm here at the invitation of my grandson. He told me to sit right up front, so I could make sure no worthless hussy bids for him."

"Oh really? Which one is he?"

"We call him M&M. That stands for Marriage Minded. He just needs to find the right girl and it's wedding bells for him."

Game over. White Spandex's eyes, in their nest

of mascara, brightened. She backed off and took another chair, across the table. At her next eager question, Nelly put her hand to her ear in the classic deaf-lady manner, and the girl turned away. Being old sometimes had its advantages.

"Grans?" Melissa stood behind her, hands on hips, green eyes flaring.

"There you are! Just look at these seats I got for us. We'll have the best view in the whole—"

"A bachelor auction, Grans? Have you lost your mind?"

"Now Melissa, that's not a nice thing to say to an old lady." Nelly sniffed, looking, she hoped, deeply wounded.

"Playing the age card. You should be ashamed."

"Well, I'm not. It's my birthday and you have to do what I want. This is what I want. Now sit down." She tugged on her granddaughter's slim wrist, but Melissa didn't budge.

"I left work early to celebrate your birthday. Which means Ella Joy is going to write her own copy for the *Six O'Clock News*, and you know what happened last time." Nelly remembered. Three slander lawsuits had resulted from the anchorwoman's aversion to the word "alleged." "So the least you can do is explain to me *why* you wanted to come here for your birthday."

Nelly sighed. If Melissa wanted to be difficult, she'd have to play dirty. "I hate to point it out, but at my age, this could be my *last* birthday . . ."

"Oh geez, Grans."

Worked every time.

Melissa picked up Nelly's purse and sat gingerly

in its place. "I know this is one of your crazy plans to butt in on my love life . . ."

"Oh, relax. Just try to enjoy yourself. You're too serious."

Nelly smiled at her lovely granddaughter. Melissa had forest-green eyes, deep chocolate hair that curled tenderly around her face, and, when she chose, a radiant smile. In this crowd, Melissa looked like a woodland violet in a field of flashy dahlias. Why should a beautiful, sweet, intelligent darling like her granddaughter have any problem finding the right man? Because—she didn't know what to look for. She went for the artsy type, graduate students and wannabe film directors, the kind of man more interested in finishing his thousand-page novel than in knowing how to treat a woman.

Nelly didn't want one more pair of wire-rimmed glasses showing up on their doorstep.

No, what Melissa needed was a prime, red-blooded, testosterone-loaded man. Someone like Nelly's dear departed Leon. She could hear him even now. *You want some sugar? Come on up here and I'll give you a big old heapful.* That's when she'd jump eagerly into his lap. Oh, the times they'd had . . .

"Look, they're starting!" Across the table, White Spandex adjusted her top and leaned forward. Revved-up hip-hop music blasted through the ballroom and a buzz of excitement shot through the crowd.

The auctioneer, a blonde with a high-voltage smile, strode to the podium and tapped on the microphone. *"Ladies, are you ready to meet the man of your dreams?"* The roar of whoops and cheers was so loud it made the silverware rattle on the tables. "Let's thank all the gentlemen who have agreed to participate tonight, and don't forget, all the proceeds go to the Widows and Orphans Fund, so don't be afraid to bid high if you see something you like! And I guarantee you will. They're all single, they're all sensational, and they're all sexy as heck! If you make the winning bid, not only will you get a romantic evening alone with your man, but if you bid on a fireman, you'll get an added bonus—a home-cooked dinner at the fire station! And let me tell you, some of these boys can cook. So let's get to it!"

The auctioneer quickly went over the instructions. There wasn't much to them. Bidders were supposed to raise their numbered paddles, shaped like fire engines, and yell out an amount. The crowd looked ready to rumble. Melissa, slouched in her chair, looked ready to disappear under the table. Nelly wanted to poke her.

"Drum roll, please!" shouted the woman. "Give a big hand to our first brave bachelor, his name is Dave, he's one of the guys over at Porter Ranch Fire Station 6 . . ." Dave from Porter Ranch, eyes twinkling, strode out onto the stage in jeans and a tight SGFD T-shirt. *Oh my!* Nelly felt faint as he began gyrating to the hopped-up electronic beat of a remixed "Light My Fire." Screams of approval rolled through the room like a fireball. He winked at the crowd, flexed his biceps, and turned to show off his muscular butt. Nelly gripped the table. The sheer energy in the room was overwhelming. Melissa, whose head could now barely be seen over the edge of the table, had a look of horror on her face.

"Bidding starts at one hundred dollars for a date with Dave. Did I mention he ran the marathon last year? This year he's going for the Iron Man race. He's fit, he's strong, and he's looking for someone to give him a nice backrub at the end of the day. Anyone here want to rub Dave's back?"

White Spandex certainly did. "I do! I do! Two hundred!" Girls from all corners of the ballroom recklessly yelled out higher and higher amounts. Before long the bidding was at a thousand dollars, and White Spandex, crushed, sank down in her seat.

The auctioneer banged the gavel and shouted, "Sold, for fifteen hundred dollars!" Whoops and hollers filled the ballroom as the winner collapsed into the arms of her friends. Dave crooked his finger and the pink-faced young woman made her way to the stage, where he brought her hand up for a gallant kiss that made her hyperventilate.

"Lucky," said White Spandex enviously. "But where that skank got fifteen hundred dollars, I don't even want to know."

"Grans, this is insane." Nelly could barely hear Melissa over the buzz of excitement. "Bidding on a man like some prize bull at a cattle auction? It's ridiculous."

"Shhh." Nelly decided to ignore Melissa for the rest of the show. "Here comes the next one."

The beefcake parade of Southern California's finest continued. All those powerful arms, those firm, flexing buttocks, those rock-hard stomachs. What about Vince from LA County Fire and Rescue, six feet seven inches of glorious sinewy coiled strength? Or José from Moorpark PD, with his laughing eyes and dance moves straight out of a strip show?

By the time Number Five was called, Nelly was ready. She'd circled and double underlined Number Five on her program. His name was Ryan, twenty-seven years old, a firefighter at San Gabriel's Fire Station 1. He liked dogs, hiking, and old-fashioned courting. He had blue eyes and brown hair, stood six foot two, and weighed in at a muscular two hundred pounds. Number Five was perfect.

And he obviously knew it. He strolled onto the stage in what seemed like slow motion as the music shifted to a slow, sensuous beat. With lazy blue eyes, he looked the crowd over, and a slow smile spread across his perfect face. From his slight slouch to the thumbs hooked casually in his jeans pockets, everything about him looked re-laxed, easy, unhurried. He didn't need to dance or swivel his hips to get attention. All he had to do was stand in just that particular way. One sky-blue eye drooped in a slight wink, and a sigh swept through the ballroom.

The auctioneer could barely be heard over the din. "Meet Ryan from the most famous fire station in the country! You've heard of the smoking hot Bachelor Firemen of San Gabriel, now's your chance to get up close and personal with one of them . . ."

Arms shot up, crazy amounts were shouted out, and still Number Five did no more than stand, head slightly cocked. Nelly had no idea what the auctioneer was jabbering about, but that didn't matter. Oh yes, she thought. *This is the one.* The bid-ding became even more frenzied, but Nelly bided her time.

"Two thousand four . . . two thousand five . . . do I hear two thousand six? Come on ladies, don't be shy . . . two thousand six in the back . . . how about two thousand seven?"

When no more hands went up, and the auctioneer was lifting the gavel, Nelly rose to her feet. "Three thousand dollars, cash!" she yelled, waving her purse in the air.

Across the table, she heard a choking sound as White Spandex, who'd given up at seven hundred, nearly swallowed an ice cube.

Onstage, Number Five's eyes, blue as cornflowers, blue as a June sky, slowly drifted to meet Nelly's. She could see, just for a moment, a shock shimmering under the calm surface of his gaze.

"Three thousand dollars, that could be a record! Anyone for three thousand and one?"

Nelly thought she saw Number Five's eyes dart around the room, looking for someone, anyone, to counter her bid.

"Going once, going twice . . ."

The gavel dropped and the shout of "Sold!" echoed through the hushed ballroom. As a huge cheer went up, the fireman's lazy lids drooped, and his chiseled lips curved. He gave Nelly the slightest nod of his handsome head, and then strolled off stage at a slow-moving pace that set hearts fluttering and pulses racing.

Nelly sank down in her chair and put a hand to her chest. White Spandex glared at her in outrage. "If that isn't the biggest waste! What are you going to do, make him rock your rocking chair? Play solitaire with you?"

Nelly could still feel the adrenaline racing

through her. Despite her skipping heart and shaking hands, she hadn't felt this good in a long time. "No, dear, I plan to give him away. To the most deserving girl, of course. Someone polite and well-mannered." She looked over to share her triumph with Melissa. But Melissa's chair was empty. Her granddaughter had disappeared.

Melissa pushed her way through the ballroom, transformed into a kaleidoscope of screaming faces and raised arms. She loved her Grans, but enough was enough. She'd wait in the lobby. If Grans came out, hauling a fireman behind her like a side of beef, she'd politely tell the guy her grandmother was suffering from dementia. Did Nelly really think she needed to buy Melissa a man? Didn't a twenty-nine-year-old woman have the right to pick her own dates? Compatible, mentally stimulating men?

She'd almost reached the exit when an overenthusiastic bidder jumped up, sending her chair skidding into the aisle, right under Melissa's feet. Crash! As she landed flat on her face on the ballroom floor, everything went dim, as if someone had fooled with the lights.

"You okay there?"

When she craned her neck to look up, she saw a man's powerful body silhouetted against the light glowing from the lobby. She wondered dizzily if she'd gotten a concussion, because it looked as if the fireman from the poster had come to life. He reached his hand to her, exactly the way the fireman in the poster held his hose. She blinked. He was still there.

The man bent down and untangled the chair from her feet. He hauled her upright. She was still marveling at the effortlessness of the move when he spoke again. "Leaving already? There's twenty more guys to go."

Dizziness was replaced by mortification. "No! I'm not here, I mean, I am here, but it's not because of—" She stopped. Her brain was just not working right. Maybe it had gotten scrambled by her fall.

"You sure you're okay?"

He had unusual eyes, she noticed. Dark gray, like charcoal. With little specks of silver. Right now those eyes were examining her far too closely. One firm hand gripped her shoulder. She shrugged it off. "Yes. I'm fine. And believe me, the last thing I'd consider doing is going to a bachelor auction."

"I see."

"No, you don't see. It's a birthday present."

"Firemen make nice birthday presents."

Was he making fun of her? "No! They don't. I mean, I don't know if they do or not, it's not my birthday, and besides, I'm not into firemen. I like, you know, writers. Genius types. Sculptors." *Sculptors?* Where had that come from?

"I hear there's an auction of bachelor genius sculptors down the street." The man's grave eyes had a little twinkle in them. He stepped back. Even in jeans and an open-collared shirt, his physicality shone through. There was something quietly powerful about him, something intense and contained. Maybe mid-thirties. A head taller than she. His face was weathered, with deep lines around his mouth, and stubble on his jaw. And those extraordinary eyes. It occurred to her that he was the only man in the place, except for the ones onstage. Of course! The truth clicked. He was just waiting his turn on the meat market.

"Are you sure you're okay?" he asked again.

"Yes. Absolutely. I don't want to hold you up."

He frowned. "Hold me up?"

"I'm sure the girls here are just dying to bid on you. You'd better get on up there."

"Oh. Well, no hurry."

So he *was* one of the bachelors. She felt a weird thrill combined with disappointment. Bachelors were, by definition, single. But bachelors selling their wares onstage were, by definition, not her type.

"I don't understand how you can do it," she blurted out. "Don't you think it's a little embarrassing? Dancing around like a male stripper, flexing your muscles and showing off your pecs or your abs or your glutes or—" She broke off with a gulp. Mentioning muscles was a mistake, because now all she could see was the hard outline of his chest under his shirt.

The man shrugged those powerful shoulders, a gesture she found annoyingly distracting. "If it's so embarrassing, don't you think anyone who does it for charity deserves some credit?"

Score one for the stranger. She scrambled for a response. "What about the girl who bids for you? It's not like you're going to marry her. You'll take her out once and never see her again, right?"

"That's the most likely scenario."

"So you let her spend all that money for one date. How could it possibly be worth it?"

The man quirked one eyebrow in the most maddening way. "Don't knock it till you've tried it."

Oh, the arrogance of the man! Macho men like him always thought they were God's gift to women. Just then, another wave of delirious screams swept the ballroom. "Your fans are waiting. Better go!"

She pushed past him. Her shoulder brushed against his and a shocking tingle raced down her arm. It pissed her off. Didn't her arm know she wasn't attracted to guys like that? It had no business reacting to a full-of-himself, muscle-obsessed fireman.

This was exactly why she belonged with a nice poet or maybe a singer-songwriter. Guys like that didn't make her feel all jangly and off-balance.

She put the fireman out of her mind and settled into a quiet corner of the lobby with a newspaper to wait for her outrageous grandmother.

Chapter Two

Maybe you could rent some *Matlock* reruns."

"Or how about that show with the old chick who solves murders."

"Don't forget the early bird special over at Bonanza."

In the captain's office of San Gabriel Fire Station 1, Captain Harry Brody, long legs propped on his desk, listened with a resigned sigh. Of course the guys would jump at the chance to torment the station's resident heartbreaker. In a few minutes he'd have to intervene. But he would pick his moment. He'd let the guys get it out of their system first.

"Don't worry, Stan," he told the lump of dozing canine flesh under his chair. "I won't let them kill each other."

Stan twitched one fire-mangled ear, but showed no other signs of concern. It took a lot to get Stan moving. For a fire station dog, he was on the lazy side. He'd even slept through the three-alarm warehouse fire that had burned his ear. Impressed by such a fearless attitude toward fire, the San Gabriel firemen had insisted on adopting him, even though the last thing Brody needed was a half-beagle, half-spaniel, completely obsessed mutt following him around.

"You'll let me know before things get bloody, right Stan?"

Brody tilted his head back and gazed up at the ceiling through half-closed eyes. Time for an imaginary cigarette. He hadn't smoked since his ex-wife had left him three years ago. But nothing focused the mind like a perfect smoke ring. So he watched an imaginary ring of smoke drift with the air currents as he kept one ear cocked toward his men.

Noisy rattling came from Ryan Blake's locker. Ryan hadn't said a word when he'd walked into the station; he didn't have to. In the magic way of fire stations, the news had gotten there long before he had. Brody had been the only actual witness to Ryan's starring moment onstage at the Hilton.

"Gettin' all hot and bothered already, aren't ya, Hoagie?" called the veteran, big-bellied Double D. Nicknames were a badge of honor for a firefighter. Ryan got his nickname from the lunch he ate every day. Double D owed his to the dog doo he'd tracked into the burning home of a local millionaire, who had then sued the fire department for ruining his carpet.

"Stuff it, Doo-doo," growled Ryan.

Double D chuckled into his Styrofoam cup of coffee. "Heard it was a record payout. What'd you go for, three K?"

"Bet she'd been saving up for a while," threw in the rookie from the stove, where he was scrambling enough eggs to feed an army.

"Oh sure, at least seventy, eighty years."

"Shut up!"

Brody winced. Ryan was nearing the edge; he could hear it in the young fireman's voice. Maybe it had been a mistake to let Ryan take part in the bachelor auction. He'd been nervous about it, which was why he'd planted himself at the back of the ballroom, monitoring the scene like a Secret Service agent. But the only bullet he'd taken was the verbal kind, from a sparkly-eyed, opinionated girl who'd gotten under his skin.

It wasn't like him to let things get under his skin. That was Ryan's territory. Captain Brody was known far and wide for his control, for his calmness under pressure. But pressure didn't usually come in the form of gorgeous, scornful green eyes.

Brody heard another bang from Hoagie's locker. He had a good idea of what his star firefighter was doing in there. The guys joked that Ryan kept a mirror in his locker, but only Brody knew it wasn't true. Whenever Ryan ran to his locker, Brody knew he was taking his own form of a timeout. Most likely he was consulting his book of affirmations, which had been given to him by one of his many, many girlfriends.

Brody had no problem with affirmations if they helped his star keep a grip on his impulsive nature.

The barrage of jokes didn't slow down.

"My granny likes bingo. She won five bucks last time."

"Bet that's how Hoagie's gal got the three grand."

"Three grand for a bite of the Hoagie!"

"For three grand, she'll be wantin' the whole Hoagie."

Okay, time to step into captain mode. Brody unfurled himself from the desk and strolled into the training room. Stan hauled himself to his feet and trotted behind him. Darn dog and his abandonment issues.

As always, the atmosphere of the room shifted when he walked in. Everyone sat a little straighter. The teasing stopped. Plenty of the gung-ho younger guys had more muscle power than Brody. But respect—that came from something else. Brody couldn't have explained it with a gun to his head. But there it was.

He surveyed his crew with a cool stare. Brody rarely, if ever, yelled. Instead, he preferred to drop cryptic statements that made everyone stop and scratch their heads. "A fire engine can't function with a kink in the hose. Anyone here responsible for that?"

The firefighters exchanged confused glances. No one had left a kink in any of the hoses at the last fire. No firefighter worth the name would do that. But not a single soul argued. They knew their captain and his ways. A riled-up Ryan would be worse than a kink in the hose.

Double D crunched his cup into a Styrofoam ball and tossed it in the trash. "Sorry, Captain."

Brody rewarded him with a curt nod, and beckoned Ryan toward the apparatus bay where the station's engine, truck, pumper, and ambulance were housed. Stan tried to follow but Double D snagged his collar.

Ryan followed after him. "I know there's no problem with the hose, Captain. You don't have to worry. I'm fine now. I've got the lake."

"The lake?" Brody quirked an eyebrow.

"The calm lake within. It's an image. Helps me keep my cool when the guys are messing with me."

Right. The affirmations. "Glad to hear it. Has the lake told you what to do about this problem?"

"What problem? You made them stop. I don't have to go crazy on them now."

Brody put an arm over his subordinate's shoulder. Ryan's easygoing appearance hid the fiery temper that Brody had spent countless hours trying to tame. The kid was a firefighting natural who lived for the moments he got to grapple with the flames. It had taken every ounce of Brody's patience and knowledge to transform Ryan into an actual firefighter instead of a death-defying daredevil. Ryan still required careful handling.

"Yes, that's true . . . for now. But the more I think it over, the more certain I am they're not going to let this go. It's too good. If it was someone else, maybe . . . but with a girl magnet like you? No, there's no chance. Any ideas?"

"I don't know. I suppose you're right," said Ryan, his blue eyes dark with dread. "Guess I'll have to teach them a lesson. Thrash someone. And I've been so good lately, you know I have."

Brody sighed. "Let's try to come up with something else."

Ryan gloomily kicked at one of the huge tires of Engine 1. "This is crap. I was trying to do a good deed."

"And you did. Three thousand dollars for the Widows and Orphans Fund. Of course, you cost me a pretty penny."

Ryan frowned. "How'd I do that?"

"I told them I'd match whatever my guys went for. I didn't know you'd be such a hot item."

Ryan tucked his thumbs in his pockets, looking skeptical. "Then why'd you put me up there, Cap?"

"Good point." Brody clapped Ryan on the shoulder. "Look, it's a great cause, and you did a good thing. Lord knows nothing could have gotten me up there. That's why I put my money on you."

"Lots of girls would've bid on you. My girlfriends are always asking about you. The legendary Captain Brody and all the lives you've saved. Too bad the girls are kind of afraid of you."

The image of the green-eyed girl from the auction surfaced again. She certainly hadn't been afraid of him. Then again, she hadn't known he was the "legendary Captain Brody."

"You could relax and smile a little, you know. You'd have girls all over you," continued Ryan.

"Nah, that's what you're around for. Who else could earn six thousand dollars for standing on a stage for two minutes? Think about that when they're hassling you. Think about it when you're on the date, if you need to."

"What date?" Ryan scuffed the cement floor. "I can't do it, Captain. You know what the guys'll do. They'll follow me around with a video camera. Put it up on YouTube. Give out DVDs for Christmas presents, for Chrissakes. I think I have to bail."

"Ryan, you have to go." Brody shook his head, as

disappointed as if he were Ryan's actual father, not the authority figure the kid had eagerly latched on to. "You can't back out now. It wouldn't be right."

"I'll pay back the three thousand. Or six thousand, whatever. I can get a loan."

"Are you nuts? Just to avoid some harmless teasing?"

"You don't know what it's like!"

"Sure I do. Everyone goes through it."

"No one teases you."

"That's because I'm the captain—"

"That's it!" Ryan broke in. "No one will tease you. You can do it!"

"Do what?"

"Go on the date!"

"What? Absolutely not."

"Why not? I already did the hard part. I got my ass up on that stage. Now you can do the easy part. You're more her type anyway."

"I am?"

"Sure! You're more . . . old-school."

Brody cocked his head at him. Ryan probably didn't realize they had less than a ten-year age difference, twenty-seven to his thirty-six. "Old-school?"

"You know, more of a gentleman. With manners and all that shit."

Brody bit back a laugh, which might make Ryan think he was going for this plan. "I wouldn't want to disappoint the lady. She's expecting the handsome young prize she bid on."

"But you're even better. You're a captain. Women love that stuff. Wear your uniform. Come on, when's the last time you went out? All you do is work on your house when you're not working here."

The kid had a point there. God, was he actually getting talked into this? "And what explanation would I give her for our little switcheroo?"

"Who cares? She probably won't even notice the difference. She's old, Cap. With glasses. One fireman's the same as another. Except you're the captain, so that's even better," he added hastily. "The best part is, no one will rag on you. They wouldn't dare."

"Because I'm the captain?"

"No, because you're . . . you."

Brody frowned and pretended to check Engine 1 to make sure the B shift had polished it properly. He didn't want to upset the white-haired woman who had bid on Ryan, but he also didn't want to send the kid over the edge.

"Seriously, Captain, I won't know what to say to her. It'll be embarrassing for her. I don't know anything about . . . knitting or that shit. Crocheting. Bingo."

"Elderly people often care deeply about politics."

"Exactly. I don't even read *People* magazine. Please, Captain. I'll do anything."

Brody gauged the extent of Ryan's anxiety. Would it kill him to go out for an evening? He hadn't dated since Rebecca had e-mailed him from an Internet café in San Diego, where she'd run off with Thorval the surfer. But this wouldn't be a date. This would be like taking his grandmother out for an afternoon at the Botanical Gardens.

He might not be able to hang on to a marriage, but he could show an old lady a good time.

"You owe me, Hoagie."

"Captain, you rock."

"I'm deeply moved."

Whistling, Ryan disappeared. Brody was left alone with his thoughts, which now went in an unexpected direction—just how did you plan for a date with an eighty-year-old woman?

Nelly and Melissa lived in the old Victorian house where Nelly had spent the last fifty-six years of her life. It was an unusual style for San Gabriel, which, like most small towns in the sunny valley northeast of Los Angeles, was filled with old, Spanish-style, stuccoed buildings mixed with newer tract homes. When Nelly and Leon had first moved in, they'd planted lemon and orange trees, and masses of jasmine, which twined up the front and back porches. The back porch held a glider where Nelly loved to rock and smell her beloved flowers. Inside were worn hardwood floors and old-fashioned crown moldings. The kitchen had vintage pink-speckled linoleum floors. It was here that Melissa, in the middle of washing dishes, faced off with her grandmother.

"Nope! Sorry, Grans, it's not going to happen. It's not your birthday anymore." Melissa tossed the hair out of her eyes as she scrubbed a pot with frustration verging on violence. She glared at Nelly, whose eyes, normally fierce as a golden eagle's, wore the "innocent" look that meant trouble.

"Don't frown. You'll ruin your looks," said Nelly automatically.

Melissa hunched her shoulder to wipe soap

suds off her cheek. "If you're so worried about my looks, you shouldn't piss me off."

"I wasn't trying to. I'm just asking you for a favor."

"Is that what it is? Nothing resembling, say, the wackiest setup known to man? You're the one who bid on him, you get to go out with him." Melissa used the hand sprayer to rinse the pot, then set it upside down on the drying rack. When her grandmother didn't answer, Melissa sent her a sidelong look.

Nelly, with a pained look, was holding her stomach, clearly waiting for a spasm to pass.

Oh, Grans, thought Melissa, her irritation evaporating. Those spasms were the reason Melissa had moved in with Nelly. When Nelly had first revealed her unspecified but clearly painful condition, Melissa had tried to convince her grandmother to move into an assisted living situation. There was no one else to help. Melissa's mother was dead, and her father was . . . her father. But Nelly had flat-out refused to leave her home. Melissa had launched a full-scale search for a live-in nurse, but every candidate with any experience had instantly recognized Nelly as a handful of hell-on-earth and passed on the job offer.

At that point, about two years ago, Melissa's own life in Los Angeles was falling apart. Her news director, the world-famous Everett Malcolm, had crushed her heart and nearly destroyed her career, not to mention her confidence. Anything had to be better than the day-to-day torment of working with him. She'd offered to move in with Nelly, and after much mulling and squawking Nelly had eagerly welcomed her only granddaughter. Melissa had quickly realized why. Nelly had seen it as a chance to set Melissa's life in order.

"What harm would it do to step out with a handsome young fireman? They make excellent husbands."

"Grans, getting married doesn't happen to be my goal in life. So sue me."

"Oh, that fancy career of yours. You think your career is going to take care of you when you're my age?"

"As a matter of fact, yes. My IRA—"

"I don't want to hear about your IRA. It's not going to drive you to the pharmacy, it's not going to rub your feet, or change your colostomy bag."

Melissa hid a smile. Nelly loved to hold up the specter of a colostomy bag, even though she herself had never had any problems along those lines.

"I'm only twenty-nine, I don't think I need to worry about my future hypothetical colostomy bag just yet."

"It's never too soon," said Nelly darkly.

Melissa's cell phone rang—the theme from *Gladiator*. She snatched it up. But if there was something worse than talking about a nonexistent colostomy bag, it was dealing with Ella Joy during one of her fits of paranoia.

"Why did you change my password, Melissa? I hate it when you do that, especially when you don't tell me."

"I would never change your password, Ella. That's not even technically possible."

Ella Joy was the diva of Channel Six news, where the slogan was "The Sunny Side of the News." Ella was personally responsible for an extra two points in the ratings. For two ratings points, Melissa was expected to let Ella treat her like a personal assistant rather than the special news segment producer she was supposed to be.

"Then why can't I get on the computer? It's like someone's trying to keep me out."

"No one's trying to keep you out. I promise. They want you to log in." *You might even do some work, who knows?* Praying for patience, Melissa walked the anchor through the steps of logging onto the newsroom computer network. "Click the enter button . . . you know, the big one on the right . . . that's it, are you in? No problem. You can call anytime, you know that. See you tomorrow." She switched off the phone and tossed it on the counter. "I wish you'd let us move somewhere with no cell phone reception."

"That girl is nothing but fluff. You're worth ten Ella Joys. Did you see that calendar they're advertising?"

The calendar, Ella's idea, featured shots of her broadcasting from various live locations in each month, January through December. The very thought of it made Melissa ill. "Let's not talk about it."

"Fine. Let's talk about this evening. I'm not feeling very well at the moment, and I have a date. I can't cancel it, so you're going to have to fill in for me."

"Date? You don't have a date." Melissa's irritation surged back. "Your last date was in 1940-something. With Gramps. And Scrabble Club meetings don't count."

"I don't know why you're taking that tone. You'll be sorry when you see your date. Such lovely blue eyes. Handsome as the cover of a magazine. You shouldn't have run out of the room before you saw who I bid on."

"Wrong. I should have run out of the room as soon as I saw that poster."

"Nonetheless, I'm feeling poorly and must take to my bed." Nelly's voice quavered. "But we can't disappoint a member of the firefighting forces, now can we?"

Melissa rolled her eyes. Nelly was not the easiest person to live with. Though she had a heart as big as Planet Earth, she was infinitely resourceful when it came to getting her way. And too stubborn to let anything go, especially her plans for Melissa's future. "Don't you think he might be disappointed when I show up, instead of the sweet, charming old hag he's expecting?"

"Don't be angry, now. It's just one evening. It won't kill you. And it would mean so much to me."

"Oh Lord in heaven, Grans . . ." A knock on the door interrupted them. "Please tell me that's not him."

"That's probably him." With surprising agility, Nelly scuttled toward the door leading to her downstairs bedroom. "You'd better answer that."

"Grans, so help me . . ." But her grandmother was gone.

From the safety of her bedroom, Nelly called, "No swearing, you don't want to create a bad first impression." She did a little dance as she closed the door halfway, so she could still see everything. Just wait until Melissa caught a glimpse of Ryan the dreamboat. Maybe he'd wear his uniform, the irresistible cherry on top of his natural-born gorgeousness. Melissa would thank her from the bottom of her heart; she'd kneel down and kiss her hand. And oh, the babies they'd have . . .

Nelly watched her granddaughter hesitate and mutter to herself. Melissa headed toward the front door, only to stop at the mirror in the entryway. Nelly quietly cackled with delight. If Melissa felt the urge to check her appearance, anything was possible. Melissa was wearing her casual clothes—black Capri pants and a paisley-patterned sleeveless top. It wouldn't have been Nelly's first choice, but everything looked good on her sweet Melissa.

Then Nelly's heart sank. Melissa was picking up her glasses. Why'd that girl have to be so darn stubborn? She refused to get contacts. Nelly swore she wore her glasses to distract her coworkers from her camera-worthy looks. "Put those down," hissed Nelly.

But Melissa set her jaw and jammed the glasses onto her face. What was she doing now, messing up her hair? Nelly didn't protest that move. She thought Melissa looked more appealing, less buttoned-up, when her thick chocolate hair danced and curved around her head. All in all, outfit and glasses aside, she wasn't ashamed to call Melissa her granddaughter. But would she be enough to catch the eye of someone as flat-out gorgeous as Ryan from Fire Station 1?

Nelly wiggled with glee as Melissa made her way toward the front door.

Chapter Three

At Mrs. Nelly McGuire's front door, Brody checked his watch and looked longingly back toward his robin's-egg-blue '69 Dodge. Maybe the old lady had already gone to bed. He could hop right back in his car and cruise back to his house (aka the construction zone), where he'd left behind a long list of unfinished tasks.

A date. For Chrissakes. The only saving grace was that his date was an elderly woman who didn't deserve to be stood up. For that reason, he'd dug out khaki pants and a nice white shirt, and hauled his father's old Dodge from under the tarp behind his garage. It would give them an icebreaker, right?

A date. Jesus. Not that he didn't enjoy women and make damn sure they enjoyed their time with him. But dating . . . no. Not for him. Unless it was with an eighty-something woman who couldn't possibly disturb his peace of mind.

One more knock on Mrs. McGuire's door, and then he'd go home and work on the wiring in his kitchen.

His attention was already back on the car when he felt his hand rap against soft flesh instead of hard oak. "Oh shit . . . I mean, so sorry, ma'am, are you hurt?" He reached out to keep his victim from losing her balance and felt the unexpected thrill of a slender arm and warm skin under his fingers. All he could see was a blur of hands protecting a dark head, fumbling for the glasses he'd knocked off her face. A face, he realized as his appalled vision cleared, that was most definitely not old. In fact, it was riveting. Maybe not beautiful, precisely, but arresting. And—familiar.

It was the girl from the bachelor auction, with the same skin like vanilla cream, stubborn jaw, vulnerable mouth, and eyes glaring a deep green at him. He realized he was staring and looked away, dropping his hands, just as the girl firmly set a pair of horn-rimmed glasses back onto her nose.

"You?" She didn't look all that happy about it.

"Are you all right? I'm so sorry. I was starting to think no one was here."

"Your eyes aren't blue."

It seemed like a non sequitur, until he remembered she was expecting Ryan. "I am aware of that, and I do apologize. Ryan, the one you bid for, was . . . indisposed. I told him I'd take his place, if that is acceptable to you . . . that is . . . to Nelly McGuire. You can't be . . . You're not Mrs. Nelly McGuire, are you?" Of course she wasn't. He knew all about his date. But still, his thoughts went wild. Maybe he'd gotten the name wrong. Maybe Ryan had seen the glasses and assumed she was old. Maybe her dark brown hair had looked white in the bright lights of the auction.

"I am not," she said firmly. "Strangely enough, my grandmother is also indisposed. Grans! Come out here."

No one responded. The girl shot him a suspicious look. "Are you in on this too?"

Brody had no idea how to answer that. He had the feeling he'd stepped into some kind of looking-glass world.

"Grans!" the girl called again. A door snapped open, and a white-haired, feisty-looking woman with golden eyes behind thick glasses marched out. So here was Nelly McGuire.

His date.

"Who the dickens are you?" She adjusted her glasses. "You're too old, and your eyes don't look blue to me."

No doubt about it, he'd fallen down a rabbit hole. "My name is Captain Brody—"

"Where's Number Five?"

Brody cast a desperate glance at the girl and was relieved to see she looked just as confused as he was.

"What kind of operation are you people running? You wouldn't be trying to fool an old lady, would you?" Nelly demanded.

"Not at all." This situation was infinitely more mortifying than Brody had feared. His whole body stiffened, and when he spoke again his voice sounded painfully formal. "Ryan Blake works under me over at San Gabriel Fire Station 1, and when he informed me he wouldn't be able to be here tonight, I requested the honor of taking his place."

"Why can't he be here?"

"Well . . ." How to put it politely without lying? "An unpleasant fire station situation came up."

Nelly's suspicious gaze scanned him, head to toe. "You're not wearing a fire captain uniform."

"It didn't seem appropriate for the occasion. If you'd like to see my identification—"

"No!" the girl broke in. "I'm sure that won't be necessary. You look like a fire captain to me."

"Melissa, he could be anyone. Just walking in off the street like that."

So that was her name. Melissa. It suited her. It would feel like honey on his tongue. Right now that vanilla skin was pink with embarrassment. Brody watched the play of expressions on her mobile face. Outrage, humor, confusion, mortification. He had the sudden thought that he wouldn't mind standing here for a while, watching her face.

"Really, Grans . . ."

Nelly ignored her. "Are you single?"

"Yes."

"Not homosexual?"

"No ma'am." By this point, the entire scene had reached such a surreal level he found himself smiling.

"How old are you?"

"Thirty-six."

"Isn't that young for a fire captain?"

"I'm very good."

Nelly paused in her inquisition, as if to say, she'd be the judge of that. "Have you ever been married?"

"Yes."

"Divorced?"

"Yes."

"Any children?"

The smile drained from his face. The one question he didn't want to answer. Ramrod-straight, he stared at a spot above Nelly's head. Rescue came in the form of a slim hand on his elbow.

"Okay, that's it!" Melissa crooked her arm in his and grabbed her jacket. "Shall we go?"

No three words had ever been so welcome. As he gratefully pressed her arm against his side, he couldn't help noticing how good she felt. He made a slight bow to the openmouthed Nelly. "It was a pleasure meeting you, Mrs. Nelly McGuire, and I'm very sorry you're indisposed. I'm sure it would have been an unforgettable evening."

"Well, I'm sure it would. Be nice to my Melissa. I'll be waiting up, so no fancy fandangos."

"I wouldn't think of it." Moving his hand to her lower back, he steered Melissa out the door.

The alleged fire captain opened the passenger door of his big blue boat of a car, waited until Melissa was settled in, then slid behind the wheel. Melissa wasn't used to such old-fashioned courtesy. Like his car, it seemed to come from another era. She had to admit she rather liked it. He didn't start the Dodge immediately, but instead let out a long breath. There was a moment of strained silence. The scent of jasmine drifted through the open windows. It was just after five in the evening, and the late October sky was a dusky pink.

"I'm so sorry," said Melissa in a stifled voice. She hated apologizing for her grandmother.

"She's something else. What's a fancy fandango?"

Was he making fun of Grans? Melissa looked over at him sharply, and once again felt that annoying tingle. He was a complete stranger, and yet when he'd grabbed her arm (after nearly knocking her over), a shiver had passed through her. And those eyes, the intense gray of charcoal, had looked into hers with such genuine concern. There was a restrained strength in the way he'd held her, the same power she'd felt when he'd plucked her off the Hilton carpet.

"She reminds me of my aunt Maggie," Brody was saying. "She raised six children alone after her husband died in a fishing accident. She took over his boat. Ran the tightest crew in San Pedro."

Melissa laughed. "Yeah, Grans is a pain in my butt, but I love her to death. If only she'd stay out of my social life."

"So I take it she bid on Ryan . . . for you?"

"Apparently."

"Then who did you bid on?"

"No one! I don't need to raid my bank account to get a date."

"Interesting."

Melissa eyed him with suspicion. The silvery bits in his gray eyes gleamed. He was definitely amused about something. "What's interesting?"

"Well, I can't help wondering why your grandmother seems to disagree."

Ooohhh, that did it. Melissa fumbled with her seat belt, all set to bolt out of the car. "My grandmother, much as I love her, has some crazy ideas that I can't be responsible for, and anyway why should I have to justify anything to you . . ."

A firm hand stilled hers.

"I'm very sorry. I didn't mean to offend you. To tell the truth, I haven't been on a date for quite a while, and my manners are a little rusty. Let's try again."

Still wary, Melissa dropped the seat belt. Her hand was tingling again, curse it. He looked sincerely apologetic, his gray eyes serious.

"I realize you wanted to save me from an awkward situation, but you have no obligation to go through with this evening. I can arrange for the donation to be refunded."

"Donation?"

"You know, to the Widows and Orphans Fund."

Right. She'd forgotten that part.

"Your grandmother's bid was very generous, and I can understand why she'd be upset that Ryan isn't here. He's very good-looking."

Melissa thought Brody did just fine in the looks department, but that wasn't the point right now. "What amount did she bid?"

"I think you should ask your grandmother that."

"*What amount?*" She used her best news producer look on him, the one that made editors tremble. But Brody seemed to be immune and returned a mild stare.

"As I said, we'd be happy to refund the donation."

"Right. So the widows and orphans are going to be deprived because I don't want to go on a date with a not-quite-as-good-looking-as-the-first-choice bachelor," said Melissa. Oh, that grand-mother of hers was clever.

"I see a couple options here. We refund the do-nation."

"Not an option."

"Or we keep the donation, but I drop you off somewhere, and you can tell Nelly we went on a date."

She eyed him. Was that what he wanted? He met her eyes with an unreadable look.

"To be honest," she answered, "I'm not a big fan of lying to my grandmother. Even though she can tell some doozies herself."

"Good." He seemed to mean it, as a slow smile lit up his rather serious face. "The final option is to enjoy the lovely evening I have planned for . . . well, for your grandmother."

Melissa considered. She could leave the car right now, and no harm done. But she realized she didn't want to. The man was attractive. Extremely so. Even though, of course, he wasn't her type. Besides, he was a fire captain. Maybe she could look at it as an interview for a future news special. "Fine. Let's get going, Mr. Bachelor Number Two. You got yourself a date."

It was a good thing the Dodge was already cruising down the freeway when another thought occurred to her. "So exactly why couldn't Ryan make it?"

At his split-second of hesitation, Melissa's eyes flashed. "Let me guess. He didn't want to go out with an old lady."

"He wasn't feeling well," said Brody, uneasily.

"You mean he wasn't feeling well enough to go out with an old lady. Of all the low, cowardly—!"

"Would it help if I said he would have been very pleasantly surprised?"

"No, it wouldn't! That makes it even worse!"

"Melissa."

"My grandmother spent good money on him, and for him to turn around—"

"Melissa!"

"—and refuse to go out with her . . . isn't that just like a man—"

"Melissa!!"

"What?"

Brody spoke in a firm voice. "I'm here. I'm very happy to be here. If your grandmother was here, I'm sure I'd be happy too, in a slightly different way. Can we just leave it at that?"

Melissa closed her mouth with a snap. How did he manage to sound so . . . right? But she had to admit she had no reason to be angry with Brody. He hadn't skipped out on his responsibilities. In fact, he had stepped in and saved her grandmother from the complete humiliation of having no one show up.

"Of course." She turned a thousand-watt smile at him and had the satisfaction of seeing something flare in his eyes before they turned back to the freeway. "Let's forget everything that's happened until now. You just picked me up, like any other date, and we're headed out for a night—well, an early evening—on the town. So where are we going?"

A smile played over his lips, and he shot her a wicked sidelong look. "Early bird special at the

Orange Tree. I have a reservation. They're very hard to get, you know. Hot ticket for the over-seventy crowd."

They were the youngest patrons at the Orange Tree by at least thirty years. Ever the gentleman, Brody held Melissa's chair for her. She peered at him through her lashes while pretending to look at the menu. He had a controlled physicality that kept drawing her eyes to him. There was something so . . . intriguing about him. He was all easy strength and restrained power. Which brought to mind something else she'd been wondering about.

"What about your real date?"

"My real date?"

"The girl who bid for you. How much did you end up going for?"

"Nothing."

She stared. No one had bid on Captain Brody? "That's terrible. If I'd been there, I mean if I'd been there to bid, instead of being dragged there on false pretenses by my grandmother, I definitely would have bid on you." In fact, he was the only one she would have considered.

"That's very supportive of you, but what I meant was, I wasn't on the auction block. I was just there to keep an eye on my guys."

Melissa's face burned.

The waitress appeared. She, like most of her customers, was on the far side of seventy, wiry and powdered. "You two youngsters ready, or ya need more time? We got a special tonight. Baked salmon. Easy on the intestinal tract. And if you want the chocolate soufflé, better order it now."

Melissa felt a fit of giggles threaten. This whole

situation was absurd. If she tried to order, she'd
lose it. She gave Brody a pleading look.

"Two specials," said Brody, who clearly had no
trouble taking command. "Two soufflés. And your
best Chardonnay."

Melissa managed to keep her cool until the
waitress left. Under Brody's curious gaze, she admitted, "She lost me at 'intestinal tract.'" The last
two words came out in a spurt of giggles. Had the
phrase "intestinal tract" always amused her, or did
Brody make her giddy? Either way, she couldn't
help it. She surrendered to the waves of laughter.

Brody watched her with a bemused smile, then
leaned in. She noticed how broad his shoulders
were. Something else she wasn't used to. "You
okay? All done?"

She nodded, wiping her eyes.

"Then let's get back to what we were just talking
about. I believe the last thing you said was, you
definitely would have bid on me."

"It was just a hypothetical."

"Then hypothetically, we could pretend this is
the date we would have had *if* I had been up for
auction *and* if you had bid for me."

"Would our hypothetical date include dinner
that's easy on the intestinal tract?" She giggled
again. Giggling was so unlike her. She hadn't even
had wine yet.

"Oh, an easily digestible dinner is just the beginning."

"Really? What's next?"

"Well, I was thinking I'd take you . . . your
grandmother . . . dancing at the Oasis. The Les Barrett band is playing, and I understand she's a fan.

And then, if she . . . you . . . still have energy, there's a movie about a Scrabble competition that's supposed to be interesting . . . What's wrong?"

Melissa stared at him in fascination. "You really thought about this. Grans loves to dance. Les Barrett is an old friend of hers. And Scrabble is her passion."

"I know." Brody ducked his head and sipped his water. "I did a little research. I've got a friend who's good at digging up information."

"That is really—" Melissa began indignantly.

"Did you know your grandmother has five outstanding parking tickets and a couple moving violations?"

"—extremely—"

"I took care of the tickets. Can't touch the violations." He seemed to brace himself for her verdict.

"—sweet," finished Melissa softly.

"Well, she did bid a lot of money."

Her face fell at the reminder. "My Grans has made up her mind to get me married off, whatever it takes. I'm sure she thought it was money well spent."

The waitress arrived and plunked a bottle of wine on their table, then filled two glasses in the no-nonsense manner of a nurse doling out medication. Melissa took her medicine gladly, a long sip of cool white wine. Maybe it would relax her. Brody definitely put her on edge.

"But you have other ideas?"

"Is that so bad? I just haven't had the best luck in the romance department. I'm better off sticking to my career." Not that things were going any better in that area. But if she thought about her life too much right now she'd get depressed. "What about you? Do you like being a firefighter?"

"Sure. What is your career?"

"I'm a news producer at Channel Six. What do you like about being a firefighter?"

"News producer." Most people were fascinated to hear she worked in the news. Not this man. His dark eyebrows drew together. "Channel Six? Ella Joy?"

Melissa made a little face, which she quickly hid with another sip of wine. It would never do to show anything less than wholehearted support for the most demanding and aggravating anchor she'd ever worked with. "Yes, Ella Joy. We work together quite a bit."

"My guys all love her. Every night at eleven, no matter what's going on, the TV gets turned to Channel Six."

"She'll be happy to hear that," said Melissa politely. "So how long does it take to become a fire captain?"

"You must be good at your job. You're a good interviewer."

Not good enough, thought Melissa. She was getting nowhere with him. Which was frustrating, since she really wanted to know more about him. "You don't talk about your work?"

"Not really, no."

"Why not?"

Brody shrugged. "I don't want to bore you."

She blinked at him indignantly. This, she reminded herself, was why she never went out with this kind of man—a man's man, who probably saw women as pretty, empty-headed decorations.

Pointedly, she adjusted the glasses on her nose. "So that's the way you think. That I can't handle it."

"Handle it?" He looked startled. "Oh. You mean . . . No, of course that's not it. Please, look at you. You're obviously very smart."

"What makes you say that?"

"I would say the glasses, but then you'd think I was an idiot who assumed every girl with glasses is smart. No, it's the way you challenge the things I say."

Melissa felt her face heat. How had this man, this stranger, this macho man, put his finger on her worst fault? "It's a bad habit. Career hazard."

"No," he said thoughtfully. "It's not because of your career. But I'm sure it helps you. You don't have to apologize for it, I like it."

"You do?"

"Sure. Same reason I like racquetball. Keeps me on my toes."

After a pause, Melissa gave a gurgle of laughter. "Likewise. Every time I think I have a handle on you, you throw me a curve."

He cocked his head at her. "You have a lovely laugh."

And there went another curve.

Chapter Four

The fire captain was truly unpredictable. Melissa never would have guessed they'd find so many things to talk about. Through their delicious, if bland, meal of baked salmon and boiled potatoes, they discussed all sorts of things, from their hometowns (San Gabriel for her, Phoenix, Arizona, for him), to their favorite movie (*Casablanca* for her, *Ben-Hur* for him), to their first loves (Betty in second grade for him, Keanu Reeves for her). Brody seemed to actually listen to her, rather than waiting for her to finish so he could describe his latest screenplay. As she talked, he watched her closely with those deep charcoal eyes. Somewhere in the middle of the second bottle of Chardonnay, while digging into her chocolate soufflé, she decided his eyes were the most beautiful she'd ever seen.

After dinner they drove to the Oasis Club and danced to the Les Barrett band, which hadn't changed their play list since about 1960. Melissa watched with awe the older couples who swirled around them on the polished dance floor. No matter how stiff in the joints, how gnarled and bent their limbs, they still moved in perfect harmony with each other. She wished she'd paid more attention when Nelly had tried to teach her ballroom dancing.

"Everything okay?" asked Brody, as they executed a slow spin.

"Great. But my Grans wouldn't be stepping on your toes like this."

"She'd probably be boxing my ears instead. That's what they did in her generation, boxed people's ears. I'm not even sure what it means."

Melissa laughed, and caught the answering flare in his eyes. Suddenly she wondered what it would be like to kiss him. If she pressed her lips to that firm mouth, would he lose that calm control of his? Bend her backward right here on the dance floor? Flushing, she dragged her gaze away from his mouth.

She'd had way too much Chardonnay. There would be no kiss. It wasn't a real date, after all. He was just doing his duty for the Widows and Orphans Fund. So why did she keep having these ridiculous little fantasies and random tinglings of various body parts?

She took a deep breath, inhaling his scent. He smelled like clean leather, like the seats in his car. Mixed with some kind of light aftershave with a woodsy aroma. She breathed in again for another dose. It wasn't enough—she wanted to push aside his white collar and bury her face in his chest. Maybe lick his skin to pin down that elusive essence of male.

What was wrong with her?

This was all her grandmother's fault. Nelly was always going on about testosterone and red-blooded men. It was ridiculous. Melissa liked a completely different type, sensitive and artsy. One of her writer boyfriends had put her in a short story. A fireman couldn't do that, could he? Of course, it had hardly been a flattering portrait. She'd come off as a money-grubbing sellout for working at a TV station. But still—it was art. Not bad for the daughter of an electrician.

She should be spending the evening with a goateed artist, not this iron-armed, enigma-eyed man twirling her around the dance floor. She should be at an art gallery or a poetry reading, or in a loft sharing a bottle of red wine and a deep philosophical discussion with someone who didn't make her pulse skip so many beats. She had to get a grip.

She stiffened her arms to put more distance between them. "So . . ." She stuck her chin out. "Isn't that a little archaic, the Widows and Orphans Fund? It sounds like something out of *Oliver Twist*."

"Does it?"

"It more or less assumes that when a firefighter dies, he'll be leaving a wife behind. What if the firefighter is a woman? Or gay?"

"I could check the bylaws, but I'm sure exceptions can be made."

"Exceptions! That's exactly the problem. It

shouldn't be an exception. It should be normal."
She glared up at him.

Brody, taken aback, played for time with a quick
spinning move. What had set her off? She'd turned
stiff as a board in his arms, and her eyes were
throwing emerald sparks at him. She really was
quite beautiful. He suddenly wanted to see more
of those sparks.

"Speaking generally, your typical firefighter is
a married man with kids." The San Gabriel station was a glaring exception, but he saw no need
to mention that.

"Then you're not a typical firefighter. At least in
that way."

"But in other ways?" He arched an eyebrow.
This should be interesting.

"Probably. Do you like football?"

"Yes."

"Cars? Something tells me that blue time machine is not your only car."

"I've also got a truck and a Toyota. And a mo-
torcycle."

"Of course you do. You listen to country music?"

"Something wrong with country music?"

Her agitation had quickened her steps, and he
found himself traveling double-time around the
dance floor to keep her from spinning off by herself. He twirled them toward a quiet corner. The
other dancers, moving at one third their pace, kept
a wise distance.

"You probably hang out in bars playing darts
and waiting for the next wet T-shirt contest. You
spend your weekends tinkering with your car,
or watching the *Pimp My Ride* marathon. If you

were married, you'd leave your wife home to do
the dishes while you go hunting with your buddies. God forbid you should ever have to change
a diaper or vacuum a floor. And the worst part is,
you have willing young girls falling all over themselves, bidding hundreds of dollars to be the next
Mrs. Fire Captain and have little fire babies." She
paused for a breath, then turned beet-red as her
words echoed between them.

"At least they'd be taken care of if I died,"
pointed out Brody. He ought to be offended. But he
was too busy watching the way her hair tumbled
around her head. He wondered if it felt as silky as
it looked.

"I apologize if I was rude," she said, nose in the
air.

"Not at all."

"So you don't deny I'm right?"

"Why should I, when you seem so convinced
that you are?"

Now those emerald sparks were firing again.
"You could at least try to defend yourself."

"Are we in a battle? I thought this was a date."

"You . . ." She gave a squeak of pure frustration.
"Don't you ever get rattled?"

"It's part of my job to not get rattled."

"But you're not on the job right now. Don't you
want to argue with me? Mix it up? Play a little racquetball?"

"Oh, later I'll probably grab some of my buddies, hit the nearest bar, and beat someone up. You
know how us firemen like a good throw down."

"See that? You'll fight with your buddies, but
not with a mere woman. Typical male arrogance."

Okay, now she was starting to get under his skin. "You really want me to fight with you?"

His men would have recognized the dangerous look in his eyes, but Melissa stuck out her chin in that stubborn way of hers.

"If it wouldn't be too much trouble."

"Okay. Let's see, the news." His voice was quiet enough not to be overheard, but forceful enough to get his point across. "You stick microphones in people's faces at their worst moments, but you make sure your lipstick is perfect first. If someone's crying, you get that camera nice and close so you can catch every moment. The first thing you want to know about a man, after what he makes, is what car he drives. BMWs or Porsches are best, but you might condescend to date a man with an Audi, if you were really desperate. You get your nails done once a week, a facial every other week, you don't mind spending five hundred dollars on a pair of shoes you wear twice. And once you have yourself a man, he'd better make sure to keep the cash flowing, because if it stops . . . you're off to the next provider."

He snapped his mouth shut. Where had that last part come from? But he knew the answer to that; he was describing his ex-wife.

Of course, Melissa had no way of knowing that. "That is completely unfair. You just repeated every cliché ever invented about the news business."

"And you're obviously completely objective when it comes to firemen."

"I'm a newsperson, we're paid to be objective."

"Then you might want to think about giving the money back, because—"

"Excuse me, mister."

"*What?*" He swung around and found himself staring down a willowy, gray-haired lady. She took a startled step back. "I'm sorry. So sorry. I didn't mean to speak so forcefully. What is it?"

"The other dancers and I would . . . Well, you're causing quite a commotion."

Brody looked around and saw the dance floor had cleared in a wide circle around them. The music had trailed off. Melissa tugged at his arm, her face bright pink.

"We'll leave immediately," she said. "We're extremely sorry."

"Very, very sorry," he repeated after her.

During the ride back to her house, Melissa stewed next to him.

"One thing's for sure," she said. "We are not compatible, not one bit."

Brody didn't argue, although he'd been having a good time despite Melissa's absurd prejudices about firemen. He would have enjoyed showing her just how wrong she was. But then he'd lost control—he, Captain Brody, whose cool under pressure was legendary on the force.

He was embarrassed. Ashamed. This proved he had no business dating. He thought he'd put all thoughts of Rebecca behind him. But she'd popped up like a mocking jack-in-the-box determined to ruin his good time.

Out of sheer, dogged politeness, he followed Melissa to her door. She stuck out her hand to shake his.

"Thank you for the nice evening. And just so

you know, my shoes cost thirty-two dollars at Payless—" But she didn't get a chance to finish. Before he knew what he was doing, Brody yanked her into his arms and covered her mouth with his. She tasted so good she made his head spin. She was warm cream, vanilla velvet, wine, and fire.

What was he doing? He was insane. This girl despised him, she thought they weren't compatible; but none of that mattered. He had to touch her, had to feel her soft lips against his. She'd probably knee him in the balls, spray him with Mace . . . but no. Her mouth opened on a sigh.

Her bare arms came around him, silky and maddening. Losing himself in the sweetness of her mouth, he let his tongue explore, feeling hers dance and twirl with his, as if they were still on the ballroom floor. This was a bad idea, a very bad idea. In another second he would lose the last ounce of his control. With a groan, he pulled away.

Her green eyes had gone all hazy, like mist over a quarry lake. She looked so beautiful he couldn't stand it. He had to kiss her again, taste that smooth skin . . . He lowered his head to press kisses into her neck, onto her cheekbones, against her ear. "Even when you were yelling at me, I wanted to do this."

She laughed. Such a rich sound, like deep wind chimes in a forest. He loved her laugh.

Was her skin this soft everywhere on her body? Just the question made him tighten with excitement. If he didn't stop now, he was going to tear off her clothes and run his hands over every curve of her body. That tempting vanilla scent was driving him insane, and so was the way she'd gone loose in the limbs from his kisses. He would have to be made of mahogany to resist.

He felt alive, fiercely aroused. He hadn't felt like this in so long he'd forgotten how to handle it. Giving in to the craziness of it, he pushed her against the front door, braced his arms on either side of her, and pressed his aching groin against her.

When she arched her body against his hips, it felt like a spark in a tinderbox. He ground himself into her. She answered with a moan and a thrust of her hips. Urgent need raced through him like a sheet of flame, obliterating every other thought.

His hungry hands flew to her neckline. She was wearing some kind of sleeveless top that had no visible way in. Too tight to pull up, no zipper that his fumbling fingers could find. How the hell did she get it on? He'd have to rip it off. But he couldn't wait. He molded her full breasts through the thin material and felt their eager tips leap toward his hands. His hands shook with the need to feel her secret softness against his palms, their tender nipples hardening under his fingers.

He was about to rip her shirt in two, when suddenly the door swung open behind her. Melissa stumbled backward. He hauled her against him to keep her from hitting the floor.

Nelly, arms akimbo, glared at them in outrage. "What are you doing to my granddaughter?"

Brody felt Melissa shake against his chest. He tightened his arm around her. "It's okay, Mrs. McGuire. Nothing happened."

"Melissa?"

Melissa raised her head. Her face was flushed,

lips swollen, glasses fogged up. "Nothing happened," she echoed in a smothered voice. Brody hoped Nelly's glasses were equally foggy. It was their only chance.

"I saw his hands around your neck! He's no fire captain, he's an axe murderer!"

"Grans, he doesn't have an axe."

"I'm not a murderer of any kind." Brody felt compelled to clarify. "I was just . . ."

"He was just . . ." Melissa trailed off.

"Adjusting her collar," Brody finally managed.

"What collar? She doesn't have one."

"I thought she did."

"Well, you were wrong, weren't you?" demanded Nelly.

"Very wrong."

Nelly seemed to be satisfied. "Well, go on with you, then."

Brody looked at Melissa, who was staring down at her feet, still trying to catch her breath. She must think he was some kind of animal. His arousal hadn't gone down a bit, despite the rude shock of the interruption. Hoping it wasn't too obvious, he backed away, then turned sideways to address Melissa.

"Thank you for a lovely evening."

"Thank you," she answered, equally polite. She gave him one quick glance, and the heat in her eyes shot directly to his groin.

Trying to think of the most unsexy things possible—the new sink he had to put in, the compost pile he'd started in the backyard—he walked quickly toward his car. When he looked back, the door had closed, and both women were gone.

He let out a long whistling breath. Holy Mother of God. What had just happened? He needed a cold shower. Or a bucket of ice. If that didn't work, his favorite channel, C-SPAN. And wouldn't Melissa gloat if she found out he was a secret news junkie.

Chapter Five

As Melissa walked through the fluorescent-lit corridors of the Channel Six newsroom the next morning, her step had a definite, unaccustomed bounce. It did not go unnoticed.

"Finally get laid?" said Nolan Chang, the young, hip, Asian-American reporter who sat in the cubicle next to hers. His phone was clamped to his ear; she could only hope he was on hold.

"Must you? Really?" It had taken Melissa a few years to get used to the raunchy humor of the typical newsroom. By now she'd learned to hold her own, but at times the X-rated joking still made her blush. She was a shy girl at heart. Then again, maybe she wasn't, if last night was any indication. At the memory, she felt her face flame.

The crazy electricity that had raced through her body when Brody kissed her! She'd melted against him with absolutely no hesitation. One minute she'd been about to explain Payless shoes to him, the next she'd plastered her body against his hard chest. When she'd felt the warm, rigid thrust of him against her hips, she'd gone wild. If Nelly hadn't opened the door when she had . . .

"You did! Look at you. That is the face of someone who did the nasty . . . the beast with two backs, the— Yes, hello, I'm calling to set up an interview with the governor . . ."

Saved by a press agent. Melissa walked into her tiny cubicle and tossed her bag into a corner. She hung her jacket on the back of her chair. Back in Los Angeles, she'd had her own office, but when she'd moved home to San Gabriel, she'd jumped down about a hundred market sizes. At Channel Six there was no one taking phone messages, no assistant to help her log footage, no promotion department to promote her investigations. And no sexy heartbreaker of a news director to ruin her life.

So what if she had to do everything herself here? So what if Channel Six's slogan was "The Sunny Side of the News"? She was in a rebuilding phase of her career.

She logged on to her computer; while it was booting up, she went through the messages on her voice mail. One viewer had called to complain about her special report on black market dog breeders. Another had called to compliment it. Fifty-fifty, not a bad response. The complainer was much louder and more profane, but she could understand why. As he repeatedly pointed out, she had put him out of business; now he was going to have to start breeding cats. Or maybe ferrets. Would she prefer that, Miss F-ing Know-It-All?

Melissa sighed and deleted the call. If the man had left a number, she would have called him back and let him vent in person. Most producers and reporters hated talking to angry viewers, but Melissa loved it. Usually people just needed to have their say, and by the end of the call they would vow to watch only Channel Six from now on. She'd even gotten some story tips from initially furious viewers. But there was a fine line between furious and abusive, and this last caller fell into the latter category.

As did the four messages from Ella Joy. "This friggin' computer system . . . I can't get on . . . someone's supposed to e-mail me something . . . I don't want to call IT, they take frickin' forever . . . why don't you get this god-awful, ridiculous computer fixed . . . I've only asked you a million times . . ."

Delete.

"Okay, I called IT, they're saying it's my fault, I don't have to take this, Melissa, I really don't, I'm supposed to be on the air in one hour, and I'm getting splotches from this stress. What's the point of a hot stone massage during my break if I have to come back and deal with this crap?"

Delete.

"Melissa, where is your freakin' cell phone number, I can never find it when I need it, I swear you do it on purpose . . ."

Delete. On the bright side, if Ella Joy was checking her e-mail, that must mean she was attempting to do some work. Then again . . .

"Okay, I'm on my computer now, and I finally opened that e-mail from the Absolut Vodka people, and you need to get me off the news this Friday night. They want me to host a party for their new Jalapeño Absolut, and of course I told them, absolutely! Get it?"

Melissa deleted the last voice mail, and gave a long sigh. How was she going to break it to Ella that she could *absolutely not* host a party for a new flavor of vodka? And why should she be the one who had to break it to her? But there was no point in whining about that. The news director was terrified of Ella, and the general manager was in love with her. Nope—all bad news had to come from Melissa.

"There you are! I called you a million times last night." Ella Joy propped one tiny hip on Melissa's desk, then crossed her legs so she perched like a hummingbird. Everything about her was tiny, except for her head with its lacquered helmet of hair. Her features were perfect for television— large brilliant blue eyes, slightly tilted; chiseled cheekbones; skin just a shade darker than her honey-colored hair. Rumor had it her father was Filipino, but she had never said so publicly. From the waist up, she was camera-ready in an electric blue blazer and chunky gold earrings. From the waist down, she was a slob in ratty sweatpants and flip-flops.

"I was out. I turned my phone off right after I talked to you."

Ella's attention sharpened. "Do tell."

"Nothing to tell."

"Well, what'd you do?"

"Ate. Danced. Went home." There must have been a self-conscious look on her face, because Ella refused to let it drop.

"Who's the lucky fella? You haven't gone on a date since that sculptor or whatever he was."

"Ceramic impressionist."

"Like I said, whatever."

"This one wasn't a ceramicist, that's for sure."

Ella's attention drifted to one of her nails, and Melissa found herself, for once, wanting to surprise her. "He's actually a fireman."

Ella's glance shot back to Melissa's. "No shit."

"Honest to God. By the way, he said you're the anchor of choice at their fire station."

Ella gave a smug smile and went back to her nail. "If your date wants a signed photo, just ask. Or maybe I'll send them a calendar."

Melissa gritted her teeth. "Great idea. So about this vodka party—"

"I already told them I'd do it, so don't even try."

"Ella, remember that integrity workshop they made us take? They specifically said we can't let anchors endorse alcohol use."

"Who's endorsing? I'm just hosting the party. No one said anything about endorsing."

Melissa sighed. Ella was truly a creative genius when it came to rationalization. "I see your point. I just worry about the little children." Ella claimed to be deeply concerned with the next generation, although Melissa had never seen any concrete proof of this.

"But honey, there won't *be* any little children at this party. It's strictly twenty-one and over."

Melissa gave up the fight—for now. "When is it?"

"This Friday, like I said on my message," replied Ella impatiently. She expected every word she spoke to be remembered like gospel. "That's why you have to get me off the news."

Friday. So she had a few days to figure out a solution. She could always threaten to put an intern on the air in her place. Ella had a mortal fear of interns—all young, all gorgeous, all single-mindedly after her job. "We'll figure something out. I have to check my e-mail now."

Chang popped his head into Melissa's cubicle. "What's crack-a-lackin', babe?" He spotted Ella. "Great numbers last night."

"Why thanks. The numbers always pop when I wear my fuchsia silk."

"Nothing to do with the black market dog-breeding story, I suppose," interjected Melissa, looking up from her computer.

Ella and Chang ignored that absurdity, and Melissa went back to her e-mail. The usual corporate memos, lectures from the news director, viewer comments, and forwarded dirty jokes. She deleted most of it and nearly deleted the misspelled e-mail with the subject line, "Pleas help cawl soon." But since Ella and Chang were now arguing over whether Starbucks would deliver, she decided even a wacko e-mail would be preferable. She opened it, and right away saw the misspellings were those of a child.

Pleas help. Our foster mother beets us and gives mony to the soshul worker not to tell. Call 557-9268 onley between 9 and 10. My name is Rodrigo. I got yore card from Juan.

Melissa felt the little hairs rise on her arms. A child abuser bribing a social worker to look the other way. If it was true, it was disgusting. It needed to be exposed. This was exactly why she'd gotten into the news business. This was why she frequently went into the worst neighborhoods and left her card with key people. The pastor at the church. The drug counselor. The barber. People who could let her know if something wrong was happening.

Brody's words came back to her, the ones about sticking cameras in people's faces and making sure her lipstick looked good. How she'd love to prove him wrong. She'd love to see Mr. Big Shot Fire Captain eat his words.

She checked her watch. Nine-forty. She'd better call the boy, Rodrigo, right away. But first she had to get rid of her bickering coworkers. "Chang, if you struck out with the governor, try Dana in the press office, and tell her I told you to call. And Ella, you really should do something about that nail, I can tell it's driving you crazy. You don't want it to distract you when you're on the air."

When Ella and Chang were gone, Melissa picked up the phone and dialed.

Before anyone could answer, the number of the news director's office flashed on the screen. She sighed. How did she ever get any work done in this place? The window to call Rodrigo was disappearing. But news directors, as a species, didn't like being ignored. She punched the button.

"My office, two seconds."

Even though Melissa dawdled out of sheer rebellion, it didn't take long to make her way to Bill

Loudon's dimly lit office. The news director was a watery-eyed, hunched little man whose salary was rumored to be seventy-five percent devoted to alimony payments. The news business was hard on marriages. Loudon had gone from market to market, Cedar Springs to Fargo to Las Vegas and on and on, strewing a trail of ex-wives behind him. The years of staring at TV screens had taken a toll on his eyesight. He kept his office so dim it felt almost subterranean. And he spent so much time in it that some wondered if he could no longer afford a house.

Melissa decided to take the initiative.

"Loudon, I'd like some extra time to work on a new investigation."

"Extra time? Take all you want."

"Not my personal time. You know what I mean. I want time off Ella duty." Part of her job as "special news projects producer" was to create showcase reports for Ella. She would research them, do the interviews, write the pieces, produce them, then drag Ella out for an hour to shoot standups that could then be inserted into the finished story.

"What's the story? Can we use it for November sweeps?"

"I'm not sure yet. It's a tip from a kid in foster care, and it's going to take some time to confirm. It may end up being nothing. Or it could blow up the whole foster care system."

"Blow up foster care," said Loudon with deep gloom. He reached for the jumbo-size bottle of pastel antacids he kept at his elbow.

"Exactly."

"Ella doesn't like stories with bad guys."

"I know."

"Channel Six is supposed to be the Sunny Side of the News."

"I know. But this could be a really important story that could save children from abuse."

He blinked wearily at her. "You're a pain in my fat arse."

"I'm really sorry. And you look like you've lost a few pounds."

"Fine. No Ella this week."

"You're a champ, boss." She gave him a glorious smile. What a difference to have an open, easy, work-only relationship with her boss. In Los Angeles, every time she'd stepped into Everett's office her pulse had raced and her heart had pounded.

"On one condition."

Of course there would be a catch. "What?"

"Heard you went on a date last night."

Melissa's jaw dropped. That was the last thing she'd expected him to say. "What . . . how . . ."

"I have my sources."

For one wild moment, Melissa imagined their sixty-year-old waitress slipping off to report a hot tip to Loudon, like some kind of secret agent.

"Does this new development in your love life mean you'll have an in with the Bachelor Firemen of San Gabriel?"

"The *what*?" Maybe all the light waves from the ten TV sets in his office had disrupted his brain function. But Loudon gazed at her expectantly, as if his words made some kind of sense. "What are you talking about?"

"That's right, you were in LA being a big shot. Our local fire station is famous. Even made the

Today show. The whole crew was in *People* magazine's Sexiest Man Alive issue. It's the only all-bachelor fire station in the country. Or almost all. And apparently they're good-looking too. Hell if I know."

Melissa put a hand to her head. Captain Brody was famous? The whole station was? And she'd spent the evening alternately yelling at him and French-kissing him?

"They had that big media blitz a couple years ago, then nothing. Apparently the captain shut it down. Won't give interviews anymore. Except about fires, of course."

Melissa remembered Brody's scathing comments about the news—in fact, how could she forget them? Except now they made a little more sense. "So why are you telling me all this?"

"You know." Loudon gave her a half wink that, with his droopy eyes, looked more like a leer.

"I really don't."

"Sure would be good for ratings to get those Bachelor Firemen back on the air. Why, with ratings like that, we could afford all kinds of investigations into foster care. Throw in the health department too. FDA, FDIC, whatever you like."

You're a twisted, loathsome man. Melissa had to double check to make sure she hadn't said that out loud. Obviously his sources weren't all that good, if they thought there was any chance she and Brody would go out again. But she saw no need to explain all that to Loudon, who blinked at her in the flickering blue light.

"I'll . . . uh . . . do what I can. In between investigating a story that could actually save lives."

"Fair enough."

On her way out the door, she paused. "Oh, I almost forgot. Ella accepted an invite to host a party for Absolut Vodka. Since I'm off Ella duty, I guess you'll have to tell her she can't."

Loudon looked alarmed, frantically wiping his bleary eyes. "Oh no, Melissa. You take that one."

"But you said—"

"After you handle this. *Then* you're off Ella duty."

Melissa groaned. "Fine."

She'd think of something. In the meantime, she needed to start making some calls on the foster care story. The story that would make Bachelor Fireman Brody grovel at her feet.

Chapter Six

Brody, crouched between two studs in the living room of his house-under-construction, dropped his wire strippers for the tenth time and swore.

"You know, Cap, most guys do things like buy a new sports car or date a sorority girl after a breakup." Ryan Blake, holding a large bag from Subway, loomed over him.

"Yeah, well, I'm building myself a new house. Better than therapy." Brody strained to reach the wire strippers. He knew his crew thought he was nuts. They were probably right, especially when it came to wiring. Home-run wires, three-way light switches, designated circuits. Why the hell didn't he just give in and call a damn professional? He had a healthy respect for good electricians; he'd put out his share of fires caused by the bad ones.

And why did he keep dropping his tools? He never dropped his tools.

He knew why. Melissa McGuire.

"What are you doing here?" he growled at Ryan.

"Thought I'd come by and help you out today."

The San Gabriel firefighters had gotten in the habit of dropping by to help with his one-man construction project. They'd watched him go through hell, and they'd been ready at any moment to spackle walls, hoist two-by-fours, badmouth Rebecca, set him up with random strippers, or come over and hang out over beers and football.

But the guys didn't know the whole story. They didn't know about the baby.

"I brought lunch too. I thought you might need some refreshment," Ryan added.

Brody gave up on the wire strippers and extracted himself from between the studs. He stood up, wiping the sweat from his eyes. "After my hard night's work?" he asked dryly.

He took the offered bag and rummaged through it for a drink. After gulping down most of a Snapple, he fished out a turkey sub and handed the bag back to Ryan. He sat down on an overturned bucket and pulled another over for Ryan.

Ryan wore a guilty look on his movie-star face. "I really owe you big, Cap. Was it . . . okay?"

"Define okay."

"Did she make you play bingo or anything?" Ryan unwrapped a ham and cheese sandwich and bit into it.

"Nope. She was very intelligent, very charming. When she wasn't yelling at me."

"Yelling at you?"

"For being a football-watching, car-driving blockhead."

Ryan frowned, confused. "What are we supposed to drive?"

"Good question. Too bad you weren't there to ask it."

"Geez, I'm sorry, Captain, I never thought it'd be like that. I thought she'd be all over you."

"Well, at the end . . ." Brody smiled reminiscently, and Ryan nearly choked on his ham and cheese.

"You didn't . . . you didn't . . . *make out* with her?"

"A gentleman doesn't kiss and tell, you know that, Hoagie," said Brody reprovingly. Ryan carefully put down his sandwich, clearly trying to process this new development.

"You mean, you dug her?"

"What's not to like about a beautiful, passionate, articulate woman?"

"Is this another one of your lessons?" Ryan sounded worried. "I'm supposed to . . . um . . . see past appearances? To the soul within, or some shit?" Brody watched the gears click with great amusement, then decided to give the kid a break.

"Well, yes, that's always wise strategy. But actually, Nelly McGuire was indisposed, and her granddaughter took her place. That seems to have been Mrs. McGuire's intention all along."

The clouds instantly cleared from Ryan's face. "Was the granddaughter hot?"

Unbelievably hot. Molten lava hot. Kept-him-up-all-night hot.

"Probably not your usual type," came his eventual answer. For some reason, the thought of Ryan with Melissa didn't sit right. Would she fall for the pretty face, as so many others had? And what difference did it make if she did? She clearly didn't think much of him, especially after he'd lost it and insulted her whole profession.

Then again, if she really hated him, would she have responded with such fire and eagerness at the end? He'd been all over her, and she hadn't seemed to mind. In fact, if Nelly hadn't opened the door . . .

He swallowed the rest of his Snapple to drown the memory.

"I bet she was smokin'. You got that look in your eye."

"I have no look."

"Yeah you do. You haven't looked like that since . . . you know."

"You know" was code for "Rebecca."

He chewed the turkey, which tasted like sandpaper. When Rebecca left, he'd realized the truth. He'd been born to command, born to save lives, risk his neck, guide his crew, school his rookies. None of that led to a happy personal life. It hadn't helped his marriage to Rebecca, and why should it be different with any other woman?

"Cap, I'm sorry," Ryan broke in. "Didn't mean to say the wrong thing." Brody caught the alarmed look on the younger man's face. He must be looking grim, as he always did when thoughts of Rebecca haunted him.

"You didn't. Don't worry. Can you get those wire strippers out of there?" Ryan jumped to his feet. "Actually, never mind." It was time to let go of the insanity. At least one part of it. "Hand me the Yellow Pages over in the corner."

Ryan grabbed the phone book that had been tossed on the doorstep a few days ago. "I know a guy. Wired my buddy's office."

"Licensed?" asked Brody, scanning the listings under "electrician."

"No, but that's why he's so cheap . . ."

But Brody stopped listening. A name in bold type caught his eye. Haskell McGuire, Electrician. Licensed and bonded. No ad, no goofy guy with a head shaped like a light bulb. But the name alone was enough to draw Brody. Could it possibly be the same family? A father, a cousin, a brother? Might as well call the man. One way or the other, he'd get an electrician out of it. And maybe another connection to the feisty, fascinating, irritating, sexy Melissa. Maybe she'd bring him lunch, maybe she'd sit on that bucket and toss her dark hair over her shoulder and—

"Cap, there's another part of the prize . . ."

Brody looked up from the Yellow Pages, and Ryan blinked. "Geez, you look like you found Jesus in there."

"Praise the Lord. You better scram, Hoagie. I gotta make a call."

"But wait. You have to hear this, Cap. We have to make dinner for her at the station. For Nelly McGuire."

"Oh, hell." He'd forgotten that part.

"Don't worry, I've been doing a lot of thinking. There's always time to do the right thing, you know."

Brody recognized one of the affirmations. "What right thing?"

"I'm going to make up for blowing off the grandmother. I'll be nice as pie to her, and to her granddaughter."

"You're inviting her too?"

"Yes, sir. You said she's hot, right?"

Brody could have kicked himself. "I think I said not your usual type."

"Doesn't matter. They're going to get the royal treatment—Hoagie-style." And he was off.

So much for that. If Ryan aimed his mojo on Melissa, Brody might as well forget her. He and Nelly would get to spend the evening watching the fireworks. Still, he needed a damn electrician. Brody dialed the number listed for Haskell McGuire.

When Melissa got back to her cubicle, her private line was ringing. *Is it Brody?* How should she act? Apologetic? Standoffish? Confused? She pounced on it, then fought her disappointment at the sound of Nelly's voice.

"Oh, hi Grans. Is something wrong?"

"There must be, you sound like someone died."

"I'm just busy, that's all. I'm at work, you know."

"Work, always work. Never mind, you're going to forget that nasty job when I tell you what's happening on Friday."

"I am?" said Melissa warily.

"We're both invited to the firehouse for dinner! Those handsome firemen are going to make us dinner with their own two hands. And we are the guests of honor!"

Dinner at Brody's fire station? A jolt of mixed

emotions shot through her. Embarrassment at how she'd insulted him. Shame at how she'd thrown herself at him. And most of all, a deep thrill at the thought of seeing him again.

"I don't know, Grans. Who invited us?"

She heard Nelly hesitate a moment. "Well, it's part of the prize."

"Oh Lord. The auction. Forget it, I'm not going."

"But you have to, Melissa. You have to drive me. You know I can't drive anymore, it's bad for my blood pressure."

Not to mention the California Highway Patrol's, thought Melissa.

"Besides, it's on Friday, and that's Haskell's meeting night."

"Friday?" That rang a bell. What was Friday? Oh right, the vodka party. An idea formed

"Let me think about it. I'll see you later, Grans."

"Well, don't work too much, sweetie. And tell Ella that pink suit made her look like a hooker."

"It's fuchsia—" But Nelly had already hung up.

Melissa gathered up a handful of Ella Joy's glossy headshots. Due to Channel Six's lack of a promotion department, she handled all viewer requests for photos. She had refused to do this until they'd been reshot. The originals showed Ella reclining on the news set as though it were a piano in a nightclub act. The new photos featured a perfectly respectable Ella smiling professionally at the camera. One of the editors had seen some of the old photos selling for ten dollars apiece on eBay, but Melissa didn't feel that her obligations extended to policing the Internet.

She knocked on Ella's office door. Her office

had the feel of a sorority girl's dorm room—piles of clothes on the chairs, even on the desk. Her mini fridge was stashed with Perrier, fruit enzyme masks, and ice cream. Ella was going through a pile of magazines, with half an eye on her TV, which was tuned to a soap opera. When Melissa knocked, Ella quickly put down her *Us Weekly* and directed her gaze toward *Time* magazine.

"Ella, do you have a minute?"

"Well . . . is it important?"

"I just need some photos signed."

Ella perked up. She took the photos and set to work with her signature hot-pink Sharpie. "Who are these for?" she asked idly.

"A bunch of strong, good-looking, heroic public servants," answered Melissa.

"Soldiers?" said Ella hopefully. The newscast was available for download on the Internet, and everyone at the station knew she longed for the day it would become a hot item for troops overseas.

"Firefighters. They're heroes too, you know. When they come back from risking their lives on the fire lines, they deserve a little appreciation and inspiration." Had she gone too far? But no, Ella was eating it up.

"Of course they do, the poor brave darlings." As Ella signed her graceful, elaborate signature on each photo, Melissa sensed her moment.

"You are so sweet to do this. I told them I'd bring them a surprise, since they're cooking dinner for me."

"The firemen are cooking dinner for you?"

"Sure. At the firehouse. It's a huge honor, I heard. They always cook for themselves, you know, and sometimes they invite people over. They actually begged . . . well, I don't want to tell you, you might feel obligated."

"What? Tell me what?" Ella's blue eyes were bright with excitement.

"Well, they begged me to see if you might want to come. I told them you were a busy woman, so I couldn't promise anything, but that I'd try to get photos for them. They're world-famous, you know. Haven't you heard of the Bachelor Firemen of San Gabriel?"

"Hell, yes! I saw them on the *Today* show. Totally hot. You had no right to say I couldn't come."

Melissa put on a look of worried concern. "I was just covering for you."

"We're talking about the best-looking firemen in the country. You should have at least mentioned it to me."

"That's why I'm mentioning it to you now. I'll just tell them you have a scheduling conflict or something. I told them not to get their hopes up. But the way Ryan looked at me with those blue eyes of his . . . you can't blame me for trying." Grans had said his eyes were blue, hadn't she?

"Who's Ryan?"

"One of the firemen. He's so gorgeous." Melissa prayed that Nelly's first-choice bachelor lived up to expectations. If he was more handsome than Brody, he must be really something.

"Was he your date last night?"

"Oh no, he's way out of my league." Melissa moved in for the kill. "The day a hottie like Ryan looks twice at me . . ." And there it was, the final nail, a challenge a beauty like Ella couldn't possibly resist.

"I think I should go, after all. It would be good PR, wouldn't it?"

"Absolutely! The best. But you're so busy, Ella . . . You're a doll, but don't do it on my account."

"Oh, pooh. I've made up my mind. Now I'm starting to think you want all those handsome firemen to yourself!"

Melissa gave an embarrassed you-caught-me laugh. "You know they won't even notice me if you're there."

"You think?" asked Ella, pleased. "Just put it on my calendar. When is it?"

"I'll go call them right away. They'll be so happy." Melissa turned to go. She waited until she was almost out of earshot before she called back to Ella's office. "Oh, the dinner's on Friday. I'll make sure someone subs for you that night."

And that, she thought smugly, was the way to handle Ella Joy. In a while, Ella would realize there was a conflict, but she wouldn't be able to bear the thought of leaving an admiring, gorgeous group of men—single fireman heroes—to Melissa's sole possession. She would find her own way to back out of the vodka party.

The only downside was that Ella would now meet Brody. Would Brody fall at her feet the way most men did? Not that Melissa cared, of course.

Chapter Seven

Melissa ripped the little black dress off her body and glared at her reflection in the bathroom mirror. What were you supposed to wear to dinner at a fire station with a man who'd nearly torn your shirt off? She didn't want to wear something that said, *Hey, big guy, come rip this off my body.* On the other hand, she didn't want something that said, *Don't even think about it.* Besides, Ella Joy would set the bar so high that anything less than a G-string would barely register with the guys. She had to reach a minimum level of hotness. The little black dress just didn't cut it. And tonight she had no intention of wearing her glasses.

She chose a slinky, silvery sweater that clung tightly to her curves and made her eyes glow like emeralds. A forest-green suede skirt and knee-high boots completed the outfit, which she hoped said, *I wouldn't say no if you treat me right, and maybe apologize for insulting my profession*. She'd worn this same combo to a fund-raiser for journalists imprisoned overseas, and a radical environmentalist had hit on her. So it had a proven track record, though in a very different crowd.

"Grans? You ready?"

"Ready as rain," answered Nelly. Downstairs, Melissa saw her grandmother was sporting her very favorite sweater, which Nelly's sister, now deceased, had knitted for her seventieth birthday. It was made from a Guatemalan design, and Nelly loved to wear various buttons attached to it: "Respect Mother Earth." "Promote Whirled Peas." Melissa thought she looked like an elderly bomb-throwing revolutionary. Or at least a troublemaker.

"You look shocking, Grans."

"Thank you."

"We'd better go. We have to make a stop on the way."

"Stop? Where?"

Melissa had deliberately left this until the last moment. "We have to pick up Ella Joy."

"What? That tramp is coming? Who invited her?"

"I did. And please don't call the anchor of the Sunny Side of the News a tramp."

"More like the Slutty Side, with that one."

"Language, Grans!" Did everyone's grandmother's talk like this?

"Melissa, you don't have the sense God gave a peanut. You want to lose Brody to her?"

"Oh, come on, he's going to ignore both of us and make a beeline toward you!" Melissa gave her grandmother a little hug and shuffled her out the door.

But Nelly would not be distracted. "It's not that you aren't a hundred times prettier than Miss Fancy Schmancy, but she's got that killer instinct. If she sees a man interested in you, she'll go for his jugular. Remember Alice May? How she nearly stole Leon out from under my nose?"

"A, he's not interested in me. And B, Ella's not some jungle cat. There will be plenty of men to go around. Maybe Ryan will be there."

Nelly brightened. "That's right! Whichever one Ella likes, you go for the other one."

Melissa pretended to consider that approach as she helped her grandmother into the car. "I suppose I could, but that would interfere with my plan to eat dinner and mind my own business." She closed the car door before Nelly could answer, and took her time walking to the driver's side. Once inside, she added, "And be nice to Ella. Don't forget she's worth two ratings points, and two ratings points could get me fired."

"Don't be ridiculous. That place would fall apart without you." The rest of the drive was taken up with a litany of complaints about how little Channel Six appreciated her Melissa, and it was only when Ella Joy slid in the backseat that Nelly was finally rendered speechless. And no wonder.

Ella was dressed in a red vinyl pantsuit the exact color of a fire engine. It looked like a slick, shiny coat of all-body nail polish. Dazed, Melissa wondered if Ella had already had such an item in her closet, or if she had bought it just for this occasion. Either option seemed absurd. Ella's honey locks were curled and piled on her head, and her smoky eye shadow made her eyes look huge and luminescent. Melissa shifted uncomfortably in her sweater, which in the last two seconds had gone from slinky to deadly dull.

Maybe Grans had been right, after all. If she wanted any chance with Brody, she should never have invited Ella. Not that she was after Brody, not at all. They had nothing in common. Except that she couldn't get that crazy kissing incident out of her mind.

It didn't matter. What chance did regular mortals have next to someone like Ella? She'd have to be content with her original plan. Eat her dinner and mind her own business. The only entertainment would be watching the firemen fall over themselves bowing down to the goddess of Channel Six news.

San Gabriel Fire Station 1 was a square, concrete building smack in the middle of town. Melissa had seen it in news reports, but since she wasn't on the daily news beat herself, she had never actually been there. The firefighters kept it immaculate and had even planted geraniums in planters out front. A fresh-faced young fireman, who looked about twelve, was busy watering the flowers, and at the sight of Ella exiting the car he dropped the hose. It went snaking across the driveway, spewing a rooster tail of water in front of them. Ella gave a little shriek, and jumped behind Nelly.

Melissa bent down and picked up the hose. She handed it back to the firefighter, but he didn't budge. He stood, openmouthed, as the water streamed onto the driveway. Finally she stood directly in his line of sight. "Hi," she said brightly. "We're here at the invitation of Ryan Blake. This is my grandmother, Nelly McGuire. And this is—"

"Ella Joy." He said it in a voice of awe. "We . . . we watch you all the time, you're the bomb."

Ella must have decided that the receiving of adulation was worth getting her strappy sandals wet. She moved from behind Nelly to greet the fireman. "Aren't you a doll? We do our humble best, and it's so nice to know it's appreciated." Bestowing her hand on the dazzled young man, she nearly bowled him over with a huge smile. *Humble best*, thought Melissa. *Where on earth had she come up with that?*

"And just call me Ella. This is Melissa, my producer."

"We're so . . . honored to have you . . . all of you." Finally he managed to tear his gaze away from Ella, and remembered his manners. "Mrs. McGuire, it's nice to meet you. I'm Stud . . . I mean, Fred. Stud's my nickname. Because I'm not, really. A stud, that is. Not compared to the others. Come on in, and I'll introduce you to the rest of the crew. They're going to be so stoked!" He dropped the hose again and took Nelly's arm. "How are you doing, ma'am?"

"Not very well, young man. Frankly, I could use a glass of water." Nelly did not look pleased with events thus far.

"Right away." He ushered Ella in front of him, with a kind of formal bow that he could have learned in dancing class. Since he seemed oblivious to the abandoned garden hose still pumping out water, Melissa hung back to turn it off. The faucet was behind a camellia bush, which left a streak of dirt on the sleeve of her silver sweater. Yet another sign that she might as well give up hope of the evening being anything other than the Ella show.

She caught up with the rest of the group as they passed through the garage-type area with four gleaming fire engines of various kinds. Fred was racing through the tour, clearly eager to present his prize guests to the rest of the squad. "That's Engine 1 and that's Truck 1. When the engine, truck, and pumper go out together on a call they're called Task Force 1. Engine 1 takes a four-man crew and carries five hundred gallons. Truck 1's brand-new, it's got a state-of-the-art hundred-foot aerial ladder. I can't go up in it, I'm afraid of heights, but man, you should see the captain. Ryan Blake's our inside man, plus we have a top man, an AO, Apparatus Operator, and a tillerman, or tiller person I should say, for Truck 1. We have a pumper and an ambulance too. We clean and polish them up every day, we take a lot of pride in our rigs. And our captain's a stickler. But it pays off, because if you get messy in one area, you might get sloppy in others, and then it's a safety issue. This station's a sparkle corps house."

He paused proudly.

"What's that?" Melissa asked, when it appeared she was the only one paying attention to his spiel.

"It means every firefighter in California wants to be at this station. Only the best of the best get to come here. We get a lot of action, lot of fires, but we have the best safety record anywhere. And everyone wants to work for our captain. He's a legend, you know."

Melissa, too curious to resist, broke the flow of his commentary. "Do you mean Captain Brody?"

His face lit up. "Yeah, that's him, have you heard of him? He's saved hundreds of lives in his career, that's why he's a legend. There's nobody like him. That's why everyone wants to transfer in here."

"Hundreds of lives," breathed Ella. "What a hero. We should do a story on him, Melissa."

"Oh, he'd never let you. He doesn't like publicity at all. *60 Minutes* wanted him on, and he wouldn't even talk to them."

"I'll just have to try to persuade him," cooed Ella in a tone that made Melissa want to wring her neck.

"Sure, I bet he'd talk to you. You're even more beautiful in person, and you're the hottest anchor on TV."

Nelly gave a dry little cough. "I'm awfully thirsty."

"Oh sure, ma'am, my bad. I get kinda carried away sometimes. I'll show you more about the rigs later. Come on and meet the others!"

They followed him down a narrow hall, then turned left toward a large common room.

"That's the training room up ahead," said Stud. "At least that's what it's called officially. We call it the TV room. Workout room's around the corner. This is where we sleep during our shifts. We work twenty-four hours on, twenty-four hours off, twenty-four on, then get four days off. Sometimes it feels like we live here. "

Looking back over her shoulder, Melissa saw a series of small, cell-like rooms with beds. Did Brody sleep in one of those? The thought made her shiver.

The training room contained comfortable couches, armchairs, and an enormous TV set mounted on the wall. It gave on to a large kitchen with a long table lined with two benches. Several firemen were kicking back watching a football game—*what else?* thought Melissa. One man stood at the stove, cooking, and another was busy laying out paper plates and handing out sodas.

The excitable Stud burst out talking as soon as he stepped into the room. "Look who came to dinner, guys!"

A roomful of heads turned and then snapped in a general double take. The firemen who were sitting down leaped to their feet. Everyone gaped at the fiery beacon of Ella. She was red meat before a pack of hungry dogs, a red flag before a herd of bulls. It wasn't just the fact that Ella was a semicelebrity, thought Melissa, watching the scene. It was the way she'd dressed, like a cartoon figure of lust, created to appeal to the most primitive part of the male brain.

"Ella Joy! . . . From Channel Six . . . We watch you every night . . . The Sexy Side of the News! . . . You are the bomb . . . You read the news better than anybody . . . Can't you get rid of that jerk who's always talking over you . . . It's Ella Joy, dude! Right here, in our station! Wait'll the 5s hear about this."

Ella Joy stood laughing, soaking it in like a hummingbird feeding on sugar water. This was the kind of moment she lived for, and she looked so delighted, Melissa didn't begrudge it to her at all. Nelly, on the other hand . . . Nelly quivered with fury, muttering a word Melissa sincerely hoped was not "tramp."

She scanned the group with superhuman speed, her heart racing.

No Brody. Disappointment formed a hard lump in her throat. So maybe she had been counting on seeing him here. It was better this way. She could concentrate on her secret mission of getting the Bachelor Firemen to come on the news. As soon as the noise died down a bit, she broke in. "Hi everyone, it's so nice of you to invite us. This is Nelly McGuire and I'm her granddaughter, Melissa. Is Ryan Blake here?"

"Hoagie! Get your butt out here!"

A vision stepped out of the kitchen. Melissa went actually, literally breathless as he ambled with a loose-hipped, relaxed stride toward them. Those eyes . . . bluer than a sunny summer sky . . . those perfect features . . . that sexy walk. It felt as if time had stopped . . . as if the world slowed down to admire him as he passed. Dazed, Melissa watched him make his way along the benches, and suddenly she felt deep sympathy for Fred. If she had a hose, it would have slipped right through her fingers. The closer he got to them, the more breathtaking he looked, and when he finally stood before them, Melissa could have sworn she heard a chorus of heavenly angels crooning overhead. But wasn't she supposed to be mad at Ryan, who had refused to show up for his date with Nelly?

Ryan took Nelly's hand in both of his. "I'm so pleased to meet you, Miz McGuire, and I want to say how sorry I am about the other night. I just hope I can make it up to you tonight with some home cooking."

"Well, aren't you the sweetest thing. As a matter of fact, I was feeling sickly myself that night."

"The captain told me. Is this your beautiful granddaughter?" His summer-blue eyes smiled into Melissa's.

That did it. She was going to faint at this gorgeous man's feet. She opened her mouth, hoping something would come out, anything, but it took Nelly's fierce hand squeeze to get the words flowing.

"Hi, I'm Melissa." And that was the end of the flow.

"So you're the granddaughter." He cocked his head at her, a speculative look in his eye. Her mind raced. What had he heard about her? Had Brody said something? What? And how could she find out?

Ryan turned back to Nelly. "Would you like something to drink, Mrs. McGuire?"

"A glass of water," she said firmly, with a venomous glance toward Fred, who was lost in the crowd around Ella Joy.

"Coming right up. Why don't you come sit down over here." He led Nelly and Melissa to a place on the bench that had obviously been prepared specially for Nelly, with a dusty-looking cushion and a bouquet of daisies in a plastic cup.

"My, you boys think of everything. I hope you're going to sit here next to us."

"Of course I will. You tell your granddaughter to save me a seat." Ryan winked at Melissa. "I'm going to go finish up this stew. You like lamb stew, Miz Nelly?"

"I'm sure it'll be just wonderful." Nelly patted his hand. As soon as he was gone, she turned on Melissa.

"Melissa, you're embarrassing me," she hissed.

"I know. I'll be okay, I promise. He just . . . took me by surprise."

"Didn't I tell you he was something else? Look at Miss Trampy-Pants. She wants all the boys to herself."

Melissa glanced over at the anchor, who was surrounded by eager firemen. The mob included a big fellow with a belly, Fred the Stud, several men in their twenties and thirties. They were all fit, rugged, muscular guys (except for the big-bellied one), and attractive as hell. But Melissa had to admit, Ryan was in a class by himself.

"I'm going to make sure Ryan stays right next to me." Nelly cackled. "I'll turn the fire hose on Ella if I have to. I bet you're sorry now that he was sick."

Surprisingly, "sorry" didn't come to mind. Ryan was gorgeous, but she couldn't imagine feeling comfortable with him. Not the way she had with Brody. Even though she'd yelled at Brody and he'd yelled back, there still had been a feeling of ease with him. Maybe that was *why*, come to think of it. He hadn't backed down, and he hadn't gotten offended. She hadn't worried about what to say, clearly. And as much as she admired Ryan's appearance, somehow she had no interest in being kissed by him. When he'd taken her arm to guide her to the bench, she hadn't felt a flicker of that electric jolt she'd felt with Brody.

Where was Captain Brody? He must have known about this dinner—captains knew that

sort of thing, didn't they? She wondered if he was
avoiding her. Fine. She'd just have to enjoy herself
with Bachelor Number One.

When Ryan returned, Melissa gave him a beam-
ing smile. He handed them blue plastic cups filled
with water, and then sat down, swinging one leg
over the bench so he straddled it. Melissa searched
for a topic of conversation. It was time to prove she
knew how to speak words in a coherent sequence.

"So Fred was saying this is one of the most
sought-after fire stations . . . do you like working
here?"

Bingo. Ryan's face lit up. "Love it. We work hard
but we have fun too. We play jokes on each other.
A couple weeks ago we put Double D's boots in the
freezer, you shoulda seen his face when he stepped
into 'em. He jumped around like his socks were on
fire. All kinds of shit like that. Cap doesn't mind,
he says it's good for morale. He says when you're
dealing with life-and-death situations, you have to
let out the pressure somehow or other."

"I know exactly what you mean," said Melissa.
"It's the same way in the newsroom. Once we moved
our anchor's clock forward, so when he came back
from dinner he thought he'd missed the news."

Ryan threw his head back and laughed. In a dis-
passionate way, Melissa admired the strong, clean
line of his throat. "Good one. I like that. Reminds
me of when we sent Vader out for takeout, and
when he got back we were all gone. Hiding behind
the station, but he didn't know that. He thought it
was invasion of the body snatchers."

Nelly chimed in and told a story about an April
Fool's prank she had once pulled on her husband,

Leon. Before long, the three of them were happily
exchanging stories, and Melissa felt as though she'd
found a long-lost brother. She even felt comfortable
enough to bring up Loudon's favorite topic.

"So I heard you guys are called the Bachelor
Firemen of San Gabriel. What's that all about?"

For the first time, Ryan looked uncomfortable.
The man they called Double D leaned over. "Look
around you. All these young studs? Single. I'm
the only married one here. Me and a guy on the
C shift. Everyone else is ready, willing, and available." He winked.

"The captain hates it when people talk about it.
But it's true," said Ryan. "We don't have a lot of
married guys. Cap was, but not anymore."

"It's the curse." Double D glanced around the
table and lowered his voice. "The Curse of Con-
stancia B. Sidwell."

Melissa nearly choked on her sip of water. She
couldn't do a news story about a curse, could she?
"Who's that?"

"Mail-order bride, selected in 1850 by one of
San Gabriel's first volunteer firemen, Virgil Rush.
His house used to stand on this very spot. He led
a lonely, solitary existence, and hoped Miss Con-
stancia from Boston would be the answer. They
corresponded a few times, then she packed up to
move West. He met the mail wagon month after
month, but she never showed up. Held up by rob-
bers, the legend says. Then she fell in love with the
leader of the gang. All the other firemen mocked
him. He ended his days bitter and alone, and sup-
posedly his last words were a curse in the name of
Constancia Sidwell against all the other firemen,

vowing they should have just as hard a time finding love as he did. And to this day, the path of true
love pretty much goes off a cliff when it hits this
firehouse."

Melissa was so caught up in the story she barely
realized that a hush had fallen around the table.
"That's a great story. Do you have any examples?"

Ryan interjected. "It might also be that we have
a lot of younger guys here. They come to Captain
Brody to get trained, because he's the best. Cap
says the curse is a load of bull."

"Yeah? Explain Stan, then," said Double D.

"Stan? Who's Stan?" asked Melissa.

"Okay, that's enough of that." A commanding
voice from the doorway sent butterflies streaking
through Melissa's stomach.

Chapter Eight

*D*amn. The sight of Melissa hanging on Ryan's every word with her lips parted and her eyes shining did unpleasant things to Brody's gut. She looked different, her creamy skin flushed pink, her hair in smooth waves. Why had he ever thought she wasn't beautiful? She was stunning. And Ryan seemed to be glued to her side.

Talking about the damn bachelor fireman curse.

On cue, Stan pressed against his leg.

"Just look at that cute doggy!"

A familiar voice stopped him in his tracks. Good thing, because he'd been about to stalk to the table and swat Ryan away from the girl he couldn't stop staring at. He wrenched his eyes away from Melissa and blinked at the onslaught of shiny red vinyl. It encased a tiny, curvy woman whom he'd last seen on his TV.

Fred, hovering at Ella Joy's elbow, jumped to attention. "Captain, look who came tonight. Ella Joy, from Channel Six! Can you believe she's going to eat with us?"

Ella offered him the kind of smile that said a night in her bed wouldn't be far off. "Captain, I like the sound of that. Call me Ella."

"Ella, from the Sunny Side of the News. Honor to meet you, Ms. Joy."

"It's my pleasure, I do love to meet my fans." She touched his arm. "Especially when they're captains."

Her seductive flattery had a hypnotic effect on him. "I'm one of the fire captains here. There's two of us. I'm Captain Brody."

"He's the only captain that counts," said Fred. Brody tore his gaze away from Ella Joy to frown at the kid. "What I mean is . . . he's higher up than Captain Kelly, and he's the one on shift right now, so right now, he's the one who counts."

"Are you the captain they were telling us about, who's saved so many lives?" Ella fluttered her eyelashes.

Brody's frown grew fiercer. "Stud, you're off tour guide duty until further notice."

"Oh, you can't blame him. I am a reporter, you know. Prying information from unwilling sources is my job."

"You must be very good at it. Who could resist you?" said Brody gallantly.

"Oh you!" Ella hit him lightly on the arm in a gesture straight out of *Gone with the Wind.* "I'm so fascinated to find out what firemen eat for dinner." She took his arm, pressing it against her breast. "I had no idea you boys cooked for yourselves."

"It's either that or starve," said Brody, escorting Ella to the table as the other firefighters trailed in their wake. "Most firefighters get to be good cooks, out of sheer necessity."

"We'd make One and Two cook, but they'd kick our asses," said Fred.

"Fred is referring to our two female firefighters. They're on different shifts, but they take their turn, just like everyone," said Brody. He could tell from the way Ella's eyes glazed over that she had no interest in the station's female firefighters. She was exquisitely, provocatively beautiful, but already he felt impatient to end his conversation with her.

He stole a glance at Melissa. The glow in her jewel-green eyes had faded. She gave him a cool look. Maybe she was still mad about the other night. He sat down at his usual place at the head of the table. Stan curled up at his feet with his chin on Brody's shoes. Fred pulled over a chair so Ella could sit next to Brody. He couldn't think of a polite way to decline. The rest of the crew, jostling for position, settled in.

"We got some fine chefs here at the firehouse," said Double D. "Hoagie ain't half bad, if you don't count the hot dog lasagna he made up."

Everyone groaned at the memory.

"Stan liked it," said Ryan.

"Stan likes anything. I caught him chewing on sheetrock the other day," said Brody.

Melissa finally spoke. "Who is this Stan everyone keeps talking about?"

"Firehouse dog. Named after—" Brody shot Double D a warning look. The last thing he wanted was more of that talk. "'Course, we're always happy when someone else cooks for us," said Double D, quickly changing the subject.

Ella's eyes slid over Double D, then back to Brody. Apparently she had no interest in the older, chubbier variety of fireman either. Suddenly she grabbed his shoulder, so tightly he winced. "I just had the most amazing idea. If you all knock my socks off with this dinner of yours, maybe we'll make a competition out of it! Melissa, what do you think? Melissa?" She leaned forward to call down the table to Melissa, who had turned back to Ryan.

Of course. Ella Joy wanted Ryan's attention on her. Brody wondered if he could get Ella and Melissa to trade seats. What were she and Ryan whispering about down there? She sure wasn't yelling at him about football and country music.

Then again, Ryan wasn't yelling at her about BMWs. God, he'd screwed things up. He had no business being around a beautiful, smart woman like Melissa. But sitting here watching Ryan put the moves on her—that qualified as torture.

Melissa heard Ella call her name. Did she really have to look in that direction again? She already knew what she'd see. Ella snuggled next to Brody as though she owned him. Brody in his captain's uniform, looking unapproachable and adorable at the same time. She heaved a sigh. Short of hiding under the table, there was no way to avoid the cozy pair.

She gritted her teeth and reluctantly turned to face them. Brody's dark gray eyes met hers with an unreadable expression. As expected, Ella was plastered to his side.

"Captain Brody," she purred. "I hope you wouldn't mind if my producer and I came in and whipped up a little something for your brave boys."

"Wait, what?" Melissa wasn't sure she'd heard right. Ella never cooked. Her usual contribution to newsroom potlucks was a chocolate truffle cake from her favorite gourmet bakery. But they couldn't feed a bunch of hungry firefighters cake.

"We should do our part, don't you think? We'll come back and cook these guys a meal they'll never forget." Ella winked at Ryan and sent a dazzling smile his way. Melissa gazed from one beautiful face to the other, two pairs of blue eyes flirting down the length of the table. So that's what was going on. Ella had all kinds of ways of grabbing a good-looking man's attention.

A general cheer went up among the firemen.

"You're the best, Ms. Ella Joy," announced Ryan.

"But wait, Ella . . ." Melissa tried to protest, but shouts of "Ella Joy!" "The Sunny Side," and "Yee-hah!" drowned her out. Her gaze slid back to Brody's, and she found him watching her with definite amusement. Her chin went up and she smiled defiantly. "I look forward to it," she said firmly. It would give her a chance to find out more about this bachelor curse.

Nelly tugged on her sleeve. "Don't let her win," she hissed.

Melissa sighed. Grans apparently expected her to hold the attention of the most beautiful man she'd ever seen even though Ella was nearby, taking off the red vinyl gloves. Worst of all, she didn't want his attention, she wanted someone else's.

Nelly shouldered her aside and tugged on

Ryan's sleeve. "Could you explain something to an old lady? What happens if there's a fire tonight?"

Ryan immediately turned back to them and eagerly explained that a certain number of them would have to leap up from the table, jump into their gear (their turnouts were already waiting) and pile into Engine 1 or Truck 1, depending on their roles. "You never can predict when or where the next fire will hit," he added.

Isn't that the truth, thought Melissa.

For the rest of the evening, Ryan devoted himself to the two of them. He refilled their drinks, made sure Nelly had first crack at the choicest pieces of lamb in the stew, and kept an easy flow of conversation going. Melissa knew he was just being polite, but by the end of the dinner, he had earned her undying gratitude. Ryan was a great kid, she decided, under all that star power.

"Kid" being the key word. Brody now . . . Brody was a man. As she chatted and laughed with Ryan, she started to feel almost schizophrenic. It was a mystery how her brain managed it, but somehow she could hear every word Brody said. She felt like a cat, with one ear listening to Ryan, the other swiveled back to catch everything passing between Brody and Ella. Ella laughed at every little thing Brody said, no matter how mundane, and each time, it was like fingernails down a chalkboard to Melissa. She risked a peek back while pretending to look for the salt shaker, and found Brody smiling down at Ella's perfect face.

Hadn't he told Melissa *she* had a lovely laugh? Maybe he liked laughs of all sorts.

She viciously shook salt into her stew until Nelly

exclaimed in horror. Wonderful. Now she was going to give herself hypertension on top of everything else. She shrugged and reminded herself that this night was about survival, not enjoyment.

"Melissa, you have to fight back," Nelly whispered in her ear.

"Stay out of it, Grans."

"I will not." Nelly raised her voice so the entire table could hear. "Ryan, did you know that my little Melissa used to be the top news producer in Los Angeles?"

"Oh please, Grans . . ."

"You know it's true. She's won five Emmys, and once she even went to New York to attend a ceremony. Some people work their whole lives and never even get to work in a big city like Los Angeles." Nelly darted a pointed look in Ella's direction. "It's like going from the minor leagues to the major leagues."

"So our Ella Joy's stuck here in the minors, huh?" chuckled Double D.

"That's a very good way to put it," Nelly said, as Melissa cringed.

"Oh really?" Ella rose to the bait. "Then what's Melissa doing here? Maybe she couldn't hack it in the majors."

"Melissa came back to take care of her ailing grandmother," said Nelly with a kind of prim sweetness that Melissa knew was totally out of character.

Melissa could practically hear Ella's teeth gnash. She couldn't help admiring the neat trap Nelly had set for Ella, but at the same time, the last thing she needed was a snippy anchor. "Ella could move away in a heartbeat, but she doesn't want to disappoint all her fans."

"That's right. I get calls all the time, but I turn them down because I'm happy where I am."

"What calls? Name one," snorted Nelly.

Taken aback by such a direct attack, Ella fumbled. Melissa smoothly came to her rescue. "My old news director in LA used to say our viewers would go crazy if we could get Ella Joy. But our anchors all had contracts, so his hands were tied." Everett hadn't actually meant it as a compliment— watching the small-town news feed, they used to laugh at some of her sexier outfits—but it was, strictly speaking, true.

"Melissa *is* a really good producer," said Ella grudgingly. "She's worked on some of my best stories."

"*Your* stories . . ." Nelly spluttered in outrage.

Time for a quick subject change. Melissa turned to Double D, on her other side, and asked him about the scariest fire he'd ever fought.

"Easy!" said Double D promptly, in his booming voice. "The time we got called up to San Berdu to help out with those brushfires. Captain wasn't with us—they put us under the county guys—"

"We aren't trained for brushfires," interjected another firefighter.

"A fire's a fire. And good sense is good sense. I'm just saying, Captain wasn't with us, and we ended up getting ourselves trapped, surrounded on all sides by the biggest son-of-a-gun flames we'd ever seen."

"Tall as skyscrapers," chimed in Ryan.

"And hot as a horny Catholic girl . . ." Double D caught his captain's look. "Excuse me, ladies. I mean, extremely hot."

"So what happened? What'd you do?" Everyone was listening now.

"We clustered together, back to back. How many were there, five, six? Hoagie, you were there. And Vader, Skeet, me, and One. So five of us. We came together, back to back, and just sprayed those flames like there was no tomorrow. We could hardly see an inch, what with the sweat, and the heat from the flames. Couldn't breathe. Took me a week to be able to say one word afterward. Throat was that sore."

"So you put out the flames?"

"Lord no. There's no putting out flames like that. They do what they're gonna do. No, the captain got a military chopper to come and get us. In the nick of time too."

Melissa looked over at Brody, who was staring absently at his cup of water. He hadn't even been there, and he'd saved their lives. "How'd you get the chopper?"

But Ella had already claimed his attention, leaning so her chest rubbed against his arm. "That's exactly the kind of story our viewers want to hear. Ordinary heroes like you. Please let me do an interview with you, Harry. I would be so very grateful." The caressing hand on his arm left no doubt as to just how grateful Ella would be.

Brody shook his head. "I don't do interviews."

"Maybe you haven't been asked by the right person yet."

"If I did one, it would be with you. How's that?"

"Did you hear that, Melissa? He almost agreed to an interview."

"But didn't," Brody quickly clarified.

"I'll tell you what. You can look at it when we're done, and if there's anything you don't like, we'll take it out."

"We can't promise that, Ella!" Melissa reminded her. "That's against our policy."

"Don't interfere, Melissa. I've almost gotten him to agree."

"It does sound tempting." Brody rubbed his jaw. "I sure could make myself look good. Maybe we could even ban certain words and topics from the interview. Say, the word 'bachelor.'"

"Well . . . I guess . . ."

Melissa saw disaster approaching. Giving an interview subject approval of the final cut was against station policy. They could be fired for that, and if someone had to take the fall, it would be her, not Ella. Besides, the word "bachelor" happened to be the one Loudon wanted on the air. She stood up quickly.

"Ella, can I speak with you for a second?" Ella, as usual, ignored her. Melissa watched Ella curl a teasing finger across Brody's hand, and suddenly couldn't stand it another second. "Captain Brody, a word in private, please?"

"Certainly."

Brody extricated himself from Ella's grasp and followed Melissa into the hallway, the dog trotting at his heels. He closed the door and leaned against it, arms folded.

Melissa, glaring at him, crossed her arms too. He raised an eyebrow, waiting.

An embarrassing moment of silence followed. With him looking at her like that, she couldn't remember what she wanted to say to him. Which made her feel like an idiot. Which made her angry.

"*Harry?*" Of all things, that was what eventually burst from her mouth.

"Yes?"

"Your name's Harry?"

"Is that what you needed to speak to me about?" He cocked his head.

"No, *Harry*, it isn't. You ought to know we can't give you final approval on an interview. Please don't encourage her."

"How should I know that? I'm just a simple firefighter. Now if you want me to rebuild an engine, or—"

"Okay, I get it. I'm sorry I said those things the other night. I was a little bit buzzed. I don't always behave correctly when I'm . . . tipsy."

His eyes darkened. "Well, that does explain some things."

Melissa flushed and wrenched the conversation back to her original purpose. "So will you stop letting Ella promise things she can't deliver?"

"Why don't you make her stop? I don't work for the Sunny Side of the News."

Melissa gritted her teeth. "She doesn't care what I say, haven't you noticed?"

"I've noticed that an extremely intelligent woman is letting herself be pushed around. Where's all that opinionated ranting and raving I listened to the other night?"

"I was not ranting. Or raving. I was expressing opinions."

"Then what's stopping you now? Just go out there and lay down the law. She doesn't seem so unreasonable."

Irritation took hold of Melissa. Who was this man to tell her how to handle Ella? "Maybe I should drool all over her. Then she'd listen to me."

"That's ridiculous."

"Do you love *her* laugh too?"

"What?"

"You've been hearing enough of it. Hahahaha-heeee . . ." Melissa mimicked Ella's trilling laugh. "You said I had a lovely laugh."

"Are you jealous?"

Melissa snapped her mouth shut. "Don't be silly," she said loftily. "I just don't want you to make a fool of yourself like all the rest."

Brody's eyes narrowed. "By the way, you do know Hoagie watches football, don't you? Or maybe it doesn't matter with that pretty face of his."

"Hoagie, as you call him, is more than a pretty face. He's a wonderful conversationalist. Did you know he studies affirmations to improve himself?"

"He's a regular Dr. Phil." A dangerous scowl appeared on Brody's face, but Melissa barreled on.

"At least he's not a Pussycat Doll."

"Ella Joy is an accomplished journalist," said Brody through clenched teeth. "Worth two extra ratings points, according to her—whatever that means."

"If I went on the air wearing the stuff she does, I'd get two ratings points too!"

"Why don't you then?"

The nerve of the man. "You're not my career adviser. You want me to dress up in red vinyl and no underwear?"

Heat leaped in Brody's eyes. He dug his fingers into her upper arms. His mouth lowered to hover an inch over hers. "How do you do this to me? I never argue. Ever. With everyone else I'm calm and in control. I get around you, and I snap."

"So you're blaming me?" Melissa fired back.

"Yes," he said, and his mouth swooped down on hers. Fire shot through her, the same unforgettable heat she'd felt that first night. His strong hands cradled her head, and a shiver shook her entire body. Those hands moved her head at will, tilting her face up to receive his kiss more deeply. She melted into a boneless, liquid waterfall of desire.

The dog whimpered.

"I blame that sweater you're wearing, and how it moves against your body," mumbled Brody against her lips.

"I didn't think you noticed," whispered Melissa. It was all she could do to get a sentence out.

"I noticed. I've been watching you all evening, with that short skirt and those . . ." He groaned. " . . . those sexy boots." One of his thighs thrust between her legs, which moved apart to make room for him. Her skirt rode up her thighs as she pressed herself against him. He muttered something else—something like "You're killing me"— then moved his warm hands to her suede-covered rear to pull her more tightly against him.

Her breath came in quick pants, and her hands roamed his back, loving the feel of those hard muscles she'd dreamed about since the other night. She ran her hands down his backside to his strong thighs, feeling his muscles clench at her touch. Her head swam. "I want you," she whispered. "Right now, against this door."

Her words seemed to set him off. He spun her around so her back was to the door, firmly placed her legs around him, and crushed his bulging erection against her groin. A stream of rough, hot whispers came next. "I want to open you up . . . touch you all over . . . make you scream . . . spread you wide . . ." All the while he kept her pinned to the door, so only her hips could move. These seemed to have a will of their own, and she felt them quiver and thrust and tease. Her blood sang, her nerves thrummed.

The dog whined and pawed at Melissa's leg.

"Stop it, Stan," Brody ordered, tearing his mouth away from hers.

"The dog is Stan?" Melissa panted.

"Our dogs are always named Stan." He nibbled at her neck, making her shudder with wild desire. "Stan!"

The dog wouldn't stop nipping at Melissa's skirt.

Through the frantic drumbeat of her excitement, she barely heard the footsteps outside the door. Then she was being yanked into the air and set down on her feet. Brody thrust her behind him just as the door opened.

"Oh!" said Fred, jaw dropping. "I . . . uh . . . was just going to the . . . Never mind. I can hold it." He turned to flee, but Brody stopped him.

"Go ahead. We were . . . um . . . just coming in."

Hiding behind his broad shoulders, Melissa pulled down her skirt and straightened her hair. Was she halfway presentable? She felt her cheeks;

still flushed. Her breath came in fast pants. And what about Brody? He hadn't unzipped his pants—thank God things hadn't gone that far—but his shirt was no longer neatly tucked in. They would just have to brazen it out.

Melissa stepped forward. "Thanks for your time, Captain Brody." She managed not to sound too breathless.

"I'll think very carefully about your suggestion. Thanks for bringing it up," Brody answered.

Bringing it up? Was that a double-entendre? She could still feel his arousal burning against her thigh. Melissa swallowed hard.

"Thank you for listening," she said. Great. Could she thank him any more times?

"I'm sorry about Stan. He should know better than to paw our guests." Brody winced as the words left his mouth. One of the firemen snickered.

Oh God, she was going to completely lose it. "That's okay," she said in a strangled voice, and hurried to her seat next to Nelly, who glared at her.

"Again?" hissed Nelly. "Just like the front door the other night!"

Melissa couldn't stop a quick snort of laughter. Her grandmother had a point. Did she and Brody have some kind of door fetish? She shot Brody a sidelong look. His hair was ruffled and his collar slightly askew. The other firefighters looked down, or sideways at each other, trying not to laugh. Ella drummed her fingers on the table. An awkward silence fell over the room.

Ryan cleared his throat. "We sure are grateful you three beautiful ladies came to dinner. Kinda hate to see it end. We might have to hold you to your offer, Miss Ella Joy. When are you going to come back and cook for us?" He aimed a slow wink at her.

Ella brightened. Once again, Melissa experienced a sense of deep gratitude toward the gorgeous Ryan Blake. "Of course, handsome," said Ella. "You just name the date."

Wonderful, thought Melissa. Another dinner. She'd have to remember not to go anywhere near a door.

Chapter Nine

An enormous golden moon hovered over San Gabriel that night. Crickets murmured, mockingbirds sang. Countless skittering creatures came alive now the heat of the day had ended. The fresh scent of night-blooming jasmine mingled with roses stole through Nelly's window.

The pain was worse at night, and instead of sleeping, she held long discussions with Leon. "Disastrous start, but I think it ended up pretty good. Two times Melissa's gone off with that Captain Brody and barely kept her clothes on. Some sparks between those two. It's true I wanted that handsome boy for her, but I've never seen Melissa act like this with anyone. You should have seen the way they looked when they came back in the room. Oh, it was sweet. And Ella's face—she looked like she was sucking on a pickled egg. She's really not such a bad girl. She's spoiled and needs a good spanking. I wish Melissa would stand up to her. But Melissa's a funny one. With all her brains, all her qualities, I don't know why she hides herself away. Not with Brody, though, I'll tell you that much. Oh . . ." The pain surged, and it was a minute before she could think again.

"Oh yeah, Melissa and Brody. I heard them talking out there in the hall—and don't try to tell me it's eavesdropping when I was sitting right there at the table—and she was letting him have it, but good. Oh, she's going to mess this up, I just know it. And don't be pestering me, I know time's running out. I've got to hurry things along. Make sure she doesn't drive the poor man away. And see that she doesn't get into one of her stubborn fits and decide he's not her 'type.' These girls today, it's a mystery to me how any of them ever gets married. Back in my day, we didn't have 'types.' Men were all about the same, until you found the one you just couldn't live without. That was you, for me. Wouldn't surprise me one bit if Brody's the one for Melissa."

Another pang struck deep.

"I know, I know. Not much longer. I'll just have to do what I can." After that, she drifted into a dream in which she and Leon shared a hot fudge sundae, and he gave her his cheeky wink, and said his favorite thing. *You want some sugar? Come on up here and I'll give you a big old heapful.*

In the upstairs bedroom, Melissa also lay awake. She couldn't have slept if she'd taken a whole case of Valium. Her body still buzzed, her skin still tingled. The way she'd behaved with Brody made no sense. She wasn't even sure she liked the man. He wasn't her type. Not at all poetic and soulful. Not artsy and creative. How could she and Captain Brody have anything in common?

Brody might look calm on the surface, but for those few seconds against the door, he'd lost his cool. To be held by him, spoken to like that . . . she'd never felt anything so thrilling. Face it, the man was hot. Disturbingly, outrageously hot.

What must he think of her? In the darkness, her face burned. He thought she was opinionated, rude, and probably, by now, a sex fiend. How could she explain that he brought it out in her? She didn't normally rant and rave. Or insult virtual strangers. Let alone nearly have sex with them in public places. What was it about him that made her so . . . uninhibited?

She had to get a grip on herself. No more wine, for one thing. She should stay as far away from Captain Brody as she could. Ella could cook her own dinner for the firemen, Melissa had better things to do. First thing tomorrow, she would tell Ella she didn't have time for another firehouse dinner—she had to work on the foster care investigation.

She'd finally spoken to Rodrigo, who seemed like an intelligent kid. He was twelve and had been in foster care since he was eight. He'd given her his foster family's name and the name of the social worker and the dates the alleged bribes had taken place. She needed to confirm all that information, which was a whole lot more important than making spaghetti for a bunch of firemen so Ella could stoke her ego.

Yep, better avoid the firehouse like a . . . well, a house on fire.

* * *

And across town, in the Airstream trailer parked next to his house-in-progress, Brody cursed the insane attraction that kept making him lose all sense. Was it because he hadn't been getting laid enough lately? Women had offered. No fireman ever had trouble attracting women. But the breakup with Rebecca had scarred him. The few empty encounters since then had left him temporarily satisfied but depressed.

And then . . . Melissa. What the hell was it with her? Of all the girls who had chased after him since his divorce, she wasn't the most beautiful. Definitely not the most flirtatious. She always seemed to be yelling at him. So why couldn't he keep his hands off her? She must think he was the horniest bastard ever. Should he call her and try to explain himself? *When I see your gorgeous skin, those eyes darting green fire at me, those soft beautiful curves you hide away, I lose my mind.*

What other explanation was there?

He couldn't imagine any two people less compatible. Even though he was a news junkie, he didn't trust newspeople. In the early days of his career, he'd been interviewed a few times, and his words had been twisted around so he hardly recognized them. And then had come the Bachelor Firemen media circus.

Even if Melissa was a great producer, why did she work at the Sunny Side of the News? That channel was a joke. Exactly the kind of "news" he detested. Hadn't they run the very first Bachelor Firemen story? No, the two of them were a gasoline leak and a lit match. For their own good, and for his reputation among his men, they ought to stay away from each other.

Several hours later, a persistent knocking on the door of his trailer yanked him out of a delicious dream involving a green-eyed, dark-haired mermaid. *This better be good.* On his days off, Brody liked to sleep late. He stumbled out of bed, pulled on a pair of sweats, and went to the door.

When he opened it, a green-eyed, dark-haired man peered in at him. "Haskell McGuire. You called the other day. Said you wanted an estimate."

Damn. Brody had forgotten about Haskell McGuire. With those deep green eyes, this man had to be Melissa's father, or some relation. The last thing he needed was Melissa's relative hanging around while he was trying to keep his distance. How was he supposed to forget about Melissa that way?

He opened his mouth to tell Haskell he'd changed his mind, but the man had a certain look about him. His hands, clutching his toolbox, trembled slightly. A recovering addict, most likely an alcoholic. Brody had known enough of them to see the signs. This man was probably working hard to turn his life around. How could Brody fire him before he'd even started?

"Go ahead and take a look around the house. I'm sure you saw it on the way in. I'll join you in a few," he said finally.

Haskell nodded and headed for the house. If he was related to Melissa, she hadn't gotten her way with words from him.

Brody made himself eggs and toast for breakfast, put on a pot of coffee, then made his way toward the house carrying an extra mug for Haskell.

He found the man squeezed between studs, tracing wires. "How's it going?"

Haskell grunted. For the first time, Brody experienced real doubt that he was related to Melissa. He sure wasn't much of a talker.

"You from around here?" He thought he heard a "yep" in response, but it was hard to tell. "I moved here from Moorpark a year ago. Been building the house since then, but it's tough going on top of a full-time job."

More silence. Brody found it kind of restful. "My wife left me, you see. I gave her the house. People said I shouldn't, but that's what felt right to me. You a married man?"

"Was."

That fit. Melissa had said her parents were divorced, her mother dead.

"Kids?"

But Haskell, without answering, put his head between two boards and peered up toward the ceiling.

What was he doing, anyway? Interrogating a total stranger to find out if he might be related to some girl? What was it about Melissa? She certainly didn't resemble Rebecca, who wouldn't have been caught dead in horn-rimmed glasses, with nothing sparkling on her body. No sequins, no dangling earrings, no diamond tennis bracelet. Rebecca would have thought her boring. So why did he find Melissa so fascinating . . . and so aggravating?

And in the meantime, he'd called this man to his house on the off chance he might be a member of that maddening McGuire family. He opened his mouth to tell Haskell he'd changed his mind and would handle the job himself. But at that moment, Haskell extracted his head from between the studs and brushed wood shavings off his work shirt.

"It's a good thing you called when you did. You made a good start, but then when you put in this three-way wire, you headed down the wrong road entirely. Easy mistake. I won't have to tear everything out. Just back to that wire."

"Sounds good. So you want the job?" What was he doing? "I need the whole house wired."

"Don't you want an estimate?"

"Can you do it right now?" Brody handed him the cup of coffee. "Got a seat for you right here." He gestured to the overturned bucket on which he usually ate lunch.

"I guess." Haskell sat down, pulled out an envelope and a stubby little pencil. He worked out figures on the back of the envelope.

Brody sat on the other bucket, sipped his coffee, and wondered if Melissa ever did her work on the back of an envelope. It seemed unlikely. He gazed out the framed, empty window. The day was going to be hot and dry, already smelling of plaster dust and sagebrush. His trailer glinted silver in the morning sun.

"Sometimes I think I'd be happier living in that thing the rest of my life," he said, half to himself.

"Could be. The simple life."

Brody glanced at Haskell in surprise. Maybe the coffee was waking up his conversational skills. If he wanted to learn more about him, now was the moment. "Are you a family man?"

At first he thought Haskell wasn't going to answer. Eventually he said, in a gruff voice, "My wife died. My daughter and I don't speak much. I blame myself for that."

No doubt about it, this man had to be Melissa's father. Not that it was any of his business. "Sorry if I got too personal."

"It's all right. At AA they say it's better to talk. I been trying to get better. Here." Haskell handed Brody the envelope and pointed to a figure on the bottom.

"That's very reasonable."

"Well, there's a reason for that. One thing I better tell you. I done some time. Two years, for robbing a liquor store. Got out three years ago. Quit drinking, been toeing the line since then. Thought you should know. You don't want to hire me, I'll understand. But I'll do a good job and you won't get a better price than that."

Haskell got to his feet. Again Brody noticed the tremor in his hands, his stooped shoulders. His heart went out to the guy. Brody knew how to read people. He had to, working with rookies, training his crew. In Haskell, he saw a man who'd been through hell, and was doing his best to put it behind him.

He looked down at the envelope. Haskell had just handed him the perfect excuse not to hire him. He wouldn't have Melissa's father around, reminding him of her. Yes, that's exactly what he should do. He opened his mouth to give Haskell the bad news.

"Thanks for telling me. Can you start tomorrow?"

Jesus Christ. Didn't he have control over his own words anymore? But watching the relieved smile cross Haskell's face, he didn't regret his impulsive decision. The guy deserved a chance.

Besides, if he hired Haskell, he wouldn't wind up electrocuting himself. Unless, he thought wryly, he touched Melissa again. That was guaranteed electrocution.

Haskell drained his coffee mug and left. Brody watched him go, mulling over the bit of information he'd revealed. So Melissa had a father who'd done time. What had that been like for her? Was that why she and her father didn't speak much? How had she gotten to be a hotshot news producer with such a rough family history? She probably wouldn't like him learning her deep, dark family secrets. But he couldn't help it. He wanted to know more. He wanted to know everything. And with Haskell working for him, he might have a chance, if he could pry the words out of him.

After her sleepless night, Melissa went to work early with every intention of researching the San Gabriel County Child Services Department. But first, as if magically compelled, she found herself heading to the tape archives. Somewhere in the rows of old tape lurked the *Today* show feature on the Bachelor Firemen of San Gabriel. Her curiosity was killing her.

When she finally located it, she closed herself in the viewing station and pushed play.

Whoever had last viewed the tape had left it cued up to the Bachelor Firemen story. A beautiful young feature reporter stood outside Fire Station 1 with the whole crew lined up behind her. Captain Brody stood next to her wearing a polite smile. The reporter spoke in a "kicker" tone, signifying the story was not to be taken too seriously.

"We're reporting live today outside a historic firehouse in San Gabriel, California, where we've uncovered a fascinating situation. Not only is this one of the most active and successful stations in the country, but it has—pay attention, ladies—the highest number of bachelors of any firehouse in the nation. Yes, believe it or not, only two of the handsome, heroic men you see behind me are married."

The show switched to a taped story. Various lingering close-ups of firefighters in action flowed across the screen. But Melissa didn't care about any of the shots except those of Brody. The man, on top of everything else, was annoyingly photogenic. The camera made his eyes look more silver than gray, striking against his dark hair. He moved with power and grace, directing his men, polishing the fire engine, hauling hose, checking equipment.

He didn't seem happy to have a camera following him, however. He kept shooting irritated glances in the audience's direction. Luckily, Ryan got the lion's share of the attention. He didn't seem to mind one bit. He kept giving the camera that sexy, slow wink Melissa remembered. It was just as devastating on tape.

The reporter continued in a voiceover, telling the same story that Double D had related at the dinner. "So is it a curse or a coincidence?" The story wrapped up and the shot went back to the pretty reporter. "Some might say it's a blessing. Imagine a firehouse filled with eligible, attractive men with no wedding rings. And not just any men. These guys put their lives on the line on a daily basis. Curse or not, we here at the *Today* show hope these sexy, heroic bachelors manage to find their happily-ever-afters."

Gag. Melissa punched the eject button and returned the tape to the archives. No wonder they'd been flooded with female attention after that report. No wonder Brody detested the news media.

Disgusted with herself for getting so distracted, she went back to her cubicle to focus on the foster care investigation. She found reports of a few complaints against the department over the years, but nothing major. When she looked up Rodrigo's caseworker, she found nothing out of the ordinary. Clicking on her tape recorder, she reviewed her phone conversation with Rodrigo.

RODRIGO: She yells at us all the time. And she has these branches sometimes.

MELISSA: Branches? From a tree?

RODRIGO: Yeah, but they're not straight like regular branches. They're long and skinny.

MELISSA: Long and skinny branches.

RODRIGO: Yeah, and they hurt a lot.

MELISSA: Where does she hit you?

RODRIGO: On the butt. Or sometimes our legs. I don't mind for me so much, but for the littler ones, I get so scared.

MELISSA: Have you ever gone to the police?

RODRIGO: Once I did, but he just went and talked to the social worker. She lied to him. He never even came and talked to me. They said I made it up to make trouble.

MELISSA: I'm so sorry this is happening, Rodrigo. I promise you I'll do everything I can.

She couldn't take his story to the police. It had already been "investigated." The police would assume she was an overeager reporter taken in by an adolescent con man. Which was a possibility. He sounded sincere to her—scared and traumatized—but she had to keep an open mind. His story might not be true. If it was, she had to find proof.

Rodrigo's foster family lived in Fern Acres. It was one of the worst neighborhoods in town. It was also where she'd grown up. When she'd first come back to San Gabriel, the last thing she wanted to do was visit her old neighborhood. But she'd forced herself to, bearing business cards, for the sake of future news tips. Now it was time for another trip.

As she walked to the far corner of the parking garage where her car was parked, she saw Ella's cream-colored convertible BMW pull into the prime parking spot, reserved solely for her. Ella hopped out, wearing a gold Juicy Couture sweat suit. With her huge Chanel sunglasses and perky ponytail, she looked like a Spice Girl. Newsy Spice, perhaps.

"Hello, slut," she called cheerfully to Melissa.

"Nothing happened," said Melissa defensively. "It was the dog, he kept attacking my leg." She planned to stick to that story, as ludicrous as it sounded.

"What is the problemo, darling? That guy was hot. Nothing like Hoagie, of course. Did you hear the nickname Hoagie gave me?"

"No, what?"

"SOH. It stands for Slice of Heaven."

"Are you sure?" Slice of Hell worked too, but she refrained from mentioning that. "He must be really into you."

"He's sweet. You don't think he's too young for me, do you?" Something like real anxiety crossed over Ella's face.

"If he doesn't think so, and you don't think so, what does it matter what I think?"

"But I don't know what I think. And he doesn't know how old I am."

Melissa reminded herself that boosting Ella's ego was part of the job. "I think you'd be the best-looking couple I've ever seen. Like Brad and Angelina."

Ella's smile returned. "Good point. Now, darling, we have to talk about the dinner. You know I don't have time to do any cooking . . ."

"I know, and that's why I think you should hire someone, a caterer maybe. I found some names and numbers, and I can set the whole thing up for you."

"No. We have to do the cooking. I said we would."

"But I've got a project I'm working on and I'm not going to be able to—"

"You can't work all the time. And it's just one evening. I have some ideas about what you can make."

"Me?" And the truth comes out, thought Melissa.

"I mean 'we,' of course, you know we're a team. But I'm not going to have much time. I'll contribute the ideas. You can execute. You're the producer, after all."

Since when did "producer" mean "personal chef"? Brody's words echoed in her mind. *Just go out there and lay down the law.*

Maybe later. "Ella, let's talk about it when I get back. I'm already late."

"Fine. I'll start brainstorming the menu."

Melissa groaned and headed to her car. Okay, so Brody would probably laugh at her pathetic non-laying down of the law. What did it matter what he thought anyway? *Put that man out of your mind!*

It took her fifteen minutes to reach Fern Acres. Driving down the main avenue, she wondered why the most terrible places always had such lovely names. Fern Acres sounded like a rainforest or a country club. But in her Fern Acres, 7–Eleven convenience stores appeared every few blocks. Liquor stores were even more plentiful. Melissa had no idea how much money her father had handed over to those liquor stores over the years. Broken glass littered the streets. Anyone who parked a car here was asking to be vandalized. The few ramshackle churches had graffiti scrawled on the outside walls. Kids gathered in vacant lots to bounce basketballs and make trouble.

Growing up in Fern Acres had been hell.

Except for Mr. Guildenback, the English teacher who had encouraged her to write, and taken her on a tour of the local newspaper. She'd latched on to the dream of being a journalist as though it were a parachute thrown from a crashing plane.

Shaking off the memories, she turned onto Alden Drive. Rodrigo's foster parents' house was located in the middle of the block. She scanned the bedraggled tract home crammed between two other houses, its front yard littered with toys. If kids were being beaten in that house, wouldn't the neighbors hear? Wouldn't they call the police?

118   Jennifer Bernard

She had checked her police sources, and there had been no complaint calls from neighbors.

At the moment, all was quiet. She checked her watch. The kids must be home from school by now. In the backyard she could make out several small figures. One kid was pushing another on a swing. It appeared to be a perfectly normal scene. Nothing out of the ordinary at all.

She gnawed at her bottom lip. Maybe Rodrigo had invented the whole thing to get attention. Maybe she needed to get him some psychological help. Maybe she needed to forget this investigation and focus on cooking Ella's firehouse dinner.

Then, just as her car rolled past the far side of the house, she noticed a tree in the front yard. A very graceful tree, unusual for the dry Southern California conditions. A weeping willow, whose long branches dipped to the ground and swayed in the breeze. "Long and skinny" branches.

Not exactly evidence, but enough to make her continue the investigation. She checked her watch. Time to get back to the station. The afternoon news meeting started in ten minutes. And she'd had enough of memory lane for one day.

Chapter Ten

*B*ack at the TV station, she dashed up the stairs to the conference room, where she found an argument in full swing. She slid into an empty seat.

"What are we fighting about?" she whispered to the intern.

"Flying the news chopper at night."

"Again?"

"It's a classic."

"News can break any time of the day, why not at night?" The nightside producer hammered home his point with annoying, rapid-fire clicks of his ballpoint pen.

"You can't see anything from the chopper at night anyway," answered Blaine, the assistant news director.

"You can see lights."

"Then why don't we just run stock footage of lights, no one would know the difference."

"That's unethical."

"So is wasting our money so people can see a bunch of lights. And stop it with the pen."

"If it's a money issue, the ratings increase will make up for the cost."

"So it's all about the ratings, is it?"

Melissa had heard all sides of the argument many times. She took out her notebook to write down her impressions of Fern Acres and the willow tree. The willow tree didn't prove anything. But her instincts told her Rodrigo was on the level. She should arrange to meet him as soon as possible. What about giving him an undercover camera . . . a lipstick camera? She'd have to check with legal. She jotted the words, "Check with legal."

Lost in thought, she barely noticed when her name surfaced in the discussion. "Earth to Melissa!" She looked up to find a ring of excited faces looking her way. Blaine grinned at her. "I love it. It will make an excellent Thanksgiving special."

"What? No!" she protested. Were they already slotting in the Rodrigo story? She hadn't even shot any footage yet. "It won't be ready by then."

"Oh come on. How long could it take?" He was already writing in his big day planner.

"It's very delicate. I don't even know if it's for real."

"Oh, it's for real. I already checked with the PIO. They're jumping up and down over there. They love the concept."

Jumping up and down at the Child Services Department? In utter bewilderment, her eyes scanned the room and caught Ella's. The anchor wore a smug smile. *Uh-oh.* "What are we talking about?"

"*Thanksgiving with the Bachelor Firemen*, hosted by our own Ella Joy. Produced by our own Melissa McGuire. Our viewers will freakin' love it. Great way to end sweeps."

"*What?* It was just going to be us cooking dinner. I mean, Ella cooking dinner."

"Well, now it's a special."

"*My* idea." Ella flicked an imaginary speck of dust off her gold sweat suit. "I'm a genius sometimes."

Melissa groaned. "I can't do it. Ask Loudon. I'm on special assignment right now."

"Don't worry," cooed Ella in her sweetest voice. "I cleared it with Bill myself. He agreed that as a special project, this falls exactly into your job description."

Melissa felt the Rodrigo investigation slipping away. How would she have any time to work on it when she was producing an on-air special? A Thanksgiving special . . . good God, would she have to cook a turkey?

"Cooking is *not* in my job description."

"Don't be silly, I'll be cooking," said Ella. "You just have to get everything ready. Then I'll do the stirring or basting or whatever. I have the most adorable apron to wear. Oh, I know! We can make Channel Six aprons, and sell them. The Sunny Side of the News . . . how cute would that be on an apron!"

"I love it," said Blaine. "Take care of it, Melissa." Melissa nodded numbly. In the old days, she would have kept arguing. But if Everett had taught her anything, it was the futility of going up against "the talent." The last time she'd tried, he'd humiliated her, and her career still hadn't recovered.

Besides, she was still reeling from the image of Sunny Side of the News aprons. What would those go for on eBay?

When the meeting ended, she headed straight for Loudon's office. How was she going to produce an hour-long special and a major investigation at the same time? They'd have to tape before Thanksgiving, which didn't leave much production time. She'd just have to beg Loudon to take her off the firefighter special.

But as she got closer to his office, her steps slowed. If Loudon heard how little proof she had in the Rodrigo investigation, he'd probably kill the story. She couldn't let that happen. Besides, he always sided with Ella in the end. Especially for a chance to get the Bachelor Firemen on the air. And besides that, if she did the special, she'd see Captain Brody again.

For reasons she didn't want to examine, that was the clincher. No matter what she'd decided last night.

Thanksgiving with the Firefighters, renamed when Melissa reminded everyone about One and Two, the female firefighters, quickly became Ella's pet project. The anchor revealed a previously undiscovered domestic-goddess side. At a preproduction meeting in her office, she announced to Melissa the menu had to be traditional, but with a twist.

Melissa, hardly able to believe her career had

come to this, suggested lentil loaf in place of turkey.

"You're not taking this project seriously." Ella pouted.

"You said you wanted a twist."

Ella tossed Melissa a copy of a cooking magazine. "Deep-fried turkey. It says here it comes out crisp on the outside, tender on the inside."

"But it's deep fried. Is that the best thing to promote to our viewers?"

"No one said anything about promoting it. We're just cooking it."

"You don't even eat fried food," Melissa pointed out.

"This is not about me," said Ella loftily. "This is about the guys. I asked Ryan, and he said they'd love it."

"Fine." Melissa gave up. Maybe they could run a viewer calorie advisory. "Did you happen to ask Ryan if they have a deep fryer?"

Ella's face lit up. "Hang on, I'll give him a call." She picked up her rhinestone-studded cell phone and pointedly waited for Melissa to leave.

Meeting over, apparently. Melissa happily left, marveling at how Ella managed to maneuver things so cleverly to suit herself. Early on, she'd announced that Ryan represented the typical firefighter, and they'd better run everything past him. Ryan got the final call on mini hot dogs for appetizers and marshmallow fudge pie for dessert. Somehow, Ella always got the job of checking in with him.

The whole project, Melissa suspected, was a way for Ella to put the moves on the hellaciously handsome Ryan Blake. Melissa's head spun at the speed with which she'd gone from producer to chef to matchmaker.

She just hoped Ryan wasn't falling head over heels for Ella. She liked Ryan, and when it came to men, Ella had a very short attention span.

With the menu finalized—deep-fried turkey, roast ham, mashed potatoes with parmesan cheese, a vegetable medley, cream of squash soup, rolls with butter, cranberry sauce, three different kinds of pie, and the inevitable chocolate truffle cake—Melissa arranged a site survey. She brought along the production manager, Kevin, a brusque man in his mid-fifties. Rumor had it he'd been injured while shooting a riot in Burma and had been given a job for life as compensation. With a job for life, he had no interest in getting along with his co-workers, and no time for fools who didn't know a satellite truck from a news van. Melissa did know a sat truck from a news van, so he managed to tolerate her. Barely.

At the last minute, Ella insisted on going along, even though site surveys were the kind of nuts and bolts part of the process she usually avoided. As the three of them walked into the station, Melissa's heart raced. Her eyes immediately flew to the captain's office. Empty. Brody wasn't in the training room either. She felt the adrenaline drain away. No chance of an encounter with Brody. It felt like a wasted trip.

Then again, she wasn't getting paid to lust after a fireman. Nope, they were paying her to babysit Ella while *she* lusted after a fireman.

She beckoned to Kevin, and they got to work

noting down power sources and likely camera angles.

Meanwhile, Ella perched on the table next to Fred and Vader. "Where's Ryan?"

"Called out to a fire. We're just here to work out." Vader leered at her. "And it sure did work out."

"But he promised he'd be here when I came!"

"A fire's a fire, Ms. Joy. Never know when we'll get a call," Fred explained.

Ella pouted. "Isn't there some way to call him back? Can't you talk to the fire truck or whatever?"

Uh-oh, thought Melissa. This sounded like trouble. She gave half an ear to Kevin's grumbling about amps and the rest of her attention to Ella's shenanigans.

"Well, yes, but—"

"Let's surprise him!" Ella waved an imperious hand at Fred. "Won't he just die when he hears me on the radio?"

"Captain wouldn't like it," said Fred uneasily. "I'm pretty sure it's against the law."

"Is the captain here?"

"Somewhere," said Fred vaguely.

Melissa's ears perked up. So Brody was somewhere. Did that mean somewhere in the firehouse?

Ella pinned Fred with her most mesmerizing smile. Melissa rolled her eyes. The poor kid didn't stand a chance.

"If he's not here, he'll never know about it. Come on. Where's that radio?" She pulled Fred to his feet.

With tightly folded lips, he shook his head.

"Come on, Freddy-weddy, where's the radio?"

"Ella," called Melissa. "I don't think this is a good idea."

Ella, of course, ignored her.

"You don't want to make me unhappy now, do you?" She traced a finger across Fred's lips.

He heaved a helpless sigh and opened his mouth. "The radio is this way." The poor fellow trudged across the room, followed by Ella, smug as could be.

"Ella, stop this!"

But neither of them paid any attention to her.

"What's going on here?" Brody emerged from the apparatus bay with a rag over his shoulder, a dark frown on his face. Melissa felt every nerve shiver at the sight of him.

"She . . . she made me . . . she wanted to talk to Hoagie on the radio."

Brody let out half a curse before snapping his mouth shut. He put one firm hand on Ella's shoulder, the other on Fred's, almost as if they were children, and maneuvered them back toward the couch. "Ms. Joy," he said, biting off each word. "I'm sure you must have forgotten that misuse of a first responder frequency could cause quite a backlash."

"It's not a misuse. I just wanted to say hi."

He stared at her, flabbergasted. Melissa got a certain amount of satisfaction from his expression. Now he'd find out what it was like dealing with Ella Joy, whose fists were clenched at her side as if she were one step from committing assault on an officer.

Brody let out a long breath. "That's very friendly of you. Speaking of which, would you be willing to sign some of your calendars? One of the guys got them on eBay. Paid a bundle for them too. Fred, show her."

At the magic word "calendar," Ella smiled graciously. "Anything for my fans."

She eagerly followed Fred toward the captain's office. Melissa, astonished, stared after them.

"How did you do that?"

"You mean, how did I keep myself from strangling her? Believe me, I've been considering it these past few days. Or are you the one to blame for this?"

The look in his intense gray eyes made her shift uncomfortably. "Blame for what?"

"The last thing I want is to put my guys on TV again. Do you have any idea what we went through last time? We had girls coming out of our ears. We were tripping over them."

Kevin perked up. "Any chance of more of that?"

Melissa and Brody both ignored him. "You think I want to do this special? It's a complete waste of my time. I have real stories to work on."

"Then why are you here? Call the damn thing off."

"I'm not the news director. Why don't you call it off?"

He swiped his hand against his jaw, leaving a streak of dirt. "I tried, believe me."

She felt a sneaky moment of hurt that he was so opposed to the special. Maybe he wanted nothing to do with her. "Well, since we're both stuck with it, how about we get to work. Captain Brody, this is Kevin Murphy, our production manager. We came here to do a site survey for the special."

Kevin barely nodded before launching into a technical tirade. "Power's no problem, you got lotsa juice here, but we got no line of sight, so we'd have to bounce a signal off Mount Wilson unless we take the sat truck. Park the truck out front, run a cable through the hallway, maybe book some time on a bird as backup in case we lose the mountain, then we got the issue of lights. I'm thinking we'll need at least four three hundreds, that's twelve amps. That going to interfere with anything?"

Brody listened with a frown of growing irritation. "The whole thing interferes. But what does it matter if we blow out our power, it's all in a good cause, right? It's all about PR. Speaking of which, I have another problem for you, Melissa."

"Don't mind me, I'm just a union guy," said Kevin. "You got coffee around here?" Brody waved an arm toward the kitchen, and off he went.

Melissa crossed her arms, bracing for a scathing lecture on the evils of the news business. The air between the two of them seemed to vibrate with tension.

"I want to talk to you about Ella."

That wasn't what she was expecting. "What about her?"

"She calls Ryan every other minute. It's interfering with his work. Can you get her to stop?"

Melissa swore, silently to herself. Was her whole life going to be devoted to making Ella behave? "Tell Ryan. It takes two, you know."

"I have. But she keeps calling him. She doesn't seem to understand that lives depend on him keeping his focus."

"So you're telling me lives depend on me getting Ella to back off?"

"I wouldn't put it—"

"I'll tell her to back off!" Kevin interrupted, back with a Styrofoam cup of coffee. "Be happy to."

Melissa snapped her notebook shut. "Kevin, I think we're done here. We'll bring a backup generator just in case. There's no way we're doing this live, so line of sight's not a factor. Forget the sat truck too. We'll do it 'as-live'—switch the show in the production truck and roll tape. Keep it simple. Can you find Ella and tell her we're leaving?"

"I'm not a message boy." She shot him a look. He shrugged and left.

"So you can take charge," said Brody, narrowing his eyes at her.

"Of course I can. I'm a producer. We're in charge."

"But you let Ella walk all over you."

Melissa flushed. "I can handle Ella. I just do it my own way."

Brody put a hand on her shoulder. The warm weight of it sent a thrill through her. "I don't mean to put you on the spot. Obviously you know what you're doing."

She swallowed hard. Right now, she wasn't so sure. All she wanted was for him to back her up against the wall again. How was she supposed to get her work done around those intense eyes and that powerful body? It wasn't humanly possible.

"Look, Brody, I'm going to be here a lot until we tape this thing, and . . ."

"Yes?"

"I know you hate it, but this special is important to the station. Not to mention my career. I have to do a good job on it, like it or not."

"Yeah, so?"

"I need to keep things, you know . . ." Somehow she couldn't get the words out.

His eyes flared with sudden heat. "I think I know what you're trying to say."

"You do?"

"You want me to keep my hands off you." Yet he made no move to remove his hand from her shoulder.

Her face flamed. "Um . . ."

He bent down until his mouth was a breath away from hers. Charcoal eyes seemed to take in every inch of her face. She bit her lip to keep herself from melting into him. She knew exactly how it would feel if she leaned against his hard chest, let those iron arms wrap around her. His smell, soap with a hint of diesel, made her heart skip one beat, then another . . .

"Whatever you say," he said. He straightened up and strode away.

Brody knew Melissa was right. He'd already told himself the same thing. *Forget about Melissa. Get ahold of yourself.* But he hadn't counted on Haskell McGuire.

Haskell turned out to be an outstanding electrician with one huge flaw. He didn't talk much, but when he did, every other word out of his mouth concerned his beautiful, bright daughter. He never mentioned her by name, but by now Brody had a good picture of Melissa's childhood. Her father was extremely proud of the sensitive little girl who had spent every spare moment studying and working, making her escape from her painful circumstances.

"She inspired me," he told Brody, as he held a

fixture steady so Brody could fasten it to the cabinet. "These lights are gonna make some nice mood lighting in here. When I was in the slammer, I thought about her a lot. She's my blood, and look at what she made of her life. If she did it, so can I."

"Of course you can."

"Just wish she could find herself a worthwhile man."

Dangerous territory. Brody kept his response to a grunt.

"She don't talk to me much, like I said, but my ma says she likes boys that don't give her any trouble."

That description sure didn't fit him. "Whatever makes her happy."

"But she ain't. Not according to my ma. Won't listen to my advice."

"Big surprise," Brody mumbled.

"What's that?"

"I said, pass that impact driver, would you?"

"Sure thing."

Haskell lapsed back into silence, while Brody veered between relief and regret. Too much talk about Melissa made it hard for him to concentrate. It was too bad she didn't get along with her father, but what could he do about it? Melissa wouldn't appreciate any interference from him.

Okay, so she wasn't like the reporters who'd hounded him when the Bachelor Firemen story had first aired. She'd struggled and worked hard to get where she was. She was great at her job, except for her annoying habit of giving in to the obnoxious Ella Joy. He wished she'd stand up to her now and then. Not that she would appreciate that advice either.

He grabbed the drill and, to Haskell's confusion, added a random screw hole to the back corner of the cabinet. Maybe the noise would chase thoughts of Melissa away.

Chapter Eleven

Captain Brody was no ordinary fire captain, Melissa quickly discovered. Over the next few days, she made several trips to the San Gabriel Fire Station for preproduction and interviews. At first, when the firefighters told stories about their captain, she accused them of exaggerating. They told her about the time he'd run back into a fire to save an unconscious, elderly man with an oxygen tank that could have exploded at any moment. Brody had disengaged the tank, and as he'd carried the man out of the building, he'd stopped twice, surrounded by flames, to send his own breath into the man's gasping lungs. Incredibly, the man had survived.

He'd saved Double D a few times. Double D's closest brush with death had come when he'd slipped on the extension ladder and knocked himself unconscious. As he'd dangled by one foot, five floors up, Brody had shot up that ladder and somehow managed to manhandle him down. And Double D was no lightweight.

"Is he so strong then? Is that how he does it?" asked Melissa. The firefighters shook their heads.

"Sure, he's strong, but it's not that. Lotta guys are stronger. He just goes right in there and does what has to be done. He thinks without thinking. Like he's in the zone."

"What's the zone?"

"Same as for Michael Jordan. He sees everything that's going to happen way before it happens, so he doesn't even have to move fast. He just moves *right*. If you see him in action, you never forget it."

Melissa sighed. If she saw him in action, she'd probably have a heart attack. Even the sight of him doing paperwork in his office did crazy things to her blood pressure.

While Brody kept his distance, the other firemen treated her like their favorite little sister. They even gave her a nickname: Hollywood. Ryan told her she should be honored.

The more time she spent at the station, the more she realized what great guys they were. And gals too, although One didn't say much and Two, the younger one, seemed to go out of her way to avoid Melissa. It embarrassed her to remember how she'd dismissed firemen as nothing more than "macho men." She loved being greeted with a casual "What's shakin', Hollywood?" She liked the way they teased her, the way they lifted heavy things out of her hands, and the devotion they all felt for their station, for one another, and for Captain Brody.

Brody led his men and women with a Zen-like calm that seemed to hold them spellbound. Every once in a while he dropped a cryptic remark the firefighters would spend hours debating.

"Hollywood, what do you think this means?" Ryan called to her as she was dropping off boxes packed with autumn leaves for decorating the tables. "The fire already exists, waiting for the right conditions."

"I don't know, Hoagie. Did you check your manual?"

"What's the point of all that education of yours?" He twisted his gorgeous face into a comical frown.

"Got me. Say it again?" He repeated the words. "I think I heard a monk say something like that once, in a documentary. Where'd you hear it?"

"The captain," he said gloomily. "Sometimes he's like a walking affirmation. Makes my head hurt. How can the fire exist if there's no fire?"

Melissa thought about it. "Maybe he means all the elements that make the fire exist, but conditions have to be right for fire to appear."

Ryan frowned into the distance. Melissa caught her breath in awe at his sheer gorgeousness. Finally he turned blazing blue eyes on her, and snatched her up in a twirl. "That's it! You rock, Hollywood. I'm going to blow the captain's mind."

"The captain is looking forward to it." Brody caught them both by surprise. Ryan quickly put Melissa down, then righted her as she swayed.

"Sorry, sir. Just having fun. No harm intended." Ryan gave a vaguely military salute and backed out of the room.

Melissa, still a little breathless, picked up her

box of leaves. "He's just excited because I helped him solve your latest enigma."

"What enigma?" Brody took the box of leaves from her.

"What is it with you guys, can't you ever just let a girl carry something? I think I can handle a bunch of dead leaves."

"But why should you have to, when you have a big strong numskull around?"

She shot him a look under her lashes. He looked particularly attractive today. Nothing set off a uniform like rumpled dark hair and a slight five o'clock shadow. "You're not a numskull. I should have known it before, but I guess it took me a while. I suppose that means I'm the numskull."

Brody shrugged. "We see what we expect to see."

"There! Another enigma. I've figured out your secret weapon. You have them all so mystified they do whatever you tell them."

"Is that why Ryan ran out of here?"

"No, that was because—" Melissa stopped, flustered.

"Because?"

Melissa searched for a tactful way to explain it. "Oh, just . . . they think . . . I'm . . . your girl. Because of what happened at the dinner. I told them that's ridiculous."

Brody frowned down at Melissa.

So his men thought they were together. No wonder they all seemed to vanish whenever he spoke to Melissa. Like now. He looked around. No firefighters to be seen. Melissa wore a self-conscious look along with a ponytail, which made her look about sixteen years old. She was wearing jeans that molded her sweetly curved hips in a way that made his own pants feel too tight. Her soft breasts pushed against her T-shirt, red with some kind of bull on it and some Asian lettering. He squinted at it, then caught Melissa's curious look.

"I'm sorry, I was just . . . looking at the bull. Looks familiar," he stammered.

"It's the Red Bull logo. You know, the drink."

"Sure, I'm a big fan of it." Gesturing toward the T-shirt, he accidentally brushed her chest, and saw her take a quick step back. He stepped back too, and clamped both arms around the box of leaves. "Believe it or not, I have no intention of groping you every time we're alone. And I'll make sure the guys know you're not, that we're not . . . I'll leave you to your leaves."

He took the box into the kitchen and marched back into his office. So much for the calm, collected leader of men. When he'd made that promise about keeping his hands off her, he'd been half joking. But it turned out to be harder than he'd thought. When he was in Melissa's presence, he seemed to either pounce on her or stammer like a teenager.

And when he wasn't with her, he watched her from a distance. He'd never known how sexy organizing a news special could be. When Melissa was at the station, he couldn't think of anything else until she left. He loved watching her in action. Melissa was the go-to person for anyone with problems or questions. If the question was too technical, she tossed it to Kevin. The rest she solved herself.

On top of the production aspects of the show,

apparently she was also in charge of the cooking itself. One day he nearly ran into her carting in plastic-covered bowls of mashed potatoes and pie filling.

"I thought Ella was cooking the dinner."

"That's right." She had a smear of mashed potato on her cheek, and he closed his fists to keep from wiping it off.

"So what's all this?"

"She can't do everything on the day of the dinner. We have to prep stuff beforehand."

"You mean, *you* have to prep stuff?"

"Is there a problem, Captain Brody?" She held the bowls in front of her like a shield. He stepped forward and saw a flicker in the green eyes hiding behind her glasses. What did she think he was going to do? Tackle her and roll her in pie filling? Not a bad idea, but instead he lifted one of the bowls from her arms.

"I'm fascinated by the process, that's all."

"Most of the cooking will be done ahead of time," she explained. "The viewers will see Ella putting the finishing touches on a fabulous meal. We're going to show the recipes, and a little bit of the process. I've already shot some of that."

"You've been busy."

"An hour-long special is a lot of work."

"For you," murmured Brody, opening the refrigerator.

Melissa bristled. "Ella does her part."

"I look forward to seeing it."

"Put it this way. Without her, the show would be a bunch of food on a table. With some camera-shy guys in uniform sitting around hoping a fire breaks out."

Brody knelt in front of the jam-packed refrigerator. Stan nosed behind him, sniffing at the fridge. "Get out of here, Stan." Sulking, Stan went to a corner of the kitchen and flopped down. "Damn Vader and his energy drinks." Somehow he managed to find a space for the pie filling in the crowded refrigerator, then reached for Melissa's bowl of mashed potatoes. Their fingers brushed and a tingle shot all the way up his arm. He jerked his hand away, and made a show of maneuvering the bowl into the fridge. What had they been talking about?

Oh yeah. Camera-shy firefighters.

"That's not fair," he said. "Some of my guys enjoy being filmed. Vader tried out for *Survivor*." He closed the refrigerator door, and stood up.

"Is he the one who happens to be working out every time we come by?"

"Yep. You probably won't recognize him with his shirt on."

"So he's planning to wear one? That's a relief."

Brody smiled. It was nice to know they could talk without him mauling her. "I have to admit, I fought against this project, but you're doing a good job with it. It's all anyone's talking about here. All the guys are excited. And the gals too."

Melissa gave a delighted smile that made Brody's groin twitch. "Thanks. I wasn't in favor of it either, but it's turning out better than I thought. I was wondering . . . we'd love to do a shot with Ella on the aerial. You know, show our viewers what it's like to fight a fire from so high up."

"Absolutely not."

The smile vanished. She pushed her glasses higher on her nose. "Why not?"

"Because I don't trust Ella up there. Because it's not safe. Because it's a misuse of expensive life-saving equipment. Do you want me to go on?"

"What if she just walks up it partway? She can stop and pose a little ways up, then we'll do a tilt to the top."

"Another shot for the calendar?"

Pink tinted her cheeks. He couldn't help it. He reached out and wiped off the streak of mashed potato. She went even pinker, and furiously scrubbed the last traces of potato off her cheek.

"It could totally make the special. Viewers love to get an inside look at stuff like that."

"Sorry." He had to admire her tenacity, not that it would change his decision. "Not going to happen."

"Maybe I should skip the aerial and do a feature on the bachelors of San Gabriel. I've been doing some research on the curse. I found out why every firehouse dog here is named Stan. It's after Con-stancia, from the bachelor curse."

Stan, hearing his name, lifted his head from its nest on his paws. Melissa bent down to scratch his ears.

"So?"

"So." She rose to her feet again, like a lawyer making her closing argument. "You could have broken with tradition and named the dog something else. Fluffy. Bunny."

Stan gave a little whimper. Brody didn't blame him one bit.

Melissa continued with a flourish. "Which leads me to believe you aren't as skeptical of the curse as you pretend. Which makes it a legitimate story. Why shouldn't I include it in the special?"

Brody took two quick steps until he was nose to nose with her. The vanilla scent of her hair nearly made him forget his anger. Nearly. "The curse is absurd. I allowed the name Stan because I didn't want to upset the guys. Firemen are superstitious. And if you say one word about bachelors in this damn special, I will pull the plug. Literally. I know where Kevin's getting his power. And no Ella on the aerial. That's final."

The sparks of green fire spitting at him could have set the building on fire. "You're being unreasonable."

"I'm being a fire captain."

She opened her mouth, then surprised him by holding her fire. "Fine." She pushed past him, the soft skin of her arm brushing against his. He watched her go, unable to tear his eyes away from the sensual sway of her jeans-covered rear.

It didn't occur to him until later that she'd given in with suspicious ease.

God, he was infuriating. Just the type she couldn't stand, ordering everyone else around in that arrogant way. If she hadn't been so furious with Brody's high-handedness, she would have followed his orders. But she told herself that he'd left her no choice. He'd said, "No Ella on the aerial." Well, there would be no Ella on the aerial. But she hadn't promised anything else.

If he got upset with her, it would be because everyone at the firehouse always followed his orders. Always.

The more she saw him in action, the more she understood why. Many of his firefighters were young and unseasoned, with fiery tempers. In this category she included Ryan. She'd seen him flare up several times. The station had the added friction of the two female firefighters, who seemed perfectly capable to her, but whose presence galled the older veterans. When quarrels broke out, she found herself, along with the others, looking around anxiously for Brody.

Three days before the taping, she asked Ryan who would be carving the turkey. Within minutes, a shoving match erupted between Ryan and Vader. Two, the other witness, rolled her pretty turquoise eyes and announced her disgust with them both. Horrified that she'd caused a fight, Melissa ran into Brody's office. "Captain Brody, I think you should get out there. Hoagie and Vader are fighting."

Brody cocked his head to listen. "Don't you have any brothers?"

"No, but I know what a fight looks like."

"How much blood is there?"

"None. They're just pushing each other. But I feel terrible, because they're fighting over the special."

He sighed. "It's not about Ella, is it?"

"Well, kind of. It's about the turkey."

"I won't make the obvious joke."

She was too worried to laugh. "Someone's going to get to help Ella carve the turkey, and Ryan thinks it should be him. Vader thinks his superior upper body strength makes him the best choice."

Brody rose lazily to his feet. "I really prefer not to interfere in these things, but since you're upset, I'll make an exception."

He strolled out of the room, as Melissa hopped to keep up. "But you interfere all the time."

"Do I? How irritating. I'll have to stop that."

"No, no, you shouldn't. They'd probably all kill each other if you let them."

"Well, maybe I should let them." They walked into the lounge, where Vader and Ryan were standing chest to chest, raring to go.

"No fighting in the firehouse," ordered Brody. They immediately fell apart, still glaring bloody murder at each other. "Outside, everyone, so we can settle this."

The firefighters streamed outside. Melissa grabbed Brody's arm. "You're going to let them fight? That's not going to solve anything."

"No brothers, right?" murmured Brody. When they had all reached the backyard, a tidy square of well-trodden lawn, Brody addressed his troops. "Okay, where's one of our married men? There you are, Double D. Who carves the turkey in your house?"

"Well, Cap, it used to be me, but my wife makes the cuts a heckuva lot better, so now she does it."

"So you're saying we should see who carves the turkey better?"

"Whoo-hoo," shouted Fred. "A carve-off! I'll get some birds." The firefighters sprang into action, and in less than two minutes a long table had appeared, on which two leftover roast chickens were displayed. Ryan and Vader were each handed a knife. No one except Melissa seemed to be bothered by the idea of sharp knives in the hands of two virile young men who had been fighting tooth and nail a few minutes ago.

"The rules." Brody planted himself at the end of the table. "The rules are, whoever can extract the most meat with the fewest number of cuts will win. Carvers, ready?"

Ryan and Vader eyed each other like knife-wielding prizefighters ready to take each other down. Melissa hoped they understood they were supposed to attack the chickens, not each other. "And . . . begin!"

They pounced on the poor chickens. The other firefighters immediately took sides, shouting out bets and heckling the two competitors. "Two bucks on Vader!" "Hoagie, go for the wings first!" "Not so deep, moron." "Try a little freakin' finesse!" Stan ran in circles around the table, barking frantically and nipping at random pant legs. If only she had a camera, thought Melissa, laughing at the sight of two big strong guys making a mess of the greasy roast chickens. The Great Turkey Carve-Off. It would make a fantastic blooper piece for the end of the special.

Vader managed to take off two wings and one leg before he pressed the knife too hard and the slippery chicken spurted off the table. Ryan raised his fist in triumph, but his bird was an even bigger mess. It looked as if a wild beast had torn it apart.

Brody, shaking his head in disgust, called a stop to the massacre.

"Both of you should seriously consider taking some lessons from Double D's wife. In the meantime, since I am the senior captain of this station,

I will be carving the turkey. And anyone who fights over this damn special again will be put on Smokey duty for the next two weeks." He turned on his heel.

"Smokey duty?" Melissa asked as he passed her.

"Instructing kids in fire safety. They actually like it, but they pretend not to," answered Brody before heading into the station. Melissa watched him go, her respect for him rising another notch. He'd managed to bring the fight to an end, prevent future fights, and entertain the guys in the process. And look damn good doing it too.

Chapter Twelve

Two days before the taping of the Thanksgiving special, Nelly slowly made her way into the nondescript office building called, innocuously, Medical Suites. Down a hall, second door to the right, Dr. Daughtry awaited her. Even though she was used to these appointments, her stomach tightened with nerves. She knew very well her time was coming. But the "when" of it—that was the question. Even though Dr. Daughtry always said he couldn't tell her that precisely, she was convinced he had the truth locked somewhere inside his head.

She greeted the nurse-receptionist, who showed her immediately into the doctor's office. The privilege of old age, or of the terminally ill; either way she had both bases covered. With bustling energy and a folder of X-rays, the ever-cheerful Dr. Daughtry strode into his office and sat behind his desk.

As always, she plastered a defiant smile on her face. That smile had helped her soldier on since she'd first gotten the news.

"Well, Dr. Death?"

He winced. "Please don't spread that nickname around."

"Where I'm going, no one's going to care."

"You're one of a kind, Nelly, you really are."

"I know that. And I know what's in that folder. What I don't know is how long I got."

He opened the folder and extracted X-rays and some typed reports. "No one can tell you that, Nelly. But I want you to look at your latest scans. This was taken a month ago. And this is the most current." He pointed to the shadowy area that she knew so well, and her face tightened. It had grown so much bigger. How could it get that much bigger in just one month? From the beginning, she'd promised herself no lies. Whatever the grim truth, she wanted to know it.

"It's growing awful fast, I guess," she said.

"Awful fast."

"How much time? Can you tell me now?"

"Less than we thought."

"C'mon, Doc, that's no way to treat a dying lady. Give me a real answer."

"No more than six months." He gave it to her simply and sympathetically, but a punch in the gut was a punch in the gut.

"Fudge. You can't hold it off? I got some things to wrap up here."

"Are you still set against chemotherapy?"

"Yes."

"Then there's nothing I can do. "

"Fudge."

"Nelly, I think it's time we spoke to your family."

"No!" she said sharply. "Not yet. It'll throw everything off. They'll be too busy worrying about me to look out for themselves. And that's what I'm trying to take care of."

"As you like, but soon you'll have to, Nelly. They deserve to know the full extent of your condition. We need to start thinking about hospice care. You're going to get to a point where you can't function at home." She nodded reluctantly. Hospice care was the last thing she wanted. If she could write the end of her own story, it would be quick and happy—meaning she'd know her family would be all right.

The hassles they put her through, that family of hers. As she waited at the curb for Haskell to pick her up, she cursed the bad luck that gave her such stubborn descendants. Why couldn't Melissa see the truth right in front of her? How much time was she going to waste before she admitted her feelings and did something about them?

She glanced up at the sky. Right now she really needed to talk to Leon. "The problem, Leon, is that Melissa doesn't know how to fight for what's hers. Even though they see each other nearly every day, they're too darn 'professional' to take advantage of the situation. Professional! Professional doesn't keep you warm at night."

A woman passed by, pushing a stroller. She gave Nelly a pitying look, but Nelly didn't care. Her conversations with Leon were her business.

"What if Ella gets tired of Ryan and decides to steal Brody away? I wouldn't give Melissa a snowball's chance in a bonfire. Not because she isn't ten times as good as Ella. Because she doesn't stand up for herself. Remember all the tricks I pulled to get rid of that Alice May you had an eye for? I'm not sorry for it either. All's fair in love and war, and that's a fact. It's a battle you gotta fight till you can't fight no more. But she doesn't see it that way. I don't know, Leon. I'm at my wits' end. If you got any pull up there, you gotta think of something. You always were a charmer. Put that cheeky smile of yours to work, if you don't mind."

Haskell pulled up and opened the passenger door of his truck. She climbed in. "Sorry I'm late. Got stuck with the captain."

"Making an old lady wait, you should be . . . did you say 'captain'?"

"The job I'm working on. Boss is a fire captain."

"Who is it? What's his name?"

Haskell shot her a suspicious look. "I probably shouldn't say."

"Oh, pish. You're not a doctor, Haskell."

"Well, it's Captain Brody over at Station 1. Helluva good guy. I'm headed back over there after I drop you off. It's his last day off and we're trying to finish the kitchen."

Nelly looked up at the ceiling of the truck, mouthing a thank-you. She knew it. Leon had come through for her. Must have been that smile of his.

As soon as she got home, she called Melissa at work. "Your dad needs a ride home from his job."

Melissa groaned. "He started drinking again, didn't he?"

"No, nothing like that. He's fine. Something

about his truck." She should have worked out a more detailed story, but she'd wanted to get this done before her nap. Dr. Death appointments always took it out of her.

"Grans, you have no idea how busy I am. This stupid special is taping in two days, and I can't even do my own work. I just had to cancel my meeting with Rodrigo to help Ella with a wardrobe consultation."

"This is after work. It's not far. And you know how much it would mean to him. He's been trying so hard, Melissa, you know he has. And you barely give him the time of day."

"Is this some plot to throw me and my father together?"

"No! I swear it's not that." Nelly loved being able to deny an accusation with a clear conscience.

Nelly heard her granddaughter's heavy sigh. "Fine. Give me the address. I'll swing by after work."

Nelly hung up, feeling exhausted. Would it help things along if Melissa saw Brody outside of work, where they wouldn't be so worried about being "professional"? Who knew? But the way she saw it, Leon had dropped the opportunity in her lap. She might as well jump on it.

That evening, Melissa arrived at a house still under construction in the lovely wooded subdivision just beyond Fern Acres. When the work was finished, it would be a nice house, she thought. Pretty location, surrounded by birch woods, the nearest neighbors barely within shouting distance. Two stories, unusual for Southern California. Gabled windows, a porch. She spotted a silver Airstream trailer parked at the edge of the yard.

She walked to the front door—or rather, the empty space framed by studs where the door would eventually be installed. Peering in, she saw no signs of life. She rapped her knuckles on one of the studs.

"Hello? Is Haskell McGuire here?"

She heard the clank of tools being put down, followed by firm footsteps. At the sight of the man who appeared, a shocked little thrill went through her. *Captain Brody*. Brody as she'd never seen him before, wearing torn jeans, a tool belt, and no shirt. Dizzy, Melissa gripped the stud and feasted her eyes.

Hard-muscled and furry-chested, he had a sprinkling of sawdust in his dark hair and on his shoulders. Oh, those shoulders, powerful and glistening with sweat. Her eyes traveled down his chest to his muscular stomach. Not an ounce of fat to be seen. Her mouth went dry, and she had a sudden urge to lick that one particular drop of sweat off his belly. She dragged her eyes up so they wouldn't stray below his belt buckle. When her eyes met his, she felt as if she'd been caught with her hand in a cookie jar.

The nerve of the man, catching her off guard like that. "What are you doing here?"

"Well, I live here, but I suppose I should have cleared it with you ahead of time. Haskell!"

Haskell hurried in, wiping sawdust off his face. "Melissa? Why are you here?"

"Grans said you needed a ride."

"Huh? Why'd she say that?"

"I have no idea. Is your truck okay?"

He shook his head. "She's up to something. Thought she seemed strange when I picked her up at lunch."

Melissa flattened herself against the door frame to let him pass. She looked back at Brody. With the first impact of his bare chest over, she could think more clearly.

"My father is working for you?"

He nodded.

Disaster. Her ex-con father, whom she never talked about with anyone, was working with Brody. Not only that, but they seemed friendly with each other. Too friendly. How much did Brody know about her family? She didn't like this one bit. "Why? I mean, out of all the electricians in San Gabriel, why?"

"Got his name from the phone book. He's a hard worker."

"Is he?" Melissa's dread grew. Her father had a knack for ruining everything. Was this going to be like the time he scared off her junior prom date by pantsing him?

"Yes. He's doing an excellent job."

"Why wouldn't he? What are you implying?"

"No reason. I just said it in case you were wondering." Then, in a blatant attempt to change the subject, "Do you want a soda?"

She refused to be distracted. "Why would I wonder?"

"No reason. I have Snapple, Coke, beer. Wanna beer?"

"Is that what you're doing, drinking beer with Haskell?"

"Of course not. I know he doesn't drink."

Melissa clenched her fists, her nails digging into the palms. If he knew that, what other embarrassing things did he know? "What else did he tell you?"

"Melissa, calm down. I know how to mind my own business." He took a step toward her, and she held up a hand.

"Oh, really?" This was getting worse and worse. She knew her father was trying to talk more, thanks to AA. "What has he told you about me?"

Brody looked uncomfortable. "What are you so worried about? I needed an electrician. He needed work. End of story." He took another step toward her. "What he's done in his life doesn't reflect on you."

"Thank you, Dr. Phil. But may I point out that you have no idea what he put me through."

"Yes I do. He's told me a few things."

Great. Complete, utter humiliation. Brody knew all about her past, all about her father, the drunken ex-con. She didn't want his pity or his sympathy. And that's what she would inevitably get. Blindly, she turned to go.

She felt his hand on her arm, and tried to shake it off. But that strong grip wasn't going anywhere.

"He's trying hard now. I've seen how hard."

"So?" She tugged her arm, but couldn't free it.

"You could try a little open-mindedness."

Last straw. Melissa spun around to face him. How dare he lecture her? Before she realized it, her free arm swung toward him, and her hand flew toward his cheek.

He stopped her just in time, with a hard grip on her wrist. "Are you crazy?"

"Maybe I am. Maybe it's in the genes." Everything she'd tried to put behind her rose up like a horror movie. Just like the old days, when she'd live in dread of her father ruining everything. "I look like him, don't I? That's what everyone used to say. Along with things like alkie's girl . . . white trash . . . welfare brat . . ."

"Stop that!" He gave her a shake. "You're none of those things."

"You probably despise me now. Who knows what he's said about me." Tears pricked the backs of her eyelids. She couldn't stand the thought of Brody, the legendary captain, the arrogant commander of men, knowing about her past.

"You've got it all wrong." He cupped her face in his warm hands and tilted it so she couldn't avoid his gaze. "You're the reason he's working so hard. He talks about you all the time. You're a . . . jewel."

Her breath caught in a hiccup. The look in those charcoal eyes made her suddenly go weak. Everything seemed to stop as they faced each other, only inches apart. Tiny details jumped out at her. The bits of sawdust caught in his dark eyebrows. The warmth of his body, so close to hers. The clean, spicy smell of his shampoo, buried under the scents of sweat and wood dust. The specks of silver lighting the unusual gray of his eyes. She leaned in, as though in a trance, and softly put her lips to his. He stood very still, but she felt his chest rising and falling with his quickening breath.

This wasn't like the other times. Before, they'd been crazed, out of control. This time, they moved at a deliberate pace that said, *I know exactly what I'm doing, I like it, and I'm not going to stop.* Feeling the gentle pressure of his mouth, she opened her lips, letting his tongue spread sweet wildfire along her tender inner flesh.

This man was not like other men, she thought as her skin shivered and her bones melted. He affected her in a way no one ever had. If she let him in, her life would never be the same.

Her father's footsteps sounded on the pathway. They pulled apart, even though it physically hurt to withdraw from him. She fought to regain her balance.

"We really need to stay away from doors," she said with a shaky laugh.

He chuckled, his muscles moving under her hands. How had her hands gotten onto his chest? She didn't move them away.

"Melissa, how would you like to—"

Before Brody could finish his sentence, Melissa felt a tap on her shoulder. She quickly dropped her hands from that tempting bare chest.

"You two know each other?" Haskell asked warily. "Or should I punch him out?"

"I know him." Melissa stepped away from Brody. "We're working together on a project."

Haskell looked from one to the other, but made no comment. "Don't know what Ma's up to, or if she's just confused, but my truck's fine."

Melissa groaned. "Did she know you were working for Captain Brody?"

"Well, I guess. Told her when I picked her up."

Melissa's face flamed. "I'm really sorry, Captain Brody. You know my grandmother's crazy ideas."

"She's determined, I'll give her that." She couldn't read his expression.

Her father cleared his throat. "Melissa, sorry if I told Ma too much." He looked so miserable she softened.

"It's okay."

In the past, she would have been furious with her father. But in this case, he hadn't exactly ruined things. The opposite, really.

She said an awkward good-bye to them both and drove away in a fog. This time, she had no one to blame but herself. She couldn't blame it on wine. She couldn't blame it on a door. She couldn't even blame it on him, since she'd been the one to initiate the kiss. Maybe she could blame it on his bare chest, which ought to be illegal, not to mention the tool belt slung around his hips. That sight would be enough to make any woman, no matter how professional, lose control.

Two days until the special. It would be a miracle if she managed to keep her clothes on until then.

The day before the taping, Ella stretched out on the chaise by her pool to refresh her tan. She yawned into her cell phone. "Hey there, beautiful," Ryan was saying. "Saw you on the news last night. You read that story about celebrity moms real well. They should have just kept the camera on you instead of showing all those ugly movie stars."

"You mean like Angelina Jolie and Gwyneth Paltrow?" Ella stretched her tiny, toned body. This phone call was boring her to death.

"Yeah, who cares about them? We want us some more Ella Joy, baby."

"Oh yeah?"

"You go tell that news director to get rid of all

that other boring stuff. It just takes away from the main event. You."

Ryan said all the right things, but still . . . something was missing. After she hung up, Ella crossed one leg over the other and gazed at her frosted-plum toenails. Damn, she felt restless. She was always restless when she wasn't on the air. She loved the moment when that magic red camera light went on. It meant she could shine the way destiny intended. It meant she could speak, live, to thousands of people, people she didn't have to listen to.

Not that she wasn't a "people" person. She preferred being with people. Being alone sucked. What was the point of trying on her new lime-green string bikini if no one was there to tell her how great her ass looked in it, and that she ought to go switch the pink Gucci sunglasses for the white Versace ones? In her dream life she would have an assistant, a stylist, a nutritionist, a manicurist, and so on. That's what she needed—an entourage. If she had an entourage, she wouldn't be lounging alone by her pool.

She sauntered back into her house, grabbed the other pair of sunglasses, and poured herself a sugar-free iced tea. Why couldn't she just relax? She worked hard; she deserved a couple hours of downtime. But her foot kept tapping, and she couldn't get comfortable on her chaise. Stupid five-hundred-dollar chaise that she'd seen in *InStyle* magazine. If she had an assistant, the girl (or eager gay guy, or hot young stud) would have thoroughly tested it before letting her purchase it.

The thought of a hot young stud made her mind

wander to Ryan. He was a sweet guy, gorgeous as a movie star, but the challenge had disappeared. Once he'd fallen for her, he seemed dull. In fact, her life seemed dull. By the end of tomorrow, the Thanksgiving special would be history. She had nothing else to look forward to. Of course, if it turned out well, it could be her ticket to a bigger market.

She flopped back down on her chaise and crossed her perfectly tanned legs, which gleamed like the sand on a Tahitian beach.

She grabbed her cell and dialed her agent. "Don, have you heard anything more about the spot in LA? I heard they're not renewing that old hag."

"Ella, I'm on my way to a meeting."

"I sure hope it's a meeting about my future. I have to get out of here, Don. I belong in Los Angeles. Can't you call that Everett Malcolm?"

"I have. No go. Won't even look at your tape. But he had good things to say about someone you work with."

"Who?"

"Do you know Melissa McGuire? He thinks highly of her. Maybe she can put a good word in for you."

Furious, she clicked off the phone. *Melissa, Melissa, Melissa.* As if Melissa would ever help her out. She'd already tried to bribe her with a hazelnut latte.

"Ella," she'd said, "I can't recommend that place as long as Everett Malcolm is news director. You can't trust him. He has no conscience. He's destroyed a lot of people's careers."

"Oh come on, you're exaggerating because you screwed him and he dumped you."

Melissa had nearly choked on her biscotti. "You know about that?"

"It's old news, honey. But that's not the main point. What about the old hag who's leaving?"

But Melissa had clammed up. "The only thing I'm going to say is that it's true Everett dumped me, but I never had sex with him."

"Maybe that's why he dumped you."

"Don't mess with him, Ella. And don't say I didn't warn you."

Ella recrossed her legs and downed her iced tea. Melissa would be no help at all. Unless . . .

An idea formed. Maybe it was time to get more proactive. All she had to do was get Everett Malcolm to San Gabriel. Once he saw her in person, he'd change his mind.

While she was on the phone with a party rental company, one thought kept running through Melissa's mind. What had Brody been about to say?

Melissa, how would you like to—? Like to what? Have dinner? Fly to Paris? Crochet a placemat? She wanted to scream just thinking about it. Had he almost asked her out? If so, why hadn't he called her later to finish the job? Or maybe it was business-related, something like, *How would you like to interview Vader in his muscle shirt?*

One thing she knew—she wanted Brody. She thought about him all the time. Even now, when she was supposed to be arranging for tablecloths and extra card tables, she was thinking about him. *If you really want Brody, why don't you just go for it? Have a fling. It won't kill you. No one has to know. No one has to get hurt. Other people do it all the time. So* what if he was recovering from being dumped by his ex-wife? A little sexual healing would be good for him. Good for both of them. So what if they were all wrong for each other? That didn't mean they couldn't enjoy each other on a physical level.

What if things had gone differently at his house? What if he'd leaned her against the door frame, opened her blouse one slow button at a time, rubbed his thumbs over her nipples? What if he'd traced warm fingertips along the curves of her torso, murmuring, "Touch me. Put your hands on me," in a rough whisper? What if she'd opened his pants, reached her hand inside, and felt his heavy, burning erection . . . ?

"Miss, did you say you wanted the ivory, or the cream?"

Melissa shook herself out of her fantasy. "What the hell's the difference?" Her whole body felt flushed and restless. And who was this idiot asking stupid questions on the phone?

"No need for that attitude. It doesn't make any difference to me what you choose."

"Sorry. Uh . . . better make them a darker color, white doesn't look good on camera." This had to stop before she made some bonehead mistake, she thought as she hung up with Party Central. Maybe she should just get it out of her system. As soon as the special was over, she was going to jump his bones. Where did this madness come from? She'd never even used the phrase "jump his bones" before. *Get a grip*, she ordered herself.

She picked up the phone to call Rodrigo. Twice now she'd had to cancel a meeting with him when some "crisis" came up with the Thanksgiving special. Before she could finish dialing, Loudon stuck his head into her cubicle. She quickly hung up. Was she in trouble?

"I'm hearing good things about the special. You're shooting tomorrow, right?"

Whew. "Yep. I think it'll turn out pretty well."

"I have no doubt. You're my ace in the hole. My clean-up batter. My consigliere."

"Are you about to dump another project on me? Because you promised . . ."

"Hang on, tiger. I'm a good guy today. If this special knocks 'em out the way I expect, there's a new title in it for you."

"And a raise?" she asked quickly. Titles were a dime a dozen in this business.

"Greedy minx."

"Stingy penny pincher."

"We'll discuss your precious pennies if and when the time comes. Make it sing, Melissa. Make it sing." And he took his drooping face and streaming eyes back to the dim office that was his natural habitat.

Melissa sat back with a happy sigh. A new title and a raise. Maybe things were finally going her way. Leaving LA for San Gabriel had been a huge step backward, career-wise. But maybe things were finally going to turn around. She'd work like crazy on the special, hold on to her professionalism until it was wrapped, get her promotion, and then jump Brody's bones. She was beginning to like that phrase.

She forgot all about the call to Rodrigo.

Chapter Thirteen

Captain Brody gazed in horror at his normally neat-as-a-pin fire station. He saw a scene of utter chaos, worse than any four-alarm fire. Piles of camera equipment filled the training room. Cables cluttered the floor, technical people snapped at anyone who got in their way. His usually confident, cock-of-the-walk firemen tiptoed around or stood in stunned clusters. He saw Vader try to inch out of the room, only to be scolded by a scruffy man in shorts wheeling a large light.

"Careful! Watch where you're going, big guy."

"Sorry," muttered Vader, and quickly rejoined his comrades. The scruffy man plugged in the light, and suddenly the entire room was filled with a white glare. The firefighters blinked and threw their arms over their eyes. Brody shook his head in disgust. How could his guys, who would run into a burning building, turn into such wimps just because they were going to be on TV?

"Hey!" he called to the lighting guy. "Could you turn that god-awful light off?"

He found himself the subject of a withering stare. "We have to get the lighting set. We're only two hours from taping."

"You're telling me that light is going to be on the whole time?"

"How else is anyone supposed to see anything?"

"We're supposed to eat dinner with giant lights shining in our eyes?"

The man shrugged. "I'm just the lighting guy. I set the light so Ella looks good, take my paycheck, and go home. Have a beer. You got a problem, talk to someone in charge." He moved to the opposite side of the room and plugged in another light. The glare doubled.

Brody groaned. He should have known it would be all about making Ella look good. "How much light does it take?"

"We'll have to play with it. Do you mind?" The man elbowed Brody out of the way.

Brody stepped back, feeling his temper rise. When he'd agreed to this project, he'd been under pressure from the fire department's public relations officer, who had emphasized the wholesome picture it would present, and the plugs for the Widows and Orphans Fund that the station had agreed to run. He certainly hadn't imagined anything like this insanity.

Fred bounced into the room and immediately tripped on a cable.

"Captain! Can you believe this? Isn't it awesome?"

"Find Melissa for me, Stud. Hollywood. I need to talk to her."

"Sure, I think I just saw her outside." And he ran off, once again tripping on the cable. Fred was probably the clumsiest of his crew, but that didn't relieve the TV people of responsibility.

A sudden shriek of feedback made everyone jump. Brody turned to the source, ready to let fly. A skinny blond girl with a ring in her nose was turning knobs on a mixer.

"Sorry, dude," she muttered as he glared at her.

"Dude?" said Brody, ominously. "How old are you?"

"I'm legal. But I'm not interested, sorry." She tapped a small microphone, and he jumped again.

"Damn it!" The word blared across the room, and startled faces turned toward him. He looked up to find a big, fuzzy microphone hovering over his head. It was attached to a long pole balanced on the shoulder of a burly man in a tie-dyed T-shirt.

Melissa's cool voice intervened.

"Hank, get that mic out of the captain's face, you know better. Dina, there's no need for the boom mic to be live right now. Turn it off. And someone come tape down this cable, it's a hazard." As her crew scrambled to follow her orders, she made her way toward Brody. She looked calm enough to be strolling through a garden party. "Hey there, Captain. Everything's going great, as you can see."

"Can I?" He scowled at her. What he really wanted to do was kick the whole lot of them out of his station. Barring that, he could at least yell

at the producer. "This is pure chaos. My guys are
going to go blind and deaf. You have a thirteen-
year-old club kid working for you, and I think she
just propositioned me—"

"No way! You're too vanilla for me," objected
the skinny blonde.

"—and don't you people have any kind of dress
code?"

Melissa seemed unfazed. "They'll get used to
the light. We're almost done testing audio. Dina
is twenty-five, and apparently not interested. And
behind-the-scenes people tend to dress however's
most comfortable. They have a tough job. Anyone
who thinks TV is glamorous hasn't seen the way
it works."

"So this is normal?" Brody shook his head. "I
don't know how you do it."

"This is more organized than normal. Come on,
I'll show you the production truck. We're going to
switch and record the show in there."

"I shouldn't . . . my guys . . ." He shot a worried glance at his crew, who were now exchanging ogling looks with Dina. But Melissa took his
hand, and how could he resist that? He followed
her through the tangle of lights and cables.

"That's Greg behind the camera, he's the best
cameraman this side of the Mississippi." She blew
a kiss at the young cameraman, a dead ringer for
Kobe Bryant. Brody found he didn't like seeing
one of her kisses aimed anywhere but toward him.
He scowled, which she seemed to misinterpret.
"I know this part's boring, but we'll be getting
started soon."

"I don't think they're bored. Bedazzled is more

like it." Her hand felt good in his, soft and cool. Too bad she dropped it when they reached the production truck. A crew of two filled the small space packed with monitors and editing machines. They pointed out the two monitors that showed what was happening in the fire station. On one of them he saw Dina showing Vader how the mixer worked. The other camera hadn't been set yet, and it was pointed directly at the hairy legs of the lighting guy.

Melissa exchanged some technical talk with the director, gave a satisfied nod, and led the way out of the production truck. "I have to check on Ella, I'll see you in a little bit," she said, and hurried off. But the next time he saw her, she had another crisis on her hands. The tablecloths were apparently the wrong color, and Melissa sent the intern to return them. When she came scurrying back, they had to quickly reset and redecorate the table.

Over in the kitchen, where Ella would be shown stirring cranberry sauce and basting the turkey, Melissa had to do some last-minute "set dressing." Brody felt a bit guilty about that—the night before, there had been a barbecue sauce incident, and no one had cleaned up properly afterward. Melissa decided there wasn't time for scrubbing, so she cleverly positioned a pile of plates and a scattering of autumn leaves over the worst of the stains.

Brody stayed out of the way, watching with bemused admiration. Melissa seemed to be everywhere at once, but never looked rushed or panicked. The intern almost had a breakdown when it turned out the new tablecloths were still the wrong color. But Melissa quickly soothed her. "As long as they're not white, we'll make it work." She spoke into her headset. "Burt, how do they look?"

She listened, then gave the tearful intern a quick thumbs-up. "He says fabulous, darling. Don't worry about a thing. Now run and take this script change to the prompter. The black-haired guy in the corner."

The grateful intern trotted away.

Ryan appeared at Brody's side. "This is something else, huh Cap?"

"Sure is. I didn't know what I was getting us into. I hope I don't live to regret it."

"Why would you? It's the most exciting thing around here since that big apartment fire last year. And no body bags here."

"Unless that lighting guy bugs me again," muttered Brody under his breath.

"And check out Hollywood. She's all over this thing. Really knows her shit."

Brody watched Melissa cross the room. She was wearing soft black pants that were probably meant for comfort, but happened to cling to her ass in a particularly sexy manner. When Brody saw Ryan checking her out, he stifled an urge to smack him.

"She does," he said. "But that doesn't mean you have to stare at her."

But Ryan was now staring in a different direction, his jaw nearly on the floor. Ella strolled in as a hush fell over the room.

Even Brody gave a silent whistle. Among the raggedy crew members and uniformed firefighters, she looked like someone from a different species, an exotic butterfly landing among a crowd of sparrows. Her hair had been molded into soft brown-sugar waves, and her eyes, outlined in smoky black, were a dazzling china-blue. Her lips shone glossy pink. A clingy dress the color of a ripe plum caressed her tiny golden body. She looked fragile and perfect, like a doll.

Until she opened her mouth. "Melissa, this intro is crapola. Who cares about the Pilgrims anymore? That was, like, centuries ago."

Melissa hurried to her side. "Little children love the Pilgrims. I think it's because of the hats. But if you want me to take out that line . . ."

"Fine, never mind. But what about—"

"You look amazing, Ella. That color really brings out your eyes."

"Thanks. Do you think it's appropriate for Thanksgiving? Rust tones seemed so boring."

"I think it's perfect. Now take your first mark, so we can fine tune the lighting." Ella obediently moved toward the pieces of tape on the floor in the dining room. She smiled at the camera and, as Dina helped her put on the mic, she whispered something sultry into it. The stage manager gave a shout of laughter. Brody realized this was Ella in her element. All the things that seemed over-the-top and absurd about her under normal circumstances seemed glamorous and fascinating under the lights and concentrated attention of a production crew.

Brody looked over at Ryan and saw he was completely transfixed. Poor Hoagie. In his lazy way, he'd fallen for Ella Joy, even though he complained about her high-maintenance ways. Ryan had been spoiled by all the girls who fawned over him, did

his laundry, filed his taxes. Brody could have told
him it was a full-time job to keep the attention of a
flirt like Ella.

Ella sent a teasing smile to the slack-jawed firefighters. "Are you guys ready to make TV magic?"
A little cheer went up from the dazzled crew.
"You're all going to be superstars, and no one's
going to remember me at all. Now gather round,
let's take a group photo before the show starts."
She beckoned imperiously toward the intern, who
dug in her fanny pack for a digital camera.

"I told you she earns her money," murmured
Melissa, at Brody's side.

"She sure is a sight to behold." He shook his head
admiringly and felt Melissa's sharp gaze on him.

"So you've changed your mind about her?"

"It's the first time I've seen her in action. Now I
see what the fuss is all about."

"Right." Melissa looked away, fiddling with
her headset. "Well, like I said, she's good. Don't
you want to be in the photo? I'm sure she'll sign
it for you."

"I'm happy where I am," he said firmly. He took
her by the shoulders and turned her to face him.
"Good luck with the show. Do you TV people say
break a leg? Or in Ella's case, a nail?"

"Very funny." Melissa smiled. "Good luck carving that turkey. Untold millions of people will be
watching."

"Trying to make me nervous? I'll have you know
I have nerves of steel."

"Any problems, just imagine the cameramen
naked."

"Not the producer?" He gave her a devilish wink and a quick flick of his eyes down her body. Imagining her naked seemed like a fine way to pass the time.

Oh boy, Melissa thought faintly. She had a show to produce, just minutes away. And now her knees felt a little shaky and butterflies fluttered in her belly. In her headset, she heard the director say, "Two minutes."

"Two minutes," she called, for those without headsets. Leaving Brody's side, she hurried to her spot next to the big monitor the guys had set up for her.

Suddenly the atmosphere turned serious. Ella took a last-minute look at the scripts she held in her hand. The stage manager settled the firemen and women into their spots. He adjusted his headset and called out, "Thirty seconds."

Everyone else fell silent as he continued the countdown. Then he gave Ella a hand gesture, and when the red light went on, she beamed a huge smile at the camera.

"Good evening, and happy Thanksgiving! We're so glad you're joining us for this very special dinner with the Bachelor Firemen of San Gabriel. I'm sure all you little children out there . . ." Melissa winced at this ad lib, but Ella took no notice. "You know all about the Pilgrims, and how they cooked the very first Thanksgiving dinner for the Native Americans who had helped them survive here in the New World. These firefighters you see behind me devote their lives to helping us survive, and that's why we decided we should cook them a Thanksgiving dinner. First, let's meet these brave men and women who put their lives on the line . . . all in a day's work."

At this point, the camera closed in on the firefighters sitting behind Ella. Melissa, watching with an eagle eye, saw their expressions of mingled self-consciousness and embarrassment, and quickly spoke into her headset to tell the director to dissolve to the prerecorded story about the station.

As the piece ran, quiet reigned in the room. Ella looked over the next script, and the firefighters sat as though afraid to move an inch. Melissa listened to the audio from the prerecorded piece. It was one of her favorite parts of the show—she'd pieced together the best parts of all her interviews with the crew.

In the piece, Ryan talked about how he could instinctively feel the flames and guess their next move. Double D told the story of the time they managed to save the local church, with a congregation trapped inside. "I figure we got an automatic pass to heaven after that one," he joked.

Vader gave Ella a ride in Engine 1. The cameraman got some great shots of Ella wearing a helmet, Ella climbing into a set of turnout gear, Ella talking on the radio.

And then came the aerial segment. They'd shot the segment very carefully. Melissa had climbed up the aerial while the cameraman stayed on the ground, zooming in over her shoulder, while Ella provided the voiceover.

"Look how high we are, and how precariously we're perched. This is called manning the ladder pipe. Now imagine you're holding a hose shooting six hundred gallons of water a minute at the flames. Someone's property is being destroyed. Lives depend on you. Sometimes being a fire-fighter is a lonely job."

Tricky editing hid the fact that Ella wasn't actu-ally on the aerial. Only one shot of the side of Me-lissa's face gave it away, but it was so quick no one would notice it. The piece turned out well, in Me-lissa's opinion. Until she caught a glimpse of Brody scowling at her from across the room.

She braced herself.

When they reached the end of the first segment, Brody instantly appeared at Melissa's side. "What the hell were you thinking?"

"You said no Ella in the aerial. I followed your orders. She never went up. Sorry"—she brushed past him—"I have to get ready for the cooking segment." She hurried toward the kitchen, where the intern was setting pans on the stove and Ella peered at the glass front of the oven to fix her hair. Brody stalked after her.

"Do you have any idea how dangerous that was?"

"Nothing happened, did it?" She fussed with the pans. There wasn't really anything for her to do—things were on autopilot at this point—but Brody didn't have to know that. "Besides, how'd you know it was me?"

"You were right there on the tape."

Why did he have to be so freakishly observant?

"You were goddamn lucky." He turned her by the shoulders to face him.

"No, I'm goddamn smart," she shot back. "I've done much scarier things than that. But I don't take stupid risks."

"Two minutes," yelled the stage manager.

"Do you mind?" Melissa glared at Brody, who still had her by the shoulders.

"We're not through with this."

Melissa shook him off and took her place by the monitor again. Her shoulder still tingled from where he'd touched her. Why did he always have to be so absolutely sure he was right? Okay, in this case, maybe he was. She shouldn't have fudged it like that. But still, did he have to be so . . . fierce about it?

An odd smell brought her back to the present. They'd reached the middle of the deep-fried turkey segment, and something didn't look right. Or smell right.

Smoke poured out of the rented deep fryer that sat on the stove. "Oh shit," muttered Melissa. She'd known that deep fryer would be trouble. That's why she'd made Ella practice the technique.

Ella blinked smoke out of her eyes and smiled brightly, gamely trying to act as though nothing were wrong. "In this case, we seem to be getting a smoked deep-fried turkey. Smoked turkey sandwiches are one of my favorite lunches . . . oh crap!"

A flame leaped into the air.

"Cut!" yelled the stage manager. Ten firefighters jumped to Ella's side, milling around her in a clamor of voices. Melissa, hypnotized, watched the flame leap higher. What if the kitchen caught fire? What if they burned down the fire station?

A stream of liquid from a handheld fire extinguisher shot through the crowd and smothered the deep fryer in white foam. At the same moment, Ella, turning to run, stepped into the path of the chemical blast. The nasty white stuff drenched her chest. She let out a shriek. "Are you crazy?"

Captain Brody, holding the spent fire extinguisher, glowered at Ella and his crew. In a room filled with firefighters, only one had the presence of mind to grab a simple fire extinguisher.

Ella danced around, shaking white foam off her body. "What is this nasty shit? This is disgusting! Get it off me! *Melissa?*"

Melissa pushed her way through the crowd to reach her bedraggled anchorwoman. "Thank God you're okay, Ella! You could have been burned . . . maybe even disfigured!" Ella gasped—Melissa had evoked her worst nightmare. Melissa gestured to the intern. "Take Ella to the bathroom. It's time for an outfit change anyway. This dress wasn't working with the apron."

As the intern helped Ella out of the room, Melissa raised her voice over the din. "Let's have a big hand for Ella Joy, everyone, what a trouper! We'll take a break until further notice. But don't go far. The show will go on."

Melissa made her way toward Brody, who loomed over his crew while they cleaned up the mess. His grim expression made her wince. So far she'd disobeyed his orders and set his kitchen on fire. How much trouble was she in? "Thanks for saving the day. I'm really sorry. I don't know how it happened. The deep fryer worked fine in rehearsal yesterday."

"Goddamn TV news," he growled in response. "I knew this was going to be trouble."

"It was an accident."

"I can't risk any more accidents." He spread his hand across her back and marched her into his office. "Melissa, I have to pull the plug on this thing."

"*What?* You can't do that. We've sold the commercials already."

"The commercials aren't my problem. My problem is how to keep this firehouse in one piece."

"But . . ." She swallowed. Loudon would be furious if the special didn't get shot. He might fire her. Her entire career would disappear in a puff of smoke from a deep fryer.

"Brody, I don't blame you for being upset. We've made a mess of your station. But you're overreacting. One little grease fire is no reason to cancel the whole special."

"My guys were so bedazzled no one remembered to grab a fire extinguisher. I can't have them incapacitated." He headed toward his desk. "I'm going to call the PIO and explain."

"It was a freak accident. They were caught off guard."

"Firefighters aren't supposed to get caught off guard by a fire."

Melissa ran to block his path to his desk. "Brody, please. It wasn't that bad. I mean, it was bad, but not bad enough to cancel the whole thing."

"Maybe not, but what's going to happen next? A freak blow dryer explosion?"

"That's not fair. Nothing's going to happen next."

"You can't guarantee that."

"Nobody can! Isn't that what fighting fires is all about?"

"Come again?" He planted his fists on his hips. At least he wasn't making the phone call yet, the one that would end her career.

Melissa scrambled for words that would make sense to this scowling man. "Fires happen. That's what you guys are for. What would life be like if fires never broke out?"

A hint of something, possibly confusion, crossed his face. "Go on."

"You can't play it safe your whole life. Isn't it better to take chances and deal with the mess afterward?"

Gray-black eyes drilled into hers. Something leaped between them. "Take chances . . . Just what kind of chances are you talking about?"

"I . . . um . . ." All her words deserted her. The breath left her body. She felt behind her for the edge of the desk, just in case she collapsed under the intensity of his gaze.

"Chances like climbing a hundred feet up in the air?"

He let his arms drop and, his eyes never leaving hers, took a deliberate step in her direction. "Do you have any idea how dangerous that aerial is? Do you know how it felt when I saw you up there?"

Spellbound, she shook her head.

"It took ten years off my life. No training. No gear. Never, never do that to me again." The heat in his gaze made her faint.

"I thought . . . you were mad because I went against your orders."

"I am. But mostly the thought of you falling from that—" He broke off. "I can't think about it."

"I'm sorry, Brody," she whispered. "I thought you were just being a jerk when you said no."

"You think I'm just an ass, don't you? What did you say before? Typical male arrogance."

"No, I don't. I mean, I used to, but I swear, Brody, I don't think that anymore." Suddenly all she wanted was to throw herself into his arms. He'd actually been worried about her. Her heart expanded like a happy balloon.

The sound of a blaring alarm punctured the moment.

Melissa snapped out of her Brody-induced trance. "The turkey's on fire again? I thought they put it out—"

Brody held up a hand to silence her.

A clear female voice spoke over the intercom.

"Reported structure fire for Task Force 1, Task Force 2, Engine 5, Engine 7, and Battalion 1. Respond to the reported structure fire at 100 Jacinto Avenue. Incident number 502, Time of alarm 19:05. We're receiving multiple calls and reports of possible victims trapped inside."

"100 Jacinto. That's City Hall," said Melissa, but Brody was already on the run.

"We're not done with this," he snapped, then joined the other firemen racing for their gear.

Chapter Fourteen

All of a sudden, no one cared about the cameras, the lights, or the TV special. Every man and woman in a uniform ran toward the apparatus bay, with Captain Brody leading the way. Melissa heard no yelling, no panic, just an intense surge of activity. Even Stan the dog knew to get out of the way.

"Let's go!" Melissa yelled to Greg, who immediately dragged his camera off the tripod and shouldered it. To the intern, she said, "Go get Ella. As soon as she's ready, bring her to City Hall. We'll take the production truck, tell her to come in her car. We'll go live as soon as we can." She and Greg ran for the truck. Normally the cameraman drove, but she wanted him to shoot the entire event, so she took the wheel while he aimed his camera out the window. As she drove, she called into the station to explain the situation.

"We're on it. Call when you're on the scene," said Blaine, the assistant news director. She knew what would happen back in the newsroom. The assignment editors would scramble to gather details on the fire. The chopper pilot would be paged. The studio crew would run to their posts. A backup anchor would throw on some powder. Ella would be the field reporter, and someone else, probably Jeff Jensen, would broadcast from the studio. Every nerve in Melissa's body thrummed with adrenaline. She loved investigations, but breaking news stories were always such a rush—as long as no one was hurt.

As they drew closer to City Hall, she saw a glowing light on the horizon. *My God, the fire must be huge.*

"Jesus," Greg muttered. When they rounded the last corner of Jacinto Avenue, they finally saw the full extent of the disaster. The graceful old mission-style building that had been San Gabriel's City Hall for the last hundred years was engulfed in voracious, leaping flames. She heard their roar and felt their hot wind on her face. The smell of smoke made her throat prickle.

They pulled up a short distance from the fire engines and Greg immediately raised the mast on the production truck. Good thing there were no line-of-sight issues from City Hall. In the meantime, Melissa dashed out of the truck. The firefighters blasted heavy streams of water at the flames, and she saw the aerial ladder being moved into position. She headed for some bewildered bystanders—they looked like office workers—who stood transfixed by the incredible blaze.

"Hi, I'm Melissa McGuire from Channel Six. Were any of you inside City Hall when the fire started?" It turned out they all were. They'd been working late on a new budget plan when one of them smelled smoke.

"We think it was from a toaster oven. It has this old extension cord . . ."

"We were just making tuna melts. How could tuna melts do this?"

"A spark is a spark, moron. I told you not to mess with that thing."

"Was anyone else in the building?" intervened Melissa, furiously taking notes.

"We don't know. We called 911 and got the hell out."

"So someone else might be inside?"

"Like we told that captain, maybe the cleaning crew. They come at night. I don't remember seeing them though."

"I saw them. No, maybe that was yesterday. Holy shit, look at that!"

They all turned. A giant fountain of sparks shot up into the night air. It looked like an exploding volcano, or a geyser of liquid sun. It lit up the entire area, including a man on top of the roof with a fire axe.

Somehow she knew instantly the man was Brody. With an air of complete mastery, calm and steady, he faced the fire. He seemed to be communicating with it, willing it toward its inevitable submission. He hacked at the roof, releasing a billow of smoke into the night air.

Enraptured, Melissa watched him until she remembered she had a job to do. She ran back to the truck. The mast was up, and Greg had shouldered his camera.

"We have to go live, now!" shouted Melissa. Blinking smoke from his teary eyes, he nodded. He gestured for her to stand in front of the flames, and tossed her a mic.

"Studio crew isn't ready yet. Jeff Jensen went jogging."

"Where's Ella?"

Greg shrugged, and focused the camera on her. "It's gotta be you. Let's go."

Melissa stood rooted to the ground. Ella would kill her if she went on the air first. But what choice did she have?

"I'll do a quick intro, then go right to the flames. Show as little of me as possible." Melissa switched on the mic. Greg nodded, and after listening to the studio countdown through his earpiece, gave her the we're-live gesture.

"We're here outside San Gabriel City Hall, where nearly twenty fire companies are battling a huge, fast-burning fire that has so far destroyed nearly half the building. Firefighters got the call at approximately seven o'clock tonight, when the fire was already well involved. I spoke to several City Hall employees who were inside when they first smelled smoke. So far no definitive cause of the fire has been determined . . ."

Melissa trailed off as shouts rose from the side entrance of City Hall. "We're going to show you the scene here for a moment, as firefighters struggle to get a handle on this devastating blaze." She motioned for Greg to keep shooting the fire, while she ran to the side entrance.

A woman covered with soot was crawling out the door on her hands and knees. Part of her blouse had been burned off. Two firefighters ran to help her, but she shook them off. She pointed back into the building. *"Mi hermano! Está adentro!* Inside. My brother. Please, please!" The firefighters looked at each other. Even though she couldn't see who they were, Melissa could imagine what they were thinking. No one in their right mind would go inside that building at this point.

"Por favor! Por favor!" screamed the woman in a shaky, smoke-roughened voice.

An ominous crash made them all jump.

"Emergency Traffic! Emergency Traffic! We have a partial collapse on the Bravo side of the building."

Melissa heard the urgent call on someone's radio.

"Everyone out, now." That must be the battalion chief.

"We're pulling out, but we've got a man still inside, Firefighter Blake. Think he spotted someone."

"Damn it!"

"I'll go after him." Melissa recognized Brody's voice. She looked up at the roof in time to see Brody disappear inside the burning building.

"Stop him!" she screamed as the firefighters around her scattered. No one paid attention.

"No," she shouted. "No!" She could barely hear her own voice over the roar of the fire and the blast of the water from the hoses. She looked around frantically. The battle against the flames went on as though nothing out of the ordinary had happened.

Shouldn't someone do something? Get Brody and Ryan out?

She saw Fred dash toward an ambulance and she ran to intercept him. Surely Fred would explain things to her. But he brushed her off as if she were a pesky mosquito.

"Fire department coming through! Get back! Out of the way!" He ran past her with a pile of blankets, a large first aid kit, and an oxygen tank. He stationed himself as close to the entrance as he could get and peered into the leaping flames. Melissa wrung her hands together. Fred was a trained paramedic as well as a firefighter. He would know what to do.

An ominous rumbling caught her ear.

"Melissa!" Greg called. She ran back toward the truck. He gestured at the east wing of the building, which seemed to be slowly warping from the white heat of the fire. No, not warping, she realized, as her brain caught up with her eyes. It was collapsing in on itself. The rumble grew louder, and she clapped her hands over her ears. A huge crash sent clouds of hot dust billowing toward them. Greg staggered, but kept the camera rolling. Melissa covered her head and squeezed her eyes shut until the assault of dust and debris had faded.

When she opened her eyes Greg tossed the mic to her, with the order to go live again. In the next moment she faced the camera again, giving the viewers a brief, poignant summary of what had just happened. She knew the east wing well; it was where San Gabriel's wedding licenses were issued, where Ask the Mayor sessions were held. A part of San Gabriel's history had collapsed. She recounted the details in a calm, informational tone, in a voice raw from smoke.

She said nothing about the other drama taking place. A reckless firefighter was trying to rescue a trapped man, and his obstinate captain had gone inside the building to pull him out. She'd seen it with her own eyes. She could report it right now, leaving out their names until loved ones could be notified. But at the back of her mind, she could still hear Brody's words on that first date. *You stick microphones in people's faces at their worst moments . . . you get that camera nice and close so you can catch every moment.* So she said nothing.

As soon as she'd finished her report and Greg gave her the off-the-air signal, she dropped the mic. "Where the hell is Ella?"

"I don't know, but you're doing great."

"She'd better get here quick. I'm not going on again."

"You might have to. Jeff's still getting dressed." But they were spared an argument by the screeching arrival of a BMW. Ella burst out and ran to meet them. She had changed into another outfit for the Thanksgiving special, a form-fitting burgundy velvet catsuit, completely inappropriate for the current situation. Melissa grabbed a Channel Six jacket from the truck and threw it to Ella while she relayed everything she knew about the fire.

She left out the fact that Ryan and Brody were inside that fiery deathtrap.

Greg handed Melissa a cell phone, and she had a quick conversation with Blaine. He wanted to go live again right away.

"All set?" Melissa asked Ella. The anchor nodded. She looked like a deer caught in the headlights, but Melissa knew she'd be fine. Despite her silliness, Ella was quick on her feet in a live situation.

As soon as Ella was ready to go live, Melissa ran to the side door. She found Fred there, hopping from foot to foot.

"You haven't seen them?" He shook his head, too worried to remember that she shouldn't be there. "We have to do something!"

"They'll be okay," he answered, as if trying to convince himself. His eyes, straining for any sign of movement, didn't shift from the doorway. Beyond it, an incandescent inferno raged, an orgy of orange and red. An occasional rat-a-tat of sparks burst out at them like fireworks gone astray. Melissa had never been this close to a working fire before, and its sheer primal energy overwhelmed her. If only she could forget that Brody, Ryan, and a stranger were inside, she might simply stand in awe at its magnificent, mindless fury. But she couldn't forget, and she stared at the doorway as if by willpower alone she could make them appear. From Fred's tense posture beside her, she knew he felt the same. She felt a sudden deep kinship with him.

A sudden burst of flames made them both jump back. What looked like a ball of fire blew open the door. And then—there was no door. She squinted through the almost unbearable light at the empty space filled with flame and splintered wood. *No more door.* How could they get out? How would they know where to go? Despair sickened her. She bent toward the ground, thinking she was about to vomit. But instead, she forced herself to stand up again. They still had a chance. They had to. Black smoke poured out of the gaping hole where the door had been, and she had to squint to make anything out. *Please, please, please*, she found herself chanting. *Please, please.*

A dark shape finally stumbled out of the thick fiery cloud. At first she thought she'd imagined it. But she couldn't have conjured up this strange shape, almost like a deformed monster. As it limped closer, the shape dissolved into identifiable forms. One man carried another over his shoulder, helped by a third man. They weren't walking so much as falling, one step at a time, hoping their feet would hold them just a few more yards.

As they reached the edge of the building, they stopped. Fred yelled at them to keep coming. Melissa opened her mouth too, but she never knew if anything came out. All she heard was the rush of the hot wind and the roaring, mocking flames. Maybe the firemen heard, because their next step was stronger, and the next. Then they reached their limit. Lurching forward, they fell to the ground in a heap. Fred ran forward, with Melissa following. Fred reached first for the man on top of the heap. It must be the janitor, unconscious. Melissa could see patches of horribly charred flesh through his tattered work clothes.

Together, they lifted him and carried him to the edge of the grass where Fred had laid down some blankets. He yelled into his helmet mic, "Two firemen and one civilian injured, need an RA!" Melissa heard sirens getting closer, and then a rescue ambulance slammed to a stop next to them and

paramedics poured out. She and Fred dashed back
to the fallen firemen. Both were coughing as they
struggled to get on their feet. Fred went to Ryan to
help him up, and Melissa ran to Brody. He didn't
seem to be aware of who she was as he clutched at
her. It took all her strength not to collapse under
his weight, which seemed twice as heavy with the
tank on his back. But she dug in her heels, and after
a few moments he stood upright next to her. He
tore off his helmet and face piece, hacking and gag-
ging. She put her arms around his chest and made
him lean his weight on her. When he resisted, she
yelled at him.

"Lean on me! Damn it, Brody!" He stiffened—
maybe he had just then realized who she was—but
then relaxed against her. In this way, half stum-
bling, half lurching, they made their way to the
treatment area that the paramedics had managed
to set up in an astonishingly short time. Paramedics buzzed around Ryan, taking his blood pressure and administering an oxygen mask. Several
more paramedics ran toward Brody and whisked
him away from her. Melissa looked around for the
unconscious janitor, but couldn't find him. Maybe
he'd already been taken to the hospital; she hoped
so. She shivered at the memory of that charred
flesh.

The next long period passed in a blur. At some
point she spotted Ella interviewing a paramedic,
and it occurred to her that she'd just participated
in a major news story. Not reported—participated.
But it didn't feel like a news story to her. It felt personal, and she didn't want it on the *Eleven O'Clock
News*. What she wanted was to stay with Brody,

to hover over him, hear his voice, look into his eyes, and know he was okay. But Greg needed her, Loudon kept calling, and the thousand demands of a breaking news emergency took over.

Slowly, over hours, the City Hall fire burned itself out. The firefighters, with a heroic effort, managed to keep the nearby buildings from catching fire. The Channel Six news team stayed on the scene until after midnight. Then Ella signed off and the news crew packed up their equipment. Through an exhausted haze, Melissa heard her coworkers congratulate one another. "We beat the crap out of Channel Two . . . did you see that shot I got of that freaking explosion? . . . Ella, you rocked, babe!" And so on. Too tired to say a word, Melissa sank down onto the ground to put her head between her knees. She closed her eyes, feeling them sting in the welcome darkness.

"Melissa! Come on, let's go." She heard Greg, but made no move to respond. She heard another voice say something, then Greg said, "All right, man," and then came the sound of car doors slamming. Dimly, she knew she ought to get up before everyone left without her.

A hand appeared in front of her face, and she grabbed on to it. Pulling herself up, she staggered, and strong arms caught her. She lifted her head and saw charcoal-gray eyes burning into hers. Though bloodshot and watery, their tender expression made her smile through her exhaustion.

"You're coming with me," Brody stated. She didn't argue. A swarm of questions came to her. How was he? Had he suffered any injuries? Why was he now wearing his regular clothes? How had his truck gotten here? But she said nothing as he put his arm around her and led her to his truck. As if in a dream, she got in, and they drove away from the still-smoldering City Hall. They drove across town, through streets oddly calm and silvered with moonlight. The rest of San Gabriel, free of fire, seemed so fresh and innocent.

Brody parked next to his silver Airstream and led Melissa inside. He made her drink a huge glass of water. It felt like heaven on her raw throat. She looked down at herself. Her clothes were black with soot. When she touched a hand to her face, it came away covered with grime. She pulled a disgusted face, which made Brody chuckle. He beckoned to her, and she followed him into the Airstream's tiny bathroom. It was barely big enough for the two of them. They pressed up against each other, two dirty, smoky, exhausted bodies.

For reasons having nothing to do with the smoke she'd inhaled, Melissa suddenly couldn't breathe.

With an intent look, Brody pulled her shirt up over her arms. He tossed it aside, then unbuttoned her black jeans. She stood in front of him in her underwear. She couldn't have spoken if a gun had been at her head. Frowning slightly, Brody unhooked her bra, then pulled down her panties. He lifted her arm, and showed her a long scratch down it.

"Oh!" she said, startled. Her voice sounded like a stranger's.

"Save your voice," Brody said in a croak.

He turned the shower on, tested the temperature, then guided her under the stream of warm water. She sobbed in gratitude as her tired, aching muscles reacted. Tilting her head back, she closed her eyes and let the water flow through her hair. She lost herself in a kind of primitive pleasure, intensified by the feeling of gentle hands massaging shampoo into her hair. Her groan of delight mingled with the sound of water hitting the shower walls. The lavender scent of the shampoo soothed her frayed nerves. Their mutual silence, after all the verbal sparring, felt like a blessing.

Opening her eyes a slit, through the steam she saw Brody standing naked outside the shower stall, leaning in so he could wash her hair. Maybe he didn't want to crowd her. Maybe he needed an invitation. She reached out a hand and pulled him gently into the shower.

Now they stood skin to naked skin. She felt the hot press of his erection rise against her thigh and twitched her hip to get closer. His breath came faster, tickling her ear, and his touch turned more urgent. His hands left her head and smoothed the curve of her back down to her buttocks.

"Wait," he whispered. One hand left her for a moment, then returned with a bar of soap. He slip-slided it over her body as she shivered with delight. Across her nipples, along the slope of her shoulders, the line of her throat. With one hand he held her hips steady while he rubbed the soap between her legs. She squirmed as the soap's smooth hardness probed her inner folds, pressing against the growing core of her excitement. Her legs parted helplessly. Then he turned her around to smooth the soap along her inner thighs, down her calves. He lifted her feet, one by one, and carefully lathered them. She leaned against the shower wall, bracing herself with her hands, as the pleasure coursed through her.

Then the soap was gone. She felt as though she'd shed a layer of outer skin, of unnecessary shyness. Warm fingers cupped her sex. She heard herself gasp into the steamy air. Then another warm hand came around to her front, dancing up her body to gather her breasts, to pluck at her nipples. Such a hand—so strong, so knowing—and big enough to squeeze both breasts together, one long finger on one nipple, a thumb on the other. She twisted in pleasure, but she couldn't move far because Brody's hard, hot body was pressed into her. He pushed one finger inside her, then another, and she eagerly pressed her backside against his erection. "God, you're incredible," he murmured in her ear. "I've been wanting this for so long."

Incapable of speech, she answered with a thrust of her hips that made him groan. She changed the angle of her body so his thumb could brush over her excited, begging clitoris. Her whole body jerked from the electric sensation. This was a bad idea, they shouldn't do this, not yet . . . Another stroke of his thumb, and all her doubts vanished. It felt so good to be in his arms, surrounded by his strength.

He held her so tightly there was nowhere for her to go. With a long moan, she submitted to that relentless, stroking thumb. His other hand molded her breasts, pulling at her nipples until she screamed into the shower wall and her body gave in to a racking, ecstatic orgasm.

After, she could have melted to the floor. But instead she turned, and met Brody's seeking lips with her own. Under the stream of water, they shared a luxuriously sensuous kiss. Melissa got hold of the soap, and now it was her turn to wash his body. This she did slowly, carefully, missing not one streak of grime or bloody scratch. His magnificent, powerful body had been through the wringer that night, and she couldn't believe he could be sexually aroused after all that. But the evidence stared her in the face as she knelt to soap his legs. She cradled his iron erection between her neck and shoulder, then moved it from side to side so she could thoroughly soap him.

When she looked up, she saw him watching her with a look of such desire her breath caught in her throat. She wanted to take him in her mouth, but somehow she knew that wasn't what he wanted at that moment. He wanted to be in her body, in her living heat, and that's where she wanted him. Gently, caressingly, she rinsed him off, taking one moment to tenderly lick the purpling tip before turning off the water.

"Do you have a bed in this tin can?" she whispered. The desire in his eyes flamed into urgent lust, and he picked her up, carried her out of the bathroom, and tossed her on the bed. Eyes heavy with excitement, legs sprawled apart, she stared up at his naked, dripping form. He stood with legs apart, erection jutting forward, charcoal eyes eating up her body.

"I can't go slow. I have to have you now," he said in a peremptory tone.

"If you go slow, I'll punch you in the stomach."

With a bark of laughter, he quickly pulled on a condom. Then, his face lit with fierce lust, he dove on top of her. She met him with equal fervor, and they joined together in a sweaty, clutching, craving tangle of flesh. He drove inside her, hammering hard . . . pumping until she moaned . . . then they rolled so she was on top, his firm hands bouncing her up and down on his arousal . . . his thumb rubbing her until she felt the waves start to come. She screamed out loud as they washed over her with electrifying brightness. His guttural shout mingled with hers as he thrust into her one final time. They flew together, clutching each other tight, on a magic carpet ride through bursting stars and exploding volcanoes. When the last wave had passed, they held each other tight as though they'd just survived a perfect storm.

Chapter Fifteen

"Holy mackerel," Melissa said, when she could speak.

"Yep," agreed Brody. They lay still, panting, for another moment, then Brody rolled off her and sat up. Melissa ate him up with her eyes. His body was bruised and battered, his eyes bloodshot. He looked sore and exhausted. And satisfied. The thought inspired a small, feminine smile. Satisfied, yes . . . so was she. She'd never felt like this in her life. That thought terrified her.

"I guess it's true what they say about extreme circumstances," she said, pulling the sheet up over her.

"How do you mean?"

"You know, about sex under extreme circumstances. It's the only explanation."

"Explanation for what?" He sounded irritated. "Here, drink some more water if we're going to talk."

He handed her a glass. She drained it, appreciating the coolness on her throat.

"We don't have to talk. It's obvious what just happened. We got carried away. We already know we're not compatible." There. It had to be said. So why did her words sound so wrong?

Brody grunted and rolled out of the bed. He grabbed the glass and walked to the kitchenette. Riveted by the sight of the muscles in his naked rear, her throat went dry all over again.

At the sink, he drank for a long time, then refilled the glass and brought it back to Melissa. "Drink," he told her.

Bossy man. Then again, she didn't mind the way he took charge in bed. Color flooded her face. Time for a subject change.

"Brody, what happened in there? How'd you find Hoagie?"

He leaned against a dresser. "Stroke of luck. I was about to turn back when I heard someone yell. It was Hoagie, trying to get that janitor to wake up. Never did, far as I know." Brody's face darkened. "Did you hear how he's doing?"

"Last I heard, he was still in critical condition. Do you think he'll be okay?"

"I don't know. He looked pretty bad. A beam had fallen on his leg, and he couldn't move. His clothes were on fire when we found him. He was already passed out from the smoke. Or plain terror."

"My God." She shivered. "I thought you weren't coming out. You and Ryan. It seemed like you were in there forever."

"If that poor man survives, it's thanks to Ryan."

"If Ryan survives, it's thanks to you."

Brody shrugged. "We were both extremely stupid."

"Probably. But could you have lived with yourself if you didn't go in after him?"

A long silence. "You can't save everyone."

Melissa finished her glass of water. Her throat already felt better. "The firemen say you've never lost anyone in a fire."

"I haven't."

"How is that possible?"

"Maybe I've made a deal with the devil."

She frowned at him skeptically. With that poker face of his, she couldn't tell if he was teasing. "What'd you have to give up, your firstborn child?"

Brody's face slammed shut, and he turned his back to her.

What had she said? "Brody . . . I . . . I'm sorry. It was a dumb joke."

He didn't seem to hear. He rummaged through a pile of clothes on the dresser. What the hell had she said wrong? He pulled on a pair of loose sweatpants. Melissa couldn't help admiring the grace and power in every movement he made, even while he was ignoring her.

Was he never going to speak to her again?

As the awkward silence went on, she jumped up to fetch her own clothes from the bathroom. No way was she going to hang around naked while he gave her the silent treatment. She pulled them on as quickly as she could, trying to ignore how filthy and sooty they were.

Brody heard her banging around in the bathroom, and cursed himself. She hadn't meant anything by that silly crack. He'd overreacted, and he knew it. And now she was headed out the door.

Maybe it was best. She'd already said they weren't compatible. Why not just let her go? It would be a hell of a lot easier than trying to explain himself. Running into a burning building looked like a breeze in comparison. And yet—

"Don't go," he said. Melissa paused in mid-exit. "You touched a sore spot."

She turned and crossed her arms over her chest. "Go on."

Brody took a deep breath. Into the burning building. "My wife, Rebecca, lost our baby. And it was my fault."

The shock rippled across her face.

He continued. "I wanted a child, and before we got married, so did Rebecca. But then she decided she wasn't ready for children. We argued . . . negotiated . . . and eventually, I won. She got pregnant. And she hated it."

"Hated it? Why?"

"She worried about losing her figure, losing her freedom, losing sleep. I couldn't understand why those things were important compared to what we were gaining. She got very depressed. She quit her job, and stayed home in bed."

"Pregnancy depression is pretty common. We did a story about it. Therapy can help." Melissa's green eyes shone with concern, which unsettled him.

"I made an appointment with a therapist, but she refused to go," he said. "She was so angry at me. Then she miscarried. Just under three months. No one even knew we were expecting a child."

He fell silent. Melissa frowned. "But . . . how was it your fault?"

"I was the one who wanted the baby. I pushed her into getting pregnant."

"You did nothing wrong. She could have said no."

"Yes. If only . . ." Why was talking about things like this so damn difficult?

"If only what?"

"Things had been different. I hated seeing her like that. I felt so guilty." He met Melissa's soft eyes, and saw no judgment, no condemnation. Just sympathy.

"What happened afterward?"

"She didn't leave her bed for a month. She was too upset to work. And eventually, she left."

That was the short version. In the long version, Brody could never make Rebecca happy after that. He'd had gone along with her every whim. The new feng shui landscaping. Which then had to be redone to accommodate the above-ground hot tub. Which eventually was moved to make room for a trampoline. While Brody advanced up the fire department career ladder, Rebecca moved from making handcrafted string purses to designing sequined flip-flops.

Until one day he'd gotten an e-mail from a café in San Diego. She'd run off with Thorval, her surfer-dude flip-flop supplier.

"I was shocked when she asked for a divorce. She was my high school sweetheart, you know. I thought we'd be together forever. But I didn't fight it. I gave her the house, which she sold."

"I'm sorry. If I had known, I never would have made that stupid joke."

Brody smiled ruefully. "Like I said, it's a sore spot. Nothing to do with you. You know, you were right, I actually started to believe in that damn curse. I know I'm a good firefighter. A good captain. Husband and father? Not meant to be."

"Oh." She looked down, biting her lip.

"Melissa . . ."

When she met his eyes, he couldn't remember what he wanted to say. "Please stay. It's too late to go home. Take those smoky, filthy clothes off and let's watch the late news. I want to see how you guys covered the fire."

"It's three in the morning. The news was over hours ago."

But she took the sweats he tossed her and pulled off her top. His groin twitched. God, was he ready to go all over again? Something about her sweetly curved body did something very primal to him. "Don't you know your own schedule? You guys re-broadcast the *Eleven O'Clock News* at three."

Melissa felt his eyes follow her as she pulled on the baggy San Gabriel sweatshirt. She couldn't possibly look very sexy in it, but that didn't seem to stop Brody from leering at her. Not that she minded. "Interesting. I thought you never watched the news." She picked up his remote and turned on his TV. "CNN. You watch CNN?"

"A little CNN, a little C-SPAN. ESPN, when they show the monster truck rallies." Another wink. Melissa noticed those endearing little winks made her stomach give a little jump.

"Are you ever going to forget about that?"

"Maybe, if you come over here and make me." He pulled her down next to him on the couch and nestled her against his side. She relaxed against him with a little sigh. Why was it she felt so good with this man? It wasn't love, or romance, or anything like that. They'd pretty much agreed about that.

"You told me you hated the news," she said.

"It's a love-hate kind of relationship." He switched to Channel Six, and immediately tensed as the first aerial shots of the flaming City Hall filled the screen. "Jesus. You don't always get the whole picture when you're in the thick of it."

"See how quickly we got our chopper up? That's because I called from the firehouse," Melissa pointed out proudly. "Of course, this means another debate about the *Eleven O'Clock News* using the chopper, but never mind that."

"Look at you, Hollywood! Lookin' good."

Melissa cringed at the sight of herself holding the mic and staring intently into the camera. Her report seemed to make sense, and she barely stumbled at all. She counted two "ums," but under the circumstances, who could blame her? Was she overdramatic? Too sensationalistic? Or too matter-of-fact? Her live shot ended, and the camera panned away from her, toward the flames. Brody hugged her to him and gave her a smacking kiss on the top of her head.

"Now that was a good news report. To the point, just the facts, no speculation, no drama. That's the way it's done! Way to go, Hollywood."

Melissa flushed at the praise. "Wait'll you see a real pro in action. I think Ella should be on next."

"Oh, I've seen Ella in action."

Melissa gave him a mock punch on the arm

and peered at the screen. "Is that Vader up on the aerial?" Braced with two legs far apart, like a captain steering a ship, he seemed to be yelling something.

"Yep, the cocky bastard."

"What's he saying?"

"Lord knows. He sings to the fire, sometimes he talks. We tune him out." Now the shot changed, and they saw the woman Melissa had seen crawling out of the building. She was crying and pointing to the side entrance. The camera jogged that direction, and then swerved to suddenly include Ella. The beautiful anchor, breathless and disheveled, leaned into the camera to grab the audience's attention.

"We've just learned that two firefighters are currently inside the building attempting the daring rescue of a maintenance worker. You just saw his sister, who told us what happened. She and her brother were both inside the building when they smelled smoke, but unfortunately they ran in the wrong direction and became trapped. Something fell on top of them and pinned the worker to the floor. His sister tried to pull him out but wasn't strong enough. She managed to make her way out of the building and call for help. One brave fireman who was already inside went to help him, but then a partial collapse trapped him too. One of the captains here on the scene risked his own life to go after him. We are right now waiting for some sign that they are still alive. Please, send all your thoughts and prayers to Firefighter Ryan Blake and Captain Harry Brody as they battle the flames to save an innocent victim's life." A crystal-clear tear ran down her beautiful cheek. The shot stayed on her as she gazed soulfully into the camera.

"Oh my God," moaned Brody. "How could she?"

Melissa stared at the television set in shock. "Oh hell."

She'd screwed up. Badly. She hadn't told Ella about Ryan and Brody, but of course Ella had found out anyway. It was news. It was part of the story. She should have told Ella. If she had, she could have made sure Ella treated the story in a professional way, instead of sensationalizing it. At the very least, she should have told Blaine, and they could have decided what to do with the information. Her first responsibility was to the station, and she hadn't done her job.

On the other hand, she hated seeing Brody's fate a matter of breathless will-he-live-or-die speculation. That's why she'd kept the story to herself. It was the kind of TV news she hated, the kind Brody hated too.

"I am so screwed," she said. "I should have reported it myself, as soon as I knew. I wouldn't have included names, of course, the way she did. I'll be lucky if I don't get fired."

"Fired? For having principles?"

"That's not the way Loudon's going to see it."

"She should be fired. Look at that," he said, disgusted. On the screen, Ella was holding hands with the janitor's sister, their heads bent in prayer. Melissa winced.

"She's expressing what—"

"She's milking it. Me and Hoagie are in there fighting to stay alive, and she's out here playing to the camera. Saint Friggin' Ella Joy. I'm going to call up your news director and tell him he can forget ever getting an interview from me or my guys. And to get all that TV crap out of my station."

"Too late," said Melissa, pointing to the TV. Now the shot showed Ryan, surrounded by paramedics. He lifted up his oxygen mask, and Ella swooped in with the mic.

"Mr. Blake, we've all been praying you'd make it out of there alive, and our prayers were answered. Can you tell us what you were feeling inside that fiery inferno?"

"Fiery inferno?" Brody brandished a fist at the TV set.

But Ryan didn't seem to mind the clichéd language. He gave Ella a watery smile. "Hi there, Ella. Aren't you a sight for sore eyes? I just thank the Lord I was able to find the victim and get to him in time. I didn't worry about myself, because I knew my captain would get me out, and that's just what he did. He's the man. Where's the captain? Is Brody okay?" He sat up halfway to scan the area, then laughed, a coughing, wheezing sound, and pointed. The camera followed his hand. Brody was already back at work, directing the firefighters to another flank of the fire.

Melissa glanced over at the night's hero. He lowered his head to his hands. "Another chapter in the legend of Captain Brody."

"Exactly."

"Does that bother you?"

"Don't want to talk about it."

He fell silent, and after a little while Melissa got to her feet.

"I'd better get back."

He shook himself off and rose to stand next to her. Leaning in, his mouth hovering over hers, he asked, "Do you want to come by tomorrow?"

Bad idea, she knew. If she saw him again, it wouldn't be the same—no extreme circumstances to get them both revved up. They'd probably both be disappointed. They should leave things as they were, a hot one-night encounter between two people completely unsuited to each other.

And yet—she nodded. "See you tomorrow."

The next day, as she expected, Melissa walked in to her office to find a Post-it on her computer ordering her to report immediately to Loudon's office.

"Trouble?" said Chang, popping his head into her cubicle.

"Hey, sorry you missed the biggest story of the year. How's your budget series coming?" asked Melissa sweetly. Chang clutched his stomach as though a knife had been plunged into it, and withdrew his head. Melissa took a deep breath. Why did TV stations have to be so gossipy—they were worse than firehouses. Head held high, she made her way to Loudon's office. On her way, she passed Ella's domain. Huge bouquets of flowers crowded her desk. Ella had seized her moment, no doubt about it. No surprise there. Ella had never bothered to hide her ambition.

In Loudon's dim office, the news director blinked up at her and gave a weary sigh. "Why do you do this to me, Melissa? With you, it's always the bad with the good. I'm starting to wonder if LA was right to let you go."

Melissa marshaled her arguments. "Loudon, be

fair. I was first on the scene. I got us there. I got us the story."

"You got us part of the story."

"The biggest part."

"Our viewers disagree."

Melissa swallowed hard. "I did what I thought was right at the time."

"You knew about those firefighters who went inside City Hall."

She nodded.

"Why didn't you tell the assignment desk?"

"I was busy. No, scratch that." If she was going to get yelled at, she might as well tell the real story. "I didn't think about it as a news story. I knew the guys who had gone into the fire, and I was worried about them."

"Do you have some sort of emotional attachment interfering with your news judgment?" Loudon peered at her with watery eyes.

"What? That's ridiculous."

"The guys tell me you left City Hall with the captain."

Oh, for Pete's sake. Was there absolutely no privacy around here? "Look, Loudon, I got us to the scene of that fire before anyone else, we kicked ass on it, I kept it going until Ella got there. I even went on the air and didn't do half bad either."

"Not at all. Too bad Ella'd have a fit if we put you on the air."

Melissa let that one pass. She didn't want to be on the air anyway. "Meanwhile, Ella goes live and actually says their names. What if they hadn't made it out? That's a horrible way for their families to find out."

"Melissa, why are you trying to interfere with my lecture? You know I have to give you one."

She glanced at him sharply, finally detecting a glint of humor in his watery gaze. "If you want to lecture me, go ahead."

"Since when did you get so feisty?"

Since she'd seen Captain Brody in action.

"Meh, forget it. You know what I'm going to say, so I won't waste our time. But I can't give you that promotion. I have to question your news judgment. And I'm going to put you on unpaid suspension for the next few days. I'm sorry. Come back after Thanksgiving weekend."

Suspension. Hot outrage swept through her. It was completely unfair. She'd done a damn good job on the live shot, and he ought to reprimand Ella, not her. But she choked the words back. Who was she, a kid from Fern Acres, to talk back to a news director? Hadn't she learned her lesson from Everett back in Los Angeles?

Besides, she'd do the same thing again. Images from last night flickered through her mind—the janitor's burned flesh, Brody's bloodshot eyes, the weight of him against her shoulder. She'd helped Brody get away from the flames. What was a promotion compared to that?

"I understand. I'll try to do better."

At the door, she turned back. "By the way, what about the special? We never finished taping it."

Loudon rubbed his bleary eyes. "The captain canceled it. I already notified the advertisers."

"Really? What did he say? Why did he cancel?" Melissa's pulse raced. What if Brody had mentioned the grease fire and the unauthorized aerial trip? He wouldn't do that, would he?

No, if he'd done that, she'd probably be fired already.

"He was upset about our coverage, about the approach Ella took," admitted Loudon.

Relief made her knees wobble. She quickly turned her face so he wouldn't see the I-told-you-so written all over it.

"I almost forgot the kicker. Captain Brody gave his permission for us to run a story on the Bachelor Firemen. I guess he felt bad about canceling after all that hard work. Good guy."

"Yes," she said in a strangled voice, before escaping to her cubicle. Back at her desk, her voice mail light blinked at her.

One message awaited her, left by Ella Joy at two-twenty in the morning. The venom in her voice nearly melted the phone. "How dare you, Melissa. You left me at that stupid fire station so you could get your face on TV. You've always been jealous of me, haven't you? If you think you can pull an *All About Eve* on me, you'd better think twice. How could you do this to me? I thought we were friends."

Melissa dropped her head to her hands. Being on Ella Joy's hit list might be worse than getting suspended. She checked her cell phone. It had been off since she'd gone to Brody's, and there were three messages, all from Ella.

She was so damn tired of dancing around Ella's ego. Normally, she would call Ella right away and explain she had no choice but to go on the air. Tell her she'd only done it under orders from the assistant news director. Remind her she'd handed off the mic as soon as Ella had arrived on the scene. Apologize for the crime of stealing airtime.

Screw that. Would Captain Brody apologize for trying to put out a fire? No way. Why should she apologize for doing her job? Besides, she was on suspension.

Suspension. The shame of it swept through her again. Suddenly all she wanted to do was see Brody.

It was Brody's day off, but he felt the heroic efforts of his crew deserved something special. Around midday he strolled into the station and spent a couple hours talking to his guys. He apologized for the canceled Thanksgiving special and made sure everyone got a personal word of thanks about the role they'd played in fighting the fire.

"Vader, I've never seen anyone work the aerial like you. From now on, I'm sending you up there, these bones are getting too old for that shit." He clapped Vader on the back and enjoyed his shy grin of pleasure. "Double D, nice job. I didn't worry the whole time I was in there chasing after Hoagie. I knew you'd keep it under control . . . Hoagie, glad to see you alive. Come see me in the captain's office. If Captain Kelly doesn't mind."

Captain Kelly obligingly went to refill his coffee mug, and Ryan followed Brody into the captain's office.

Brody dreaded this conversation. Ryan was a notorious hothead, and Brody had to lecture him about going after the janitor. But since he probably would have done exactly the same thing, a scolding felt hypocritical. In the end, he said simply, "You know better. Never veer off alone. Ever. We both could have died in there."

"I know, Cap. But, you know—"

"I ought to put you on suspension."

Ryan went white.

"Tell me one thing. Were you trying to impress Ella Joy?"

"Captain!" Ryan's jaw dropped in horror.

"Hoagie?"

"No. I—she wasn't even there." He hung his head.

"So you looked for her."

"Yeah. But I didn't go in because of her, I swear, Cap. I forgot all about her by then." His face went red. "And she sure pissed me off afterward, when I saw the TV report."

"Okay. Like I said, I'm glad you're alive. Try to keep it that way. And the next reckless, dumbass move you pull, that's it. Automatic suspension."

"I got it. Thank you, Cap. I'll be good."

After that, he spent a few minutes fending off Hoagie's fervent thanks for saving his life. "Thank me by being more careful."

"I will, Cap, I promise. Well, I'll try."

"All I can ask."

Just before Brody left the station, the San Gabriel Good Samaritan Hospital called. Captain Kelly handed him the phone. Brody listened, and then slowly replaced the receiver.

Despite all efforts to revive him, the janitor, Diego Hernandez, had died.

Chapter Sixteen

Brody stalked out of the firehouse, brushing off the pats and sympathetic murmurs of his crew. For the first time in his firefighting career, he'd lost a life. Images of the man's blistered, blackened body haunted him. He should have gone in faster, found him sooner.

Back in his Airstream, he opened a bottle of Scotch and downed a quick shot. The liquid scorched his mouth and throat. He welcomed the burn. His second shot blurred the pain of the first. He started to pour another shot, but a knock on the door interrupted him.

Damn it. Was Haskell here to start the upstairs? He couldn't let the man find him in the process of getting drunk. He capped the bottle and stuffed it in the cabinet, then downed a glass of water. "Who is it?"

"It's me," came a soft, female voice. *Melissa.* He

didn't want Melissa finding him drunk either, but on the other hand . . . God, he wanted her. Needed her.

He strode to the door and opened it. He didn't even give her a chance to say hello before sweeping her into his arms and whirling her to the bed. "Melissa," he groaned against her soft neck. Her skin smelled so delicious, he wanted to lick it, kiss every sleek curve of her body.

He tossed her on the bed, feeling like a pirate claiming his prize. She gazed up at him with wide green eyes. "Brody, are you okay?"

"I don't want to talk. I just want to be with you." *Touch you. Bury myself inside you. Forget everything else but you.* He ripped off his shirt and unzipped his pants. He was already hard, just from the scent of her skin, and the sight of her stretched across his bed. She had on a sleeveless blouse with about a billion buttons. Could he rip them off? Would that upset her? Was she already upset by his manhandling?

When her hands went to her top button, he let out a breath of relief. "Here. I'll do it." He straddled her, one bent knee on either side of her hips. He saw her eyes flick to his raging erection. Hands shaking, he attacked her buttons one by one. As her creamy flesh was exposed, a kind of madness came over him. He bent his head to her soft breasts, devouring her nipples with greedy strokes of his tongue. She tasted like heaven, like forgiveness, like every good thing in the universe. She moaned and twisted under him. God, she was beautiful.

He had to get inside her or he'd lose his mind. His hands went to her pants, but he was too crazed and fumbled at the zipper. Melissa pushed his hands away and unfastened them herself. As soon as the enticing dark curls between her thighs appeared, he yanked her hips to his mouth and dove into the sweet wetness.

She was ready for him. Already. He lapped at her slick folds. Circled the hot, hidden kernel at the heart of them. He gripped her thighs, which quivered under his touch. Her little cries and frantic movements drove him on. He loved seeing her like this, giving in to her need, surrendering to him. The intensity of his desire for her shocked him. He'd never felt this way, not even . . . His thoughts scattered as he felt her orgasm pulse through her. She thrashed against the bed, pushed against his mouth, and he couldn't stand it anymore.

He fumbled for a condom, then plunged into her body, still vibrating from her climax. Oh yes, sweet oblivion. Blissful release. He could live forever like this, ravaging her flesh, losing himself inside her, tasting her sweet nipples, stroking her skin until it shivered.

But forever would have to wait. Two strokes, and he came like a rocket. On and on it went, his body rigid with ecstasy, his mind emptied of everything but pleasure.

When the last spasm had been wrung from him, he sprawled on top of Melissa's trembling, damp body.

Holy fucking crap. As he surfaced, those were the only words that came to mind. Melissa tapped her fingers across his back. "Um . . . yeah, as I was about to say when I knocked, hello, and how was your day?"

Brody groaned and rolled off her. "Sorry."

"Don't be. I loved it. I'm just glad it wasn't the Avon lady at your door."

"I sure hope you're joking. I wouldn't attack just anyone like that." He forced a laugh. Had he made a fool of himself? Shown his need too clearly?

"I was joking. But seriously, what happened? You seem different. Upset. You're usually so calm." She brushed her tumbled hair away from her face.

"Melissa," he tucked a strand behind her ear, "I don't think I've had a minute of calm since I met you."

Color swept across her cheeks. He loved seeing that flicker of pleasure in her expressive eyes.

"The janitor died. From the City Hall fire. I'm surprised you don't know."

"I got suspended."

"What?"

"It doesn't matter. I decided to use the time to work on an investigation."

He laughed. "You are one of a kind. You're going to work while you're on suspension?"

She lifted herself on her elbow and tangled a finger in the damp hair on his chest. "I'm sorry about the janitor."

"Yeah. Turns out I can't save everyone."

"Are you okay?" The worry in her eyes gave him a funny feeling. Hernandez's death had thrown him for a loop, but he didn't want her thinking he couldn't handle it. He was Captain Brody. He could handle anything.

"I'm fine. Maybe this will teach my guys a lesson and they'll stop diving into fully involved fires, assuming I'll save their stupid asses."

"But you probably will," she pointed out, dancing her fingers down to his navel. "You can't help it."

"I will if I can. But now they know I'm not Superman."

"Oh really?" Melissa murmured wickedly. "I might have something to say about that." She lowered her hand to his already hardening erection.

"Maybe I am, when it comes to you," he said with a groan and pulled her on top of him.

Much later, when they'd sufficiently slaked their thirst for each other, something occurred to Brody. Maybe the curse—invulnerable firefighter with a crappy personal life—was over. Maybe things had changed. Maybe he deserved someone. Maybe he deserved Melissa.

But next time, he'd take his time and show her how much he appreciated her.

When Melissa knocked on the door of the trailer the next evening, she was greeted by the sight of Brody in an apron, thrusting a huge bouquet of wildflowers at her.

"Wow, for me?" she said, a thrill rippling through her. Just seeing him, his storm-gray eyes smiling into hers, made her shiver. On top of that— flowers.

"For the Avon lady, but you got here first."

"Trying to make me jealous, Captain?"

"Sure. I want you to try to win me back from that man-stealing Avon lady."

"I can try," she said dubiously. "But they make some really good products. How's this?" She leaned in and took his bottom lip between her teeth. "If you ever"—she nibbled his lip—"mess

with her again"—she sucked on his tongue—"I'll
have to get seriously"—her tongue flicked inside
his mouth—"disgracefully"—she tugged on his
upper lip—"naughty."

When she drew back, she was more than satisfied with the way his breathing came fast and his
eyes darkened. "Put that bouquet down," he muttered. "It's in my way."

She tossed it onto the TV and went into his arms.
Being held by him felt so right, so perfectly magical, it nearly brought tears to her eyes. His warm
body against hers felt like home. All her worries
about work, about Ella, vanished as if they'd never
existed. The only thing that mattered was the solid
heat of him against her. She ran her hands down to
his backside and giggled as she felt the strings of
the apron.

"You've been cooking?"

"Yes, but I have a better idea now," he said with
an eyebrow-waggling leer.

"Me too." Under the apron he wore baggy
sweatpants, and she deftly pulled them down to
his knees. His underwear went next, and then
there was nothing between his rising erection and
her but his apron, which now stood out in front of
him like a tent. She took a step back and cocked
her head.

"That is surprisingly . . ." Her voice caught.
"Sexy," she finally managed. In response, the apron
rose even higher. "I didn't know a man could look
this good in an apron."

"Martha Stewart's got nothin' on me."

"Do you cook as good as you look?" There was
pleasure in drawing this out, in standing close to

each other, not touching, but enjoying each other with their eyes, their playfulness. Brody kicked his sweatpants off and stood in his bare feet.

"I'm feeling underdressed. Take off your blouse," said Brody. Melissa's throat constricted. Their eyes met for a long moment, and she felt weak from the lust-filled promise in his eyes. Slowly her fingers rose and moved to her top button. Her breath came faster as the buttons fell away. When her blouse lay open, she felt his hot eyes roaming over her skin. "Show me your breasts," he breathed.

Unable to speak, she drew down the material of her bra to expose her breasts. Her body quivered as a slight movement of air passed across her skin. Her nipples tightened and puckered. "So beautiful," he said, eyes dreamy and intense. With both hands, he reached for her nipples and touched them tenderly. For such a gentle touch, it sent a spark of lightning through her. With a gleam in his eye, he cupped both her breasts and lightly rubbed her nipples with his thumbs. Her eyes half closed, she swayed toward him.

"Maybe you should take off that apron," she whispered.

"I bet you say that to all the guys," he joked, with a little tweak of her nipples that made her jump. In revenge, she lifted up his apron and bit her lip at the sight of him, massively aroused. Meeting his eyes, she saw the unmistakable challenge in them. She took hold of his erection, and gently drew him toward her.

"It looks like dinner's ready," she breathed. She untied the strings of his apron and pulled it off him slowly, making a striptease out of it.

"Help yourself," muttered Brody in a choked voice as she knelt before him. He leaned back against the wall of the trailer as she licked, stroked, and teased him into a state of frenzy. Her hands roamed his body, weighing his balls, fingers digging into his backside. Where did this craving for his body come from? She wanted to feel every part of him, touch every part with her fingertips, her tongue, the inside of her mouth. When he started to buck against her, he firmly pushed her head away and fought for control with gritted teeth.

"Get up here," he growled.

She rose to her feet, only to find herself airborne as he lifted her up against his body.

"Put your sweet legs around me," he said intensely. She did so, her skirt pushing up her legs, and felt his iron hardness burn against her thigh. Bending his head down, he undid the front clasp of her bra with his teeth. He immediately engulfed one breast in his mouth, while his hands made their way inside her panties. Her head jerked backward as his mouth clamped onto her nipple and sent pangs of pleasure down to her belly. She felt the scrape of teeth against her and arched her chest toward him, wanting more of this exquisite joy, more, more, as much as he could give. When his mouth left one throbbing nipple and greeted the other one, she moaned aloud.

"Brody, Brody . . ." she heard herself say. "It feels too good, I can't stand it." He chuckled and pressed her against his erection.

"I'm just getting started." He lifted her ass with his powerful hands and sat her on the counter. His hands were all the way inside her panties, his fingers buried deep in her folds. Now he pulled one hand away, and drew the crotch of her panties to one side to expose her flesh.

"Look at you," he said wonderingly. "So wet." Indeed she was. She felt the moisture drip out of her, onto his thumb as it pressed against the small kernel of flesh crying out for his attention.

"Oh please," she gasped, and opened her legs further.

"That's it, my darling. I want to see you open and begging for me. I want to hear you scream when I put myself inside you. I want you wild for me. You'd better hang on tight, honey." Urging her on with his whispers, he brought his proudly erect shaft to the burning entrance of her body. Looking down, Melissa caught her breath. How could he possibly fit that huge, glistening thing inside her? But then he gave a thrust of his hip and impaled her.

Immediately she soared into another world of velvet darkness and fountains of stars. She came right away, with a loud, groaning scream. After a moment of amazement that it had happened so quickly, she felt Brody's strong hands lift her up, then slam her down on his erection. And unbelievably, she felt a new pleasure growing deep inside her. She leaned forward and sank her teeth into the muscle of his neck—not enough to hurt, just enough to make contact with him.

He was so strong. He held her up with one hand spread beneath her ass, while the other massaged her breasts. He felt one breast, then the other. "I love the feel of you," he whispered in her ear. "Your sexy nipple poking against the palm of my hand. Makes me want to . . ." and he demonstrated with a quick thrust of his hips that made her cry out. The sound of her growing pleasure seemed to send him into overdrive, and suddenly the hand on her breast disappeared, and his two hands came under her, manipulating her, moving her up and down like a rag doll as he plunged deep within her. So deep, she almost thought her body would break apart.

But it didn't. Only her mind did, exploding into a thousand pieces of unthinking bliss. Through her own haze of ecstasy, she heard Brody shout her name as huge spasms shook his body. She opened her eyes and saw his head thrown back, his eyes half shut into slits of darkest shining gray. With a last thrust, a last groan, he collapsed limply against the wall of the trailer and let her slide down his body.

On her feet again, she leaned against him and wrapped her arms around him. She rested her cheek against his chest and felt his heart racing against hers. Why had she thought this amazing connection was due to extreme circumstances? Unless wearing an apron counted as an extreme circumstance.

The black hairs on his chest tickled her mouth, and she blew softly against his skin.

"Sweet Melissa," she heard him murmur. Was she really sweet? "Sweet" sounded so dull, so . . . vulnerable. But Brody could call her anything he liked. He could do anything he liked with her. And if that wasn't vulnerable . . . yes, when it came to him, she was definitely vulnerable.

She felt so relaxed around him, so incredibly at ease. It had never been this way with Everett.

Everett had made her feel many things—from giddy excitement to the lowest despair—but she'd never felt comfortable with him. She couldn't joke around with him, she couldn't act silly and goofy. With Brody, she could do all those things, and also discuss something as serious as the janitor's death.

But Brody wasn't her type at all. Right?

Over the next few days, Melissa forgot to worry about "types." She found herself living in a new world, a world in which only two people really mattered, her and Brody. Thanksgiving passed in a blur, without any fireman specials. Other people floated in and out, talking to her about her investigation, or nagging her about the dishes (Nelly). But none of that felt real. The only thing that felt real was Brody's trailer, and the heights of bliss the two of them attained inside that silver nest. They did everything inside that Airstream. For such a small space, they took full advantage of it.

She squeezed herself onto the tiny countertop, and he bent between her spread legs, licking and nibbling until she screamed for relief. Lounging around watching the tiny TV, he fingered her inner folds until the silky moisture soaked his hand. He pulled her up on his lap, so the rough material of his pants rubbed her from below, while he stroked her from above. She shamelessly ground her hips into his strong thigh. With his other hand, he tugged at her nipples until she jerked and cried out her release. Melissa was sure she'd never come during an AT&T commercial before.

One time she knocked on the door and found herself staring at a blindfold Brody held toward her. She nodded her wide-eyed consent, and the next moment she was in total darkness, her other senses wide awake to the feel of Brody's strong hands undressing her, turning her, stroking her. She lost all sense of where she was, even what she was. All she knew was she was lost in a sea of endless sensation, with waves of bliss crashing over her. When she came back to herself and tore off the blindfold, she found she was bent over the arm of the couch, breasts crushed into the cushions, ass high in the air, Brody still buried deep inside her. Nothing seemed too wild anymore, nothing seemed forbidden.

They couldn't keep their hands off each other. But as great as the sex was, they found plenty of time for other things. Inside that trailer, they were able to say everything to each other. She told him about Everett, how he'd destroyed her confidence and sent her fleeing back to the familiar safety of San Gabriel.

"I was such a little idiot, I really thought he loved me. But he was just toying with me."

"Did you love him?"

"I was dazzled, that's all. I'm just a kid from Fern Acres. He's a legend in the news business. I couldn't believe he even noticed me. But he saw me as a naïve little girl, not a woman."

"You, not a woman? Is he blind?" Brody stroked his hands over her curves as they cuddled in their favorite spot on the couch.

She drew his head down and kissed him passionately. Brody's kisses were just the right medicine to chase away the bad Everett memories trying to sneak back into her mind. "Oh, who cares about him? He's screwed up enough of my life. Do you know how hard it was to take such a big step backward?"

"Yes, and I'm kind of glad you did, or else I never would have met you. Maybe I should thank the bastard."

She laughed, and showered his face with kisses.

"Just a wild stab in the dark, but did Everett do something to make you lose confidence in yourself at work?"

She drew away. How had he hit so close to the mark? "What makes you think that?"

"It's always bugged me that someone as smart as you doesn't stand up for yourself."

"You sound like my grandmother."

"Ouch. But you haven't answered my question."

Memories flashed across her mind. Everett's office . . . star reporter Barb Nelson . . . the most humiliating moments of her life . . .

She shuddered. "Can we change the subject? Any more talk about Everett, I'll have to wash off in the shower."

"A fine idea." His leer made her giggle helplessly. And thankfully, he dropped it.

Later, as he was chopping carrots for beef stew, he told her how he had hired Haskell because of his last name.

"That's a little creepy."

"But it paid off. I've spent a lot of time with your dad, wiring the house. He talks about you a lot."

She turned on the faucet to wash the potatoes. "Oh?"

"Can you blame him? You're a superstar, Hollywood."

"Well, no thanks to him."

"Maybe."

"What does that mean?"

"Would you have worked so hard if it weren't for him?"

Melissa brandished the potato peeler at him. "That's ridiculous. You don't know what it's like."

"No? What's it like?" He asked the question almost casually as he tossed the carrots into the stew pot.

"Always feeling like you don't belong, like you have to work ten times as hard, and if anyone finds out the truth about you, you'll be out on your ass."

"Aha."

"What do you mean, aha?"

"So that's why you put up with Ella's crap. And everyone else's."

Oh, he was infuriating, with that annoying calm, that irritating . . . bare chest, those sexy baggy running shorts. His thick hair was ruffled from their latest romp, and his eyes narrowed in concentration as he stirred the stew. Looking at him, she felt all her fury melt away.

"That's so annoying," she said. "Just when I'm about to get mad at you, you do that."

"What?" he said, glancing up absently.

"Look so goddamn gorgeous."

"I'll try not to," he said dryly. "It shouldn't be too hard. Hoagie's the heartbreaker."

"Good," she said, wrapping her arms around him.

"Good?"

She answered in a whisper. "I don't want to get my heart broken again." She closed her eyes tightly against his chest, and felt his hand tangle in her hair. But as she breathed in the warm, spicy scent of his bare skin, she knew her heart was already in major trouble. But she couldn't be in love, could she?

She didn't want to think about love. Sexual ecstasy was one thing—she trusted Brody completely with her body. But she wasn't about to go giving her heart away to any old handsome fireman who came along. No, she couldn't possibly be in love. Just because she thought about Brody a hundred times during the course of the day . . . just because she only felt alive when she walked into that trailer . . . just because she stored up a full day's worth of funny incidents to share with him at night . . . just because she told him all her painful secrets . . . none of that meant she was in love with him.

If anyone thought otherwise, they kept it to themselves. Even Nelly kept her opinions to herself these days. One evening—during one of Brody's shifts—Melissa came home to find the kitchen scented with freshly baked molasses cookies. She stared in disbelief.

"Grans, are you okay?"

"Sure am. Want some cookies?"

"I don't know. What's in them?"

"Rat poison. Really, Melissa, you have the most insulting ideas about me. I used to bake for Leon every Sunday." *And maybe that explained why Leon had been twice as crotchety as Nelly,* thought Melissa as she gingerly bit into a cookie.

"Not bad," she said, surprised.

"I made a few batches. You can take some to Captain Brody."

"Aha! I knew there was a hidden agenda."

"Hidden nothing. It's going pretty well with you two, and I'm pretending not to notice you're doing the deed with no ring on that finger." Nelly gave her a scolding gesture.

Melissa nearly choked on her cookie. "Don't go old-fashioned on me now, Grans. I know you better than that."

"Fine. I just hope you're being safe. Take the cookies."

"I am, and I will, thanks!" She gave Nelly a big kiss and began filling a plastic baggie with cookies.

Nelly watched, filled with a strange premonition. Her mother had made molasses cookies for her when she'd first started walking out with Leon. Leon had proposed soon after. This bit of memory had floated to the surface during a night of relentless pain that kept her from sleeping. Would molasses cookies make Brody propose to her darling Melissa? At the very least, making the cookies had made her feel normal. It proved she could still function at home. That she didn't have to think about a hospice yet.

Something was going to happen soon, she could feel it in her bones. She just didn't know what.

Chapter Seventeen

Ella Joy was in the worst mood of her life. And that was saying something. First, *Thanksgiving with the Firefighters* got canceled. It had gone so well, up until the turkey disaster. She didn't understand why they couldn't finish the taping another day. Loudon had the nerve to blame her. Apparently he'd gotten a call from someone at the fire station—he wouldn't say who—who hadn't liked how she'd handled the City Hall story.

"But they're heroes now, because of me!"

"They're heroes because they ran into a burning building."

"But no one would know about it if it weren't for me!" Ella couldn't believe the injustice and idiocy she had to deal with. Luckily, she and Loudon both knew he feared her, so the unpleasantness hadn't lasted long. But it had completely ruined the pleasure of her triumph, and had caused her to hurl one of her bouquets—the lamest one, nothing but boring daisies—against the wall of her office.

Then there was Ryan, who'd been all over her before the fire, and whom she had single-handedly turned into a hero. In return, he'd knifed her in the back by giving an interview to Channel Two. *Channel Two*. Who were they, compared to Ella Joy? She'd left messages at all his numbers, and gotten no call back. When she'd called the fire station and Fred had answered, he'd spoken rudely. In fact, he'd put the phone down and never come back.

She blamed Melissa for all of it. Melissa had betrayed her, blown the fire story and gotten suspended, and yet people kept talking about what a good job she'd done with the live coverage. They also kept talking about how she'd disappeared with the hot fire captain. On top of that, she had some big investigation cooking, something she hadn't bothered to tell Ella about.

The only bright spot was Melissa's suspension. It provided the perfect opportunity for Ella to kick off her plan.

She strolled into Melissa's cubicle. "Looking for glossies," she announced to the nearby reporters. Luckily, they were all busy with . . . whatever. With her back to the opening, blocking the view from the corridor, she picked up Melissa's phone and dialed the number she'd memorized.

"Yes?" a rich, gravelly voice answered.

Ella did her best to imitate Melissa's husky voice. "Hi Everett. This is Melissa."

"Melissa. I was wondering who was calling from San Gabriel. I've been thinking about you lately."

"Oh really?"

"Imagine my surprise at the sight of your lovely face reporting live from a fire. Didn't I always tell you to give on-camera a shot?"

Ella ground her teeth. She didn't want to hear about that. "I've been thinking about you too. I'm sorry about the way things ended." Her palms went sweaty. She was improvising, which could lead to disaster. Or it could lead to the biggest break of her life.

"That gladdens my heart, my little nectarine."

Nectarine? That would have sounded cheesy, if not for his cultured, sophisticated voice, with that hint of Ivy League in it. "Actually, I was hoping you might be coming to San Gabriel sometime soon. I have an idea for you. A great idea."

A short silence. Ella held her breath. "A Melissa McGuire story might be worth a trip to the Valley. Can you give me a hint?"

"I have to show you. It's too big. Besides, I was . . . hoping to see you."

"I'm intrigued."

Did he sound suspicious? "Well, I was thinking we could try to find some closure." That sounded like something Melissa would say, right? "Do you know when you might come?" It would be better if he came before Melissa's suspension ended.

"How about I surprise you."

"Oh Everett." Ella mimicked Melissa's throaty laugh. She'd always envied that laugh. "You know how my schedule gets. I have so many commitments and I like to be on top of everything."

"Excellent quality in a producer."

Ella made a face at the phone.

"Fine. I'll give you a call when I'm on my way to the station."

"I look forward to it," she purred.

After she hung up, Ella took an extra fifteen minutes to figure out how to forward Melissa's calls to her phone. She couldn't afford to miss that call. It took only one lucky break to launch a career into the big leagues. But she wasn't going to leave it to luck. When Everett Malcolm saw her in person, he'd fall at her feet. He'd beg her to take over the *Six O'Clock News*. He'd put her on billboards on every freeway in Los Angeles. They'd shoot real promos for her, the kind with film crews and catering. She'd get her own makeup artist. She'd buy two houses—one in Beverly Hills, and a little getaway retreat in Malibu.

She chased away her twinge of guilt with a vision of her future entourage.

In the snug Airstream, Melissa lay basking in Brody's arms.

"How come I never call you Harry?" she mused.

"Because I wax my legs?"

"You do?"

"Does it feel like I do?" He rubbed his leg over her naked hip.

"Mmm. Whatever you do, don't change it now, Harry." She heard the deep rumble of laughter in his chest.

"Can I tell you a secret?" He traced a finger along her collarbone.

"Is it deep and dark?"

"As the La Brea Tar Pits."

"Shoot."

"My real last name is Brod. No Y."

"That doesn't seem so deep and dark." His leg moved against her hip in a lazy, unhurried way that lulled her into a dream.

"Put it together."

"Harry . . . Brod. Harry Brod!" She sat straight up. "Your parents named you Harry Brod? Like a hairy broad?"

"Yep. Don't hurt yourself mocking me."

"I'm not . . . It's just . . . Hairy Broad! I'm in bed with a hairy broad!"

"Not for long, if you keep that up," he teased.

"Sorry. Brody. I can see why you changed it."

"Actually, I only changed it for Rebecca. She refused to be married to a Harry Brod."

"That's silly . . . I'd be proud—" She realized where her sentence was headed, and broke off. She'd almost said, *I'd be proud to be married to Harry Brod.*

Married. Did she really see herself married to Brody? She sank back on the bed next to him. Impossible. Married to a fire captain who ran into burning buildings? Married to a man who had never written a short story, never sculpted any ceramic table art? Was she crazy?

On the other hand, she'd be married to a man who made her laugh, who constantly surprised her with his quick mind, who was strong, loyal, revered by his subordinates; a man who rocked her world with his touch. What could be more wonderful? But she didn't love him, did she?

"What are you thinking about?" he asked, lifting her chin with a finger. "You got so quiet all of a sudden."

"Nothing," she said quickly. "Just this investigation I'm working on." But she wouldn't meet his eyes . . . couldn't meet his eyes. If she did, he might see the confusion written across her face. This couldn't be love, could it?

She'd never felt anything like this before. When she thought about Brody, a feeling of peace and rightness came over her. When she looked at him, joy tingled all the way to her fingertips. He made her feel free. Free to say what she wanted. Free to fight with him, if she wanted. Scream in ecstasy, if she wanted. And she did. She wanted all those things. She wanted him.

But love?

He'd never said anything about love. He'd said he wasn't cut out for a personal life. What they had was hot sex between two people with completely different lives. She'd sworn not to let herself be so vulnerable ever again. And yet, here she was. Falling for an enigmatic man she hadn't even met a month ago.

She realized Brody was saying something to her. "Sorry, what?"

"I said, it must be a fascinating investigation. What's it about?"

She told him about Rodrigo. "I kept getting distracted by that damn Thanksgiving special." He rolled his eyes at the mention. "But now I'm focusing entirely on him. I'm supposed to meet him tomorrow. It's my first day back at work."

"And you think he's telling the truth?"

"I believe he is. But I'll know more after I talk to him face-to-face."

"Where does he live?"

"Fern Acres. My old neighborhood."

He was quiet for a while. "If it's true, I sure hope you nail those bastards."

"Me too. This is the kind of story I've always wanted to work on. When I was growing up, I saw so many things in that same neighborhood, but nobody ever cared what went on there. The only time a news reporter came was when there was some kind of gang murder. They wore their bulletproof vests and got out as quick as they could. I never thought what happened to us mattered to anyone. Now I have a chance to actually help some kids living there. I just hope I do it right."

"You will. I know you, Melissa. You're solid gold, through and through. And you're smart. Those evil bastards better watch their asses."

"Oh, Brody . . ." Melissa buried her face in his chest and snuggled herself into his arms. Words bubbled up, words begging to be spoken. *I love you.*

She wouldn't let them out, she absolutely refused. *No, I don't, no I don't! It's not like that.*

Is it?

The next morning, Melissa poked her head into Nelly's room, reassured to see her sleeping peacefully. She paused a minute to watch her grandmother. Did her breathing sound a little rougher than normal? Nelly muttered and moved restlessly on the bed. Melissa smiled. Her grandmother was just fine. Feisty as ever, even in her sleep. She should stop worrying so much.

Besides, she was too happy to worry about anything. Her suspension was the best thing that could have happened. She'd spent the whole time working on her foster care investigation and hanging out with Brody. Now she could tackle her first day back at Channel Six with a fresh attitude.

Whistling, she started the coffeemaker, then jumped in the shower while the coffee brewed. Since she'd been spending time with Brody, she'd mastered the quick morning routine. Short shower, drink coffee while dressing, eat a jelly-filled breakfast bar while she dried her hair. The phone interrupted her flow, and she ran downstairs to answer it.

"Yes, hello?" she said impatiently.

"Morning, Melissa, it's Haskell."

"Oh. Hi, Dad." The word "Dad" caught her by surprise. For years now, she'd called him Haskell. Maybe she could have a fresh attitude with him too. "What's up?"

"Calling to see, well, hope you don't mind if I ask. Say no if you want. Truck broke down. Need a ride to Captain Brody's. I've got a meeting today too, don't know what to do about that."

The familiar exasperation surged. Would her father ever get his act together? But Nelly and Brody both kept telling her how hard he was working. And he needed those meetings.

"I'll tell you what. You can drop me off at work and take my car. Just pick me up after your meeting."

"Yeah? That's great, Mel. Appreciate it."

She hung up slowly, amazed at how good it felt to soften toward her father. Now if she could just get along with her impossible anchorwoman.

When Melissa arrived at work, she knew right away that something was off with Ella. She seemed wired and nervous, and she refused to meet Melissa's eyes during the morning news meeting. She must be up to something, but Melissa refused to get distracted from her story.

She spent the morning preparing for her interview with Rodrigo. At noon she walked to the Starbucks around the corner from the station. As soon as she saw him, she felt certain he was no liar. For one thing, he looked scared. He was a clean-cut kid, thin and wiry. Dark curls fell over his wide-open eyes. She spotted a bruise on his arm.

"Miss McGuire?" he said, bouncing to his feet.

"Hi, Rodrigo." Smiling, she sat down at the table he'd picked, and saw that he had no drink in front of him. "What can I get you?"

It took a minute to convince him to order something, but eventually he admitted to liking hot chocolate. The warm drink seemed to relax him, and before long the details of his life story came pouring out. Poverty-stricken parents, no health care, father had died of blood poisoning, mother had buckled under the weight of caring for five children. She'd gotten sick, and gone back to Guadalupe, a broken woman. The younger kids had returned to Mexico with her, but Rodrigo had stayed. After living on the streets for a while, he wound up in the foster system. He was smart, Melissa quickly realized. He spoke English perfectly, even though he'd lived in California for only five years.

"Would you be willing to wear a hidden camera, if I can arrange it?" she asked.

"I think so. But would she find it? How will we hide it?"

"We'll work that out. The important thing is to catch your caseworker taking money from your foster mother."

"No problem. I know exactly when she does it. First Friday of every month."

Melissa looked at her daybook. "Wow, that's this Friday. Let's meet again on Thursday. I have to get permission to use the camera, and I need to talk to some technicians about the best way for you to wear it."

"Thank you so much, Miss McGuire. I'll do anything you say to do."

"Just make sure no one finds out you're doing this. I want you to stay safe."

"I promise." His dark eyes looked so wide and eager she couldn't help smiling.

"We'll stay in touch over the next couple of days, then. If anything happens, you call and let me know."

"I will." He pulled a crumpled bus schedule from his pocket. "I better go. Hey, what kind of ride you got?"

"My car? It's a blue Volvo, an old one."

"Four-door sedan?"

"Yep."

"I saw you drive by the house, right after I first called you."

Melissa had to laugh at the way guys, no matter what their age, always noticed cars. "Did anyone else notice?"

"Nah. I did, because I was looking for you. I

knew you'd want to check out the hood. I was worried it would scare you off."

"Nah," she said, echoing him. He smiled broadly at her, and left.

The boy trusted her, Melissa realized. He trusted her with his story, and with his safety. It was a humbling thought, but inspiring, too. The kind of thing Brody would appreciate. She pulled out her cell phone and punched in Brody's number.

He took a while to answer, and when he did, his voice sounded very strange. "I'll have to call you back. Something's come up."

"Of course. But you don't have to call me back. I'll just come by after work."

"No, better wait until I call." And he hung up. Melissa snapped her phone shut. Her stomach went tight. He'd never turned down a visit from her before. His voice sounded different too. Distant. Like a stranger.

Something was wrong. She knew it.

Brody stared at the woman on his front step as if she were a ghost. Rebecca stood before him. *Rebecca*. The girl he'd fallen in love with at the age of fourteen. The girl he'd protected from her nasty stepfather, the girl he'd married at the age of nineteen, the woman who'd walked away from their life without a second glance. She still had that wide-eyed, deer-in-the-headlights look that had drawn him to her. But now she wore an anxious look and had new wrinkles at the edges of her eyes, new blond streaks in her hair.

And a new baby growing in her belly. He stared

at the small but unmistakable bump pushing against her clinging maternity tank top.

Trust Rebecca to find a way to make maternity clothes sexy.

Maybe that was her newest money-making scheme. Red-hot mama. Mamacita. MILF maternity clothes. *Stop, stop it. Don't let her make you crazy again.*

"Sorry to just show up like this," said Rebecca. "I had nowhere else to go."

Nowhere else to go? She had the whole world, didn't she? When she'd left, she'd told him anywhere was better than here, with him. But his protective instincts were too powerful to let him say that. On autopilot, he stepped back and let her in. He still held his cell phone, and vaguely remembered talking to Melissa. He followed Rebecca as she looked around his living room.

"Your place looks good," said Rebecca. "You've done a lotta work."

"It's not finished yet."

"How not finished?" In the kitchen, she trailed a hand along the counter. His counter. He fought an impulse to slap her hand away from it.

"What do you mean?"

"Finished enough so I can stay here?"

"*What?*"

Before he could explode, she turned and faced him head-on. "I wouldn't be here if I had a choice, so just get that straight. I'm desperate. I'm pregnant."

"I can see that," he said in a thin voice.

"This one's sticking around. Unlike its daddy.

Thor kicked me out and took all the money from the flip-flops. He claims he came up with them, which you know is a lie, but his brother-in-law's a lawyer, so I'm screwed. I've got nowhere, Brody. Just let me stay for a little bit, until I can figure something out."

"That's a lot to ask, don't you think?" This came out in a mild tone that bore no relation to what Brody was feeling. What he wanted to say was *You think you can dump me, throw me over for another man, then waltz back in without so much as a phone call? You're insane.*

"Brody, I'm pregnant. Think of the baby, not me." She cupped her hand around the side of her belly.

Who was she to tell him to think of the baby? She'd hated their baby. Their baby had been a burden to her. As if she could read his thoughts, she broke in. "I'm on antidepressants this time. Turns out I had real bad depression before. I didn't get it back then. This time it's different."

Sure, it was different. It wasn't his baby. It wasn't his business. He turned his back to her so he could think.

What if he turned her away and something happened to her baby? He'd never forgive himself. Her miscarriage still weighed on him. What if this was a chance to make up for that? If he did this thing for her, he could stop beating himself up about the baby they should have had.

So what if she'd screwed him over. That didn't mean he should refuse to help her.

But he couldn't live in the same space with her either. He scanned the house. The back bedrooms had already been enclosed. The plumber had hooked everything up two days ago. No kitchen yet. If she could live on takeout, without cooking, no reason why she couldn't camp out here.

"You can stay. Only until you get on your feet. You're on your own for food." He indicated the still-unfinished kitchen. "Nothing's working in there yet."

"I won't get in your way, I promise. Thank you, Harry."

"No, you won't get in my way," he snapped. "I'm not staying here, I'm in the trailer." As he turned to head to the Airstream, he caught the quick flash of disappointment in her eyes.

Disappointment because they wouldn't be sleeping in the same house? What was she up to? After all this time, did she want him back?

He slammed the newly hung door behind him. His marriage to Rebecca was over. Dead and gone. She'd killed it, or maybe the miscarriage had. Whatever it was, he felt nothing for her anymore. He'd help her out, she'd go on her way, and that would be that.

He completely forgot to call Melissa back.

Chapter Eighteen

*ack at the station, Melissa asked Greg to show
her how to work the tiny lipstick camera. His
lesson seemed to take hours, but she kept
checking her watch and seeing that no time at all
had passed. Why didn't Brody call? He never forgot
to call. Sometimes he called twice a day. What had
happened? Greg flicked her arm, and she jumped.

"Huh? What?"

"I asked," he said with exaggerated patience,
"whether this kid wears a baseball cap. A lot of
them do, you know, backward or sideways."

"Oh. I don't think so. He didn't have one on."

"What was he wearing?"

Melissa couldn't remember. It seemed like days
since her meeting with Rodrigo. "I don't know. I'll
call him and see if he can wear a cap."

"That'd be best." He showed her how to mount it
on a cap, then packed the camera away in its case.

"You okay, Melissa?"

"Of course. What do you mean?"

"You seem distracted. Trouble with the fire captain? Those guys are tough. Gotta play hard to get with them."

Too late now. "I'll try and remember that."

"You're a precious gift from God, remember that too."

"Oh really?"

"That's what my mama tells me every time a girl dumps me."

"Brody didn't dump me." *Yet.* "Anyway, who says we're even dating?"

"Everyone. But don't trip, I won't tell anyone he dumped you."

"He didn't . . . ! Argh." But she had to laugh at his teasing.

"There's that beautiful smile. Just keep smiling, girl. Precious gift from God, don't forget."

"I hate you, Greg," she said, giving him a big hug. "And thanks for your advice."

Back in her cubicle, the phone squatted on her desk like an evil black toad. She jammed it into her drawer so she wouldn't have to look at it. Where was Brody? What had happened to him? Maybe she should call him back, instead of waiting. But bugging him was pointless. He'd call her when he could. She should trust him. Have a little faith. Too bad Everett had crushed the faith right out of her. But Brody was so different from Everett—loyal, straightforward, honest.

If only he would call.

Haskell left his AA meeting feeling unusually optimistic. He didn't often speak at the meetings. But today, in the sunny community hall where he'd spent Friday nights and most lunch hours for the last three years, he'd gotten to his feet and talked about Melissa. How she'd lent him her car, and what a huge step that was. Years ago, when she'd still been in college, he'd given her a car so she could drive to her journalism classes. But then he'd gotten drunk, "borrowed" it, and wrecked it. He'd felt so awful that he'd gotten drunk again, started a bar brawl, and wound up in jail. She'd had to take the bus to bail him out.

So cars were a sore point, and it meant so much that Melissa had let him take her car without any nasty comments about the past. He'd shared this with the group, and had received genuine smiles of gladness. These people cared about him. His mother cared about him. Captain Brody cared about him. And maybe . . . just maybe his daughter did too.

Whistling, he drove back up Brody's driveway. He loved the days he worked at Brody's house. The hours passed so pleasantly, with just the right amount of conversation—not much. Of course he knew that Brody and Melissa had something going on, but he and Brody never discussed that. If asked, Haskell would have said Brody would make a fine son-in-law, but no one was asking him. He kept his own counsel and focused on the job. He'd finished the wiring, and now he was helping Brody with other odds and ends. This afternoon they planned to tackle the kitchen cabinets.

He got out of Melissa's car, checked it over to make sure he'd done no inadvertent damage, and strolled past the Airstream toward the house. He saw Brody moving around in the trailer. Must be finishing his lunch. No problem; he'd go ahead and get all the tools together for their afternoon's work. Save time. He opened the door and stopped in shock.

A pregnant woman sat perched on a bucket of spackle. She was gorgeous. Long hair streaked with blond, tanned skin, sexy outfit. Kinda like Bo Derek or Cheryl Tiegs, one of those old-time calendar girls.

"Oh!" She started to get to her feet.

"Please don't," he said quickly. "I'm here to work."

"You're helping Harry out?"

"Yeah. Wiring and other stuff."

"Good thing you're here then. Any chance you can get that fridge hooked up? Harry said the kitchen's not done, but it'd be nice to at least have some Cokes around. Or beer, for you hardworking guys." A tentative smile accompanied this last comment, but Haskell ignored it.

"You're . . . staying here?" This came out in a tone that seemed to offend her.

"Yeah, what's it to you?"

"Nothing. Surprised, is all."

"Really? Didn't you know Harry was married?"

Haskell gave her a narrow stare. Brody didn't talk much about his personal life, but he would have known if the captain was married. "Married to *you*?"

"Yeah, nosy. Married to me. So I suggest you take a look at that refrigerator. It'd be nice to have it working before the baby comes. And we'll definitely need a washer and dryer too. I'll start making a list."

Haskell did not like her. Not one bit. And right

now, he didn't like Brody much either. Without comment, he turned on his heel and walked back out to Melissa's car.

"Hey! Come back here!" she called, but he ignored her and got into the car. It wasn't his business, but he wasn't about to let his daughter get blindsided. He'd done enough damage to her over the years. The last thing Melissa needed was to get hurt again. He headed for Channel Six.

"Are you trying to ruin *everything*?" In the station parking garage, Melissa whirled away from her father. "Why are you doing this?"

"I don't want you to get hurt, Mel."

"Too late. This *hurts*."

"I thought you should know. I better go now."

Melissa ignored him. Part of her knew she was being unfair. It wasn't his fault a pregnant woman claiming to be Brody's wife was staying at his house. It wasn't his fault she felt like a neutron bomb had just dropped on her. But she couldn't look at him.

"Maybe there's a good explanation."

"I don't know, Melissa. She wanted me to get the fridge going, and the washer-dryer. Said she needed them for the baby. She's sticking around. And she's definitely pregnant."

Melissa had the childish impulse to cover her ears and yell, "Lalala."

"I'm real sorry. Did I do the right thing, telling you?"

"Yes . . . I don't know . . ." She clenched her fists hard enough to feel her fingernails dig into the heels of her hands. "I hate this. I hate it."

"I better go now. Do you want your car back? I can take a bus."

She shook her head violently. "Just go."

Her dad got in her Volvo and backed up, like someone leaving the scene of the crime. Melissa wheeled around in a frantic little circle, wishing she were anywhere but here, in this moment, facing *this*. Her dad was right. What explanation could there be? Maybe the woman wasn't Rebecca, and Haskell had misunderstood. Or maybe the woman wasn't Rebecca, but some other woman Brody had impregnated. Or maybe she was Rebecca, and the baby was Brody's.

She could think of a million explanations, but the only one who knew the truth was Brody. And Brody still hadn't called to tell her about any of this. Maybe he had no intention of calling her. Maybe he planned to blow her off. Why hadn't he told her himself?

It's not as if they had a real relationship. He didn't owe her a thing. He could do whatever he wanted with whoever he wanted, without running it past her. They were just two people having sex.

So why did this hurt so much?

Gritting her teeth, she headed back up to the newsroom. She still had to get some work done before the end of the day. God only knew how she'd be able to concentrate. She should never have gotten involved with Brody. Yet another arrogant male trampling all over her feelings.

As if she'd conjured a demon, she spotted a familiar brown leather jacket in the doorjamb of her cubicle. It was draped over the shoulder of a tall, lean man. Grizzled, gray-blond hair. Head cocked in that arrogant way. The man's head turned, and over his shoulder he gave her that wry smile that had always caused such a riot in her insides.

"Melissa," Everett said in that devastating, gravelly voice. "You're a sight for famished eyes."

Famished eyes? Melissa took refuge in a sarcastic grammar critique. *Who says things like that?* Everett Malcolm, that's who. Globe-trotter, adventurer, securer of interviews with world leaders and renegade drug lords, legendary newsman, manipulative heartbreaker. Everett Malcolm, who had crushed Melissa's heart and tossed her aside like an old orange peel. Made her lose her confidence, just as Brody had said.

Everett shifted his body to face her, and behind him she saw Ella in her favorite pose, perched cross-legged on Melissa's desk.

"What . . . what are you doing here?" she said faintly.

He looked mildly surprised. "You invited me, remember? A bit of a surprise, but an entirely welcome one."

Melissa gaped at him. Invited him? Why the hell would she invite Everett anywhere? Especially here to the most gossipy newsroom on the planet, where already all work had stopped and all eyes were glued to the little scene playing out. Behind Everett, Ella put her hands together in a pleading gesture.

Quickly, Melissa connected the dots. *Unbelievable.* Ella had, apparently, invited Everett to San Gabriel, and now expected Melissa to cover for her. Talk about nerve. Melissa opened her mouth to give her the ripping she deserved, but Ella pulled out her two-ratings-points, queen-of-the-newsroom look that always made Melissa hesitate.

Ella hopped off the desk and slinked to Everett's side. She linked her arm through his. "Everett and I were just talking about what a fantastic job you did on the City Hall fire. I don't know how many people have told me what a great team we make."

Melissa found her voice. "Team?"

"Yes, team," Ella answered quickly. "Like I told Everett, I like to give credit where credit's due. When someone does good work for me, I go straight to the news director and I make sure something comes out of it. Promotion, raise, something. My news director trusts me inplicitly."

In-plicitly? Melissa saw Everett smirk at Ella's error. But she was more interested in Ella's hidden meaning, which was pretty obvious. If Melissa refrained from busting her, Ella would make sure she got that promotion Loudon had dangled in front of her.

How many games could one tiny, ambitious anchor play? Did she think Everett would actually hire her? Melissa was sick of Ella's ridiculous ploys. If Ella wanted Everett, for whatever reason, she could have him. The two of them deserved each other.

She shrugged and turned to leave. The next thing she knew, firm footsteps sounded behind her. Everett took her by the shoulders and whirled her around. His world-weary, bleached-blue eyes looked down into hers, and the old magic that had ruled her life for two roller-coaster years gripped her. He smiled that wry smile, and bent his head toward hers.

* * *

When Brody heard the sound of a car pulling out, at first he'd thought it was Rebecca, deciding to move on. But it was Haskell. He must have come back early from lunch.

He must have seen Rebecca.

Brody bounded into the house, where Rebecca leaned against the kitchen sink, opening a can of Diet Coke. She took a sip and made a face.

"Warm Coke tastes like spit-up, I swear. Don't you think a fridge would be nice to have in here?"

"I told you there was no kitchen."

"I know, but how hard is it to plug in a fridge? Your little helper there acted like I asked for the moon." She took another sip, made a disgusted face, and poured the rest down the sink.

"It's not"—too late—"hooked up." The Coke poured out onto the floor. He knelt down to wipe the mess up with some work rags. Rebecca backed away, giggling.

"Oopsy, I'm sorry, Harry. Pregnancy brain. I do the dumbest things sometimes."

"What did you say to Haskell? The man who was here."

"Nothing. Just about the fridge."

"Did you say who you were?"

"Not exactly. He didn't introduce himself either," she said defensively.

"Not exactly? Come on, Rebecca, don't fuck with me. Tell me what you said, or you're out of here." He gave her his steeliest look.

"I didn't tell him shit. I just asked whether he knew you were married or not."

Brody swore as he swabbed the puddle of Coke.

He had to get out of here. Get to Melissa before Haskell did. Or if he'd already gotten there, he had to repair whatever damage had been done.

"Here," he said, and thrust the Coke-soaked rag at Rebecca. "Clean up that mess while I clean up your other one. Damn you, why couldn't you have stayed in San Diego?"

On the way to the TV station, he tried Melissa's cell, but she wasn't answering. He seemed to hit every stoplight, every construction zone, every spot of gridlock in the greater San Gabriel area. Jet packs, he thought fiercely. He should have his own private jet pack for moments like this. Of course Haskell had gone to warn his daughter that her lover's pregnant ex-wife had shown up. God knew what she was thinking by now. *If only he had called her earlier.*

But it would still be okay. He would explain, and she would understand. Melissa was intelligent— she would get it. She wasn't the hysterical, drama-loving type. He loved that about her, along with that mile-a-minute brain of hers, which was totally at odds with her wild, hot sexuality. He found the combination irresistible. He'd explain everything, she'd understand right away, and they could go back to having crazy hot sex in his trailer.

As he ran into the newsroom, he skidded to a halt at the sight of Melissa wrapped in the tight embrace of a tall man in a leather jacket. She didn't seem to mind one bit. No, indeed. The man was kissing her, and she was kissing him right back. Those soft lips that just last night had traveled his body with tender hunger, that had tasted his erection, licked his neck, were now intimately entangled with another man. His head spun with a sick, murderous fury.

"Melissa's a little busy right now."

He snapped out of his rage and found Ella pouting up at him, her entire body practically hanging on his arm. She seemed to be trying to drag him out of the newsroom.

"I can give her a message. Not that I'm an errand girl, of course. But for you, I'll make an exception." She tugged on his arm.

"What are you doing?"

"Out of the goodness of my heart, I'm trying to keep you from making a fool of yourself. Do you think Melissa wants you here right now? She hasn't seen Everett Malcolm in forever. She's always jabbering on about him. She must be like a kid at Christmas right now."

Brody took another quick, painful look at the still-ongoing kiss. Ella had a funny idea of what kids did at Christmas. He could have shaken off the petite anchor like a fruit fly, but he allowed her to push him toward the exit stairwell. *Everett Malcolm, the news director.* Melissa hated the man, didn't she? Apparently not. The image of her snuggled in the man's arms mocked him.

Getting the hell out sounded like the best possible idea right now. He went, after a vicious sideways slam of his fist against the wall of the stairwell.

Melissa, wrapped in Everett's arms, felt bile rise in her throat. Someone made a sound—possibly one of the many newsroom employees avidly watching the show—and she broke away from the kiss.

How had she let herself be touched, for even one moment, by the man who had caused her so much pain? She wiped her mouth with the back of her hand to get rid of the feel of Everett's kiss, but it burned with a mocking fierceness. So did Everett's gaze. *I own you,* his look seemed to say. *You will never get over me.*

A movement at the edge of the newsroom caught her eye. A familiar-looking flannel work shirt fluttered in the doorway, then disappeared. Horror shot through her. Could that have been Brody? Ella sauntered toward her.

"Ella, was that Captain Brody?"

Ella shrugged. "For a second, it was. He bolted out of here quick enough."

"Shit." Melissa ran toward the door.

"Melissa! Bad idea!"

She ignored Ella and bounded down the stairs two at a time. In the parking garage, she saw Brody's truck moving toward the exit. She ran toward her own parking space, but it was empty. Of course—her father had her car.

Never mind. She could still catch Brody. She ran after his truck, shouting his name. By now he'd almost reached the exit, but he turned his head at the sound of his name. Their eyes met. Melissa stopped in her tracks, pinned by two hard gray spears. He revved the truck, and sped out of the garage.

Melissa, panting from her mad dash, kicked the tire of the nearest car, a ratty old Toyota. How dare Brody look at her like that, when he didn't know the whole story? Besides, he was the one with a pregnant woman hanging out at his house! What right did he have to judge her? What was he doing here, anyway?

He'd probably come to tell her he was getting back together with Rebecca. What else would be so urgent? It was the only explanation that made sense. Brody would be too honorable to break up with someone on the phone. He would do it in person, even if that meant coming to see her at work.

Thank God she hadn't fallen in love with him.

They'd had a wild few days in bed, but what did they have in common, really? Okay, so they'd had some amazing conversations. She'd felt closer to him than she ever had to anyone.

But he'd loved Rebecca since the age of fourteen. How could she compare with that? Was she destined to always be second best? Second best in Everett's life, second best to on-air talent, second best to her father's drinking.

"Hey!" A voice interrupted her. "Back away from my wheels."

"I couldn't help myself," she said sarcastically. "Your car is such a chick magnet."

The editor, whose name she couldn't remember, shot her a wounded look and brushed past her.

"Sorry," she muttered. There was no need to be mean to innocent bystanders. It wasn't the editor's fault that Brody had decided to get back together with his ex. Melissa dragged herself back up the stairs to the newsroom.

On the stairs, she passed an assignment desk assistant, and snapped at her too. *Get a grip*, she lectured herself. *Brody's just one man, and come to think of it, not at all the right one for you. You need someone brilliant and artistic, intellectual and dynamic. Someone like . . .*

As soon as she walked back into the newsroom and saw Everett, her heart sank. Everett had every quality she'd just listed. But he was also dishonest, self-absorbed, and in the end he'd been outright cruel. Everett was not right for her. Neither was the screenwriter who'd left her a message earlier today, after disappearing for eight months without a word. Neither was the sculptor who had sent her an invitation to his show opening—the show that had taken up so much of his time he'd decided not to date until it was over.

Only one man would do for her now, and that man had just driven off in his truck, with a look that cut the heart right out of her.

Crap. Double crap. She *had* fallen in love with him.

She couldn't face the newsroom right now. Or Everett. Or Ella. She fled to the bathroom.

In the back corner stall, she perched on the toilet and wiped away tears with squares of toilet paper. Crying in the bathroom—the last time she'd done that, Everett had just broken up with her. She'd never forget that mortifying moment in his office with Barb Nelson, star political reporter.

"Everett, I insist you take her off the campaign special. She blew my confidential source in the vice president's office. Not literally, of course, as far as I know."

"No, I didn't! I wrote exactly what you told me. You even spelled out his name."

"Why would I burn a source like that? It doesn't make any sense."

"Now, ladies, no catfights allowed. I don't want

blood on my carpet. Barb, give me a moment with Melissa."

Barb had left, and Melissa had been confronted with Everett's coldest stare. "I have to take you off the special. I can't upset my star reporter."

"But I didn't do anything!"

"Barb has a five-year contract and an international reputation. You're an okay producer. Need I elaborate further?"

"Crushed" didn't begin to describe her sense of betrayal. Was she really just an "okay producer"? Was that how Everett saw her? Or was it just another mind game?

She hadn't learned the truth until her last day of work.

Someone knocked on the door of the stall. "Everything okay in there?"

"Yes." Her voice wobbled. "That time of the month. I get really emotional."

Whoever it was slid a Kit Kat bar under the door. "Better than painkillers."

Melissa felt a fit of giggles coming on. The giggles grew to a laugh. She opened the chocolate, took a nibble, and let the sweet comfort spread through her. How had her life gotten into such a mess? Brody gone, Everett back, her career once again hanging by a thread.

Well, she was done letting her heart get broken. From now on, Rodrigo would get all her attention. She dumped her pile of tear-soaked paper in the toilet and flushed.

Chapter Nineteen

*E*lla saw Melissa come into the newsroom and
back right out again. Good. She needed a little
more time to get Everett firmly hooked. It had
been a nasty shock to see Everett kiss Melissa so
passionately. Then Brody had shown up and she'd
had to get rid of him before he scared Everett off.
She'd kept her cool and handled the situation, but
she had to keep emotions out of this. This was
business. This was her career.

She'd heard the stories about Everett Malcolm.
He'd left Harvard to sail single-handedly around
the world in a catamaran. In a famous article for
the *New Yorker*, he'd described the huge storm that
had capsized the tiny craft. The article had been
made into a movie, and he'd finished his Harvard
education as a celebrity. As a foreign correspon-
dent, he'd been sent to prison in Myanmar, then
written a best-selling book about the experience.

He had been married at various times to a former child star, a princess from an obscure Arab country, and the daughter of a senator.

He was a fascinating man of the world, and now she had him in her office, all to herself.

She traced a finger up Everett's arm. "Lovers' quarrel?" she said provocatively. He glanced down at her with a vague look of annoyance.

"Not precisely. We haven't been together in some time."

"But there's history."

"Indeed. Not my most shining moment, unfortunately."

Ella spotted an opportunity. "I may be able to help you. I know Melissa pretty well by now." Everett's arrested gaze scanned her face. With a beckoning tilt of her head, she strolled, hips swaying, into her office. After a slight hesitation, Everett followed. She arrayed herself in her chair, and propped her legs up on her desk, one ankle over the other. In the process, her tight skirt slid up to mid-thigh, which earned a quick glace of appreciation from Everett.

"Melissa," she said, tapping her finger against her bottom lip, "brainy or not, is just like any other woman. We all want what we can't have. We all want what another woman seems to have."

"Interesting observation. Does it apply to you as well, Ms. Ella Joy?"

It was the first time he'd spoken her name, she realized with a small thrill. And now he was giving her his full attention, with those sardonic blue eyes and devilish smile.

"I want what I want. I don't pay attention to

other women," she answered, one eyebrow raised.

"Fascinating. And what do you want?" He put his hand on her thigh, just at the edge of her skirt. She shot a nervous glance at the open door, and he reached over and pushed it closed. Ella realized her bluff had been called. She had Everett just where she wanted him. But that intent stare of his unsettled her.

"What if I said you?" she said in a teasing tone.

"Me?" he answered with mock surprise. "But you just met me." His thumb pushed back the edge of her skirt, revealing the tender golden skin of her inner thigh.

"Well, sure, but . . ." Her voice wobbled. She didn't like the way he made her feel, so out of her league. "I've heard a lot about you."

"Have you? Are you wearing underwear?"

Her mouth dropped open on an outraged gasp. This was not going according to plan. She was used to men worshipping her, not asking her crude questions. Her heart raced. "Of course . . . I am."

"Take it off."

She gaped at him.

"I thought you wanted me." His hand on her thigh made her feel weak.

"I didn't say that. I said *what* if I did?"

"And if you did, I would insist you take off your underwear. If you didn't do so, I might not believe you. I might think you had a different agenda. I might wonder if you're playing some kind of game. So . . . why don't you take off your no doubt very expensive panties and let me see you."

Oh my goodness. What had she gotten herself into? If she'd wanted a challenge, that's what she was getting. Everett's thumb circled across the flesh of her inner thigh, creating the most amazing sensations. She definitely wasn't used to that.

Ella didn't care much for sex. She found it messy and embarrassing. She only had sex when it furthered her ends. This would most definitely further her ends. If she slept with Everett, he'd be more likely to give her a chance. He would at least have to give her an interview. And who knew where else it might lead?

And there was something else. Something she'd never felt before. She felt weak in his presence. Unable to deny him what he asked. Unable to resist the dark challenge in those commanding bleached-blue eyes.

She bent her knees toward her chest and reached under her skirt to pull down her red silk panties. Keeping her knees together, she inched the panties down her legs in as provocative a manner as possible. She might not like sex much, but she had long ago perfected the striptease. His eyes, glued to her every movement, heated up. When the panties were off, she lifted them in the air with one finger. With a wink, she tossed him the panties. He put them in his pocket.

"Now pull up your skirt and touch yourself," he ordered.

"What the hell?" No one ever ordered her around. But under his demanding gaze she subsided. *Put up or shut up*, he seemed to say. She pulled up her skirt. Her naked backside rubbed against the fabric of her chair in a way she found surprisingly arousing.

"Good girl. Now widen your legs. God, you are

something else. Look at you. You're absolutely perfect."

His admiration relaxed her. She let her head fall back on the edge of the chair as she gave herself up to his gaze, her legs propped apart for his viewing pleasure. His eyes ate her up.

"Didn't I tell you to touch yourself? Damn it."

Ella jumped, and before she knew it her hand flew to her crotch.

"That's it. I want to see you wet. Move your fingers. Do it."

And she did it. With shaking hands, she fingered herself. For a moment she couldn't believe she was here in her office, exposing her most intimate parts to the most famous news director in the country. She felt weak, helpless . . . and more aroused than ever before in her life. As he watched with hungry eyes, she rubbed herself until she felt slick and slippery. Then he pulled her wrists away from her body. He stared at her for a long moment while she throbbed. Holding both her wrists in one hand, he pressed the heel of his other hand into her heat. She jumped, and bit back a gasp. He ground his hand against her as she writhed wildly. Just as she reached the edge of orgasm, he pulled his hand away. She gave a squeak of protest. He looked down at her heavy eyes and drenched crotch.

"I'm staying at the Hilton. I'll keep these panties. Don't put on any others until I tell you to. Do not satisfy yourself. Come see me tonight, after the show." And he closed her legs, with one last teasing tweak of her aching crotch.

After he'd gone, it took a while for Ella to stop shaking. Who was he to boss her around? She was supposed to be the one in charge. This had never happened to her before.

And yet, for the rest of the night, she followed every one of his commands. For the first time in her life, she anchored the *Eleven O'Clock News* without any underwear on.

That night, a tap on the door made Brody jump eagerly out of bed. It must be Melissa, here to explain herself, explain why she'd been passionately kissing Everett Malcolm. Since Brody had peeled out of the garage, he'd cooled off a little. He'd overreacted—perhaps because Melissa brought out his impulsive side. Maybe he'd taken her by surprise. Maybe it had begun as a polite, glad-to-see-you kiss. If she had a good explanation, he would listen. He was a reasonable, fair man. Ask any of his fire crew. Willing to listen, willing to forgive.

In his boxers and bare feet, he padded to the door. He thought about pulling on a sweatshirt, but he knew how much Melissa loved his bare chest. If it gave him an edge, he'd stay half naked. And if things went well, he'd be entirely naked before the night was over.

The first smile since he'd seen what he now thought of as The Kiss tugged at his lips, but it disappeared when he opened the door. Rebecca stood before him in a clinging nightgown, a thin cotton robe wrapped around her.

"What's wrong?"

"Nothing, honey. It's just hard to sleep sometimes, you know, when he starts kicking."

"He's kicking?"

"Yeah. Wanna feel?" Before he could object,

she grabbed his hand and put it on her belly. Sure enough, he felt something bump against his palm.

"Lively one, feels like."

"Sure is. I hope he calms down once he's born."

"It's a boy?"

"I think it is. Just a feeling, I don't know for sure. I can't afford the test. Hey, it's kinda cold out here, ya know."

After a brief hesitation, Brody stood back and let her in. He threw on his sweatshirt and went to the stove. "Want tea or something? I can heat up some milk."

"I'm dying for a cup of coffee, with a shot of rum."

A sharp look made her teasing smile disappear. "I'm just joking. I'm doing everything right this time, Harry. I swear I am."

"I'm sure you are, Rebecca," he said heavily. *This time*, as opposed to when it was his baby. He filled a teapot with water and turned on a burner. "So what happened with Thorval?"

"Oh, T is just a jerk. He didn't want a kid. Begged me to get an abortion. But . . . you know. I just couldn't. Not after what happened before." He heard the pain in her voice, and for the first time began to soften toward her. In the back of his mind, he'd always wondered if she'd been relieved to miscarry. Had he misjudged her all this time?

"He didn't understand?"

"He didn't give a shit. Said get rid of it, or get out. So I left."

"And came here?"

"No, I just went to a hotel. He felt real bad after that and came after me. Said he'd thought about it, and he wasn't one to ditch his responsibilities and all that. But I'd been thinking, and I said to hell with you and your responsibilities. Then I came here."

Brody frowned down at the teakettle. He didn't want to look at Rebecca, but he could picture her perfectly. Her eyes would be wide and vulnerable, her lips slightly trembling. She'd always known how to bring out his protective streak. He'd married a fragile, frightened girl who clung to him as if he were her personal knight. She seemed different now. More grown up. Sharper. She had a harder edge than when he'd seen her last. And yet she was turning to him again, as she had since junior high.

"What made you think of me?"

"I know you think I sound nuts."

"Did I say that?"

"You're looking at that teapot more than me."

"The teapot didn't dump me for a flip-flop sales-man."

"Don't be mean, Harry. The flip-flops were just to support his surfing career. Did you ever think maybe we just got married too young?"

"We were definitely young." Maybe she was right, but all he'd wanted back then was to take care of her.

The teakettle whistled. Brody poured boiling water into two mugs and dropped in the teabags. "Sugar?"

"Yes, honey?"

"Don't do that." But his voice had no conviction. He put a teaspoon of sugar in her mug and stirred it.

"Why not, Harry? I never forgot you," she said softly. "Did you forget me?"

"No. But I've moved on."

"You met someone?"

"Yes."

"Is it serious?" Brody didn't answer. He and Melissa had never talked about their feelings for each other, or their future. Maybe it was too soon, or maybe she didn't have feelings for him. They'd gotten so close to each other inside this trailer, but they had never taken their relationship into the real world. They hadn't wanted to. They'd only wanted to stay cuddled in their little nest, talking, laughing, loving.

But the word "love" had never been spoken by either one of them. And then there was The Kiss.

"Because if it isn't," Rebecca continued, "it could be just like it almost was, like you always wanted it. We could be a family."

Brody, still as stone, stared into his mug of tea. So that's why she'd come back. Finally he spoke. "Why?"

"Cuz you'd be the best father. Out of all the men I've ever known. Maybe you don't love me anymore. And I don't know what I feel, with all these crazy hormones. But I know my baby would be the luckiest kid in the world with you for a dad. And who knows, maybe we can fix things between us."

Dad. Father. At her words, all the deep longings he'd buried came flooding back. Of course he wanted to be a father. He always had. But he'd convinced himself family life wasn't for him. Now here she was, offering him exactly what he'd always wanted. Wife and child. Tied up in a pretty package. Only one catch: It wasn't his child. And they didn't love each other. At least she was honest about that.

"What if we can't 'fix' things between us?"

She shrugged. "We'll do the best we can, for the baby. We didn't do so bad, before."

No, they hadn't done so bad. But they hadn't lain in bed talking about nothing for hours on end. They hadn't shared their most humiliating third grade moments, or talked about their first crushes. He felt a sudden longing to hold Melissa, to watch the laughter dawn in her forest-green eyes, to hear her whisper his name. How could he be with anyone who wasn't Melissa? The truth swept over him like a tsunami. He was in love with Melissa. Fatally, inescapably in love. Maybe it had taken Rebecca's appearance to make him see it.

But were his feelings the most important thing in this situation? What was the most honorable course of action? Maybe he owed Rebecca for what she'd gone through in the past. And then there was the baby. A baby he could help. They needed him, Rebecca and her child. And maybe, whispered his most secret fear, this was as close as he would get to happiness.

"Give me some time," he said gruffly. "This is a little sudden."

"Yeah, sure. I'll be here. Over there in that lonely house." She lifted herself out of her chair. "I'm ordering Italian tomorrow night, why don't you come by?"

He nodded mechanically.

"And tell some of the guys, Hoagie and Double D, whoever you want."

"No!" He didn't want his crew to know anything about this. They'd seen how he suffered after the breakup. And now they all loved Melissa. He didn't want to hear their opinions.

"Okay, fine, grouchy."

After she left, Brody got back into bed. He covered himself with sheets that smelled of Melissa's lavender and vanilla scent, and laid his head on a pillow that had one of her long, dark hairs clinging to it. If he accepted Rebecca's offer, he would never again feel Melissa's softness, never see her eyes sparkling as she aimed one of her snappy comebacks at him. Could he bear it?

Then again, did he have a choice? She'd been kissing Everett Malcolm. Maybe, he thought as he punched the pillow, they were together right this very moment.

Nelly heard Melissa stomp into the house and toss her shoulder bag on the floor, in that untidy habit of hers. She pulled on her housecoat and padded out into the living room. "What are you doing home?"

"It's nice to see you too," said Melissa.

"Where's Captain Brody? He's not on shift tonight."

"I'm going to ignore the fact that you know his schedule, and point out that Captain Brody's whereabouts at any given moment are not my concern."

Oh Lord. When Melissa talked like that, like some college professor, it was always a sign of trouble. "What happened?"

"Happened? Nothing." Melissa tripped over her shoulder bag and kicked it out of the way. "I think we should rearrange the living room. It's bad feng shui. We should get rid of the couches and all that potpourri, just put carpets and pillows on the floor. Like Turkey. Or is it Morocco?"

What on earth was the girl chattering about

now? "No one is changing anything in this living room," Nelly said darkly. "Not until I know what's going on."

"You really want to know what's going on? You're sure?" When Nelly nodded stubbornly, Melissa threw the words at her like live grenades. "Your precious hero fire captain turns out to be the rat of all rats. The worst of the worst. On the bright side, Dad did the right thing for once."

"What are you blabbering about? You're not making sense."

Melissa told her everything that had happened, from Haskell's eyewitness report to Brody's look of contempt.

Nelly's heart sank. Lord, what a tangle. She felt a stab of pain in her stomach, and, without thinking, addressed it out loud. "You, back off and let me breathe."

"I'm sorry," said Melissa, looking confused.

"Not you. Although I'm not at all happy with you. Why'd you let that lowlife kiss you?"

"I don't know. It's like this power he has. I can't explain it."

"Well, you'd better figure it out, if you want Brody back."

Melissa brushed away a tear. "You don't get it, Grans. He's back with his ex. She's pregnant. He always wanted a baby."

"So? You want babies too, right?"

Even though she'd been so focused on her career, now the answer seemed obvious. "Of course."

"You're going to have to go to him. It's the only way. You want that trashy ex to steal him away?"

"It's not that simple. Not if there's a baby. Besides,

I've got other things to think about. My investigation, for instance. That's all I care about right now."

Nelly shook her head. Oh, this was a disaster. Melissa and her damn career. She was proud of her granddaughter, but there was more to life than TV news. As for Brody, she knew him well enough by now to know that he would probably sacrifice his own happiness for the sake of a baby. "We have to find out what's really going on over there."

Melissa shook her head. "Stay out of it, Grans." A tear spilled over, then another.

"Stop fretting, Melissa, you're giving me a headache. Go to sleep now. All these tears are bad for your skin."

"Whatever you say. As long as you stay out of this." She walked over to Nelly and hugged her, then drew back. "Grans, are you okay? You feel so skinny. Are you eating? What did you have for dinner? Let me whip you up an omelet or something."

Nelly scowled at her granddaughter. "I don't need one of your fancy fandango omelets. All I need is to get this mess sorted out. Don't worry about me. Go to bed."

"I will, as soon as you do. Do you want any Sanka, or water, anything at all?"

Nelly gave a gesture dismissing all comforting liquids as worthless swill, and let Melissa guide her to bed. She allowed her granddaughter to fuss over her and tuck her in. No point in telling her another sleepless night lay ahead. At least tonight she'd have something to chew on. As soon as possible she'd send Haskell over there to see what was what.

Chapter Twenty

Around midnight, Ella knocked on the door of the penthouse suite of the San Gabriel Hilton. Her breath came fast as she listened to the padding of Everett's footsteps. He opened the door wearing jeans, bare feet, and a blue cashmere sweater that made her fingers itch to fondle it. Everything about him looked so . . . rich. Classy. He exuded wealth, power, and privilege, which, for Ella, were the most intoxicating of all pheromones.

When she stepped into the apartment, her five-inch heels sank into the plush carpet. She had on the same tight cobalt suit she'd worn on the air. And still no underwear. "I did what you said."

"I know," he said arrogantly.

"How do you know?" she asked, indignant.

"Don't you get it? I know you, Ms. Ella Joy."

"We barely just met."

He laughed softly. "You're rather adorable. It's a pity."

"A pity?'

"That you're such a mercenary little creature."

"That's insulting."

"Perhaps. But we can talk about that later. Do you like this room?" He gestured around the suite. It was spectacular—a large sitting room, palatial bedroom, balcony looking out over the pool.

"It's nice enough." Ella pouted. Even when he was insulting her, she preferred it when his attention stayed on her.

"Let me show you around." She could barely hide her impatience as he showed off the minibar, the giant fruit basket, the private Jacuzzi. He hadn't even bothered to touch her yet. What kind of game was he playing? When they reached the balcony, with its sweeping view of the twinkling lights of San Gabriel, he leaned his long body against the railing and gazed down at the pool twenty floors down. Even at this late hour, several people floated in the water, and a few lounged in the chaises. "Ah, the little people. How they must envy us, here in the penthouse suite. Is life worth living in anything less than the penthouse suite?"

"Not unless you're doing everything you can to get there," came Ella's emphatic answer.

"That's my girl," said Everett approvingly. He turned so he was leaning his back on the railing. "Unzip me."

She raised her chin defiantly. This afternoon he'd left her high and dry, and she could still feel the ache. Now he wanted her to . . . When he speared her with an impatient look, she scurried toward him. What was this power he seemed to have over her? She unzipped his jeans. His half-aroused penis spilled out.

"Good," he said. "Now, down on your hands and knees."

"What?" She wasn't going to kneel down for any man. But then again, she didn't want to blow her chance. "Someone might see."

"It's the penthouse suite," he said. "The privilege of money. This is the life you're striving for, remember?" Oh, she remembered. "No one can see us. And I want your mouth on me. We're wasting time."

Which meant she was wasting her big opportunity. A blow job had to at least get her on the noon show. Besides, there was something so compelling about him. It made her stomach go fluttery, and her sex burn. Breath coming fast, she knelt down on all fours. She had to lift her head high in order to reach his erection. In this position, she could feel her skirt riding up. Her still-bare crotch was now exposed to the open air, and she felt the breeze of a door opening. Inside her mouth, she felt him getting harder.

"Just put it over there."

At the sound of Everett's voice, she froze. She heard movement inside the suite, soft footsteps, and the door closing again.

"Don't stop just because the bellboy got an eyeful of the most beautiful ass I've seen in years," whispered Everett.

But she was paralyzed with humiliation, and couldn't go on. With an exclamation, he pulled her to her feet. He ripped open her blouse, sending buttons flying. Her hands flew to hide herself. She hated her small breasts and would rather die than have him see them. But he pulled her hands away and stared avidly at her bare torso.

"Perfect," he breathed. "All nipple. Just the way I like them." He turned her so her stomach pressed against the railing. "Arch your back. Show the little people what perfection looks like." He rolled her nipples roughly between his thumbs and forefingers and she cried out from the sudden painful pleasure. "That's right, let them hear. I want the whole world to hear you moan." Another rough hand dove between her legs. Her skirt had disappeared—apparently he'd ripped that off as well—and he nudged her legs apart with his knees. He pressed her lower back so her ass pushed upward.

"Maybe I'll call room service again," he said roughly. "I'll let them watch while I make your sweet ass shake." Her legs were spread wide as he pushed three strong fingers into her. "Maybe I'll let the busboys have a taste, when I'm done. Just a taste though. They can suck your nipples."

Busboys sucking her nipples. She shuddered with a kind of sick fascination. "No . . ." she protested. "Please . . ."

"Then do exactly what I say. Stick those tits out. Pull on your nipples. That's right. Stretch them out. Here, like this."

He demonstrated with his own fingers, wet with her scent. A jolt went all the way to her crotch. He put her hands on her breasts, where his had been, then lifted her ass higher in the air and spread her

lips apart. From behind, she felt him sheath himself deep within her. Her whole body throbbed.
"Pull those nipples. Show the world those tits, let
them all see you dance and moan. Do it!"

She pulled hard on her own nipples as he thrust
deeper inside her, again and again. She forgot her
embarrassing position, the risk of being seen, or
worse, recognized. Or maybe . . . maybe that risk
was what made her whole body feel so alive, so
excited. She fondled her nipples shamelessly, and
screamed out loud as his thumbs worked against
her flaming clitoris.

"Now come!" he growled in her ear. "Come
now!" He squeezed her crotch as he plunged to the
hilt one last time, and her body arched in a fierce
spasm as she shouted her long-delayed pleasure
out loud to the world. Heads looked up. She heard
someone laugh. But none of it mattered as her body
sang with a bliss she'd never known.

The bellhop, it turned out, hadn't seen a thing. The
door to the bedroom had blocked his view.

"How dare you," Ella fumed, when they had
adjusted their clothing and returned to the suite.
"You made me think . . ."

"I told you I know you," answered Everett,
calmly pouring them each a snifter of brandy.
"You're an exhibitionist. Having other people
watch you is the biggest turn-on you know."

Ella didn't answer. She didn't like the feeling
that he knew her better than she knew herself. On
the other hand, he'd given her a sexual experience
the likes of which she'd never known. "Is that what
you do? Figure out what turns women on?"

"And why not? No more powerful feeling exists than to have a beautiful woman at your mercy." He said it in a light tone that nonetheless made her shiver.

"Is that what you did with Melissa?"

"No," he said brusquely. "Melissa and I . . . that was different. I managed to curb my worst instincts with her. At least in the sexual realm."

"Oh really? I heard you broke her heart."

"Did I?" He ambled to the room service cart, and sampled a strawberry. "Better her heart than her spirit."

"What the hell does that mean?" said Ella peevishly. Why on earth was she wasting her time talking about Melissa? How could she shift this conversation to address her needs?

"It means even the devil pulls his punches sometimes." He brought a platter of cheese and crackers to Ella. "But I'd rather talk about you, at the moment. You're the reason I'm here, correct?"

Busted. At least he was smiling. "There's nothing wrong with being proactive."

"No, indeed. Well, I think you've earned this." He opened a silver case and flipped her his business card, with a name and number scrawled on the back. "Glen Woodman is my human resources guy. Give him a call and mention that I sent you. You may also tell him I said to treat you right. Now be a good girl and be off with you."

Ella bristled at the sudden dismissal, even as she slipped the card into her satin clutch. She made a fuss over closing the purse and gathering up her wrap while she tried to figure out what was bothering her. Hadn't she gotten what she'd wanted?

An interview at the Los Angeles station! It was the chance she'd been working toward. Just get her in that interview room and she would blow them away. Of course she wouldn't be put on the major newscasts right away. But she would get hired for the morning show, or the noon show, one of the more insignificant newscasts. In a year, she'd move up the ladder, maybe to the five o'clock news. Then it was just a matter of time until she dominated the LA news market the way she ruled San Gabriel.

And Everett would be her boss. She shivered. The thought made her mouth go dry. She would owe him . . . well, anything he wanted.

She left the hotel room, receiving nothing more than a careless nod of farewell and a yawn from Everett. Halfway down the hall, her cell phone rang.

Everett's gravelly voice growled in her ear. "I've decided to stay in town a few more days. I'll expect you back here tomorrow at three."

"The afternoon news meeting's at three. I can't."

"Entirely your choice, of course." And he hung up.

What a devil. She tossed the phone into her clutch. Was he trying to make her mess up at her job? She didn't have the Los Angeles contract yet. Melissa's warning came back to her, the one about him "ruining people's careers." Phooey to that. Melissa just didn't know how to handle a man like Everett Malcolm.

At Starbucks, Melissa handed the tiny lipstick camera to Rodrigo. Tomorrow the caseworker would show up to collect her blood money.

"It's so small," he said, in an awed voice.

"The last thing we want is for someone to spot it. The cameraman suggested you hide it in a baseball cap. Do you ever wear one?"

"Sometimes. But she makes me take it off in the house."

"That won't work then. You can always clip it to your shirt." Every time she'd seen him, including now, he was wearing a T-shirt. Today's shirt had a picture of a skateboarder in mid-spin. Where could a camera, even a tiny one, hide on a T-shirt?

"What about here?" Rodrigo clipped it to the crucifix that hung around his neck.

"No, it's too visible. Do you have a watch?"

"Yeah, but it's broken." A shadow crossed his face, and Melissa imagined the scene that might have resulted in a broken watch.

"That's okay, as long as the wristband is fine."

He nodded.

"The camera might blend in with the watch. You can clip it to the band. It's not the best spot, but it might be the best we can do right now. But do you think . . . do you think it might get broken again?" she asked, as delicately as possible.

"Nooo . . . I can make sure it doesn't."

"Okay then. Put it on the watch, the way I showed you. Don't forget it's there, but try not to give yourself away either. Do you think you can manage that?"

"Yes. I'm going to hide in the closet anyway. They'll never see me. But there's a hole in the closet door, and I'll just stick the camera up to the hole."

"You've planned this out," said Melissa, pleased. "Really good thinking, Rodrigo. I'm proud of you."

He ducked his head at the praise.

"It's safe, in the closet?"

"Sure. Safe as anywhere. If they see me, I'll say I'm playing hide-and-seek with the younger ones. And I will be. I already told them I'd play a game with them today."

"That's wonderful, Rodrigo," said Melissa warmly. "You're a smart kid. And you're very brave."

He flushed, and shook his head. "No," he mumbled. "If I was brave, I'd stand up for myself. And for the others."

She reached over the table and put a hand on his shoulder. "You *are* standing up for yourself. Not very many kids would have the courage to do this. I'm really proud of you, and really glad you came to me. Here, I got you this." She handed him a disposable cell phone. "It has 911 programmed in, and it has my number. If anything happens, just press one or two. One is 911, two is me. Got it?"

He nodded, appropriately awed by her serious tone. "Nothing's gonna happen though. I got this dialed in."

"All right." She smiled. "Just be careful. Pretend I'm a fussy old grandmother."

"Yeah, right." He snorted, and she was delighted to see a smile brighten his thin face. After carefully tucking the tiny camera deep inside his pocket, he headed off to catch his bus.

Melissa trudged back to the station. Without Brody, there wasn't much to look forward to. Since the scene with Everett, four days ago, she'd heard nothing from Brody. Those four days felt like four years. Obviously, she was never going to hear from him again. She would just have to accept that and move on. Move forward. Just another heartbreak— the world had seen a million of them. Big deal.

The afternoon news meeting was about to begin and, with a heavy heart, she opened the conference room door and settled into her usual seat. Producers and reporters were still trickling in. No sign of Ella yet. The buzz of news gossip filled the room. Listening with zero interest, Melissa learned that a freelancer who had been let go from Channel Six was now anchoring the morning newsbreaks at Channel Two. The City Hall fire had been ruled an accident. Had anyone else seen Ella skip off after the show last night? And the night before? Yes, and one of the photographers had seen her BMW pull up outside the Hilton. Everett Malcolm was rumored to be staying there.

Melissa froze. Ella was hooking up with Everett. Of course.

It was déjà vu all over again. She should have seen it coming.

She gripped the conference room table as the humiliating memory came crashing back.

Her last day at work in Los Angeles. She'd made up her mind to confront Everett once and for all. She had to talk to him, make him see what he meant to her. He was her mentor, her teacher, her idol. After a quick knock on his closed office door, she'd slipped inside. At his desk, Everett had jerked in alarm.

"What are you doing, Melissa?"

"Everett, you know I love you," she'd burst out. "I thought you loved me too."

"I said you were sweet and adorable. I meant it."

"Why wouldn't you sleep with me?"

"This isn't the time, Melissa."

But she'd refused to be stopped. "I wanted to, but you wouldn't. Why not? Just to toy with me?"

Something had flinched across Everett's face. "Really, this is the worst possible moment . . ."

Then a familiar face had risen from under his desk. Barb Nelson. Lipstick smeared, she'd brandished a pen in one hand.

"Here's the pen I was looking for, Everett. It rolled under your desk. It's my favorite pen, I sure would have hated to lose it." Barb had come around the desk with a hip-rolling stride and brushed past Melissa. "Oh, Melissa, I hear you're leaving us. Better luck next time. One tip for the road. Knock before you spill your guts."

Melissa had stared numbly at Everett, before fury washed over her. "I could bust you. I could tell human resources."

"Don't make a scene. A halfway decent producer wants to take on a world-famous news director and an internationally known reporter? Don't let your ideals run away with you, my dear."

She'd left Los Angeles with a broken heart, shattered self-confidence, and the belief that "talent" always held the trump card. "A halfway decent producer"—those words felt branded on her forehead. The only small moment of satisfaction had come when Nelly had called Everett and verbally ripped him to shreds.

That was then, this was now. Did it matter to her what Everett did? Back then, she'd been bedazzled by the man. Now, he meant nothing to her, except as a reminder of her second-best status. Still shaky, she slumped back in her chair. Ella and Everett could screw their little brains out as far as she was concerned. Two people more perfect for each other, she couldn't imagine.

Bill Loudon stepped into the conference room, and everyone scrambled to attention. He rarely attended the news meetings, leaving mundane details such as daily news content to the assistant news director. He took a seat at the head of the table and cleared his throat. As he surveyed the suddenly alert faces around him, Melissa noticed he avoided meeting her eyes.

"Where's Ella?" he said with a frown. No one answered. "Never mind. I want to let you all know in person before the e-mail goes out. We're doing some restructuring. Long overdue. Starting Monday, all special investigations and projects will be under the direct supervision of Blaine." He indicated the assistant news director, who didn't bother to hide his smug smile. "Our own Melissa McGuire will work exclusively with the top anchor here in San Gabriel, who I need remind none of you, and she would remind you herself if she were here, is Ella Joy. Since the City Hall fire, ratings on the *Eleven O'Clock News* have gone up another point, and a compelling case can be made that it's due to Ella. We need to capitalize on this momentum. I want Ella fronting at least one field report a week. Melissa, this will be your responsibility."

Melissa stared at him with burning eyes, but still he refused to meet her gaze.

"Any questions?" he said, in a tone that discouraged any such thing.

She should keep her mouth shut. Accept the change in duties and soldier on. Make no waves, like a good little "halfway decent producer." But she didn't. "What will my title be?"

"Same. Anything else?" He looked around the table.

Again, her mouth opened on its own. "What about my salary?"

"That's for another conversation." Melissa knew what that meant. Translation: same. It didn't matter anyway. They could double her salary, and it wouldn't make any difference. She rose to her feet.

"No," she said. In the sudden silence, she heard the blood singing in her ears.

Loudon's weary gaze traveled reluctantly back to her. "Please, Melissa. Sit down. Don't make a scene."

Don't make a scene? *Don't make a scene?* Exactly what Everett had said, while he was driving a stake through her heart and her career.

"I'll damn well make a scene whenever I damn well want to. If you think I'm just going to sit still while you turn me into Ella's little news slave, you can kiss my ass." Out of the corner of her eye, she saw a ring of shocked faces around the conference room table. Loudon's eyes widened; it might have been the first time she'd seen them fully open.

"Oh, I know what you're thinking. Hardworking little Melissa, just shuts up and does as she's told. The only one who can put up with Ella's crap.

Well, no more. I kicked ass on that fire story, and I kick ass on every other story I do, and if you can't see that, you have your head up your ass even more than most news directors. So you can take your precious little title and your nonexistent pathetic raises and do you-know-what with them."

She gathered up her papers and marched out of the room. She'd said the word "ass" four times in one tirade. Too bad Brody missed it; he would have laughed his ass off.

Then it sank in. She'd just quit her job.

In the safety of her cubicle she dropped, shaking, into her chair. The red light on her phone blinked. Her computer hummed. This morning's Starbucks cup teetered precariously on the edge of her desk. She threw it in the trash. She'd have to clear out her desk. Blindly, she started piling up papers. Her career, for which she'd struggled so hard, was over. You couldn't leave two news stations under tumultuous circumstances without paying for it.

Chang stuck his head into her cubicle. "You okay, loudmouth?"

"Leave me alone."

"What'd you get, a personality transplant?"

"No, I got a clue. I'm not letting anyone walk all over me anymore. And that includes you!" She turned on him. "Next time, knock before you walk into my soon-to-be-former cubicle."

"Dude!" he protested. "This is me, Nolan. When did I ever do you wrong?"

"Sorry," she muttered. "Not a good day. Will you do me a favor and tell Ella I'm outta here?"

"Tell Ella what?" Ella sauntered past Chang and

perched on Melissa's desk. She wore her fuchsia suit, but the blouse was partly untucked, and she had a general air of disarray about her. Her lipstick was smudged. She looked, thought Melissa with disgust, like an ad for some kind of trashy liqueur.

"I'm gone, that's what."

"What? Absolutely not. I'll talk to Loudon. He can't fire you without my consent."

Melissa shot back. "I'm not fired. I quit."

"Well, I'll talk to someone. You're not leaving, and that's final."

"Ella!" Melissa jumped to her feet to face off with the anchor. "I am done. Done. No one here has any say in what I do anymore. Especially you. So get out. Go kiss Everett's ass, and get your little interview. Maybe if you're really lucky and your guardian angel is watching out for you, you won't get the job. If you do, don't say I didn't warn you. Then again—silly me. If anyone can handle it, it's you."

She hauled Ella off her desk and gave her a push toward the cubicle door. Chang barely managed to get out of her way, and had to catch her as she stumbled. "Damn, Ella, you smell like—"

"Never mind," Ella snapped as she twitched her arm away from his grasp. She stalked back to her office. Every flimsy wall in the newsroom shook as she slammed the door shut.

Melissa, shaking from the aftershocks of all her outbursts, stuffed her personal possessions into the cardboard box that held the recycling. Photos of her and Grans, postcards from various friends, some inspirational quotes. This was right, she knew it. It was about time she started to stand up for herself. *Stand up for herself.* Rodrigo had used the same phrase.

Oh crap. Rodrigo. How could she help Rodrigo if she had no job? He was, at this moment, about to risk everything to get the footage she needed. And as a former employee of the Sunny Side of the News, there would be absolutely nothing she could do with it.

Chapter Twenty-one

*B*rody strode through the station, ignoring all attempts at friendly greetings, and shut himself in his office. These days, not even Stan was allowed in. The poor dog whimpered outside the door. Brody buried his head in his hands. Everything felt wrong. Rebecca had been living in his house for four days. On every one of those days, he'd wanted to ask her to leave. But he couldn't bring himself to do it. Protecting Rebecca had been second nature for so long.

But he didn't want her. He wanted Melissa. With Melissa, he felt alive. He could let down his guard, he could laugh. With her, he didn't have to be the invincible commander. Except in bed, of course.

His groin throbbed. He missed Melissa with a fierceness that kept him awake at night. She kept coming to him in his dreams, a soft-skinned goddess with magical eyes.

Someone knocked on the door. "Come in."

Ryan poked his head in. He looked nervous.

"What's up, Hoagie?"

"I just thought I'd . . . Well, to tell you the truth . . . That is to say . . . What I mean is that . . . You know . . ."

Good Lord. What was wrong with the kid? "I can't even begin to guess what you're talking about." He fiddled with a paperweight on his desk, hoping Ryan would take the hint and leave.

"No, I know. How could you?"

"How could I what?"

"Guess. You couldn't."

"And I won't. Is that it?"

"Yes. I mean, no, darn it! Here it is." He gestured with one hand, as if presenting a gift. "Be grateful for each moment, for it is a gift from the universe."

"What?"

"Be as the wave on the ocean. The wave doesn't notice when it begins, and when it ends."

"Excuse me?" Had Hoagie smoked something before work?

"Be happy in the here and now, because the past is gone, and the future may never arrive. Suffering is the greatest of all teachers. From suffering comes compassion. The night is darkest just before the dawn." The affirmations came tumbling out of him like rocks skipping down a mountainside.

Brody didn't know whether to be touched or offended. "Well . . . um . . ." Touched won out. Ryan had a good heart. "Food for thought. Thanks."

"You know, if you're having problems with Hollywood . . . well, do you want any of us to talk to her?"

So that's what this was about. He should have known. "Why would I want that?" Brody scowled, but Ryan didn't back down. He'd never lacked guts.

"We all really like her, and sometimes you can be . . . Well, we know you really well, so if you did something to make her mad, I could explain it to her. Maybe she doesn't understand—"

"Rebecca's back," interrupted Brody, punctuating his shocking statement by plopping the paperweight back on the table.

Ryan took a step back. "Back? Back here?" He looked around wildly, as if expecting to see her emerge from a corner.

"Back with me." He couldn't manage to bring one bit of enthusiasm to that announcement. Once the words were out, it sounded like a death sentence.

"Oh."

"Got an affirmation for that?"

Ryan's jaw tightened. Brody knew he'd never liked Rebecca. "Sure, but they might have some curse words in them."

Brody felt a smile crack his face—the first in days. "We're here for you, Captain. No matter what."

"I appreciate it, Hoagie. Now get the hell back to work."

After Ryan left, Brody's brief smile disappeared. He'd said the words aloud, so it must be true. Rebecca was back in his life.

She'd settled herself into the main house with a worker-bee attitude that implied she had no intention of leaving any time soon. Her clothes were everywhere. One bedroom had become her crafts room, where she was busily turning out new versions of the famous flip-flops. She'd set up a computer and fax machine to take orders.

She spent most of her time on the computer, and most of that time was spent arguing with Thorval. They had long, angry e-mail exchanges about the business and God knew what else. Hours later, she would still be fired up, fizzing like a firecracker, anxious to relate every heinous thing Thor had said.

But she was trying hard to patch things up, putting together nice meals from takeout and inviting him up to the house. After dinner, despite her broad hints and increasingly provocative lounging outfits, he took himself off to the trailer.

There in the Airstream, where the air still had a tang of vanilla and every surface held a memory of the sensual wonders of Melissa, he'd watch TV until he finally fell asleep. Funny that before this, his deepest desire had been for Rebecca to admit her mistake and beg him to take her back.

There's an affirmation for you: Be careful what you wish for.

Now it was happening, almost exactly as he'd fantasized, and it brought him not an ounce of joy. But what could he do? He couldn't abandon her now, not with a baby coming. Maybe the baby would change her. Make her more . . . coolly intelligent, more sweetly vulnerable, more cream-over-fire, more forest-green-eyed. More Melissa.

Stop, he ordered himself. *Melissa is gone. Don't torture yourself.* He looked at the scheduling calendar. Thursday. He had tomorrow off. And all weekend. What would Rebecca try to pull if he was around all weekend? He'd better stick to the Airstream.

On Friday afternoon, while scrubbing the Airstream bathroom, he heard Melissa's Volvo drive up. He would have recognized that coughing, rattling noise anywhere. His pulse raced and he scrambled to get the yellow rubber gloves off his hands.

But when he opened the door he found not Melissa, but Haskell, who looked like he'd rather be anywhere else.

"Good to see you, Haskell."

"Yah." The man shifted from foot to foot. Brody wondered if he too was about to spout some affirmations.

"Can I get you some coffee? Tea?"

"Nah."

A long silence followed, during which Brody decided to make himself some coffee. Haskell followed him into the trailer and sat at the kitchen booth while Brody ground the beans, boiled the water, and pulled out a mug.

"You sure you don't want any?"

"Yah."

Brody shrugged and poured boiling water over the filter. Talking had never been Haskell's forte. If he had something to say, he'd get to it when he got to it. When Brody had finally settled back at the table, mug in hand, Haskell cleared his throat.

"So, you don't got no one to make your coffee for you?"

At first Brody didn't get it. Who would make his coffee for him? Then he understood, and almost laughed out loud. Haskell was asking about Rebecca.

When he didn't answer right away, Haskell blurted out, "Nelly wants to know. My ma."

"Nelly sent you to find out if anyone's making my coffee?"

"You know how she is."

Haskell, looking miserable, fiddled with the salt shaker. Brody racked his brain for a way to let him off the hook. For the second time that day, should he say out loud that Rebecca was back in his life? If he said it to Haskell, it would be irrevocable. Melissa would know within an hour. Maybe it would be better that way. It would help him put thoughts of Melissa aside. Yes, that's what he should do. This was the perfect opportunity. But when he opened his mouth, the words refused to come. He snapped it shut and willed himself to try again. Nothing. Absolutely nothing. Mystified, he started to try one more time, when a commotion outside made both men jump up.

"Harry!" he heard Rebecca yell. "Harry, get out here!"

Haskell and Brody ran outside. Rebecca stood on the front steps, shrinking back in horror from a small, bloodied figure. She was shrieking and clutching her belly. "This . . . creature is trying to attack me! Get him away from me!"

The kid—just a boy—shook his head and held up his hands to show he meant no harm.

But Rebecca kicked at him. The boy stumbled backward.

"Rebecca, stop that! He's not trying to hurt you." He ran to the boy, who was nearly unconscious and mumbling deliriously. Ignoring the blood, he grabbed him before he fell. "What's your name, kid? What happened?"

"What do you care what his name is?" cried Rebecca. "He tried to hurt my baby!" Haskell put a hand on her shoulder to calm her down, but she shook him off.

"No!" mumbled the kid. "No, no. Don't let her kick me."

"Relax, kid, no one's going to hurt you," Brody told him. "What happened? Who are you?"

"My head . . . the camera . . . Melissa! I want Melissa." And he passed out.

The kid wanted Melissa? His Melissa? Brody remembered the investigation she'd been talking about, the boy who'd been abused. He pulled out his cell phone to dial her.

"This is Melissa."

At the sound of her voice, he felt more alive than he had in days. "It's Brody. I think the kid you were talking about is here. It looks like someone beat him up. He's asking for you."

"Oh my God. Where are you? Shit, my dad has my car again."

Brody glanced at Haskell. "I'll go get her," Haskell said instantly.

"Call 911 too. I'll be there as quick as I can."

"Harry, what the hell is this? Why aren't you trying to help me instead of him?" Rebecca's voice quivered in that way that used to send him rushing to her side.

"You didn't just get the crap beaten out of you."

She sucked in a breath at his tone. He never

spoke to her like that. "And who's this Melissa? This lowlife's mother? How do you know her?"

Brody ignored her, although he was tempted to march her inside the house and order her to get a grip on herself. Instead he focused on the kid. "Can you say your name?"

He opened his eyes a slit. "Yes. Rodrigo Juarez."

"See? He's probably illegal. We should call the cops," said Rebecca.

"Go get some ice, Rebecca. In the fridge in the trailer."

Rebecca looked mutinous, but he'd used his most commanding fire captain voice. As soon as she'd left, Rodrigo let out a sigh and relaxed.

"How's your head feeling?"

"It hurts. Not too bad. Where's Melissa? I saw her car. That's why I came here."

"She's on her way. Do you want to tell me what happened?"

Rodrigo shook his head, then winced in pain. Brody held him. Rebecca came back with some ice cubes wrapped in a paper towel. She crossed her arms, pouting, while he applied it to Rodrigo's head.

When Haskell drove up, Melissa jumped out before the car had even stopped. Brody drank in the sight of her. Even with a pale face and her dark hair tumbling out of its ponytail, she looked beautiful to him. He saw her take in the scene—Rodrigo in his lap, Rebecca behind him.

Damn it. He'd forgotten about Rebecca.

Melissa dropped to her knees next to him. "Is he okay? Did you call 911?"

"Yeah, they should be here any minute."

"This is all my fault."

At the sound of her voice, Rodrigo's eyes opened again. "I'm sorry," he moaned. "I messed everything up."

"No, no." Melissa's fierce, bossy tone sent a chill down Brody's spine. "Don't say that. You're the bravest kid I know."

"She hit me so much, worse than ever . . ."

"Shhh. You don't have to talk now."

But he didn't seem to want to stop. The sentences came out in short gasps. "I hid in the closet . . . I put the camera up, just like we said . . . the social worker lady took the money . . . then after she left I came out of the closet. I was so happy because it all worked out. Then she saw how happy I looked and got mad. She beat me, bad. She'd been drinking a lot. The watch slammed against the wall and came off my wrist. I don't know what happened to the cell phone. It's gone."

Melissa's face was absolutely white. "I'm so sorry, Rodrigo."

"Not your fault. She always gets nasty like that when she drinks too much."

Melissa picked up his hand and stroked it. "You're so brave. I'm so proud of you. How'd you end up here?"

"After she kicked me out, I walked for a long time, all bloody and all, but no one stopped to help me. That's how Fern Acres is, you know. Then I went through some kind of woods and come out on this street. I saw your car. I figured this must be your house. I couldn't believe how lucky I was, like a miracle. Like God was looking out for me.

Then that crazy lady came out and started kicking me." He started to get upset again, but Melissa shushed him.

"Forget about that now. Just lie back and rest. It's going to be fine."

"What's going to happen? Do I have to go back there? What about the other kids?" He clutched at Melissa's hand.

Melissa wanted to cry at the terror on Rodrigo's face. It was bad enough thinking she'd nearly gotten him killed. No way was she going to let him go back there. She shot Brody a desperate look.

"I can call some people," he said quietly. "I'll make sure he doesn't go back there. And we'll get the others out too."

"But the story . . . the camera . . ." Rodrigo whispered. "I messed it all up."

"Don't worry about that. I'll figure out a different way to do the story. And it was such a tiny camera anyway." She forced a smile. The camera was covered by the station's insurance, but did her current nonemployed status change things? She'd worry about that later, along with the question of exactly how she could tell Rodrigo's story with no footage and no job.

"Oh, wait!" said Rodrigo. He stuck his hand in his pocket and came up with a shattered wristwatch. "Maybe it will still work. I made sure I got it."

Amazed, Melissa took it into her palm. "You're something else, Rodrigo."

Ambulance sirens blared in the driveway. Rodrigo looked so scared she promised to meet him at the hospital.

Once the ambulance arrived, the paramedics

took charge of Rodrigo. Haskell reached a hand
down to help Melissa up. She took it gratefully.
Anything to keep from looking at Brody and the
beautiful blond pregnant woman who hovered
behind him. As soon as Brody stood up, she linked
her arm possessively in his. "Sorry I got the wrong
idea about the boy. Blame my crazy pregnancy
brain."

Melissa forced a smile—at least she hoped it
was a smile. "I'll try to explain that to him."

"I'm Rebecca," she continued. "And you must be
Melissa."

"Yes."

"And did I hear you call Harry's helper Dad?"

Harry's helper? Whatever. "Yes."

"So that's how you know Brody?"

Melissa darted a look at Brody, who was frowning in a distracted kind of way. Clearly, Rebecca
knew nothing about her. Brody hadn't bothered to
mention her. Then again, why should he? It had
been a brief, passionate interlude that meant nothing to him.

"Let her be, Rebecca," said Brody quietly. "Why
don't you go inside and have a rest?"

"A rest? But I'm not tired."

"I'd think you would be, after such a traumatic
event." Despite the edge in his voice, she made no
move to go inside the house.

"That's sweet, but I'm fine now. Y'all want a soda
or something? We have a bunch of Snapple, and
some Diet Coke. I'd make you some tea, but this
big meanie here refuses to hook up the stove yet."

Melissa felt something give way inside her. Any
secret hope of a misunderstanding evaporated.

Clearly, Rebecca was living here with Brody, acting like the lady of the house. It took all her pride to keep from bursting into tears on the spot.

Haskell tugged at Melissa's arm. "Ambulance is about to leave. I'll drive you to the hospital."

"Thanks," she said gratefully. She couldn't stand another minute of this.

As they left, Brody called after them, "Melissa, I'll let you know what I come up with for Rodrigo."

Without looking back, she nodded. Why look back, when she knew what she'd see? Handsome firefighter, gorgeous wife, baby on the way. A pretty picture, with no room for Melissa.

Chapter Twenty-two

As soon as they'd reached the road, Haskell asked, "You okay?"

"Yes," she said in a strangled voice. But all the awfulness—Rodrigo so beaten up, Brody with Rebecca—overwhelmed her. "No."

She tightened her throat to keep the tears back, but it didn't work. They spilled over, dripping down her face.

"Aw, Mel. Don't cry."

"I'm not. I won't. I just keep screwing everything up."

"Don't say that."

"I should never have let him take that camera."

"Beating would have happened with or without the camera. She'd been drinking."

Melissa looked over at his grim profile, struck by the lines on his face. The flashing lights of the ambulance ahead of them tinted his skin red in a rhythmic on-off pattern. "Take it from a drunk. This wasn't your fault. You did good, Melissa."

"Aw, Dad." More tears flooded her vision. "You're trying to make me feel better."

"Too little, too late, I know." His wry smile made her put her hand on his shoulder.

"No, it isn't. It means a lot."

They both fell silent. Melissa tried to imagine how much strength it must take to kick a drinking habit. "Dad, I'm . . . well, I'm glad you're doing so well. And I'm sorry about before, at the station."

"I quit for you."

"What?"

"Wanted you to know. Nothing else could have made me stop drinking. So don't go thinking you aren't worth anything."

Stunned, Melissa barely noticed the ambulance peel off toward the ER entrance while Haskell drove to the visitor entrance. How had he known that's how she felt? She'd never talked to her father about any of her feelings.

He stopped the car. "Want me to wait for you? You can take the car."

Melissa collected herself. "You don't have to wait. It might be a while. But I'll take the car. I've got to go see someone after this."

"Sure thing. I'll grab a cab."

He got out. "Hope the kid's okay. See you later, Mel."

She watched him walk away with that one-step-at-a-time deliberate stride he'd developed since going into rehab. She rolled down the window and leaned out. "Thanks, Dad. For everything."

* * *

"Ma, it's bad," Haskell told Nelly, shaking his head over his mug of coffee.

"How bad?"

"As bad as it could be. Looks like the woman's moved right in. Melissa saw them. Seems pretty torn up about it."

Nelly busied herself with the newest batch of molasses cookies she was baking. Clearly the situation called for as many cookies as she could churn out. If her interference caused another heartbreak for Melissa, she'd never forgive herself. She should have left well enough alone. She could practically hear Leon saying, "I told you so," with that caustic laugh of his. *Oh Leon, how did I get this wrong?*

"What's she like?" Nelly asked.

Haskell shrugged. "Not much to my taste. Fake. She was hollerin' up a storm, and I don't think the captain thought much of that."

Nelly brightened. "Sounds like a pain in the butt."

Haskell gave a hearty nod. "Big pain. Felt bad for the captain. What are you going to do, Ma?"

She shook her head. "I've done enough."

"What do you mean?"

"Poor Melissa wouldn't be in this fix, eating her heart out, if it hadn't been for me. Your father would be ripping me up one side, down the other right about now."

"No, he wouldn't," Haskell said with a conviction that took her by surprise. "Well, he might be, but he'd be wrong."

"Why do you think that?"

"I'm not the sharpest pencil in the box, but I know Melissa, and I know the captain. Better even than you do. Those two love each other, but they're stubborn. It's like getting two porcupines together. You gotta do something, Ma."

Nelly gave her son a sharp look. She was so used to thinking of him as a drunk, she hadn't noticed the progress he'd made. Now he sat in front of her, concern for his daughter shadowing his lined face, and she remembered the time Melissa had run away from home when she was thirteen. Nelly had taken her in. Haskell had been so enraged he'd broken one of Nelly's favorite chairs and told Nelly to stay out of his daughter's life. After that, she hadn't seen Melissa for two years.

Now he was actually more worried about Melissa than about himself, and he was asking for Nelly's help. How could she turn him down?

"Ma?"

"I don't know, son. I can't think of anything more to do. They might have to figure this out for themselves."

Haskell gave a sad shake of his head. "Then they don't stand a chance. I don't see how they can work themselves out of this mess. But that woman's no good for the captain, I'll tell you that. She's a handful of trouble. And that bun in her oven sure as heck wasn't put there by the captain, and I don't see why he should take on another man's child, when he don't even love the mama. He can't love her, cuz he loves Melissa. He'd be doin' it out of duty, that's all, because that's the way he is. Which just goes to prove what I already know, that he's about the only man I'd say one hundred percent is the right one for our girl." And he shuffled off, leaving Nelly openmouthed at witnessing the longest speech to pass his lips in years.

But what could she do? It would have to be something dramatic. Something that would shake them up. Open their eyes. Put the fear of God into them.

She turned on the oven to bake her cookies. As the flame lit, an idea flared to life.

In her office, with the door closed, Ella poured herself a glass of low-calorie champagne and picked up the phone. On her desk sat the business card Everett had given her. It was more than a business card; it was a ticket to her personal paradise. The name written on the card was Glen Woodman, but it might as well be Saint Peter. Or was it Paul? Whichever saint let people into heaven.

She lifted her plastic champagne flute into the air and toasted herself. Time to celebrate. Once she called Glen Woodman, everything in her life would be different. Good-bye, small-market blues. Hello, entourage.

And boy, had she earned it. Not that it hadn't been fun. She'd never expected the kind of pleasure she'd experienced with Everett Malcolm. But pleasure couldn't take the place of her true dream, which was to be catered to and turned into the star she was meant to be.

She took a long sip of her champagne, then dialed the number on the card, singing each number under her breath as she touched it. "Eight-six-two . . ."

"Channel Thirteen," answered a smoothly professional voice.

"I'd like to speak to Glen Woodman, please," said Ella, equally professional.

"Could you repeat that name, please?"

Ella read it carefully off the card. "Glen Woodman. He's in human resources."

Silence while computer keys clicked. "I'm sorry, there is no Mr. Woodman at this station. Can I connect you with someone else?"

"There is no Glen Woodman?" The words didn't make sense to Ella.

"No."

"Since when?"

"There never has been. Who is this? Can someone else help you?"

"Everett Malcolm gave me this number."

A short silence. When the woman's voice returned, it sounded like she was trying not to laugh. "Mr. Malcolm's not available. Would you like to speak to his assistant?"

Ella hung up the phone as an avalanche of rage crashed over her. The oldest trick in the book. A variation on the one-wrong-digit-in-a-phone-number trick. Oh, Everett Malcolm deserved to be roasted in a deep fryer for this one.

She ran down to the parking garage, hopped in her BMW, and roared off. So what if she had no plan of action? If a burning desire for revenge counted for anything, Everett was toast.

After hours sitting with Rodrigo, Melissa screwed up her nerve and called Everett. The story was far more important than her history with her news director.

This time, she was prepared. When he opened the door of his penthouse suite at the Hilton, she dodged his attempt to kiss her on the cheek. That kiss in the newsroom had made one thing perfectly clear. She was over Everett Malcolm. Way over.

"Don't bother," she said. "This is strictly business." He opened his mouth for one of his trademark wry rejoinders. "And I don't mean that in a wink-wink, nudge-nudge kind of way. If you have any vague memories of what it's like to be professional, this would be a good time to brush the dust off them."

He stared at her with that look of surprise she kept getting lately. "What's gotten into you?"

"Honestly, Everett, what do you care?"

"I always felt badly about how things ended."

"Aw. The guilt must have been unbearable." She went to the coffee table, which looked like the best place to set up her laptop.

Everett followed. "There were twinges."

"I hope Barb made it feel all better."

"This is absolutely fascinating. The evolution of sweet Melissa."

"Oh, get over it. Are you interested in this investigation or not?" Pushing aside a fruit basket, she opened her laptop and spread her notes out on the coffee table. She related to him each step of the foster care investigation. As she spoke, Everett's flirtatious smile vanished, replaced by the alert look of a journalist on the scent of a blockbuster story.

"My temporary title is 'Innocence Betrayed: Fraud in the Foster Care System,'" she concluded.

"Great story," he said thoughtfully. "But it doesn't sound much like the Sunny Side of the News."

"No, believe me, they don't want this story.

Loudon was just letting me work on it to keep me happy. Now he doesn't care about keeping me happy."

"And I do?"

"Despite everything, I believe you care about the news."

"I do. That, in fact, was my original reason for coming to San Gabriel, besides being tricked by your anchor. I saw your live shot."

So much had happened since then, it took a moment for Melissa to remember what he was talking about. "Oh, you mean the City Hall fire? I was only on for a few minutes."

"You did a stellar job. As soon as I saw you on the network feed, I knew it was time to lure you back to the big leagues."

"*What?*"

"I want you back in Los Angeles. Back at Channel Thirteen."

"But . . ." There were so many "buts," Melissa didn't know where to start. "I thought I was just a 'halfway decent producer.'"

"Excuse me? I never said that." Everett reached for the fruit basket and popped a grape in his mouth.

"Oh yes, you did."

He shrugged. "Well, it must have been in the heat of the moment. You're a superb producer, always have been."

Melissa drew a hand across her forehead, feeling dizzy. Just like that, her deepest trauma dismissed.

"Well, what about Barb?"

"Barb doesn't run my news department. None of your replacements have been up to snuff. She admits as much."

Melissa stared at him, her mind racing. Go back to LA? It was what she'd been working toward. It would mean the resurrection of her career. No more Ella stories. No more Ella calendars. But . . . she'd have to leave Nelly. What would her grandmother do without her? Who would she boss around? *And what about Brody?* Irritated, she shook away the thought of Brody. What did he have to do with anything? Brody was back with Rebecca. Beautiful, pregnant Rebecca.

"Why didn't you?" she suddenly asked.

"Why didn't I what?"

"Sleep with me." Until this moment, she hadn't realized how much it had bothered her. Everett slept with everyone, as far as she could tell. Why not her?

"Well, I could tell you it was because I thought too highly of you to toy with your heart in that way."

Melissa snorted. "And you'd expect me to believe that?"

"It was part of the reason. But mostly, truth be told, Barb would have cut my balls off. She doesn't much care what I do outside Los Angeles, but she protects her territory."

All that heartbreak she'd gone through, all that angst, for such a pathetic reason.

Melissa looked down at her laptop. Maybe this *was* her chance to put her career back on track. Maybe going back to LA, now that she felt nothing for Everett, would be a good move. But somehow it just felt so . . . wrong.

"All I want to talk about right now is Rodrigo. Do you want to see the footage he shot?"

"Yes, I want to see the footage. We'll have the other conversation another time."

She opened her laptop and clicked on the video file she'd downloaded from the lipstick camera's memory card. As Everett watched the footage, she knew he was hooked. Melissa had already seen it several times, but it still made her sick. The exchange of money was so blatant, so callous. Rodrigo had also managed to get shots of his foster mother beating a little girl, who was no more than three, with willow branches.

"And this boy is willing to go public?"

"Absolutely. He's in the hospital right now, waiting to be interviewed. He's the real thing, Everett. He's a hero. He's doing this for the other kids in his foster family."

"Well, this footage is outrageous. I've never seen anything like it. But there are invasion of privacy issues."

"True, but we can use it to confront the caseworker and the foster mother."

"Do you have any corroborating witnesses?"

"A neighbor. And a former caseworker who suspected. She's willing to go on camera."

She had the goods on this story; she knew it and Everett knew it.

"I think we can use this in LA, even though it's not local. As long as Channel Six doesn't mind giving us the rights."

Melissa recognized the opening gambit of a negotiation. "It's local enough. We're only a few hundred miles away."

"No one in LA cares about San Gabriel."

"They'll care when they see this footage."

They began arguing over whether it should be a week-long series or a special report, whether it was better for the *Five O'Clock* or the *Eleven O'Clock News*. It felt amazingly good to argue with Everett. She never would have dared in the old days, when she was Everett's awed, innocent junior producer.

She got so wrapped up in their discussion, the bang of the door opening barely registered, until Everett spoke.

"Why, Ms. Ella Joy. Such an unexpected pleasure."

Melissa's head shot up. Ella Joy stood in the doorway like an avenging angel in a leopard-patterned silk suit and stiletto heels. Her blue eyes blazed like lighter fluid on barbecue coals. Melissa hoped her suit was too tight for hidden weapons.

"Unexpected? *Unexpected?* You think I'm going to put up with that kind of crap?" Ella planted her hands on her hips.

"I rather think you'd put up with any kind of crap to get where you want."

"Well, you're wrong. I mean, you're right, but not that. That doesn't get me anywhere."

He threw his head back in a laugh.

Melissa looked from Ella to Everett. "This scene feels kind of familiar. What'd you do now, Everett?"

"Me? I was an unwitting pawn in this ambitious young anchor's web."

Melissa laughed. "Everett Malcolm, unwitting pawn. I like the sound of that."

"Have I already mentioned that you've changed?"

"You think so?" said Melissa.

"I'm not entirely sure I approve."

Ella stomped her foot. "Do you mind? This isn't about *Melissa*."

Everett turned his attention back to Ella. "Oh? What's it about?"

"Glen Woodman."

Melissa closed the laptop. "Maybe the two of you need a little time alone."

Everett put on a look of mock alarm. "You'd leave me at such a precarious moment?"

"Absolutely. I'll be out on the balcony."

"Don't get too close to the railing. The bellhop might see you," said Ella in her nastiest tone.

"What?"

"Control your bile, my dear," said Everett.

Melissa tuned them out and walked onto the balcony. It was hard to miss the secretive, hot look that had passed between Ella and Everett when she'd said the word "balcony." Obviously they were hooking up. It didn't surprise her. Of course Ella would have made a play for Everett, and of course Everett would have jumped at the chance. What did surprise her was how little it bothered her.

Had Ella fallen for him? Everett had a way of playing to a woman's secret fantasies. For Melissa, it had been to make her feel like she was a legitimate talent, a real newsperson despite her background. The first time he'd sat down with her and broken down one of her scripts, her heart had melted. It was only when she'd fallen in love with him, and, fool that she was, worn her heart on her sleeve, that he'd turned away from her.

How had he snared Ella? Or had Ella been the one to snare him? Then again, what difference did it make to her? She wanted only one thing from Everett—put Rodrigo's story on the air.

Deciding that she'd given them enough time to fight it out, she strolled back into the room and cleared her throat. "Ahem."

Everett had Ella backed up against the wall. She could barely see Ella's tiny body behind his lean one, but she heard her little moans.

Everett pulled away, with an actual look of embarrassment—something Melissa didn't think she'd ever seen on that suave, cynical face before.

"I'm sorry to spoil the fun, but I'm here on business, and I'm a busy woman." Never mind that she was unemployed.

"Call my office tomorrow," said Everett. "We'll work out the details."

"Wait one minute," said Ella sharply, straightening her skirt. "You aren't pulling a Glen Woodman on her, are you?"

"Who is this Glen Woodman?" asked Melissa.

"No one," said Everett.

"You got that right." Ella brushed past him to corner Melissa. "You can't trust this bastard."

Melissa tried to squirm past the tiny anchor, but Ella seemed to be channeling a pit bull. "That sounds familiar. Didn't I tell you that all along?"

"I know, I should have listened to you. But you know how I am." She spoke over her shoulder to Everett. "And Everett, I don't care how hot and bothered you get me, I'm still going to beat you." Back to Melissa. "Melissa, I know all about your investigation. And you know damn well that it should be airing on Channel Six. It's a San Gabriel story. It belongs on a San Gabriel channel. And you used San Gabriel equipment to shoot it."

Melissa felt her jaw drop. "How do you know about it?"

"Seriously, do you think anything happens in that newsroom that I don't know about? The only thing I don't know is whether the kid got the footage, and I'm guessing that's what you and Mr. Big Shot were looking at."

"You know, Ella," said Melissa thoughtfully. "You should seriously think about getting into the news business."

"I'll tell you what, I *am* thinking about it. I've got a brain like everyone else, you know."

"Don't get carried away, now," Everett said nastily.

"Shut up, you!" Ella stomped a stiletto-booted foot on the thick carpet, and Melissa could have sworn the sound of a whip hissed through the room. She took the opportunity to slip under Ella's arm and make her way to her laptop.

Ella whirled around. "I'll tell you what's going to happen. Melissa is going to bring that story back to Channel Six. I'm going to be the anchor who exposes corruption in the foster care system. And I'll be doing it for all the little children of San Gabriel."

"Except the ones with intact families," said Everett.

"I said, shut up! Melissa, you heard him. He's cynical, he doesn't care about anything or anyone, he uses people, even innocent people . . ."

"Innocent people like you?" said Melissa skeptically, putting her laptop back in its case.

"No. Like you."

Melissa's startled gaze swept up to meet Ella's. Was that something kind of like sympathy in those beautiful china-blue eyes?

"I probably deserved what I got, messing with Everett. But I sure as hell know you didn't."

Melissa wondered if she was supposed to be touched. Ella Joy, coming to her defense. Sympathizing with her. Only to further her own purposes, of course. "Don't try to tell me you're looking out for me."

"I know I haven't always treated you right. But this isn't about me or you. It's about doing what's best for the little children of San Gabriel." She clasped her hands like a saint praying to heaven, then added, "With the extra bonus of screwing with the man who screwed with us."

Melissa nearly choked trying to hold back her laughter.

"Very touching," mocked Everett. "But female solidarity can't compare to the lure of the second biggest market in the nation. Melissa, you came here to make a deal. I'm willing to negotiate. *Eleven O'Clock News*, four-part series. You're the executive producer."

"And who's the producer, Glen Woodman?" mocked Ella. "Don't make any deals with that devil, Melissa. We don't want *him* getting our story. I'll get you everything he's offering, and more. I promise. I'll get your job back for you. No, I'll get you a better job. Whatever you want, I'll get it for you."

Melissa looked from one to the other. They might have been made for each other. Two ambitious, selfish, manipulative, spoiled people. She gathered up her notes and stuffed them in her laptop case. "Will you promise me something, both of you?"

Two gorgeous heads nodded.

"You can have all the sex you can stand, but please don't reproduce." They gaped at her as she closed her case with a satisfying zzzzip. "As for the investigation, I'll get back to you."

And with that, she figured "sweet Melissa" was officially history.

Chapter Twenty-three

T he next morning, for the first time in days, Nelly woke up with no pain clawing at her gut. It was five in the morning. She walked into the kitchen and opened the window. Leaning out, she took deep breaths of the fresh night air. The intoxicating scent of jasmine filled her senses. When was the last time she'd enjoyed the beautiful flowers she and Leon had planted?

"I've been so worried about Melissa, I forgot the simple things, like how delicious that jasmine is. Even if it is a girl flower, like you used to say."

A hunger pang gave her another surprise. Nothing but pain had come from that region of her body in weeks. Before she put her plan into action, she decided to make her favorite breakfast, never mind that it was still dark out.

"Time for some oatmeal, Leon. Best way to start the day."

Her mouth watered at the thought. She put a

cup of oats in a pot, then added two cups of water. She turned on the burner, and stared fondly at the flame that leaped at her command.

Fire was going to help her get Brody and Melissa back together.

When the oatmeal was done, she added raisins, brown sugar, and cinnamon. She rummaged around the cupboard for walnuts, chopped up a handful, and threw them in too.

The first mouthful was bliss. She closed her eyes to savor it. It tasted of comfort, a mother's love, a child's contentment. This was the breakfast her mother had made for her, and the breakfast she'd made for Haskell. Even Leon had grown to like it, though he was more of an eggs and bacon man. She ate slowly, savoring every nausea-free bite.

After she'd finished her oatmeal, she made one phone call, asked one question, and nodded with satisfaction at the answer. The captain would be in at nine. The timing had to be perfect.

"I got half an hour, Leon. I think I'll conserve my energy."

She settled in on the living room couch with a paperback. It was one of her favorites, *Love's Wild Fury*, about a Viking princess and her passionate, decade-long love affair with a supernaturally strong ship's captain. The princess had ice-blond hair and glittering green eyes, but as Nelly read, half dozing, the blond hair morphed into a rich dark brown, and the princess began to occasionally wear glasses. The captain started commanding his ship while wearing firefighter gear, and he never seemed to lose his cool, with those intense charcoal eyes of his.

The princess and the captain, when they weren't falling lustfully into each other's arms, were always at each other's throats. The princess kept waving a sword in the captain's direction. *Don't fight him*, Nelly urged silently. *He loves you, can't you tell?* But the princess didn't seem to hear, so she whirled the sword over her head. It sliced through the air and flew out of the princess's hand. "Nooo!" screamed the princess, and dashed after it. But it was too late. The sword sang through the air with eerie purpose, and embedded itself in Nelly's stomach.

Nelly woke up with a guttural cry. She clutched her belly, expecting to see gallons of blood pouring out of her. No blood, just the old pain, with a grim new face.

"Oh, Leon! This is bad. Real bad."

Now she knew the pain in her stomach had been holding back all this time. *This* was the real pain. Impossible to fight, impossible to bear. But she would have to bear it, just a little while longer. Nothing was going to get in the way of her plan.

She put the cordless phone in her pocket, grabbed some matches, and went out the back door. Grabbing the back of the glider for support, she made her way, step by painful step, across the porch. She wasn't too worried about what would happen to the glider or the porch. Brody would get here in time.

She'd chosen the backyard for a reason; it was as far as possible from the front bedroom where Melissa slept. There would be no risk of Melissa hearing as she dragged the garbage can next to the back porch. After taking a deep breath for strength, she knocked the can over so the trash spilled to the ground. The can made a dull thud as it hit the grass, and she held her breath, afraid she'd woken up Melissa. But all was quiet inside the house.

As Nelly arranged the trash in a trail to the wooden railing of the back porch, she smiled fondly at the memory of poor Leon, bless his heart, trying to burn down their work shed for the insurance money. It hadn't worked, and they'd both learned not to mess with fire. Except in dire circumstances. Like now.

"It's okay, Leon. I know what I'm doing. Don't you be nagging at me."

She found the lighter fluid next to the barbecue grill. The more she moved around, the better she felt, but she couldn't count on that to continue. It was a lucky reprieve. A sign she was doing the right thing. She sprinkled lighter fluid along the trail of trash, and on the porch railing. After giving it a moment to soak in, she took the cordless phone out of her pocket.

"San Gabriel Fire Station 1, please," she told the operator.

"Is this an emergency?"

"Not yet."

"Excuse me?"

"Well, if you don't connect me, it will be an emergency. But right now, I can't say as it is. Is that too complicated for you?"

After a brief, offended silence, the operator put her through.

"Fire Station 1, at your service." Nelly relaxed. She recognized that voice. Ryan, the blue-eyed cowboy. She could still see him strolling across the stage of the San Gabriel Hilton while all the girls went crazy. With a satisfied smile, she lit a match and tossed it on the trash. Flame flared instantly.

"Ryan, it's Nelly McGuire. Can you put me on with Captain Brody?"

"Ms. McGuire, it sure is a treat to hear your voice again. What can the San Gabriel firefighters do for you?"

This was no time for flirting! Nelly anxiously watched the eager flames eat their way through the trash. "I need the captain."

"Well, Cap's off today, but I can get you Captain Kelly. Plus we've got a fire station full of guys who'd love to help you out."

Brody was off? Her heart sped up, her breath came in pants. Why, oh why, hadn't she specified *which* captain was coming in at nine? It wouldn't do for Captain Kelly to come to Melissa's rescue. No, no, no. It had to be Brody. Brody was supposed to rush over and rescue them. Only seeing Melissa in danger would make him see how much he loved her. "Page him!" she said desperately as the flames reached the porch railing. "Fire! Melissa's trapped inside!"

Then pain squeezed a ruthless fist around her heart. She dropped the phone and fell to the ground.

At the same moment that Nelly was dreaming about a captain in firefighter gear, Brody was knocking on the door of Casa de Rebecca, as he now called it. No one answered his insistent knocking. Damn her, where had she disappeared to? And how had she managed to lock him out of his own house?

It had taken him long enough to figure out the

answer to the Rebecca situation. The last thing he needed now was a delay.

He prowled around the house, peering in windows, until he spotted Rebecca in the spare bedroom. She bent, scowling, over her computer. It looked like she was hard at work—if someone could be hard at work while wearing a feathery, nearly transparent robe. Fortunately, he hadn't installed the windows yet, and nothing but heavy plastic covered the empty gaps in the wall. He ripped away a corner of the plastic and hoisted himself through the empty frame.

Rebecca looked up with a startled frown. With a visible effort, she forced a smile. "What are you doing?"

"I'm calling your bluff." He swung his body completely into the room, leaned back against the window frame, and crossed his arms.

"What bluff? I don't know what you're talking about."

"Let's get married. Right now. I called up a friend who has one of those online minister's licenses, and he's on his way over."

"What?" She looked desperately at her computer as if the entire Internet had betrayed her.

"Aren't you the one who said it could be like it almost was? We could be a family?"

"Yeeess. But—"

"But what? You've been living here like you intend to stay. You know I'm not the kind to live in sin."

"But Harry . . ." He found her alarm almost comical. "We aren't living in sin. We're like roommates. We aren't *doing* anything."

"I am aware of that."

"Are you saying you want to start having sex? But the baby . . ."

"Exactly, the baby. At some point the baby might want brothers and sisters."

"We can worry about that when the time comes, can't we?" Her eyes darted to the side, checking her computer once again.

"He's not there," said Brody.

"Who isn't . . . what . . . what do you mean?"

With one part of his mind, he knew he shouldn't be enjoying this quite so much. On the other hand, it felt too damn good to finally be free of Rebecca and his need to protect her. He knew the exact moment things had changed for him—when Melissa crouched over Rodrigo's battered body, while Rebecca clung to him in fake terror. He'd known it was fake. He'd pulled enough people out of danger to know what real terror felt like when he held it in his arms. How dare she use a beaten boy to gain sympathy for herself?

At that moment, everything had looked very clear. It wasn't the first time Rebecca had tried to manipulate him. The other times it had succeeded. Now he knew the truth.

Things hadn't worked with Rebecca because she was utterly, completely selfish. Even if he never saw Melissa again, she'd shown him the truth. He *could* have a happy personal life—but not with Rebecca.

Now his ex-wife was looking everywhere but at him, like a child caught stealing candy, and he couldn't help enjoying it.

"Thorval isn't there. That's why he isn't emailing you, and why you aren't having online sex with him at the moment."

Rebecca's jaw dropped open. "You heard us?"

"No windows," he said apologetically, with a gesture at the open frame.

"It wasn't anything . . . we just got carried away . . . It's safer than actual sex . . . better for the baby. And you didn't seem interested. If you are . . ." Rebecca let her feathery robe fall open just a bit.

"I'm not."

"Then why . . . why are you doing this?" Rebecca snatched the robe closed, and a few feathers drifted into the air. With her eyes filled with tears, she looked like a lost duckling. In the old days, he would have been at her feet, petting her, comforting her, soothing her. But those days were over.

A knock at the front door made her jump. "Harry, I can't . . . I can't marry you."

"Really? Why not?" he said, moving toward the front door. "The minister's here, ready to go."

"Because I don't . . . because I love . . . Oh, you're being horrible! I hate you! You have no compassion, no sensitivity, no . . ." Her voice followed him as he left the room. When he returned, followed by a giant man with bleached-tip hair and thick muscles bulging through his tank top, she broke off from her long list of his failings. "Thorval!"

She leaped to her feet and launched herself into the giant's arms, with Brody stepping aside just in time. Did he feel a tiny pang at the joy in her face, and the way the two of them clung to each other? To be perfectly honest with himself, he did—a pang of regret that he and Rebecca had never been able to make each other happy like that.

"Lady B, boy did I miss you, baby." The blond man covered her face with surprisingly delicate kisses.

"Me too, T, me too! But how did you know? Why'd you come here?"

"Your ex here called me up. Dude's not such a bad guy, you know."

"Thanks," said Brody. They both ignored him.

"He found some little sayings for me. What'd you call 'em? Little quotes, you know, words of wisdom through olden times."

"You mean like affirmations?" Rebecca wrapped her legs around his waist, like a feathery vine around an oak tree. She leaned back to peer at his face.

"Ding-ding! That's the word, my petite. She's a whiz with words," he told Brody. "These affirmation thingies really did a number on me. Especially the one about the ocean, because of my expertise in water sports. Helped me work through some issues, you dig? I'm not scared about the baby anymore. Be as the wave, baby, be as the wave."

"Oh T, I don't know what you're talking about, but I don't care. I love you so!" She snuggled her head between his broad shoulder and his chin, and he nuzzled the top of her head.

"Me too, baby, me too. I'm never letting you scamper away from me again. Me and the baby are going to be tight as a couple of sand fleas. I already got a boogie board for the little guy. He's going to be the Tiger Woods of surfing. That's another thing your ex thought of."

"Harry, you're a genius! How can I ever thank you?"

"You don't have to thank me."

In Brody's pocket, his pager jumped. He was off-shift, damn it. The station could survive for a few more minutes without him. He ignored the beeping.

"I know! T, why don't we name the baby after Harry! I always liked the name Harry," said Rebecca.

"Sure, babe, whatever you—"

"No, no," said Brody hastily. "I absolutely refuse. Besides, what's your last name, Thorval?"

"Mats. In Swedish, it means 'gift of God.'"

"Harry Mats, Rebecca?"

"Okay, maybe that's not such a great idea," she said quickly. "We'll find another way to thank you." She slid down from Thorval's chest, and held a hand out to Brody.

"There's no need. I'm happy you're happy." But he took her hand anyway.

"No hard feelings?"

"No hard feelings."

"Will you go to Melissa now?"

Brody pulled his hand away from hers. "Melissa's with someone else now. An ex."

"Oh Harry. Exes aren't always what they seem, you know." And with a last peck on his cheek, she danced back into Thorval's arms. "Take me home, you big kahuna."

As Thorval carried Rebecca over the threshold, like a wedding night in reverse, Brody heaved a sigh. Now he could get back to life as normal—or at least, normal before the appearance of Melissa. The station, his house, station, house.

Again, his pager beeped.

It had better be important. He pulled it out, and

saw the flashing code that meant an emergency. Damn it! Running into the Airstream for his cell phone, he cursed himself every step of the way. The one time he ignored a page, of course it would be an emergency. What was he, some kind of rookie?

Ryan answered his call on the first ring. "Captain, where are you? The McGuires' house is on fire. Engine 1 and Truck 1 are already headed over there, but I knew you'd want to know . . . and Nelly McGuire said for me to page you, which I would have done anyway, because she said Melissa's trapped inside the house . . ."

Brody was already out the door, running at top speed for his truck. "My turnout's at the station, can you get someone to take it to the house?" he yelled toward the phone, which he tossed into the passenger seat as he jerked the key in the ignition.

"It's already in the rig, Cap."

"Paramedics?"

"On their way."

"Hoagie, you're a champ."

"Drive safe, Cap."

As he reached over to end the call, he nearly swerved off the driveway. Idiot. He couldn't help Melissa if he wound up under a pile of metal on the side of the road. *Just let her live, God, let her live.*

The "curse" flittered through his mind. Was this what happened when a San Gabriel firefighter dared to dream of real love? *I won't ask for anything else. Just let her live. I'm begging.*

A strange smell woke Melissa up. It had a bitter taste that made her throat tingle. At first it made her think of the nightmare she'd been having, in which City Hall was burning down with Brody inside. But as she came awake and her head cleared, the smell didn't go away. In fact, it grew stronger.

Smoke. Fire. Had Nelly set something on fire in the kitchen? It was time to get her grandmother to stop messing around with the burners. She jumped out of bed and raced downstairs, hollering as she went.

"Grans! What happened? What's burning?"

No answer. Her grandmother's bedroom door was open. She poked her head inside. It was empty. Nelly must be in the kitchen. But no one was in the kitchen, and no burners were on. She spotted an empty bowl in the sink. The oatmeal had been left out on the counter. So Nelly had been in the kitchen. Had there been a small fire, which Nelly had managed to put out? Melissa frowned at the stove. She saw no signs of charring or blackening on any of the burners.

"Grans!" she called again. No answer.

A sound caught her attention. A sound from outside the house—a kind of flickering, flapping sound, like a sail in the hissing wind. She padded through the kitchen to the door that opened onto the back porch. She opened it, screamed, and slammed it shut. A pillar of flame was shooting from the far end of the porch.

And then it sank in. The back porch was on fire. And she had no idea where her grandmother was. "Grans!" she shouted, opening the door again to peer past the flames. On the backyard lawn, she made out the shape of a body, still and limp, wearing her grandmother's lavender cardigan. A trail of smoldering ashes led from the fallen body to the porch.

"Grans!" she screamed again. "Wake up!" Her stubborn grandmother must have tried to put out the fire by herself. Melissa darted out onto the porch, but a wall of heat stopped her. She ran back into the house. On her way through the house, she looked for the phone, but the cradle was empty. Her cell phone was all the way upstairs. No time to get it. Barefoot, still in her tank top and pajama bottoms, she raced out the front door and around the side of the house.

It seemed to take forever to reach that still body. When she dropped down on the dew-soaked grass next to Nelly, pure fear streaked through her at the look she saw frozen on her grandmother's face. She looked desperate, or maybe terrified. Her skin was a sickly shade of bluish-white. Melissa felt for a pulse in the loose folds of her neck. "Please, Nelly, please be alive, please be alive." The heat from the flames on the porch shocked her. It felt like noon on a midsummer day, not the beginning of December.

After an agonizing moment, she felt a faint pulse. "That's good, Grans, you're still alive. Now wake up, darling, we have to get you out of here." She gently shook the frail body and patted Nelly on the cheek. But the unconscious woman showed no reaction. "That's okay. That's okay. I can carry you. You probably weigh about as much as a cat."

Nelly might look fragile, but she still weighed over a hundred and twenty pounds. Melissa gathered her in a hug, and tried to lift her to her feet, only to fall back to the ground under the weight.

As the two of them tumbled to the grass, she spotted the cordless phone that had been hidden under Nelly's body.

"Oh, Grans, were you calling for help? Why didn't you just yell for me?" She reached for the phone to call 911, but at that moment the flames on the porch gave a terrifying bellow. The fire had reached the roof. If the whole house caught fire, she and Nelly would never be able to get out of the backyard. She had to get Nelly out, now.

Melissa left the phone alone and crouched next to her grandmother. She pulled Nelly onto her back, and tried to wrap her grandmother's arms around her neck. But Nelly slipped off, almost rolling onto the hot ashes on the lawn. Melissa snatched her away from the ashes just in time.

"Oh Grans, please," she begged, panting. If this didn't work, she'd have to drag Nelly across the lawn, and she didn't know what kind of injuries her grandmother had. How did those firefighters do it? They just picked people up as if they weighed nothing. How did Brody do it?

The thought of Brody gave her a burst of energy.

"Let's try this one more time, Grans." This time, finally, blessedly, it worked, and she staggered to her feet with her grandmother draped over her back, cardigan-covered arms dangling over her shoulders. As a burst of heat fanned the backs of her legs, she took one step forward, then another, and then stumbled to her knees. She groaned with frustration and crawled forward on hands and knees across the grass, her grandmother on her back.

The fire roared like an angry lion and the bitter

smell felt thick in her throat. Her world shrank to the square of grass in front of her. If she could just get that far, then she could focus on the next square. But the next square of grass seemed so far away, and the voracious heat beat against her body. The world had no more air. Her body had no more strength. Everything shimmered and began to go black.

Then, in the blurry darkness, a powerful figure appeared in silhouette. Manly and dynamic. A hero in action.

It had to be a hallucination, of course. She would have laughed, if she'd had any air in her lungs. The poster from the bachelor auction was coming to her rescue.

Chapter Twenty-four

Melissa felt her grandmother's weight being lifted off her. Someone hauled her to her feet. "Come on," said an urgent voice. "I'll take her. Are you all right, Melissa?"

Brody. Worried gray eyes scanned her. She blinked at him. The poster wasn't a hallucination, or rather, Brody wasn't a poster. She tried to clear her head. Where had he come from? It was as if he'd parachuted down from heaven.

"Grans," she croaked.

"I've got her." Brody turned his attention to the limp figure in his arms. He tilted her grandmother's head back and listened closely to her breathing.

For the first time, it occurred to Melissa there might be something wrong with Nelly, that she hadn't just fainted from the heat and fear. Brody jogged to the street, carrying her grandmother lightly in his arms. She scrambled after him, wanting to ask what he'd heard, what might be wrong, but sobs choked her and she couldn't get out a single word.

A battalion of vehicles converged on the house in a circuslike blaze of flashing lights and clashing sirens. She recognized Engine 1, and saw Vader and Two jump out. "It's the back porch and the roof," she told Brody, as they reached the paramedic van. He gave one quick gesture to his crew, and they hauled the giant hoses around the side of the house.

Brody seemed more concerned with Nelly. He handed her off to the paramedics, who immediately strapped her to a gurney in the back of the van and attached a battery of electrodes to her.

"What is it? What's wrong with Grans?" Panic gripped her. Everything was happening in some kind of time warp. It had probably been no more than a few minutes since she'd woken up to the smell of smoke, but it seemed like a lifetime.

Brody put his hands on her shoulders and gently turned her to face him. "I think she may have had a heart attack. She's alive, and the paramedics are giving her an injection to stop the clotting. But we won't know the full situation until the doctors examine her."

Melissa stared at him in sheer bewilderment. "Heart attack?" she whispered. "Grans doesn't have a bad heart. It's her stomach."

"Her stomach?"

"Pain in her stomach. But she says the doctor says it's no big deal."

"Who's her doctor?"

Melissa searched her frazzled memory for the

name. Nelly had always insisted on going to see the doctor by herself, and had rarely even mentioned his name. "Daughtry," she finally said. "Dr. Daughtry. I don't know his first name."

Brody relayed this information to the paramedics, then drew her away from the van. "Are you okay? No injuries?"

She shook her head. "No, nothing. It all happened so quickly. She'll be okay, won't she? She has to. You saved her, and you never lose anyone."

Brody didn't answer directly. "You did really well, Melissa. You kept your head."

"No, no, I should have thought of a heart attack. I should have called 911. I should have—" She was interrupted by a rough shake from Brody that made her squeak.

"Stop. She had already called the fire station. You did exactly the right thing. If you hadn't gotten her away from the fire, she might have burned to death." After one last squeeze, he drew away. "Now come on, hop in. I've got a sweater in here somewhere."

"Hop in?" she said, confused, as he led her by the hand toward his truck.

"We're going to the hospital. The ambulance is leaving."

"You're coming with me?" Why did she feel so stupid, like she was one step behind everything he said?

"Unless you have some objection."

She shook her head. Did Rebecca know he was here? But that was a stupid question. He was a firefighter. Just doing his job. "Don't you have to stay and put out the fire?"

"No, they've got it under control. It's not much of a fire," he said with a slight smile.

She attempted a smile in response, but it felt more like a gruesome twisting of her mouth. "Could have fooled me. Is this what you guys call the growth phase?"

"Very good. Been doing your homework. But don't worry, it'll be out before it gets to stage two." Brody helped her into his truck. Which was a good thing, since her body felt so strange and heavy, as if she were walking through molasses. He draped a man's crewneck sweater over her shoulders—it smelled like smoke, like everything else in his truck—then slid into the driver's seat.

"How come I feel so weird, like I can't move right?" she asked him.

"It's the aftershock," he said briskly. "I've seen it many times. You'll feel better in a few minutes. Just rest until we get to the hospital. I have some extra socks in here somewhere too."

Right. She was still barefoot, and her feet had little bits of wet grass all over them. She leaned her head back against the headrest. A sudden thought jerked her upright again. "Oh! I should call my dad."

"I already did. He's meeting us there."

Brody had taken care of everything. He'd thought of everything. Melissa let her eyes drift shut. It felt like being on a magic carpet. She had absolutely nothing to worry about.

Except Grans.

She spent the rest of the ride praying for her grandmother.

At the hospital, Brody quietly took command. He shepherded her through the reception area, got an update on Nelly's condition (critical), and settled her into the waiting area with a cup of coffee. Cream, one sugar. How on earth could he remember how she liked her coffee at a moment like this? But she was beyond questioning anything about Brody. If someone had asked her, she would have said he must be a superhero with mystical powers.

After making another call on his cell phone, he eased into the seat next to her with a sigh.

"I just called your father again. He's about fifteen minutes away."

"Thanks." She felt suddenly guilty for taking up so much of his time. "Is this . . . I mean, is there anywhere else you should be?"

"No, nowhere. But . . ." He hesitated before finishing. "Is there anyone else you want me to call?"

She searched her mind. "I can't think of anyone," she said with a shake of her head. He gave her a probing look. "Her husband's long dead, I told you that, right? It's just me and Haskell. Dad." This seemed to satisfy him, since he sat back with a little smile. She gave him an offended look. Was he smiling because poor Nelly didn't have more surviving family members?

Then the light bulb turned on.

Brody had been asking about Everett. He wanted to know if she wanted to call Everett. She nearly laughed out loud. Even when she'd been in love with Everett, she never would have expected him to rush to her side in a crisis. Besides, Nelly hated Everett. "That man is no good for anyone" had been her mantra. Nothing would be more guaranteed to upset her than Everett showing up at her bedside. She could just imagine Nelly bolting upright on her hospital bed, giving Everett a big old roundhouse slap on the cheek, and falling back into unconsciousness while nurses and doctors buzzed around her.

Brody, on the other hand, had earned Nelly's approval almost right away. Almost. "Remember Nelly's first words to you?" she asked him.

"Sure. Something along the lines of 'Who the hell are you, and how come you're dating my granddaughter and not that handsome blue-eyed hunk I paid for?'"

Melissa winced. "I guess that's about right."

"We never took her money, you know."

"What do you mean? What about the widows and orphans?" She eyed him, sitting so comfortably next to her, as if there were no place he'd rather be than in this fluorescent-lit, disinfectant-scented waiting room.

"Don't worry, they got their donation. I took care of it."

Melissa's face flamed with embarrassment. Had Brody refused to take Nelly's money because they'd slept together? Or had he made the donation out of guilt, after he'd ditched Melissa for his ex? The whole thing was humiliating.

Two white-coated doctors with grim expressions came through the door of the treatment room. Melissa and Brody both jumped to their feet. She grabbed Brody's hand. As the doctors approached, he hugged an arm around her shoulder.

"You must be Melissa," said one of the doctors, shaking her free hand. "I'm Dr. Daughtry. I've been treating your grandmother for some time now.

This is Dr. Swenson, the emergency room doctor."

"This is Harry Brody, my . . . fire captain." God, she sounded like an idiot. The two doctors were a blur. She hoped she wouldn't have to identify them in a lineup later. "Is Grans okay? Is she going to be all right?"

"Your grandmother is awake and wants to see you, but she wanted me to tell you the full extent of her situation first."

"Situation?" She didn't like the sound of that.

"How much do you know about your grand-mother's condition?" he asked.

"You mean the heart attack?"

"No, the stomach cancer."

"Cancer?" The word sent a cold shock through her. Brody's arm tightened around her.

"Your grandmother has terminal stomach cancer. Her heart attack was the result of pain and extreme stress. She's known for some time that she's in her final months, and has refused radi-cal life-saving measures." The doctor adjusted his glasses and looked down at his clipboard.

"Say it so we can understand," said Brody, in that commanding voice no one ever disobeyed.

"I'm sorry, but we don't expect her to survive the night."

No. *No.* The words sank into Melissa's numb brain. Feisty, ornery, bossy Nelly, not expected to survive the night? *Life-saving measures.* What had the doctor said about life-saving measures? "Let me talk to her. I'll convince her. You can do some-thing to save her, right?"

"Honestly, very little, even if she accepted treat-ment. The cancer is quite advanced. She's been living in nearly constant pain for the last few weeks."

"Why didn't she . . . why didn't she . . . ?" *Tell me*, she wanted to say, but couldn't get the words out. The waiting room spun around her, and she heard Brody say quietly, "Give us a moment, please," and then the doctors left, she buried her head in Brody's chest, and his arms closed tight around her as shuddering sobs shook her body. She fought to get control of herself, but the grief had a life of its own. She gave herself over to it. After some time, when the sobs had subsided into hiccups, and she lay trembling in Brody's arms, she came back to herself enough to hear him whispering in her ear.

"Nelly needs you now, Melissa. She wants to see you. Can you do it?"

She nodded, and pulled back to wipe her face. Her hands were shaking too much to have any effect, and Brody gently drew them away to take over the job himself. With the sleeve of his soft flannel shirt, he patted the wetness from her cheeks. "The bathroom's right over there. Go in and wash your face. It'll upset Nelly to see you like this."

"Yeah, you're right." Melissa took a deep, shaky breath. "She's probably going to be cracking jokes and bossing me around."

"This is her time. Let her do as she likes."

She clung to the calm command in those dark gray eyes, to the strength in the hand that still held her shoulder. "Will you go in there and tell Grans I'm coming? And tell her Dad is on his way too."

"Of course I will. Don't take too long though."

She didn't have to be told why. Melissa hurried into the bathroom.

Brody followed the doctors into Nelly's room. Nelly certainly didn't look like the end was near. She sat bolt upright, a scowl on her face, a rubber electrode clutched in her fist, a nurse flailing helplessly by her bed.

"Oh, it's you." She greeted Brody. "What's this crap they've got all over me?"

"The usual. They're trying to keep you alive for a few more hours."

"But I told them—"

"They know. This is just for monitoring. Now let the nice nurse put it back on."

After measuring the calm authority in his face, she grumpily handed the electrode back to the nurse. Brody gave her a surreptitious scan while she lay back and allowed it to be taped to her chest. Her bones looked so frail, her skin nearly transparent, as if her body was halfway to heaven already, with only her fierce, eaglelike gaze left behind. As soon as the nurse left, Nelly turned those eagle eyes on Brody.

"Where's Melissa? Where's my son?"

"Haskell is on his way. Melissa's in the bathroom. She's had quite a night, what with saving you from your own stupidity. Why'd you set that fire, Nelly?"

She didn't bother to look guilty. "I should have known you'd figure it out. Does Melissa know?"

"No. She has enough to worry her."

"You're a good man, Captain Brody. Are you going to come through?"

"Come through?" He frowned. "This isn't about me. What were you up to, Nelly? There's going to be an investigation, and I don't want Melissa hurt by the findings. I need to know the truth, so maybe I can help you."

"I'll tell you. If you tell me something." When he gave a short nod, she continued. "Who told you about the fire?"

"Ryan. He paged me."

"And he told you Melissa was trapped?"

Brody nodded.

"And what did you feel?"

That he would have thrown himself into the flames to save her. That if he couldn't save her, there would be no reason to save himself. That the entire world centered on one house, one bedroom, one irreplaceable woman who needed him.

His face must have given away his emotions, since she gave a satisfied grunt. "That's why I did it."

"What?" Brody strode over to her bedside and loomed over her. "Are you telling me you risked Melissa's life to . . . to . . ."

"Get you to admit you love her. Worked, didn't it?"

Brody clenched his jaw. "If you weren't already . . ."

"Dying? But I am dying. If I weren't, I could have let you two bumbling kids take care of your own business. But you left me no choice. Hand me that water."

Brody, kicking himself for nearly losing his temper with a woman in her waning hours, poured her some water and carefully brought it to her. She sipped from the glass, and a few drops of water spilled down her face. Brody found a box of tissues on the bedside table, and used one to gently dry her chin. At his touch, she closed her eyes.

"You know, when I met my Leon, I couldn't stand the sight of him. I thought he was arrogant, pigheaded, irritating. He came to a dance at the community hall. I grew up in a tiny little town, you know, and our little dances were the only thing to do on a Saturday night. I went with another boy, but Leon just cut right in. I thought it was mighty high-handed of him, but what I hated even worse was when he cut in on my friend Alice May too. Alice May was my best friend, but right then I could have slapped her right into the ground. He called me Nellikins, like I was a little girl. I was only seventeen, but I thought I was all grown up. After that, I could never stop thinking about him. Sometimes I hated him, sometimes I didn't."

She paused to take a deep, raspy breath, and Brody wondered if she was going to fall asleep. But after a few moments, she continued her story. "When he asked me to run off with him, I didn't know if I loved him or not. But I didn't see how I could marry anyone else if all I could think about was Leon. So I said yes. And we sure had a lot of fun times. He wasn't always a good man, my Leon, he lived on the shady side of the street a lot of the time. There were plenty of times I kicked myself for linking myself up to such a character. But I knew I never really had a choice, not if I was going to be honest. I never stopped thinking about him, you know. I still think about him today, even though he's dead these ten years. So I guess I do love him."

"He was a lucky man," said Brody, which made her chuckle weakly.

"Oh, he would have given you an argument about that. According to him, I was the biggest trial any man ever saddled himself with. Stubborn as a rash, he used to say. Never did as I was told. I ran him a pretty dance. But then he'd turn around and tell me his life wouldn't be worth a gob of spit without me, and I thought that was a very pretty thing to say, for a rough man like him."

"Sounds like you made a good match."

"I guess you could say that. Back in my day, we just fumbled and stumbled around. Didn't know what we were doing. Someone came along who had a nice-looking nose, or maybe you liked the way his smile lifted up one corner of his mouth, and the next thing you knew, you were married and churning out babies. Today, you young people think you got all the time in the world to find somebody. Tell me the truth, now, Captain Brody. Is that ex of yours back to stay?"

Taken by surprise, Brody hesitated. Things with Melissa were nowhere. He didn't want to give Nelly false hope.

"It's a simple question, Brody," said Nelly sharply. "Yes or no?"

"No," he finally said. "She's gone."

"Ah." Nelly breathed deeply, as if a heavy weight had been lifted off her shoulders. "Did she leave on her own, or did you give her some assistance?"

"I got the man she really wants to come back."

Nelly glanced up at the ceiling with a triumphant glare. "See that, Leon? You gotta understand, Brody, if I had set my girl up for a heartbreak like that, I'd never forgive myself. And Leon would scold."

"I do see that," said Brody, gravely. "I have no

intention of breaking Melissa's heart. Her heart is taking her in a different direction."

"Everett?" snorted Nelly. "If you think that, you're even more of a bumbling fool than I thought."

Brody ignored the insult. "Last I saw of him, they looked pretty darn happy to see each other."

"Are you going to argue with a dying woman?" said Nelly indignantly. "I'm telling you she doesn't give a hoot for him. You're the one she can't stop thinking about."

"But . . ."

"Ah!" she held up a forceful hand. "No backtalk. Now, do you love my Melissa or not?"

If a meteor would just crash into the hospital and hit her on the head, Melissa would be forever grateful. What did Nelly think she was doing, putting Brody on the spot like that? Nelly knew he'd gotten back together with Rebecca. And Brody was taking a long time to answer the question. He was probably trying to think of the most tactful way to let Nelly down.

"Grans!" she said from the doorway. "Take that back!"

Brody spun around at the sound of her voice, but she couldn't look him in the eye.

"Why should I take it back? It's a perfectly good question." Nelly gave her the feisty glare that meant anything could come out of her mouth next.

"Brody, I'm sorry. My grandmother has no manners."

"You're going to insult a dying woman?"

"Low blow, Grans."

"When you're dying, you get to say anything you want!" Nelly popped up in her hospital bed like a jack-in-the-box. "Brody, answer the question!"

"Brody, don't say a word!" Melissa felt her face flame. How had this gone so wrong? In the bathroom, she had schooled herself on the attitude she should take with Nelly. Loving, tender, but not sentimental. No gushing tears. No sobs. And certainly no angry yelling.

"Ladies," Brody said, obviously trying to calm them down. It didn't work. They both turned on him.

"Stay out of it!" ordered Melissa. Brody began to back out of the room.

"Where are you going?" Nelly demanded. "You stay put and answer my question."

But if anyone could stand up to Nelly, it was Brody. He met her eagle stare with his own calm gray one. "I think you two need some time alone. I'm going to track down Haskell. He just paged me. I'll be right back. Just don't kill each other in the meantime."

When he was gone, Nelly sank back into her pillows. Melissa's anger melted away. She stepped to Nelly's bedside, and saw the way the pulse fluttered in her throat. Her cheeks looked so sunken, her eyes feverish and exhausted. "I'm sorry, Grans."

Nelly reached for her hand and squeezed it. She seemed too exhausted by her outburst to say anything more. Melissa was shocked by the dry, claw-like feel of her hand. "I got so scared when I saw you lying out in the yard. Why didn't you wake me up when you saw the fire?"

Nelly shifted on her bed. "Well, I . . . I just wasn't thinking clearly, honey. All's well that ends well."

Ends well. The phrase made Melissa's tears threaten again. She fought them back. "I won't scold you this time."

"I should hope not," sniffed Nelly. "Scold me, indeed."

For a moment they held hands in silence.

"You know I'm proud of you, right, Melissa?"

"Don't, Grans, please." She'd never be able to keep the tears away if Nelly talked like that.

"I just wanted to say that, before I get into what I really want to say."

Uh-oh. If this was about Brody, Melissa didn't want to hear it. She tried to draw back, but Nelly clung tightly to her hand. "Listen to me. Don't be a damn fool idiot, you promise me? If I have to die thinking you're going to toss away the best man I ever met in my life, and I'm including Leon, since he wasn't always a good man—I'll be mad as a preacher at Mardi Gras. Before I die, I want you to say you love him, and you'll marry him, and start making me some great-grandbabies."

Melissa fought to keep her voice calm. She didn't want to spend her last hours with Nelly fighting. "He's not mine to toss away, Grans. And even if he were, it's not fair to pull this on me. Brody and I never talked about love or marriage or anything like that. It was just a fling. If it weren't, he never would have gotten back together with Rebecca. Without a word to me about it."

Nelly groaned and laid her head back on the pillow. This was never going to work. She shut her eyes, blocking out the stubborn green-eyed gaze of her granddaughter. In its place, the image of Leon danced in front of her. In her mind's eye, she saw Leon give a little shake of his head. He was telling her the dying couldn't have everything their way. And she knew he was right.

"I'm sorry, Melissa love," she whispered. "Guess I get a little carried away now and then."

Immediately Melissa brought Nelly's hand to her mouth and kissed it. Her granddaughter's kisses felt like gentle feathers floating onto her hand. "No, Grans, I don't mind. Get carried away all you want. Order me around all you want."

Nelly opened one eye. "Does that mean you'll think about it?"

Melissa laughed, and held Nelly's hand to her cheek. "Think about marrying Brody? I think about it all the time, all on my own. I'm not entirely hopeless, you know."

"Good." Hazily, Nelly remembered another important thing she had to tell Melissa. It had to do with that other woman. "She's gone, did you know that?"

"Who's gone?"

"Alice May," said Nelly. "He doesn't care about her."

Melissa looked puzzled.

"He told me he sent her away." Nelly continued, trying to make her understand. "I knew he'd do the right thing. I could tell from the beginning that he was crazy for you. Now just take care you don't mess it up."

"Okay, Grans," said Melissa patiently. "I won't mess it up."

Nelly didn't like the sound of that answer. Was Melissa patronizing her? Her granddaughter put a glass of water to her lips. She pushed it away. "You gotta fight, remember that. Did I ever tell you what I did to Alice May?"

"Yes, you spiked her punch, you broke off the heel of her shoe. I remember."

But Melissa still didn't seem to be getting the message. She smoothed out the bedsheet Nelly had rumpled. Who cared about bedsheets at a time like this? Nelly grabbed her arm to make her stop.

"Didn't you hear what I said, girl?" she said, sharply. "The other one is gone."

"I know, Grans, I know. Alice May is gone."

"No! Not her. The other one!" But Nelly, for the life of her, couldn't remember the name of Brody's ex-wife. She hadn't thought it important at the time. Now it seemed like the most important thing in the world. Her mouth working, she struggled to come up with the name. Melissa grabbed the water glass and held it to her mouth.

"Shhh, Grans. Lie back now. Take a sip of water. Please. Everything's going to be okay."

Nelly gulped the water, her throat closing convulsively around the cool wetness. "Promise me . . . promise me . . ." she whispered, clutching at Melissa's hand.

"You don't have to worry anymore, Grans. I promise." Melissa's eyes were so beautiful, like secret pools of green deep inside a forest. They had such a look of love in them. Nelly suddenly knew everything would be okay.

She sighed, and her entire body seemed to surrender. As she closed her eyes, Melissa knelt down next to her. A soft cheek rested on Nelly's hand. Gentle hands smoothed her arm.

When Nelly opened her eyes, after a long argument with Leon about the curtains in their new home, she saw her son, Haskell, gazing down at her. How solid he looked. How . . . fleshy. She felt a shiver of distaste for this world, which held such heavily breathing, thick-bodied, vigorous creatures. Leon wasn't like that, was he? No, not anymore. Her Leon awaited her without the burden of all that flesh. And soon she would fly to him, soaring freely and joyfully.

But for another brief moment, this world still tugged at her, with all its problems and attachments. "Haskell," she said, her voice barely a whisper.

"Ma."

"You're a good boy. I don't know where you got it from."

Haskell smiled broadly. "I don't know about good. But I'll keep trying. One day at a time."

"Good boy," she repeated. This was how she'd wanted it. Quick and happy. Did she have anything more to say? She couldn't think of anything. All those problems, all the worries that had preoccupied her for years—her son's alcoholism, her granddaughter's pain, her anxiety about Melissa's future happiness—now seemed supremely unimportant. It was all going to be fine.

A giggle escaped her. What a joke! What a grand joke the world was. You spend years fretting and plotting, only to find, in the end, that everything was going to be just fine, with or without you. If only she had known this earlier.

I told you so, she heard Leon say with his caustic laugh.

He was talking back to her. For the first time in so many years, she heard his voice.

Oh, get over yourself, she told him crossly. *You always think you know everything.*

I know enough, you old busybody. If you'd minded your own business, you'd have spared yourself a heap of trouble.

Maybe, she agreed. *But I wouldn't have had nearly so much fun.*

Fun, you want fun? You want some sugar? She could hear the cheeky wink in Leon's voice, see the grin on his dear face. *Come on up here, love, and I'll give you a big old heapful.*

She laughed and laughed. She couldn't wait to see Leon again. And then it came to her that the time for waiting was over.

Nelly McGuire gave the beloved faces around her a wide smile and pressed Melissa's hand. Releasing one final, grateful breath, she floated away from her body and jumped eagerly into Leon's waiting lap.

Chapter Twenty-five

*I*n the days after Nelly's death, Melissa went a little crazy. For some reason, she found herself in long, one-sided conversations with her ornery deceased grandmother.

"You sure know how to make an exit, Grans. Set the house on fire. Call out the whole darn fire department. I bet everyone up in heaven is quaking in their shoes, wondering what kind of trouble you're going to make next. Did you really have to resort to arson to try to fix things up for me? And I thought the bachelor auction was bad enough. I'll tell you right now, if you're up there plotting your next move, you'd better take a big step back and, I don't know, consult with an angel or something. And when they tell you to leave well enough alone, you should pay attention for once in your life. Or your afterlife."

The problem was, she was so used to her grandmother's bossy ways that she didn't know what to do with herself now. The house felt so empty without Nelly. And she had nowhere to go—no job to take up her time. Rodrigo's story sat in her computer, forgotten once again. Other than attending to the details of Nelly's memorial service, she spent her time drifting around the house in her rattiest sweatpants. The monologues, which had the same badgering tone as their real-life conversations, helped fend off the sadness.

Haskell had turned into a pest since Nelly had gone. He called Melissa every day, sometimes several times a day, just to check on her. They both knew Melissa had been much closer to Nelly than he had. Haskell mourned his mother, but mostly he seemed to worry about Melissa. That was a first.

"Dad, I'm fine," she said, during his third phone call of the day. "We knew she was sick."

"Not as sick as she was."

"And that's the way she wanted it. She didn't want us making a fuss over her."

"First time Nelly McGuire minded being the center of attention."

"You know what I mean. I would have made her stay in bed, or go to the doctor every time she had a pain."

"Did you eat breakfast?"

Heavy sigh. "Yes, Dad."

"I was thinking about making that lasagna you like tonight. With eggplant."

"I don't know, I should get some work done . . ."

"I'll bring it over. Around seven."

"Okay." Resigned, she forced herself to change out of her sweatpants so her father wouldn't become even more worried about her. Haskell served her lasagna, sat with her in comfortable silence as they ate, then took himself off. And strangely, she did find his presence comforting.

Several of her former coworkers at Channel Six also called to leave their condolences, but she let the answering machine handle those calls. There was no one she wanted to talk to. Well, there was one person, but Brody seemed to have gone back to his regular life. The life with the ex-ex-wife and the baby on the way.

Three days after Nelly's death, the sound of hammering woke Melissa up. Indignant, she stalked to the source of the noise at the back of the house. She squinted at the sight of Brody, Ryan, Vader, and her father.

"What are you guys doing?"

"Fixing the damage," called her father, carrying a load of shingles up the back stairs.

"No! It's fine. It doesn't need to be fixed."

Brody swung down from the roof. He wore his tool belt and looked so sexy Melissa wanted to hit him. How dare he come to her house, all gorgeous and unattainable? "Melissa, your roof has a large hole in it. You can't just leave it like that."

"Says who? This is Southern California. It never rains."

"It does in January."

"It's still December." She folded her arms across her chest and glared at him.

"Which is the month before January."

"There's thirty days in a month."

"But only twenty days left in this one." Brody was now scowling right back at her.

"Sometimes it rains in December," Ryan said reasonably, poking his head over the gutter. Brody shot him a look, and he disappeared from view.

Haskell put down the shingles and stood next to Brody. "Roof's gotta be fixed. Wouldn't be able to sleep if it ain't."

"Fine. Fix the roof. Do what you want. But leave . . . the porch . . . *alone*. And don't touch the glider." With a glare blurred by tears, she surveyed the group, and marched back into the house.

Brody slammed a fist into the charred porch railing. What had he done wrong? He was trying to help her, be there for her. A phone call hadn't seemed enough, so he'd come up with the idea to fix the roof, which was apparently the last thing she wanted.

Haskell put a hand on his shoulder. "She's not herself. Give her some time."

Brody would have disagreed with the "not herself" part—that argument was vintage Melissa. But giving her some time, that made sense, even though it went against all his protective instincts.

He took a deep breath, adjusted his tool belt, and climbed up on the roof. He'd wait until Melissa wasn't crazed with grief, then break it to her that she belonged with him. As long as that Everett Malcolm wasn't in the picture, he could wait.

Even though it was just about killing him.

After a while the hammering stopped, and when Melissa ventured back outside, Brody and the others had left. As agreed, the porch hadn't been touched, but the roof was patched and water-tight. The glider, charred but intact, swayed in the evening breeze.

What was wrong with her? Some very kind men had shown up to fix her house, and she'd sent them away in a ridiculously rude manner.

"I know you think I'm a fool, Grans. I just didn't want them to fix everything up. I mean, you burned that porch down for me. How dare they try to fix it? I know, I know, I sound like an idiot. I ought to call the fire station and thank them. Or send a card."

Instead, she went back to bed. That night it rained.

In the morning, Melissa couldn't believe how rude she'd been to Brody. He was thoughtful and helpful and so sexy it hurt, and how had she thanked him? By yelling at him. Now he probably hated her. Who could blame him? She was one hundred percent sure she'd never see the man again.

She was wrong. Brody came to the memorial service. Along with every other member of San Gabriel Fire Station 1 who had been granted the time off. Ryan came, and Vader, and Double D, and Fred, and Two. They wore their uniforms, which made them look splendid and solemn, none more so than Brody, tall and powerful, his captain's hat under his arm. Standing in a cluster in the small chapel, they attracted quite a bit of attention from the other guests—members of Nelly's Scrabble Club, the few old friends who'd managed to outlive her, a few Channel Six employees. She spotted Bill Loudon, her cameraman Greg, and Ella Joy in a tight black dress.

How Nelly would have loved all this attention, thought Melissa. As she and Haskell settled into their seats in the front pew, she squeezed her father's hand.

"She woulda been crowing like a rooster," he said with a wry smile.

"Did you invite the firefighters?" It hadn't occurred to her to send a notice to the fire station.

"The captain called and asked. Said his crew wouldn't miss it."

Melissa couldn't speak through the sudden lump in her throat. Of course Brody would think of asking. Even after the way she'd treated him, he did the classy thing. She looked at the line of firefighters, her gaze flying to meet Brody's. He inclined his head toward her with a hint of a smile. Maybe he didn't hate her after all, she thought hopefully. He drew someone else forward. A small boy with a bandaged head.

Rodrigo! Melissa smiled her first real smile since that night in the hospital. She gave Rodrigo an eager wave, which he returned. He looked so much better, still bruised, but without that beaten look in his eyes. No thanks to her. Since Nelly had died, she hadn't done anything about Rodrigo's story. To tell the truth, she'd forgotten him until this moment. How terrible.

But then the sweet lilting sound of a Les Barrett tune, played by a blue-haired lady on the organ, filled the room, and again her gaze met Brody's.

They'd danced to this tune on that hilarious first "date." He winked at her, at the memory, and she suddenly felt like laughing.

Quickly turning away so she wouldn't embarrass herself, she fixed her eyes on the big photo of Nelly mounted near the lectern. In the photo, Nelly's hair was in tight curls that seemed to jump off her head, and she wore a blouse that Melissa happened to know she'd worn only once. Melissa had wondered what Nelly was up to that day, but Nelly had refused to say.

Her grandmother sure had a pile of tricks up her sleeve. She fought another wave of laughter, knowing it would lead to tears. For Nelly's sake, she refused to cry. When she got home, back under the covers, she could cry all she wanted.

Was that a frown she saw on the photo of Nelly's absurdly perky face? *I won't cry, Grans,* she reassured the photo, and thought she saw the frown disappear. *I'm losing it,* she thought hysterically. *I'm talking to a photo.* She dragged her eyes away from Nelly and focused on the minister behind the lectern.

"Dearly beloved, we are gathered here to remember our dear friend, mother, and grandmother, Eleanor Danielle Erskine McGuire. Please be seated." A shuffling of feet followed as the assembled group obeyed. While the minister continued, Melissa's gaze returned to the photo. She tuned out the eulogy, and instead heard the voice of her grandmother.

Didn't I tell you he's the best man I ever met? Look at him, sitting there so handsome and strong. If I were younger, I'd give you a run for your money.

"Grans, you're dead. It would be no contest."

I don't know about that. You might as well be dead, for all the good you're doing.

"I'm allowed a grieving period."

Pshaw. Grieving shmieving. I'm happy as a tick. You're the one who looks like death warmed over.

"Oh, so you have a whole new set of puns now."

Listen to that man, boring the whole room to death.

"And another one. You can't stop, can you?"

Don't change the subject. What are you going to do about Brody?

"Do about him?"

I insist you talk to him. You have to thank him for coming. It's only polite.

"Of course I'm going to thank him! What do you think I am?"

Let's not get into that. No need to quarrel.

"Right, this isn't the time or the place."

You did well with the memorial, I'll give you that. It's just how I wanted it.

"You're welcome. I worked hard on it."

Well, you worked on it, anyway. I've seen you work a lot harder.

"Grans!"

I tell it like I see it. That's okay, I had this mostly planned ahead of time anyway.

"Yeah, I know. There's a word for bossy people like you."

I'm not going to quarrel. When this is over, you go back to work, and you do it right.

"Sure, Grans."

You aren't patronizing me just because I'm dead?

"Hell, no."

Language, Melissa! But she thought she heard her

grandmother laugh. *There goes your father. Listen up!*

Sure enough, her father stood at the lectern, about to speak. She knew what was coming. She'd given him Nelly's favorite Emily Dickinson poem to read. But to her surprise, he ignored his assignment and addressed the crowded pews in his own words.

"It's no secret that I gave my ma a heap of trouble growing up. But she never gave up on me. And that's the way she was. She just kept on going and going, until time ran out on her. She left a couple things unfinished down here. But I'm not going to let the ball drop. Ma, I want you to know I'm not giving up neither. Love you."

As Melissa stared in amazement, Haskell made his way back to the pew. "What about the poem I gave you?"

"Had something to say." He shrugged. "Besides, you might need it."

"No, I've got a whole thing that I wrote."

As she rose to take her turn at the lectern, he pressed the poem into her hands. "Take it."

When Melissa reached the lectern and gazed out at the sympathetic crowd, all the words she had written, memorized, and rehearsed flew out of her head. She went completely, totally blank. How had her father known? The chapel fell silent.

Silent as the grave, she heard Nelly say.

"Stop that! I'm trying to speak here."

Well, get on with it then.

But still nothing came out of her mouth. She looked around, desperate, and caught Brody's eye. He was scowling at her. *Scowling.* How dare he scowl at a moment like this.

Furious, she opened her mouth. Finally, something actually came out.

But instead of her speech, Emily Dickinson's words filled the chapel. " 'Hope is the thing with feathers . . .' " Melissa recited.

Afterward, she barely remembered sitting back down, feeling her father's comforting hand on hers, enduring the rest of the service.

When it was all over, she and Haskell stood in the chapel's foyer while the mourners filed past with murmurs of sympathy.

"Teleprompter," said Ella, helpfully. "Next time, try the prompter. And call me, we have to talk."

"Nice dress," said Melissa.

"Gucci. I liked your grandmother, even though she wasn't exactly nice to me."

"Well, she had a big problem with your fuchsia suit."

"Really?" Ella frowned, no doubt pondering this beyond-the-grave fashion critique.

"Ella." Melissa lowered her voice so no one else could hear. "Are you sure about . . . you and Everett?"

A strange look came over Ella's face. Almost tender. "Sure, I'm sure. He's a devil, but he suits me. And I won't make your mistake."

"What's that?"

"I've decided not to work for him." Ella winked. "I've got another plan in the works. I'll let him be the boss in bed, that's all." And she tripped off.

Work for him. Melissa vaguely remembered another message from Everett, reiterating his on-air job offer. Should she leave San Gabriel, now that Nelly was gone? Melissa's head began to throb. She closed her eyes and rubbed her forehead. When she opened them again, Rodrigo and Brody stood in front of her.

Brody. Brody had scowled at her when she'd blanked out on her speech. She wanted to yell and scream at him. Pound her fists into his broad chest. Tackle him to the floor. Instead she addressed the boy at his side. "Thanks for coming, Rodrigo. How are you doing?"

"A lot better. I got a new foster family. The captain knows them."

"They're good people," said Brody.

"The captain came for dinner, and he told me about your grandmother, and asked me if I wanted to come today. I'm really sorry."

"Thanks," she said, managing a smile. While she'd been buried under the bedcovers, Brody had been watching out for Rodrigo. She made herself meet his eyes. "And thanks, Brody."

"How are you holding up?" he asked, the warm gray of his gaze making her shiver.

"Pretty good. Except for forgetting my speech."

"Beautiful poem, though."

"I suppose it could have been worse. I could have set the lectern on fire."

A crack of laughter from Brody sent heads turning. "It would have been a nice tribute."

"Yes, and I would have been perfectly safe, with so many firemen here. That's thanks to you, I hear."

He shook his head. "It was their idea. Your grandmother made a big impression on us. She won't be forgotten." He bent over and kissed her cheek, and he and Rodrigo moved on. When Brody shepherded Rodrigo out of the chapel, it seemed as if the light suddenly dimmed.

As the endless procession of well-wishers continued, all Melissa could think about was that kiss. No, not a kiss. A peck on the cheek. What did that mean? Was it all Rebecca would allow? Was it a sisterly, friendly kind of kiss? Or did it mean he still had some feeling for her? He couldn't exactly get passionate at a memorial.

The rest of the event passed in a blur, except for one cryptic comment from Ryan. He too kissed her on the cheek—his kiss left no tingle—and as he did so he whispered in her ear, "Happy days are here again. You-know-who is gone."

She drew back, shocked. Was he referring to her grandmother? Ryan fumbled an apology. "That's not what I . . . Oh geez . . . I was talking about *her*, you know . . ."

Vader elbowed him aside. Ryan wandered off, still mumbling under his breath.

Much later, when she was back home soaking in a hot bath, Melissa felt Nelly rapping her on the head.

Why don't you listen to Ryan, if you won't listen to me?

"What now? I'm trying to take a bath."

Don't you remember what I said back at the hospital? About the other one being gone?

The hospital. Nelly talking about Alice May. Saying how "the other one" was gone.

In a flash, the pieces came together. How had she been so dense? "The other one" was Rebecca. Nelly had gotten the names confused. She'd been talking about Rebecca. Rebecca was gone. So why hadn't Brody come to her? Explained that she'd left? Taken Melissa into his arms and kissed her senseless? Thrown her on the bed and ravaged her? What was stopping him?

Everett. Was that Nelly talking, or her own brain? Didn't matter. The answer was so obvious she didn't know how she'd missed it. Her grief must have distracted her.

Don't go blaming it on me.

"Sorry, Grans. Now shush, I'm trying to figure this out."

How could Brody possibly think for one second that she would go back to that rat Everett? It was true that she'd never explained about Everett's kiss. There hadn't seemed any point, when he was back together with Rebecca. Besides, the kiss meant absolutely nothing.

But did Brody know that?

She went over everything that had happened since that kiss. Brody had helped her get Rodrigo to the ER. Found a new foster home for him. Carried Nelly away from the fire in the backyard. Helped Melissa during those agonizing hours at the hospital. Fixed her roof.

Don't forget my memorial service.

Right. He'd called Haskell about Nelly's service, and spread the word among his crew. And Brody had done all these things even while believing she was back together with Everett. He'd done them because he cared about her. Because she was grieving and couldn't do them for herself. He'd done them quietly, in the background. Not for attention, or for glory. He'd only wanted to help her.

Maybe he didn't write epic poetry or recite Tarantino films by heart, but Brody was the best man she'd ever known. And she loved him with all her heart.

What did he feel for her? Her father's words came back to her. "Don't go thinking you aren't worth anything."

She stood up in the bathtub, letting the water stream off her body. There was only one way to find out what Brody felt for her. One last time, she addressed her grandmother.

"Yes, I know, Grans. Time to go fight for my man."

Chapter Twenty-six

*B*ut first she had to take care of a few other things. She visited Rodrigo at his new foster home and was thrilled to see how well he'd settled in. He looked bright-eyed and full of excitement about his new life—new family, new school, new friends.

He showed her his bedroom, decorated with posters of soccer players and death metal bands. The tidiness of the room seemed almost poignant, as if he was afraid he'd have to leave if he made a mess. In time, she hoped, he'd relax and finally feel secure.

She sat on the edge of the bed while he showed her his new Wii console. "Rodrigo, how do you feel about the story now? Maybe you'd rather let the past go, and focus on your schoolwork, and all your new buddies."

"No," he said fiercely. "I want to do the story."

"Your foster mother's been charged for what she did to you. The other foster kids have been taken away from that house. No one will ever be sent there again. I promise you."

He thought that over. "It's not enough. People should know about the bribes."

"It might be hard for you. Reliving what happened. Having your friends know."

He ducked his head, twisted his hands together. "If we don't do the story, then I got beaten up for nothing. Are you backing out?"

"No," she said quickly. "I'm not backing out. I've been a little distracted since my grandmother died, but I'm back now, and if you want me to do the story, I'd like nothing better. But I had to see how you felt."

"That's how I feel," he said with a determined nod.

Her next stop was Bill Loudon's office. She sat across from his desk while he eyed her with sympathetic, watery eyes.

"Melissa, if you want your job back, we have a lot of details to work out. I've already given your former title to Blaine, and we've had some cutbacks since you left. I know what Ella told you, and what she promised. No matter what she said, I can't bring you back at your old salary, I'm sorry to say."

"Loudon, you can take my old salary and shove it."

"My, my," he said, surprised. "Full of sass today, aren't you."

"Did Ella talk to you about the foster care investigation? 'Innocence Betrayed: Fraud in the Foster Care System'? She's pretty set on doing it. If I take it to Los Angeles, she'll throw a fit like you've never seen."

"Ella Joy doesn't run this news department."

"That would be news to her," said Melissa dryly. "She may not run it, but if she wants something, I sure wouldn't bet against her."

Loudon wiped his weary eyes. "She has a bug up her ass about this story. God help me if I can understand it."

"Never underestimate the fury of a woman scorned. She's doing the story, Loudon. Just accept it. Besides, you don't want Los Angeles horning in on our territory, do you?"

He sighed. "Hardball, huh? So where does this put you? I have to find another title for you?"

"Don't bother. I found my own title."

He eyed her warily. "I feel a gastrointestinal attack coming on."

"Independent producer. Executive producer of any story I bring you. Complete freedom to pursue any investigations, plus complete access to Channel Six's resources. You get right of first refusal on any story I do. Ella gets to choose which stories she wants to front. If she passes, I will front it myself. You pay me by the story."

And she named her amount. Loudon couldn't deny it was fair—respectable, but not greedy. "You can afford that?"

"My Grans left me a little money." In fact, it was more than a little. Nelly had divided everything equally between Haskell and Melissa, but Haskell had instantly signed it all over to Melissa. Of course she'd protested, but her father hadn't budged.

"I don't need it, and it's better if I don't have it. Nothing but trouble in my hands. I'll leave it all to you when I shove off anyway. You'll make good use of it, I know." She'd given him a long hug, her first since the age of ten.

"There's one catch," said Loudon.

Melissa waited. Her dream job was so close . . .

"Ella's leaving the station when her contract's up in two months."

"Really?" She vaguely remembered Ella mentioning a plan at Nelly's memorial service.

"She's making the jump to Los Angeles."

"Everett actually hired her?"

"No, no. She's going to the competition. If she gets them two extra ratings points, they'll beat FOX News."

Melissa's head spun just thinking of the implications. Ella versus Everett in the ratings. Ella *with* Everett in bed. Everett with Barb in bed. Barb versus Ella in the ratings. Any way you added it up, Everett was screwed. And not in the good way.

Not her problem. "I guess I'll front my own stories then. I think I proved myself with the City Hall fire."

"I can live with that, unless whoever replaces Ella wants to front one."

"Deal."

"Good."

"And that brings me to my final condition," continued Melissa.

"Will it never end?" Loudon wiped his gloomy eyes.

"I never got to do that story about the Bachelor Firemen of San Gabriel. I did some research and shot some footage. I'd like that story to be my first report."

"Are you teasing me?"

"No."

"You're stringing me along, aren't you?" He popped a pale green antacid into his mouth.

"What do you mean?"

"You really want your first story to be about the dismal living conditions of elderly immigrant Hmong who don't speak English and need to be subtitled."

Melissa had to laugh. "Maybe that's next. For now, how about some gorgeous, heroic, single firemen."

Loudon wiped his eyes. "Melissa, you are, hands down, the best producer I've ever worked with."

Serious or not, she'd take that compliment. Melissa briskly shook his hand, left his office, and let out the breath she'd been holding. It was like a miracle. No more news meetings. No more newsroom politics. No more Ella wrangling. No more hiding in the background. She'd do the stories she wanted to do, when she wanted to do them. Except that it wasn't a miracle—it was called standing up for herself. Fighting for what she wanted.

She stopped by Ella's office on her way out. No matter how irritating, egotistical, and shamelessly ambitious Ella was, Melissa owed her a debt of gratitude for . . . well, for being Ella. She wasn't in yet, so Melissa wrote her a quick note. Chang interrupted. "Some security guard's gonna get fired. Who let you back in the building?"

"Special invitation. Get used to it, babe."

He stared. "Seriously, are you back? What's the haps? Is you in or is you out?"

"Stay tuned for another turn of the Sunny Side of the News."

"Ha ha."

"Tell Ella to call me when she gets in."

"C'mon, Melissa, I got to feed something to the grapevine."

"Tell them I may be looking for some freelance help, production and editorial, so if anyone needs extra cash, they should get in touch with me."

After she'd finished editing the bachelor story, she went down to the studio and taped her intro and wrap-up.

When she'd finished taping, she went home and waited.

An electrical fire at an old walnut farm outside town kept most of San Gabriel Fire Station 1 busy that night. Brody, Ryan, and Double D were the only firefighters in the lounge when the *Eleven O'Clock News* started. When he heard the familiar theme song begin, Brody went to lift weights. The last few days, everything associated with Melissa had become painful and tender, like a fresh bruise.

His plan to wait wasn't working at all. For one thing, he thought about her all the time. At the memorial service, he'd seen the lost, dazed look in her eyes and longed to take her in his arms and soothe away her pain. When she'd blanked out at the lectern, it had taken all his strength not to rush up there and whisk her away. How long was he supposed to wait? A week? A month? A year? What if Melissa forgot about him while he was patiently waiting?

The newscast was halfway over when Brody heard a shout from the TV room.

"Captain, get back in here!" called Ryan. Grumbling, sweaty, Brody stalked back to the TV room and stopped at the sight of Melissa's face filling the screen. At the bottom of the screen was a banner that read, "The Bachelor Firemen of San Gabriel."

For a moment, Brody was so riveted by the sight of Melissa the way he remembered her, he didn't notice what she was saying. The old Melissa was back. Her eyes glowed forest-green, her full lips smiled. Even with her horn-rimmed glasses, her beauty seemed to leap off the screen. Why did she wear glasses, when it didn't matter one way or the other? With them or without them, she was beautiful and brilliant.

Finally he tuned in to her words.

". . . my research into the history of San Gabriel Fire Station 1 does raise a few questions about the supposed curse. Parts of the legend are true. San Gabriel does have an unusual number of unmarried firemen. Oddly, that's been true since the turn of the last century. Whether or not San Gabriel's firefighters are more or less good-looking than average, I'll leave it to you viewers to decide."

The camera panned over a group of firemen stripped to their T-shirts, hosing down Engine 1.

"In this reporter's very biased opinion, you'd have to search a long time to find firefighters as attractive as ours. Of course, looks aren't everything. I've been lucky enough to spend time with the San Gabriel firemen, and I can personally vouch for their above-average skill, courage, daring, team spirit, and thoughtfulness."

A close-up of Ryan clapping Vader on the shoulder came next.

"So you might well wonder, why are so many of these outstanding men still single? Is there truth to the curse after all? The results of my investigation are inconclusive, but I have formed a working theory. Unlike the original Bachelor Fireman, Virgil Rush, San Gabriel firemen don't remain bachelors all their lives. They do fall in love and marry. But just like Virgil, their path to true love seems to be rockier than the norm. So, ladies, I hope you'll follow my example. If you fall for one of these men, fasten your seat belts because you're in for a bumpy ride. But take it from me, they're worth it." She winked. "Melissa McGuire, reporting for the Sunny Side of the News."

Brody couldn't move. He couldn't stop staring at the TV screen, which now showed a commercial for some cleaning product. Ryan and Double D whooped. "She's talking about you, Captain!" yelled Ryan.

"Ain't no doubt," agreed Double D. "Didn't know Hollywood had it in her."

"What are you going to do?"

What was he going to do? Getting his body to move would be the first step. He mumbled something to his firefighters about paging him in an emergency, and ran to his turnout.

His turnout? He didn't question it. He pulled on his pants and coat, and thrust his feet into his boots. Feeling like the Michelin Man, he squeezed behind the wheel of his truck. As he drove, he thought about how brave Melissa was to go on TV and bare her heart the way she had. She'd always said she didn't want to be on the air. But she'd been perfect. She'd almost sounded like . . . well, like Nelly. Maybe Nelly had left behind a little of her own fearlessness. Or maybe Melissa had it all along.

Just before midnight, he knocked on her door. For a long moment, no one answered and he waited alone in the cool, jasmine-scented moonlight. Then the door opened and Melissa appeared. He had a blurred impression of dark hair pouring over bare shoulders and green eyes blinking at him in surprise.

"You're in your turnout gear," she said blankly.

"You wore your glasses," he answered nonsensically.

"They help me think straight."

"Likewise."

They stared at each other. "I saw the news," he finally said, and thought he saw her blush.

"Will you please take that off? I can't talk to you like this," she said, gesturing at his turnout.

"Why not?"

"It makes my knees go all weak and funny."

He threw down his jacket, pushed the suspenders off his shoulders, and stepped out of his gear. Down to T-shirt and shorts, he swept her into his arms. She felt so good there, he wanted to stay like that forever. "Better?"

She buried her head in his chest. "Oh, Brody. I've been so stupid. I shouldn't have yelled at you about the roof."

"You were grieving."

"I didn't know Rebecca was gone. It was torture seeing you there."

His arms tightened even further around her.
"I'm sorry for that. I thought she still needed my
help. It's hard for me to walk away from that."

"Because you're so honorable. You took care of
Rodrigo."

"You're the one who gave him a chance."

"I'm trying to apologize!"

"Well, stop." But he stopped her himself, with a
long kiss, deep as the ocean, warm as the sun.

Nestled in his strong arms, with his steadfast
heart beating against hers, Melissa's head spun
with joy. "Rebecca's really gone?" she whispered
when his lips finally left hers.

"I got hold of the man she really loves. And who
loves her. They're good together. Not like—" He
broke off.

Melissa had her own confession to make. "Everett's gone too. What you saw in the newsroom . . ."
But she couldn't think of the best way to explain it.

Once again, Brody saved her. "Does he still want
you? Because if he does, I'll fight him for you. I'm
a peaceful man, but I think I could kick his ass."

"Really?" The idea of Brody beating up Everett
was so appealing that she giggled. "That's okay. I
think Ella might take care of that for us."

"She's just the man for the job."

"Oh Brody, I do love you so."

He cradled her face in his hands, rubbed a rough
thumb across her cheek. "Do you? Because you
know I'm a simple, old-fashioned man. If someone
tells me they love me, my next thought is flower
girls and reception halls."

She couldn't speak. What did he feel toward

her? He still hadn't said. And she couldn't help it. She needed to hear it out loud. She was a journalist, after all. Words mattered to her. Right now she felt like she'd stripped herself naked—in front of a man in uniform.

"You know I put this gear on without even thinking. I only figured out why just now."

"Why?" She frowned at him. Why on earth was he talking about his gear at a moment like this?

"There's a few things I know I'm extremely good at. Fighting fires, saving lives, being a fire captain."

"You're the best. Everyone knows it."

"But saying what's in my heart—that's not my strong point. Maybe I thought the turnout would make me irresistible. Do my talking for me. If I was really lucky, maybe a fire would break out so I could ride to your rescue."

Smiling, she lifted up his heavy jacket as though to help him into it. But instead she deliberately, provocatively, tossed it aside. "I'm not in love with a fire captain. I mean, I am, but that's because it's you. I'm in love with you, Harry Brod. I don't care how many fires you put out, or how many legends people tell about you."

"You don't, huh?" He advanced toward her with a relentless step. She backed away. "What about the legend of how the fire captain's heart was captured by a beautiful green-eyed princess—for the grand sum of three thousand dollars, cash?"

She winced. "Can't we forget that one?"

"Okay, how about the legend of how the princess rescued the fire captain from eternal loneliness and a lifetime of monster truck rallies?"

Another wince. He took a step closer.

"Don't you want to hear how it only takes one look at your face to make the whole world shine? Or how the smell of your skin makes my heart melt like . . . like cadmium? Or how I would throw myself into the pits of hell if it could save one hair on your beautiful, extremely intelligent head?"

By now she had run out of room, and felt the backs of her knees press against the arm of the couch. She nearly stumbled, but before she fell he lifted her in his arms and nestled her into the cushions of the couch. He braced himself over her, one muscular arm on either side of her head.

"You're wrong," she said breathlessly. He frowned. "It is your strong point."

He looked at her blankly, until he remembered his own words. Then he laughed. "Oh no, princess, that's just a tiny bit of what's in my heart. But if you let me, I'll spend the rest of my life trying to spit out the rest."

Laughter burbled from her lips. "Face it, Captain. You have a way with words."

He bent his elbows so his body lowered and his beautiful gray eyes blazed into hers.

"It's not just words. When I love, I love hard. You're stuck with me for good. In your news report, you didn't say what happened at the end of the bumpy ride. You didn't say what it takes to break the curse. But I know."

He brushed his lips across hers with tender intensity. "True love. The kind that doesn't go away because of a few disasters along the way. I love you, Melissa."

The last tiny piece of her heart flew to him, and she knew she belonged to him forever.

"Flower girls, did you say?" she whispered.

His eyes blazed even brighter. "As soon as possible. I'm not about to let any other news directors swoop in on the woman I love."

The words filled her with a warm serenity, like rich hot chocolate flowing through her veins.

Brody looked up at the ceiling. "Subject to your approval, of course, Ms. Nelly McGuire."

Melissa tugged on his sleeve, and he looked back down at her. "Nice idea. But Grans has promised to stay out of it."

He nodded thoughtfully. "She's absolutely right. She got us this far, but I think we can take things from here."

She curled herself into his lap and inhaled the wonderful scent of man. Her man. "You know what I'm more worried about?"

"What?"

"The rest of the guys. You've broken the curse. One less bachelor fireman. Now what's going to happen?"

Brody rested his chin on her head. "Oh no, you don't. I train them, I keep them alive. After that they're on their own."

"Heartless." The steady heartbeat under her ear proved her wrong.

"On the other hand, you might want to make that Bachelor Firemen story a regular feature. Your viewers will want updates. Girls are probably already lining up at the door of the firehouse. Good thing you snapped me up first."

She sighed happily. "Very good thing. Those poor girls don't know what they're in for."

They snuggled for a long while. "Brody."

"Hmmm." He stroked his hand down her back until it met bare skin. She shivered in anticipation.

"Any bets on which fireman is next?"

Next month, don't miss these exciting new love stories only from Avon Books

A Blood Seduction by Pamela Palmer
Quinn Lennox is searching for a missing friend when she stumbles into a dark otherworld that only she can see. She has no idea of the power she wields . . . power that could be the salvation or destruction of Arturo, the dangerously handsome vampire whose wicked kiss saves, bewitches, and betrays her.

Winter Garden by Adele Ashworth
Madeleine DuMais's cleverness is her greatest asset—one she puts to good use as a spy for the British. When she meets Thomas Blackwood, her partner in subterfuge, duty gives way to desire and she discovers their lives are no longer the only things in danger.

Darkness Becomes Her by Jaime Rush
Some might say Lachlan and Jessie don't play well with others. But they're going to have to learn to, and quickly. Because they are the only two people in the world who can save each other— and their passion is the only thing that can save the world.

Hot For Fireman by Jennifer Bernard
Katie Dane knows better than to mix business with pleasure, but when she finds herself working side by side with Ryan, the sexy heartbreaker of Station One, playing with fire suddenly feels a lot like falling in love.

REL 0512